NEW YORK
Brides

A Rural Refuge Nurtures Romance in Three Complete Novels

PAMELA GRIFFIN

BARBOUR
PUBLISHING

Dear Reader,

God's unconditional plan of love encompasses everyone—those who seem perfect and those who obviously are not. The truth is, everyone falls short of the mark of perfection, and God will be perfecting His children until the day of His return. One of my greatest pleasures is in writing about men and women who are considered pariahs by a society that often looks at them through a set of disparaging glasses. People don't always give second chances or offer acceptance, but God never fails to do so. No earthly sin is so great that it cannot be forgiven; no person is so physically or emotionally flawed that God does not look upon him or her with love and see inner beauty. I enjoy writing about the outcasts and their stories, illustrating how God's constant, tender love can soften and change even the bitterest and hardest of hearts. It is my hope that you will enjoy all the wonderful and colorful people who inhabit Lyons' Refuge as much as I took pleasure in shaping them and writing their stories. May God always fill your heart with His love and acceptance.

Pamela Griffin

Heart Appearances

Dedication

As always I dedicate this book to my Lord Jesus,
who looks beyond my imperfect outer shell
to the loving heart that seeks only to serve Him.
Also, thanks to my critique partners,
who are always so willing to lend a hand.
You girls are truly the best, and I never could have done it without you.

Chapter 1

1919

Darcy Evans was having a bad day. What's more, she certainly didn't need the added nuisance of a meddlesome porter hovering at her heels. Hugging her battered satchel, which contained the one spare dress the reformatory allowed upon her dismissal—all she had in the world—she turned and eyed the man suspiciously.

"Can I take that for you, miss?" The hefty porter raised shaggy eyebrows and held out his huge calloused hand.

"No." Her reply was stiff, to the point. Why couldn't he leave her alone? He'd been watching her since she stepped off the train at Ithaca and began pacing the platform.

The porter tipped his cap and moved away. Darcy sighed with relief and scanned the area with expectancy. The afternoon sun edged the trees and surrounding buildings with harsh white light, and the burnt-coal smell from the smokestack lingered in the damp air. Black specks of cinder from the departed train still floated through the sky, though she'd been waiting on this platform for what seemed an eternity.

Oh, pigeon feathers! Had Charleigh really forgotten her? What other explanation could there be for her not meeting the train?

A slight smile tipped Darcy's mouth as she thought of her redheaded friend. When Darcy first met Charleigh in a holding cell in England, she was confused, to say the least. To discover Charleigh had turned herself in to Scotland Yard went against every survival tactic Darcy had been taught by Hunstable and Crackers—two childhood accomplices who'd shown her all she needed to know about surviving on the streets of London.

Charleigh had exhibited a strange peace, a calm relief—as though she were actually happy to pay for her crimes. Something about the secretive woman had drawn Darcy, like a starved cat to a cooked leg of pheasant. At first she'd been a little put off by Charleigh's talk of Jesus and salvation; but after two years at Turreney Farm, Darcy saw something in Charleigh she'd seen in no one else. A peaceable attitude. A glow in her eyes. A knowledge that God loved her—no matter what. And Darcy wanted what she'd seen.

Still, after Charleigh's sentence was over—three months before Darcy's—it had been easy for Darcy to slip back into the old life. All too soon she found herself back in the reformatory, serving a second sentence for drunkenness and petty theft. Near the end of her term, the barrister who'd represented Charleigh arrived with a letter expressing her desire to have Darcy come to Lyons' Refuge—the reformatory for boys that Charleigh's husband had founded in upstate New York—and help there. Darcy had readily agreed. There had been a lot of what the barrister called "legal matters" to wade through, but soon Darcy found herself on a steamer headed for America.

And now here she was, after coming all this way and traveling for five days, with no one here to greet her.

Frustrated, Darcy plopped down on the wooden bench along the station wall and slapped her hand to the crown of her floppy black hat.

Had Charleigh really forgotten her?

Grimacing, Brent Thomas picked up the mesh sack from the driver's seat with his thumb and forefinger. He marched over the damp ground with the odorous parcel and flung it into the nearby field, wishing he knew which of his nine charges had thought it amusing to place a bag of dung on the wooden seat. He entertained a fairly good idea of the culprit's identity but wasn't certain. Furthermore, he couldn't discipline every boy at the reformatory for one child's prank, though he knew his mentor would have had no compunction in doing so. Professor Gladsbury was a stern instructor, and though Brent had appreciated the elderly man's wisdom, he'd never agreed with his strict methods of discipline, such as the harsh raps on the palm with a willow stick. And yet, on days like today...

"Brent! Wait!"

Mrs. Lyons' shout halted him as he finished wiping off the seat. He turned to watch the headmaster's British wife hurry down the three porch steps, waving an envelope in her hand.

Brent was already late for the station, having had to change into his one spare pair of trousers after his encounter with the reeking bag. Absentmindedness often made him act without being aware of his surroundings—seating himself without looking, for instance. Something the culprit was sure to know.

He offered a penitent smile. "I'm terribly sorry, Mrs. Lyons, I realize I'm late to collect your friend. Would you like me to post that while I'm in town?"

She brushed a fiery lock of hair from her face. "Yes, please," she said after she'd caught her breath and handed him the envelope. "Now, do remember, Brent. Darcy's been through a great deal, so she might not be quite—shall we say, personable, at first. But Stewart and I have prayed, and we feel God wants her here at the refuge. That's why we've done everything to make such an occurrence possible, including sending money for her passage."

Brent nodded, uneasy. Why was she telling him this? He knew most of it. He wasn't certain he was altogether in favor of bringing an ex-felon to help out at a reformatory for young boys, but he trusted Stewart's judgment. Furthermore, Stewart's wife, being an ex-felon herself, was certainly a changed person from the woman she once described.

She grinned. "You're probably wondering why I'm sharing this with you. The truth is, well, you're a wonderful instructor to the boys and a rock of support when my husband is away. Stewart and I know we can depend on you—with our very lives if need be. Why, I don't know what we would've done without you when Stewart went to France to fight in the war. You've become more than a schoolteacher to us. You've become a friend. . . ."

Brent could feel the dreaded "but" coming.

"But, well, you're a trifle stuffy. And Darcy isn't the sort of person you're accustomed to."

Stuffy? She thought him stuffy? Just because he believed in dressing impeccably and using drawing room manners at all times? So he did make sure everything went into its proper place. It didn't necessarily make him "stuffy." He removed his spectacles and cleaned them with the crisp handkerchief he'd placed in his pocket for that purpose.

"Oh dear," she murmured. "I've offended you, haven't I? I shouldn't have spoken. I simply wanted you to be prepared. Darcy isn't a woman with social graces—such as the women whose company you're accustomed to. That's the only reason I spoke—to prepare you. I never intended to injure your feelings."

"That's perfectly all right." He replaced his glasses and folded his handkerchief into thirds, tucking it back into his pocket.

"I wish I could go with you, but of course someone has to stay with the boys. Between Irma and me, we'll have our hands full."

He attempted a smile. "No explanations are necessary, Mrs. Lyons. I shall deliver your friend to you with all expedience." Still smarting from her comment, he added, "And I'm sure we'll get along splendidly."

❧

Darcy sat on the bench and kicked at the wooden planks with the toe of her scuffed shoe. Hunger gnawed at her insides. Remembering the brown paper bag of walnuts she'd bought at the wharf before boarding the train, she pulled the small sack from her valise. Setting a nut on the platform before her, she pulled up the frayed hem of her black skirt several inches and brought the heel of her shoe down hard on the shell.

With satisfaction, she heard the resulting *CRRRAAACKK* and bent to scoop her treat from the ground. She pulled the shell fragments away, popped the nutmeat into her mouth, and chewed with unabashed delight. Sensing someone watching, she turned her head sharply to the side.

A well-dressed young man stood nearby. He stared at her in horror, his blue eyes wide behind the wire-rimmed spectacles perched on his rather long nose. His light hair was combed neatly under a bowler hat, and a clean and pressed dark brown suit covered his slim form.

Darcy suddenly felt like a mangy cat next to this fancy-dressed bloke. Her woolen skirt was moth-eaten, her non-matching jacket was threadbare with ugly patches at the elbows, and she'd stuffed an old piece of cloth into the toe of one shoe to cover the hole as best she could. Her chin went up in defense. "Well, whatcha lookin' at, guv'ner?"

He continued to gape, then slowly shook his head. "Excuse me, but you aren't Miss Evans, are you?" He sounded as though he believed he'd made a mistake, and he turned to go.

"Aye, that be me!" Darcy shot to her feet, tossing the shell remnants to the ground. She brushed the residue from her palms onto her skirt. "'Ave you word on Charleigh? Is she comin' ter get me?"

He faced her again. Something like pained acceptance filled his eyes before he answered. "Not exactly. She sent me. I'm Brent Thomas, the schoolmaster at Lyons' Refuge."

Darcy gave a short nod and looked beyond him. Her eyes narrowed in suspicion. "Where's yer buggy? I don't see it."

"I had an errand to run. My wagon is on the other side, next to the post office." He let out a long, weary breath, shook his head, then closed the few steps between them and bent over, putting his hand to the handle of her bag. "If you'll follow me, Miss Evans—"

Darcy reacted quickly. She wrested the valise away from his grip, knocking him off balance. He fell against the bench with a surprised groan. Straightening, he rubbed his leg where it had made contact with the sharp corner of the bench and regarded her, his eyes wide in disbelief.

Darcy felt a momentary pang of guilt. "I like ter carry me own baggage," she explained. Head held high, she strode from the platform and turned the corner in what she hoped was the direction of the buggy.

❧

Brent stared after the tiny woman in rags, walking with the air of a queen. He shook his head. What had Stewart and Charleigh gotten themselves into? What had *he* gotten himself into?

Hurrying after the woman, Brent watched as she threw the valise onto the wagon seat. Grabbing both sides, she vaulted herself up next to the baggage in a most unladylike manner and flopped down. He briefly closed his eyes. Charleigh had tried to warn him, but he'd been too intent on her remark concerning his stuffiness to pay much heed.

"Guv'ner, hain't we goin'? I'm a mite 'ungry, I ham."

Brent winced. Her brutal attack on the English language was nothing short of criminal. The way she dropped h's and added h's where they weren't supposed to be thoroughly unsettled him. In addition, her vowels came out sounding like other vowels. It was a wonder he could understand a thing she said.

"Yes, I'm coming," he muttered, striding to the driver's side. Carefully he stepped up into the wagon and lowered himself onto the bench. With meticulous precision, he smoothed his suit coat and pants and adjusted his hat before grabbing the reins. Feeling her stare, he turned her way.

Her thin face wore an expression of humorous disbelief; both black brows arched high above her dark eyes.

"Something amuses you, Miss Evans?" Brent asked in a controlled voice. He guided the horses down the road leading to the lane that would take them to the reformatory.

"Nothin', guv'ner. Nothin' ter squawk habout anyways."

Brent concentrated on the drive.

The minutes passed in blissful silence. Autumn had come in a blaze of glory, wrapping the trees in a cloak of fire. The sky held a grayish white cast, as luminescent as a pearl polished to a fine gleam. He felt a poem coming on and wished for his journal.

CRRRAAAACKK!

Startled by the explosive thud—which shook the wagon seat—Brent whipped his head toward Darcy. Bent at the waist, she retrieved something from under her boot. She straightened and looked at him. Seeing his horrified gaze upon her, she hesitated and then held out her hand. A mangled walnut lay in her dirty palm.

"Would ye loik some, guv'ner?"

"No, thank you." Brent faced front again.

Social graces? The woman didn't know the meaning of the term. Furthermore, judging from what he'd seen of her character thus far, her housekeeping and culinary skills were likely nonexistent. He doubted she could read or write. So why had Charleigh wanted to bring her to the States so desperately?

A ghastly thought hit Brent, making him gasp as if someone had punched him in the stomach. Surely Stewart and Charleigh wouldn't do such a thing to him. No, Brent was only borrowing trouble, conjuring up all manner of ridiculous scenarios. Besides, nine small hooligans were enough for any schoolmaster to contend with.

CRRRAAACCCKK!

He braced himself against the wagon seat, closed his eyes, and sighed. It would be a long drive.

❧

The wagon eventually neared a wooden fence. Darcy could see a wide field of grass beyond the slats and a large stone and wood house in the distance. She sat up straighter and craned her neck. A sign at the open gate welcomed her, and she struggled to make out the words. The first word—"Lyons'"—she recognized. It had been in the letter from Charleigh. The second word was harder, and she drew her brows together, sounding it out as Charleigh had taught her years ago.

Puzzled, she turned to the man beside her. "What's 'refug'?"

"What?" He glanced her way, incredulous, as if she'd just asked him what color underdrawers he wore instead of the meaning of a simple word.

"Refug. What the sign says."

Brent sighed again. "That's refuge. Lyons' Refuge. The name of the reformatory."

"Oh." Darcy studied her new home.

A white picket fence enclosed vast grounds, where several horses grazed. Neat rows of vegetables grew on a small patch next to the two-story house. Dormer windows made the place look homier, and bright flowers spilled from window boxes in profusion. As she watched, a buxom red-haired woman opened the door and stepped onto the porch. Even from this distance, Darcy recognized her friend.

Before the wagon rolled to a stop, Darcy grabbed her bag with one hand, put her other to the back of her hat, and jumped to the ground, ignoring Brent's warning to wait. She raced across the wet grass to meet Charleigh coming down the steps. The two women hugged each other tightly.

"Oh, Charleigh, don't ye look grand!" Darcy exclaimed once she pulled away and eyed Charleigh's plump figure and rosy face. "Married life agrees with ye, hit does."

Charleigh smiled. "Now, let me look at you." She scanned Darcy's scarecrowlike form and frowned. "The reform still skimps on clothing allowances, I see. And meals."

"Hain't so bad," Darcy insisted. "Hat least I got me a spare dress. Some girls don't get that. Has for food, well. . .I ham a mite 'ungry."

Charleigh laughed. "Of course you are! Come along." She hooked her arm through Darcy's and led her to the porch. "Irma has prepared a special meal to welcome you. And about clothing, I have some dresses I can no longer wear. We can alter them to fit."

Darcy halted. "Charleigh! You're not—"

"No," Charleigh said, shaking her head. Pain filled her eyes, but she gave a wobbly half smile. "I was, but I lost the baby two months ago. And another at the beginning of the year."

"Oh, I ham sorry. I ought not ter 'ave said a thing."

"You didn't know." Charleigh squeezed Darcy's arm. "It's the one thing I wish I could give Stewart—a child. But maybe I never can." Her brow furrowed, a ghost of the past flitting across her face. Darcy had seen it often when they shared a room at Turreney Farm.

"Charleigh?" Darcy prodded softly.

Charleigh blinked, and a bright smile replaced the frown. "Just listen to me—all gloom and doom, and on your first day here! Come along, and let's see you fed."

❧

Brent watched the women enter the house. Then, remembering the reason for his delay to the train station, he stepped down from the wagon and strode to the vegetable patch. Three boys knelt in dirt furrows, pulling up turnips under an older boy's watchful eye.

Herbert, a recent admission to Lyons' Refuge, flickered an uneasy glance at Brent. His freckled face reddened, and his gaze zoomed back to the vegetable in his hands as he slowly dropped it in the bucket beside him. He'd always been as easy to see through as a windowpane. His every action pointed to his guilt.

Joel dusted his hands on his trousers and met Brent's inquiring stare with a steady, questioning gaze. To a stranger, his angelic face, clear blue eyes, and halo of white blond hair would have labeled him an innocent. Yet Brent knew better. Joel was often the mastermind behind pranks. He could lie through his teeth without flinching, a convincing look on his face the entire time—confusing the questioner and making him feel at fault for even asking the boy if he was involved in any wrongdoing. That his father was a con artist serving time in prison came as no surprise.

And then there was Tommy. Brent inwardly sighed. Poor lad. A clubfoot disabled him, and he was wont to jump to another's suggestion of mischief in the hopes of being accepted by his peers. He swiped away a lock of mousy brown hair from his forehead and studied Brent with solemn dark eyes that held a world of pain. The boy had been thrown out by what was left of his family, scorned by many, and later found scavenging in the streets. Stealing the grocer's apples had been his first offense, but Stewart had taken pity on the lad when Judge Markham presented Tommy's case and had brought him to Lyons' Refuge more than a year ago.

"Boys, there's something I wish to discuss with you. Samuel, please unhitch Polly from the wagon and tend to her."

"Yes, sir." Samuel, one of the original members of Lyons' Refuge, moved toward the horse, his expression curious in the eye not covered with the black patch. He'd come quite a ways from the boy who'd set fire to a farmer's field years ago. Upon coming home from fighting in the Great War, blinded in one eye from shrapnel, he'd sought a job at the refuge and did whatever was needed of him.

Brent produced his most stern gaze as he assessed the three young culprits in his charge. "As to the matter of what I found on the wagon seat earlier—and I'm certain all three of you know to what I refer—I wish to know which one of you was responsible for leaving me that undesirable gift."

Herbert sniggered nervously. Joel affected his usual innocent pose. Tommy looked down at his hands.

Brent lifted an eyebrow, crossing his arms. "Very well. If none of you will admit to the crime, then all may suffer for it. I suspect the smaller boys didn't have a hand in this; but if I don't learn the truth soon, I'll be forced to inflict group punishment."

Tommy's glance shot upward, then dove to his hands again. "I did it, Mr. Thomas," he admitted in a low voice.

Joel gave him a look of disgust, Herbert one of surprise.

Brent doubted Tommy was the only boy involved; but before he could comment further, Irma called from the porch.

"Look lively, boys! Dinner's a-waitin'."

The three shot up from the ground at the cook's announcement, grabbed their pails, and scuttled like fleeing mice. Tommy shuffled behind, trying to keep up.

"Stop where you are!" Brent's shout halted them in their tracks, and they turned, fidgety. "This conversation will resume after the meal. Is that understood?"

All three nodded, obviously relieved to have escaped judgment for however long it lasted. They tromped up the steps and disappeared through the doorway.

Shaking his head in frustration, Brent followed. If the past three hours were anything to go by, he would be better off returning to his room at the back of the schoolhouse and staying there for the remainder of the evening. Surely things couldn't get any worse.

The moment the thought crossed his mind, Brent released a humorless laugh. Then again, at Lyons' Refuge, anything was possible. And with the unpredictable Miss Darcy Evans afoot, Brent had an uneasy feeling the absurd would soon be considered the norm.

Chapter 2

The tantalizing aroma of roast beef and potatoes teased Brent's senses as he approached the dining table. Her face now free of soot, the newcomer sat next to Charleigh and stared ravenously at the platters of steaming food Irma set down. Brent took his usual seat, one catty-cornered across from Darcy, and she glanced at him.

He was struck by the intense midnight blue of her eyes—eyes so dark he'd thought the irises almost black earlier. But the electric lamps overhead revealed a trace of bluish purple in the dark orbs, something he hadn't noticed until now. Irritated that he *should* notice, Brent looked away, shook out his napkin, and placed it on his lap.

Once the boys were seated, with freshly scrubbed hands and faces, Charleigh bowed her head. "Merciful Lord, we thank You for this bounty. We ask You to bless everyone at this table, and thank You for granting safe passage to my friend, Darcy. We most humbly pray for Stewart's safe and speedy return to us from Manhattan. Amen."

A chorus of "amens" sounded. Clinks, scrapes, and muted thuds followed as helpings were scooped onto plates and platters, and dishes were passed among them.

"Tell us about your voyage, Darcy," Charleigh said from the head of the table. She spooned peas onto the plate of the youngest boy, Jimmy.

He screwed up his pixie face. "Don' want no peas."

"Hush," she admonished, "and eat them like a good lad." She turned her gaze Darcy's way. "Did you encounter any problems aboard ship?"

Darcy shook her head. "Nothin' 'appened—nothin' ter squawk habout, anyways," she said, her mouth full. "But it liked to scare me witless when I 'eard a bang, and hit turned hout to be a clumsy crew member, what dropped a box o' books on deck!" She laughed with unsuppressed glee. "I thought someone were takin' a shot hat us and the war 'ad started all over again."

Brent grimaced, carefully cut a bite-sized portion of meat, and slipped it into his mouth.

"Why does she talk so funny?" a boy said in a loud stage whisper to his peer. "And look at that ugly dress."

"We're not s'ppose to talk with our mouths full," young Jimmy informed Darcy with a superior air. "Mrs. Lyons says it ain't proper."

Brent looked up from his plate. Darcy appeared ill at ease as she fumbled with her glass of cider.

"Jimmy," Brent said, "children are also not supposed to correct their elders. Or speak unless they've been spoken to."

"Yes, sir." Jimmy bowed his head.

Brent looked Darcy's way. She studied him, clearly puzzled, creases in her milk white forehead. Uncomfortable, he looked away—to Charleigh.

A gleam of wonder lit her eyes as she looked back and forth between him and Darcy, a soft smile on her lips.

Brent focused on his plate, determined to keep his mind on his meal. Was it so unusual that he'd taken up for the poor guttersnipe? He'd always possessed something of a soft spot for the underdog. That was one reason he'd taken the job of schoolmaster to a bunch of misfits who'd each experienced short careers as a hooligan. The other reason had involved his brother Bill.

Darcy cleared her throat, and Brent looked up. She straightened in her chair, shoulders back, her chin lifted in a regal position. With as much dignity as Brent imagined she could muster, she spoke to the boy across from her and two seats down.

"Would you *pleeease* pass the Uncle Fred?"

Stunned silence met her startling request—followed by the boys' raucous laughter. They collapsed over their plates, holding their sides as if they would burst.

"She wants to eat Uncle Fred!"

"Poor ole chap—wonder who he is?"

"Is she a cannibal, too?"

"What's a 'cabinnal'?"

"Boys!" Charleigh stood and clinked her spoon against her glass, demanding attention. "If you can't behave like proper gentlemen, then you may march to your rooms and do without supper. Is that understood?"

They quieted, a muffled snort escaping now and then. Straightening in their seats, they again focused on dinner.

"That's better." Charleigh sank to her chair and replaced her napkin on her lap. She threw an apologetic look to Darcy, whose color rivaled that of the beets in the serving dish.

"I–I'm a mite tired," she mumbled. "Hit were a long journey. I'd loik to go to me room now."

"Of course. I'll have Irma send you up a tray." Charleigh's troubled gaze went to Brent. "Would you mind taking Darcy's bag to her room?"

Remembering the previous and painful incident at the station when he'd tried to assist with her valise, he turned a wary look Darcy's way. "If she'll allow it."

Darcy nodded, eyes downcast. "Hit's at the bottom o' the apples an' pears."

Brent stared, uncomprehending. "Apples and pears?"

"She means stairs," Charleigh explained.

"Well, why don't she just say so?" Joel demanded. "Is she loony?" His question led to more chortles from the boys.

"Joel, that's enough!" Charleigh leveled a steady gaze at the culprit. "Darcy speaks Cockney, a rhyming slang I also grew up with. It's popular in the East End of London. Uncle Fred is the term for bread. And as for your insolent remark, you may march to your room this minute, young man. In this house we don't use spiteful words to hurt another person's feelings."

Joel glared at Charleigh, then Darcy, but obediently rose from the table and left. Darcy stood, tears making her huge eyes sparkle. "I really ought ter go lie down, Charleigh. No need sendin' a tray. I hain't as 'ungry as I thought."

Charleigh's expression was sympathetic. "Irma, if you'll watch the boys, I'll show Darcy to her room."

Frowning, Brent secured Darcy's bag and followed the women up the carpeted staircase. Life at Lyons' Refuge had indeed undergone a drastic change. And he had a sneaking suspicion it wasn't for the better.

❧

The next morning, a tap sounded on the door. "Darcy? May I come in?"

Darcy turned from brushing the tangles out of her thick dark hair. Morning sunlight streamed into the cozy attic room through the small, arched window, casting her in a golden pool of floating dust motes. "Aye—ye may."

Charleigh opened the door and smiled. "Did you sleep well? Is the room to your liking?" She moved to the iron bedstead and sank to the mattress. "Oh dear. It's dusty in here, isn't it? I do apologize. I thought the cleaning had been taken care of. I'll tend to it right away."

"It weren't bad. And I don't mind tendin' to me own room, to help any way I can."

Darcy twisted her body around on the chair so she could get a better look at her friend. Charleigh seemed upset, distracted; maybe she regretted bringing Darcy to America. Especially after what happened last night. "Did you want ter talk with me?"

Charleigh clasped her hands around one crossed knee. "Yes, Darcy, I did. There's really no easy way to say this, and I certainly don't want to hurt your feelings, but. . ." She trailed off.

Lifting her chin, Darcy prepared for the worst.

"After what happened at dinner last evening, I've come to the conclusion that certain measures must be taken in order for things to run smoothly here. Children can often be cruel without meaning to be. The boys at Lyons' Refuge can be cruel on purpose. Many of them are hard, bitter—coming from situations that would melt the hardest of hearts."

Darcy nodded. Having come from just such a situation, she understood completely.

"First and foremost, I want you to know that I love you as you are." Charleigh smiled. "But in order to be understood—as well as to understand—I think it beneficial that you learn the proper way to talk here in America."

Darcy wrinkled her brow, uncertain if she should feel slighted, hurt, or relieved. Her manner of speech had never been a problem, though at the reform she'd been forced to drop the popular Cockney phrases. Nervousness at being in a new place had probably led her to say them without thinking last night. Ever since she'd arrived in the States, she'd felt buffeted by the peculiar yet precise way these Americans spoke. Even Charleigh's British accent was polished, like the high gloss of an apple—whereas Darcy's was as rough as a potato just dug from the earth.

Charleigh leaned forward, covering Darcy's hand with her own. "Darcy, if it was just me, I'd never suggest it. Yet, not only the boys, but also the whole town, will look at you askance. I've discovered that people often judge harshly what they don't understand, and I don't want you hurt. I want you to feel comfortable here. This is your home now."

Darcy gave a slight nod.

Charleigh's smile grew wide. "I'll help you with manners and deportment, as well as correct you when you use slang and the wrong pronunciation of words. I'd also like you to further your education in reading and writing. There's nothing wrong with increasing one's head knowledge."

At this, Darcy's heart lightened. She'd always wanted to read books, dreamed of it, wished she could flip through the pages with ease as Charleigh had always done. But Darcy could barely stumble over a paragraph. The little time Charleigh ferreted from daily chores to teach her at the women's reformatory hadn't been enough.

"Are ye certain you'll 'ave the time, Charleigh? Seems like an awful lot you're tykin' on, what with running the reform and tykin' care o' the boys."

Charleigh rose and averted her eyes, smoothing the wrinkles from her skirt. "Actually, Brent would be much better qualified to teach you. I'll suggest he tutor you for an hour every day once the children finish their lessons."

Darcy drew a soft breath. Brent Thomas teach her? She didn't think she could abide him looking down his nose at her day after day in confined quarters—and alone yet. True, he'd rescued her from total humiliation at dinner last night, but the blue eyes behind the spectacles had been full of pity. And Darcy wanted no man's pity! Yet she did want to learn all she could about reading and writing.

"Can I tyke the class wi' the others?" Darcy asked.

"After last night, I'm not sure that would be wise."

"I'd like ter give it a try. And Charleigh—I don't want to be a burden. Maybe

Cook wouldn't mind 'aving me 'elp? I learned to bake some hat the farm after ye left."

"Yes—that would be splendid. I'm sure Irma would welcome any help. As to the other..." Charleigh pursed her lips in thought, then nodded once. "I'll discuss your request with Brent and see what he says."

❧

Brent stared at Charleigh, his forearms resting at either side of the open book on his desk. Certainly he hadn't heard her correctly. It had been a long morning. Fatigue must be clouding his mind.

"Well, Brent? Will you do it?"

The screeching sound of chalk on slate made him wince. He looked across the room toward the offender, who was writing for the twenty-second time, "I will never again place bags of horse manure on wagon seats or any other vehicle. But I will leave the manure in the field where it belongs."

"Tommy, you may go for now," Brent said. "You can resume the one hundred sentences later this afternoon."

"Thank you, Mr. Thomas." Relief sweeping his features, the boy set down the chalk and limped from the room.

Brent turned his gaze to Charleigh, who stood in front of his desk. He adjusted his spectacles with thumb and forefinger. "Now let me see if I understand you correctly, Mrs. Lyons. You wish for me to train your friend in the rudiments of grammar, reading, and penmanship by allowing her to attend my class?"

Charleigh beamed. "Yes, that's right."

Brent held back a groan. "Judging from last night's fiasco, are you certain that would be wise? Maintaining order in this classroom is often a delusion. Don't you think bringing in a young woman—who obviously is far below the boys academically—would only create further problems at best? At worst, total chaos?"

"Darcy assures me that she would feel more comfortable in a classroom environment. All I ask is that we give this a try. If it doesn't work, then of course we'll arrange an alternative method."

What alternative method Charleigh had in mind, Brent didn't want to know, though he could hazard a guess.

Charleigh shifted her weight to her other foot. "Please, Brent. Darcy is special to me. She has been ever since I met her in a holding cell in London. From then on, every day with her endeared her to me all the more. I want to help her by seeing to it she receives the education she needs to coexist with the townspeople, as well as those here at the refuge."

Brent pondered her words, his hand reaching for a nearby fountain pen and repeatedly tapping first one end, then the other, on the desk. Charleigh's husband had been there for Brent when he was fresh out of college, full of hopes and

19

dreams. His brother's criminal activities became known not two months after Brent graduated—a horrible shock to the entire family. Because of Bill's folly, Brent was denied every position he applied for that summer. Only Stewart had entrusted him with his first teaching position—ironically at a boys' reformatory. Only Stewart had shown faith in him when others had snubbed him.

Brent thought about Darcy at dinner last night. Something about the little wren twisted his heart, though he was loath to admit it. Would this one good deed be such a difficult task?

He let the air escape his lungs and set down the pen. "Very well, Mrs. Lyons. You may tell Miss Evans that I'll expect her in my classroom tomorrow morning at eight."

Charleigh gave him a brilliant smile. "Thank you! I'm certain you won't regret it."

Brent watched her hurry out the door as though afraid he might change his mind. A picture of the vivacious and impulsive Darcy Evans suddenly invaded his thoughts, and he closed his eyes.

Regret it? He already did.

❧

Ten minutes before class was to start, Darcy nervously tramped to the small, shingled building set off from the main house. Inside, desks sat in three neat rows. A huge chalkboard stood beside the schoolmaster's desk, with a shelf of chunky books along the wall behind it. The only source of light came from a window near the teacher—and the few lamps bracketed to the board walls. In the corner, an ancient-looking potbellied stove gave off welcome heat.

" 'Ello!" Darcy directed an uncertain smile at Brent. He looked up from his desk, gave a vague nod, then turned back to writing something in a thin book.

The smile slipped from her face. She may not be the queen, but didn't she deserve some type of common courtesy? A hello in return? Or a polite "Good morning"?

"Whatcha doin', guv'ner? Today's lesson?"

"No," he muttered, his gaze never straying from the book.

When nothing else was offered, she sighed and scanned the desks. "Where ham I ta sit then?"

"Wherever you like," he returned, his gaze still plastered to that book.

Blowing out her breath in a loud burst of frustration, Darcy plopped onto the nearest bench and tried to squeeze her legs underneath. The desk was much too low and settled on her skirt. Drawing her brows together, she swung her legs out to the right, then settled her elbows on the desk—but now her body was twisted sideways. This would never do!

"Guv'ner?"

He sighed. "What now?"

She crossed her arms on the desk and glared at him. "I don't see 'ow I'm to learn to write good hif I 'ave to stoop like an ole woman to do it!"

"What?"

To her satisfaction, he raised his head, looking startled. He eyed the table where it hit below her waist. His brows gathered. "I'd forgotten about that. The desks were custom-made by one of the locals. He fashioned them for small boys."

Her chin lifted. "Which I hain't."

"Which I'm not."

Her brow creased in confusion. "What?"

"Which I'm not. If I'm to teach you proper grammar, we may as well begin now."

"An' what about the desk, guv'ner?"

With a sigh, he slammed his book shut. "I suppose, until we find something more suitable, you'll have to move up here with me."

If he'd asked her to parade around the room in her bloomers, she couldn't have been more shocked. "With you?"

He tilted his head. "Unless you have a better idea? My desk seems to be the only one that's the right height. And, as you've pointed out, it's important to maintain correct posture when learning penmanship. Take that chair in the corner. The boys should be along any minute." He began moving stacks of books off one edge of his desk and onto the floor.

Darcy hesitated, then went to retrieve the chair. Noisily, she dragged it across the planks, set it in position, walked to the front of it, and plopped down again. "All right. Now what?"

He looked away from sorting a stack of books and adjusted his spectacles. Sunlight pouring in from the window made the curling edges of his still-damp hair glisten. Up close, his eyes were bluer than she remembered, and the fact that she noticed made her fidget.

"I suppose we should see just how far along you are academically before the rest of the class arrives."

"A–ca–dem...?"

"In your schooling." He set a slate in front of her and slapped a piece of chalk on top. "Write your letters, if you please."

Darcy could do that. She had used a pointed stick in the reform's garden and scratched letters into the dirt while Charleigh watched. Eagerly, Darcy picked up the chalk and began forming each letter, sucking in her lower lip in concentration. She ran out of space when she still had five more to go and turned the slate so she could squeeze some along the edge, then turned it again to print upside down along the top.

"Finished!" she exclaimed, triumphant.

Brent turned from sorting the books to look. His eyebrows lifted. "Hmm. Next time don't make your letters so large, and you won't run out of room. Overall, it's adequate, I suppose."

She frowned and looked at the slate. Adequate? What did that mean? It didn't sound good.

"Now, let's hear you read." He opened a book to the first page and slid it in front of her.

Darcy hunched over, brow furrowed, and studied the black print. "A Boy's. . . Will. . .by. . ." Her brows bunched further. "Row-burt. . .Frost." She lifted her gaze to his, expecting praise for her success.

"That's Robert Frost," he said, closing the book. "With a short O. All right, that'll do for now."

That'll do? Darcy frowned. "So, ham I to learn from that book?"

"Hmm?" He looked up from jotting something down in another book. "Oh, yes, I see what you mean. Perhaps it's not suitable for a young woman. I hadn't thought of that. I'll look into acquiring more adequate literature for your schooling."

Adequate. There was that word again. Darcy had a feeling she would grow to despise it.

A flock of young boys burst through the schoolroom door, as noisy as a gaggle of geese. Their chattering and guffaws ceased when they saw Darcy.

"What's she doin' here?" the one Darcy remembered as Joel said. He frowned at her, probably blaming her for his being sent to his room without supper.

"Is she gonna teach us?" the smallest boy, Jimmy, piped up. "Is that why she's sitting at your desk, Mr. Thomas?"

"Ha! Her teach us? She can't even talk right."

"Then why's she here?"

Pulling the cap off his white blond hair, Joel let out a spiteful laugh. "I'll bet I can guess why she's sitting at his desk, all right. She's Teacher's new pet." He elbowed a gangly dark-haired boy next to him. "An' you know what that means with the likes o' her, don't ya? Smoochin' in the cloakroom, I reckon. Don't ya think so, Ralph?"

The dark-haired boy chuckled. Heat raced to Darcy's face as a few nervous titters filtered through the room.

"That will be enough!" Brent stood and rapped his ruler sharply on the edge of the desk, then snapped his forbidding gaze to Joel. "For your impertinence, Mr. Lakely, you may come an hour early to the classroom every day for the rest of this month and start the fire in the stove."

Joel's mouth tightened. "Yes, sir."

Brent released a weary breath and set the ruler down. "Nor will I have any slang in this classroom."

"Yes, sir."

"And you may apologize to Miss Evans."

"Wha—" At the teacher's lifted brow, Joel cut short his indignant reply. "Yes, sir. Sorry, Miss Evans," he clipped, his eyes glittering with hate as he looked her way.

Brent sank back to his chair. "As to the numerous inquiries regarding Miss Evans's appearance in our classroom, she is to learn alongside you gentlemen. And I trust you *will* behave like gentlemen?"

Grumbles and groans met his query. Darcy gazed over the room of scrubbed faces—some curious, some suspicious, a few of them openly hostile—until she found a pair of kind brown eyes underneath a long swatch of mousy brown hair. The boy offered her a tentative smile. Darcy returned it. Perhaps things would soon improve.

"Pull out your slates and we'll begin today's lesson." Brent adjusted his glasses.

Darcy reached for the slate but in her haste knocked it off the desk. It hit the planked floor with a resounding clatter, eliciting another round of chortles from the boys. Her gaze whipped to Brent's weary one.

Then again, perhaps not.

Chapter 3

Astreak of branched lightning zipped across the nighttime sky, making an erratic slash beyond the thicket at the eastern side of the house. Soon, a distant crash followed. Brent stood on the covered porch and listened to the rain beat down on an overturned barrel, similar to the sound of many drums. From behind, a muted yellow light shone on the porch. He turned to see who had joined him.

Looming over Brent by almost a foot, Stewart Lyons, the headmaster of Lyons' Refuge, came through the door. Premature gray sprinkled his hair, but his strapping build was that of a youth's. His hazel eyes lifted to the sky. "It looks as if the storm is passing."

Brent nodded. "It would appear so."

The light vanished as Stewart closed the door behind him. "That Darcy is something else. Imagine her saying that my fiddle playing reminded her of a rummy's who used to play at the tavern. She's certainly not afraid to speak her mind, is she?" Amusement laced his words.

"No, she's not." Brent returned his gaze to the rain. In the past weeks since he'd taken on the task of schooling her, he never knew what she would suddenly say or do next.

"Your situation reminds me of a play an acquaintance of mine attended years ago."

Brent winced. *Don't say it.*

"*Pygmalion,* I think it was called. Ever hear of it?"

Brent closed his eyes, resigned to his fate. "I remember reading the review. It's a play by Bernard Shaw, set in London, about a Cockney flower girl and a professor of diction."

"That's right. Though you hardly remind me of the irascible Henry Higgins—at least from the way my friend described him." Stewart grinned.

Brent managed a smile. Well, that was a relief. Or was it in the same league as being considered stuffy?

The two men continued to stare at the storm, watching the lightning move northeast. When Stewart again spoke, Brent detected a somber tone in his voice. The trickling sound of rain falling from the eaves added to the dreary mood.

"I received a letter from my family in Raleigh today. My father is ill. It sounds serious."

"I'm sorry to hear that." Brent studied Stewart, whose hands were now shoved into his pockets. He looked more tense than usual, still staring into the dissipating storm.

"Thank you." Stewart glanced his way. "I'd like you to take my place while I'm gone—if I go. I haven't made a solid decision yet. I wanted to talk to you first. If it became known that three women were running the reform—two of them former felons and one an old woman—the state might take the boys. Judge Markham already considers our methods of reform unconventional. It took a great deal of persistence on my part to get his support when I first got started. Especially since the idea of reformatories was still so new and my concept was so unlike the others."

"If you do go, how long will you be gone?"

"I have no idea. My parents and I were never close, one reason I came to New York with my cousin, Steven. After his suicide, my family turned against me. But that's all history now." He sighed. "With Father ill and likely to die, I feel I've no option but to go to them. It's my duty. My oldest brother died in the war, and I'm the only son left." Stewart's words trailed off. "So many good men died. So many."

Uncomfortable, Brent looked away. Stewart never talked about the fighting he'd seen, and Brent preferred it that way. He settled his hat more firmly on his head. "I should return to my room. I have papers to grade."

"And about what I asked—would you be open to taking on the job of temporary headmaster, as you did during the war?"

Brent nodded. "Of course. You can depend on me."

"Thank you, friend. You're a good man."

Brent moved toward the schoolhouse and released a self-derisive laugh. A good man? Hardly. If the truth were known, he was a coward. When the Great War had been in progress, the prospect of fighting terrified him. Guns and grenades were not for him.

All through childhood, Brent's peers had labeled him "lily-livered." An appropriate title, to be sure. He lacked the bravado that made men like Stewart, who'd won a medal for saving his company of men, a hero in people's eyes. Moreover, it hadn't boosted Brent's self-esteem when, after being drafted, he was rejected for having flat feet. Even a plausible excuse for being unable to fight didn't erase the belief Brent fostered that had he been accepted, he would have abandoned his company in the heat of battle and fled. Like a lily-livered fool.

Unlike Stewart. The town's war hero.

❧

Darcy wiggled her back against the plump cushion, enjoying the fire's warmth. The boys sat in a semicircle on the rose-patterned carpet around Charleigh, who sat in a rocker, reading from a book. Nine pairs of eyes watched Charleigh's face as she brought Louisa May Alcott's words to life: " 'You cannot be too careful; watch your tongue, and eyes, and hands, for it's easy to tell, and look, and act untruth.' "

Darcy hid a smile at the rapt expressions on the boys' faces. Four weeks ago, when Charleigh first started reading *Little Men,* she'd been met with groans and complaints that it was a "sissified book." She ignored their objections and each Sunday evening read one chapter aloud. Soon the little scamps sat entranced, eyes shining, eagerly waiting to hear the latest goings-on at Plumcrest—the school that was as odd as Lyons' Refuge and also contained a variety of boys, some with quirks much like theirs. Darcy overheard the lads talk one night and knew that each identified with a certain boy in the story, and each looked forward to hearing what his character was up to next.

Darcy's gaze swept the nine upturned faces. A hint of innocence glimmered, even in the older ones' eyes. These boys were just boys, after all. Not miniature hooligans, as some of the townspeople whispered. Many of these lads had been dealt a hard lot in life and had done what they could to survive. How well Darcy understood them.

When Charleigh first explained how she and Stewart ran the place—by discipline mixed with love—Darcy had been perplexed. She'd been sentenced to only one reformatory—and that one for women. But the strict matrons, daunting schedules, and never-ending work could not equate with life at Lyons' Refuge. Here, Charleigh and Stewart treated the boys as if they were their own, though strict discipline was administered to those who didn't abide by the rules. In the two months since Darcy had arrived, she saw Lyons' Refuge more as a home for boys than a true reformatory.

Daily schedules included chores, schooling, and then more work around the farm. Filling meals cooked by Irma and Darcy satisfied the boys, who later would gather for thirty-minute devotions with Charleigh and Stewart, then hurry off to an hour of studying lessons before bedtime. Saturdays were much the same, with the exception of no classes, which gave more time to finish lessons Brent had assigned. And Sundays were days of rest at Lyons' Refuge.

Up early, Stewart and Charleigh took the three youngest boys to the country church a few miles away in Stewart's noisy motorcar, while Brent and Darcy took the rest in the wagon. Afterward they returned home to another sumptuous meal, and the boys were allowed a couple of hours' free time to do pretty much as they pleased. Before bed, Charleigh sat in the rocker by the fire, with the boys gathered around, and read them a chapter from God's Holy Word. She then picked up a book—sometimes Charles Dickens or Robert Louis Stevenson or another author's work. But always it was a story to fuel every boy's imagination and make each face glow with anticipation.

The front door opened, letting in a blast of cold, snowy air; and Darcy looked toward the foyer. Brent walked in, his spectacles immediately fogging from the warm room. His bowler hat, scarf, and coat were speckled with white. He pulled off his glasses and glanced at Charleigh, whose back was to him, then at Darcy. Putting a finger to his lips, he shook his head, then quietly moved to the back of the house.

Darcy hesitated for two full paragraphs of the story before rising and going in search of him. The others didn't notice her leave; or if they did, they paid no attention.

She found Brent in the kitchen, pulling the loaf of bread from the bread box. He turned upon hearing her footsteps.

"Hello," Darcy said, remembering to pronounce her "H" as Charleigh had taught her. "We missed you at dinner."

He gave a slight nod. "I had grades to average. The time slipped by me unawares." With a knife, he sawed two pieces from the rye loaf and set them at precise angles on a plate.

Darcy noticed he wasn't wearing his spectacles. Without them, his eyes appeared much bluer and brighter. Flustered that she should pick up on such a thing, she looked away, to the table. His glasses lay on top.

Not thinking, Darcy plucked them up. She raised them to the light, peered through the fogged lenses, rubbed them on her skirt, and, curiosity getting the best of her, slipped them on.

"Aaeee!" she squealed. "Things appear as they did years ago—when I was about in me cups!"

Heat rushed to her face when she realized what she'd blurted. Though she'd learned much about manners since coming to Lyons' Refuge, too often the past slipped out to embarrass her.

Brent said nothing. After a moment he cleared his throat and lifted the spectacles from Darcy's nose. "Yes, well, they aid me in my vision impairment."

She watched as he slipped them back on. He looked at her for a few seconds before turning to butter his bread.

"I have some stew in the icebox for you," Darcy said. She opened the one door of the tin-lined wooden contraption where Irma stored perishable food. Blocks of ice kept the interior cold. "I'll heat it on the stove and dish you up a bowl."

"No, really, the bread is enough."

"It won't be no bother," Darcy insisted, pulling the container off the shelf and slamming the door shut.

"Really, Miss Evans, there's no need—"

Darcy swung around and crashed into Brent, who'd come up behind her. The uncovered beef stew splashed onto his pristine linen shirt and tweed vest. Involuntarily, Darcy dropped the pan, her hands flying to her mouth in horror.

The pan hit the floor, splashing the wooden planks, her skirt, and Brent's neat, creased pants with the rest of the brown juice.

Darcy's shocked gaze flew to Brent's. His eyes were filled with what looked like pained acceptance—something she'd seen many times. He moved his once-shiny brown shoe to dislodge a potato slice that rested on top.

"Perhaps I'll forgo dinner tonight. I'm really not as hungry as I thought." His smile was feeble at best.

"I–I'm sorry," Darcy stuttered, backing up. "Really, I ham." Slowly she shook her head, then hurried from the room.

Brent watched her go, his mind a tangle of thoughts that resembled Charleigh's wild ivy growing on the windowsill. Perhaps he shouldn't have said what he had. With a heavy sigh, he reached for the dish towel, dampened it with water from the pump, and blotted his clothes, attempting to remove the stains.

Darcy remained an enigma. One minute she was bold and brassy, saying whatever she pleased; the next she was as sensitive as a child whose pencil drawing had been ridiculed by an unfeeling adult. Brent was frankly astounded at her intelligence and at how quickly she learned. She wasn't far from catching up to the boys in her studies. Grammatically and in areas of deportment, Charleigh had worked wonders with her. Though, of course, the young Miss Evans still had a great deal to learn.

Brent never knew what to expect from the British spitfire. She was a cyclone in his well-ordered and perfectly planned existence. A cyclone that tore from the roots everything proper, staid, and orderly, in Brent's estimation, and replaced it with impulsiveness, disorder—and a zest for living and having fun.

He glanced at the spill on the floor and bent to mop it up with the dishcloth. He'd never experienced fun or even been allowed to play. His parents had raised him with a rigid code of conduct—so severe that it sent his brother running from home before his sixteenth birthday. Brent shook his head, sobering at the thought of Bill and the life of crime he'd chosen. Bill and he had been so close once. . . .

Releasing a forceful breath, and with it any bitter thoughts of what might have been, Brent rinsed out the towel and laid it over the rack by the counter. He shrugged into his outerwear and left by the back door.

Chapter 4

With unabashed delight, Darcy crunched into her apple. Her eyelids slid shut. "Mmmmm. . .I think apples is—are—my favorite fruit of all. Next to oranges an' pears. An' maybe plums."

"Didn't you like them pies, Miss Darcy?" young Jimmy asked.

"Well, the mincemeat pie we had for Thanksgiving sure was good, it was; but I think the fruitcake we ate earlier today topped 'em all."

"I like oranges best," Tommy said as he limped to her chair near the Christmas tree.

She put her arm around him, bringing him close. Tommy was Darcy's favorite of the boys, reminding her of Roger, a lame child who'd been in her young band of thieves. As she'd done with Roger, Darcy took Tommy under her wing.

He pulled a shiny silver whistle out of the darned sock he held, then tipped it over to let several jacks and a ball fall into his palm. "Isn't this just the greatest, Miss Darcy? Mrs. Lyons' pop sure is a nifty guy. I never had no toys gived to me before I come to this place."

"Yes, he is a nifty guy," Darcy agreed, remembering her first meeting with Michael Larkin and his wife, Alice. He accepted her immediately, despite her way of talking; and Darcy soon realized the Irish bear of a man had a heart as gentle as a cub's. A huge contributor to the reform, Michael visited often, seeming to adopt the boys as his grandsons.

Darcy looked past the tall green fir—decorated with stringed popcorn, cut-out cookies, and colorful paper chains the boys had made—to where Charleigh sat beside her father on the sofa. Stewart stood nearby, his back to them, and stared out the window at the falling snow. Charleigh and her father were in deep discussion; and from the looks of it, the topic was serious. Charleigh shook her head in reply to something Michael said. He patted her hand; and she swiped a finger underneath her eye, pasted on a smile, and stood. "Well, boys. What say we have some gingerbread and hot cocoa to end this Christmas Day?"

Loud cheers and whoops met her suggestion.

She put up her hands for quiet, then turned to Darcy. "But first I'd like you to read the Christmas story. Every year we take turns. Since this is your first year with us, I'd like you to do the honors."

The juice from the apple seemed to evaporate in Darcy's mouth, which went stone dry. "Me?" With difficulty she swallowed the chewed bite. "Maybe Mr.

Thomas should read instead." She cast a hopeful glance at Brent.

"Please, Darcy," Charleigh insisted. "You've come so far in your education since the day you arrived. I'd love to hear you read." Her gaze encompassed the children scattered on the floor. "Wouldn't we, boys?"

A chorus of mumbled agreements filled the room.

From beside the fireplace, Joel blew his new whistle, catching everyone's shocked attention. His smile was wide. "Aw, Mrs. Lyons, don't make her read if she can't do it." His clear blue eyes held a smirk as they turned Darcy's way. "I mean, we don't want to embarrass her or nothin'—like when she read aloud from *Paradicee Losit* her first week at school. Or at least that's how she said it."

"Joel." Stewart turned from the window, giving the boy a warning look. "Hold your tongue."

Darcy's lips thinned at the unwanted memory; and she glared at the scamp, who sat on the carpet, legs crossed, and stared innocently back. She turned her gaze to Charleigh and held out her hand. "Give me the book." She'd show the little rapscallion.

With an encouraging smile, Charleigh handed her the Bible, showed her the passage, and rejoined her father on the couch. Darcy took a deep breath and briefly closed her eyes, delivering a hasty, silent prayer that she wouldn't get any of the words wrong.

" 'And it came to pass in those days, that there went out a de–cree from Cae–sar Aug–us–tus that all the world should be. . .taxed. . .' "

She continued to read, sounding out the longer words. But she was certain she didn't mispronounce a single one. The simple yet fascinating story of Christ's birth produced an awed hush in the room, despite the halting manner in which the events were told. Even Darcy felt a sweet peace as she read the words, " 'Fear not: for, behold, I bring you good tidings of great joy, which shall be to all people. For unto you is born this day in the city of David a Saviour, which is Christ the Lord. . .' " Darcy paused for a moment. " 'And sud-den-ly there was with the angel a mul-ti-tude of the heav-en-ly host praising God, and saying, Glory to God in the highest, and on earth peace, good will toward men.' "

She looked up from the book. No animosity or mockery shone from Joel's eyes now. They were soft and wondering, like a child's. Sometimes it was hard to remember he *was* only a child. And suddenly Darcy knew she would do what she could to help the boy escape a life such as hers had been. How to go about such a task was the mystery. For surely trying to help such a stubborn lad would be a chore more taxing than any duties she'd had at Turreney Farm or the cooking she did at the refuge.

Irma cleared her throat. "I never get weary of hearing that story, and it seems I hear something different with each tellin' of the tale." Wiping her eyes with the edge of her apron, she turned in the direction of the kitchen, then stopped and faced them, her gaze sweeping over the room. "Well, what are you just sitting there and staring for? Look lively, laddies! Hot cocoa's awaitin'."

Her reply had the effect of a trumpet at reveille. The boys clambered to their feet, whistles and jacks forgotten, and shot toward the kitchen. Even Stewart's remonstration to "hold it down" seemed softer than usual. He moved across the room and took hold of his wife's hand, helping her from the sofa.

Charleigh cast a glance Darcy's way. "Coming, Darcy? I can try to save you a cup, but with that crowd, I can't offer any promises."

Darcy shook her head. With one hand, she closed the Bible and set it on the piecrust table beside her. "Apples is enough for me. I prefer fruit and nuts and the like."

Charleigh smiled and left the room with Stewart, and Michael and Alice followed.

❦

"Aren't you going to join the party?" Darcy asked Brent when they were the only ones left in the parlor.

He shook his head. "I've never had a penchant for such festivities."

She propped her elbow on the chair arm and rested her chin on her palm, studying him where he sat in a stiff-backed chair. "Not sure what a 'penchant' is, but if it means you don't like to have fun, why not?"

"Excuse me?" Brent lifted his eyebrows in astonishment.

"Fun. F–u–n. Fun." She threw him a wicked smile. "See, I can spell it, too. But spelling don't—doesn't—do me much good if I can't live it. Just spelling words and reading 'em don't do much of anything. You got to live 'em, too."

Baffled, he merely shook his head.

Darcy leaned forward, tucking her wrists in her skirt between her knees, her half-eaten apple still in one hand. "I'll bet you're wonderin' how a girl like me could have had any fun in her life."

"The thought had crossed my mind," Brent admitted. "Lyons' Refuge is in a class by itself, it's true, but I know most reforms are quite strict."

"See there!" She rolled her eyes as if he wore a dunce cap. "You got to tyke what fun you can find in life when you can find it. Now at the women's reform it was harder, I'll admit, and things wasn't one bit pleasant. Just ask Charleigh; she'll tell you. I learned to look for fun in the small things—like when I was hoein' the vegetable patch, and a butterfly would flutter past me face. I'd watch it and imagine I was ridin' on its back, seein' everything it saw beyond the gates of the reform. Do you know what I'm sayin'?"

Brent nodded, though he had no idea what she was talking about.

"When I was with Hunstable and Crackers—they was two of the gang, a few years older than I and smart as the dickens—they taught me how to have fun. Especially Crackers, our leader. He could pick any pocket and had a fondness for crackers. That's why we called him Crackers. He stole 'em from the grocer's barrel. Practically lived on 'em, he did!" She laughed.

"I hardly see how thievery could be classified as fun. You've seen what wages it brings."

"No, that's not the fun I was talking about," Darcy said and sighed, shaking her head in exasperation. "I'm gettin' to that. Stealin' was the same as survivin' in the East End, 'specially if you was a child. Me mum died when I was young, and me stepfather—well, let's just say he weren't a nice man. He'd get drunk and come after me. One day I had enough. I ran out and never went back. I was ten at the time. That's when I joined up with Crackers and Hunstable. They found me sleepin' in the street under a newspaper." She shrugged one shoulder, crunched another bite of her apple, and smiled as though the event hadn't been of any real concern to her.

Brent stared, uncertain how to reply. This was the first time he'd been given a glimpse into Darcy's past. Though his childhood could never be called easy, his physical comforts had been met. He was stunned at the hardships some children endured. Children such as Charleigh and Darcy had been, and the boys at Lyons' Refuge.

"Tell me about Crackers's idea of fun," he said softly.

She cocked a surprised brow and peered at him as if trying to discern whether he was truly interested, then gave a nod and swallowed her apple. "There was this organ grinder, see, and he had this monkey—it wore a red satin jacket with shiny gold buttons. Such a lovely thing—that jacket. I always did say one day I'd have me one so fine. Anyhow, Crackers dropped bits of crackers to form a trail, and the monkey found it and followed. The four of us had a grand time with that monkey before the organ grinder caught us and give it to us good."

"Four of you? You mentioned only three."

Darcy's expression sobered. "There was another. Roger had a crippled leg after falling off a wall. Sometimes Crackers and Hunstable took turns carrying him on their backs when Roger got tired of walkin' with his stick. Roger couldn't steal nothin' for the gang, bein' a cripple like he was, but we took care of him. He was four years younger than me, like me own little brother."

"And where is he now? Still in London, I presume?"

She stared into the fire. "Roger weren't strong. One hard winter, he died."

Brent flinched. Her soft, short sentences revealed more than she was aware. He had no experience when it came to offering sympathy—especially to young women—and felt completely out of his element.

"I see. Well, at least you seem to have a few good memories," he said lamely.

A smile lit her face again. "I do at that. So tell me, guv'ner, have you any brothers or sisters?"

The question hit Brent like a slap in the face. He'd never talked to anyone about Bill, though Stewart, of course, knew the basic facts. Yet something had happened between him and Darcy in these last few minutes, something that had strangely and irrevocably drawn them closer together. She had shared a painful portion of her life, and Brent felt he should reciprocate.

Before he could question his rash decision, he spoke. "I have one brother. Bill left home when he was fifteen and later joined up with a felon who ran a numbers racket. I talked to Bill once, almost a year ago. He sent me a letter and asked me to meet him in Manhattan."

Brent sighed, took off his spectacles, and wiped them with a handkerchief. "I tried to talk to him, to persuade him to listen to reason, but he would have none of it."

❧

Darcy had no idea what a numbers racket was, but it must be awful from the look on Brent's face. "I'm sorry, guv'ner. I'll ask the good Lord to keep a watch on 'im."

He lifted his startled gaze. "Thank you, Miss Evans. I would appreciate your intercession."

Her tentative grin evolved into a full-blown smile. "Well, not sure I know what that fancy word means—my, but you know a lot of 'em! But if it means prayin', then you can count on me for that, guv'ner."

He continued to look at her, his eyes almost tender. "Yes, I believe I can. From what I've seen, you are a most dependable young woman." He cleared his throat, as if embarrassed, and stood. "I should return to my quarters. A blessed Christmas to you, Miss Evans. Incidentally, your reading is much improved." He moved hurriedly to the foyer, grabbed his hat and coat, and walked out into the swirling bits of light snow.

"And a blessed Christmas to you, guv'ner," Darcy murmured, feeling as if she'd just received an unexpected gift. She stared at the closed door, took the last bite of her apple, then headed to the kitchen to help Irma with the dishes—and maybe sneak another slice of that fruitcake Irma had made.

❧

January and February brought more snow. The old potbellied stove that warmed the schoolhouse malfunctioned, spewing out gray smoke and sending everyone outside into the frigid air, coughing and hacking.

To the best of Brent's analysis, something had gotten clogged high in the stovepipe—too high to remove. Since none of the men were adept at fixing things, they decided to wait until spring to either have the fifty-year-old stove repaired or buy a new one. In the meantime, Brent relocated to an empty room in the boys' wing of the main house. To have him so near day in and day out flustered Darcy, and she often found herself dropping things or saying things she shouldn't.

Lessons continued, though not with the previous schoolroom order, since teaching was administered in the parlor. The boys sat on the sofa, chairs, carpeting—wherever they could find a spot—and took their lessons from Brent. Reading and reciting filled long hours. When they weren't studying, they did their chores. Yet with nine boys and five adults sharing a minimal amount of space for weeks on end, petty fights soon erupted. Tonight, Darcy happened to be the only adult in the room.

She wrapped her short arms around Joel's slim waist and, with as much brute strength as she could muster, pulled the wiry lad off Herbert while the two other boys in the room stood and watched. The redhead had a black eye. Once Darcy released Joel, Herbert flew at the blond scamp.

"Oh, no, you don't!" Darcy clutched a handful of the boy's collar at the back. He fought to break loose, hurling malicious threats and trying to lash out at Joel, whose face bore nary a scratch.

"What's going on here? I heard the ruckus from all the way upstairs." Charleigh hurried into the room, her skirts clutched in both hands. Seeing the troublemakers, her mouth thinned. "Joel, you may march yourself into Mr. Lyons' office this minute. Herbert, tell Irma to fetch you a steak for that eye; then you may join Joel."

"He started it," Herbert whined.

"Hardly," Joel shot back.

"I don't care who started it! Do you hear? *I don't care.*" Charleigh's eyes shot sparks and her breathing was labored. "Furthermore, I don't wish to hear another word out of either of you or you'll get extra job duties for a month. Now, go."

Flabbergasted, Darcy stared at her friend. Charleigh was usually so calm when dealing with the boys. Yet tonight she looked as if she were ready to rake the whole lot of them over flaming coals.

Samuel, the young man who'd come to the refuge after the war, hurried into the room, followed by three of the boys. Upon seeing the situation, he herded the children out, also putting a firm hand to both Joel's and Herbert's shoulders to prevent further fighting.

Darcy moved to stand in front of her friend. "Charleigh," she said, her voice low, "what's ailin' you?"

"How did you—I mean, why should you think something's ailing me?" Charleigh averted her gaze to the fireplace.

"I've known you too long, luv. Now, let's go make us a nice cup of tea, and you can tell me all about it." Putting an arm around her friend's shoulders, Darcy steered Charleigh toward the kitchen. "I made some lovely apple cinnamon muffins this morning, too."

They found the room unoccupied; and Darcy set about fixing the promised tea, though she noticed a coffeepot warming on the stove, probably left there by

Irma. Darcy wrinkled her nose. She preferred tea with plenty of lemon.

Once the beverage was made, Darcy set a muffin in front of her friend, grabbed an orange from the bowl, and took a seat across from Charleigh. "Now, tell me what has you flutterin' about like a mad, wet hen." The allusion didn't bring the desired smile Darcy hoped for.

With jerky movements, Charleigh plucked up her spoon, stirred, then set it back down on the saucer. Her eyes were full of pain when she looked up. "I think Stewart's leaving me."

"Leaving you?" Darcy repeated in disbelief.

She nodded. "The letter from his family was the excuse he needed. Oh, I don't mean to sound heartless—I do care about his father's health, and I know he needs to go to them. But, Darcy, I don't think he's coming back. I failed him, you see, and now he wants out."

"Failed him?" Darcy repeated, feeling like an echo.

Charleigh looked down. "I can't give him children. We've been married four years, and in that time I've lost five babies. I—I never talked about my past when we were together at Turreney Farm, I know."

Darcy waited, expectant. Charleigh had been closemouthed about her private life and why she'd been sentenced. Darcy never asked, since it had been an unspoken code among the convicts to mind one's own affairs. But she'd always wondered.

Charleigh released her breath in a heavy sigh. "In a nutshell, I lived with a man—a criminal—for three years. I thought we were married but came to find out the ceremony was a sham." She paused, obviously finding it difficult to say the rest. "The night the *Titanic* sank, he beat me; and the next morning, on the *Carpathia*, I miscarried our child."

Darcy listened, stunned.

Tear-filled eyes looked into her own. "Eric ruined me, Darcy. I've known it for some time. It's because of him and his abuse that I can't have children. And Stewart wants a son and daughter so badly. What am I to do? I'm losing my husband, and I'm helpless to do anything about it." She buried her face in her hands, sobbing quietly.

Darcy vacated her chair and knelt beside her friend, putting her arm around Charleigh's shoulders. "You're wrong, luv. Stewart adores you. Why, just to look in the man's eyes I can see as plain as the nose on me face that he's smitten with you."

Charleigh didn't answer.

"He feels duty bound to help his family but is obviously torn on the proper thing to do. Go to them or stay home with you, his wife."

"I suppose. But, Darcy, what if he decides to go and doesn't come back? We've. . ." She looked down at her lap. "We've quarreled lately. Since he came home from the war, he doesn't act the same. He rarely talks to me anymore, and

I feel it's because he wishes he'd never married me."

"I disagree." Darcy laid her other hand over her friend's cold one. "War changes people, luv. There's no tellin' what Stewart saw in France. Give it time. And, Charleigh, you need to seek the faith that ye somehow lost and start believin' God to work things out. I'm not too smart yet on how one's supposed to act as a Christian, but I do pray for everyone in this house each and every night."

A wisp of a smile tugged at Charleigh's lips. "Oh, Darcy, you're such a dear friend." Her eyelashes flitted down, then up, her expression guilty. "Unfortunately, I can't say the same about me. I was overbearing when you first came. I'm afraid I've grown accustomed to supervising nine boys with criminal records and have become domineering in my attitude. Forgive me for not asking if you wanted to change rather than practically ordering you to do so."

"Oh, but I'm not angered, Charleigh," Darcy was quick to assure. "Not one bit. So don't you worry none. Actually, I'm glad you forced me hand. I never would've had the courage to ask the favor for meself—since I felt beholden to you for bringin' me here all the way from London. And you were right; it never hurts to gain head knowledge."

Charleigh smiled. "For being four years younger than I, you're so much wiser, Darcy."

"Maybe in some things but not in others. Even with the trainin' you've given me, I still have problems with the way I talk; and I often find meself sayin' things that make Mr. Thomas's hair about turn white, judgin' from the shock that suddenly sweeps 'cross his face. Have you ever seen his mouth drop open? Sure is a sight for such a dignified gent!"

Charleigh giggled, the sound cheering Darcy. Her friend would be all right. She was a survivor, as was Darcy.

"I'll admit, and please don't take this wrong, but seeing the two of you together is—how do I put this? Amusing at times." Charleigh's eyes sparkled with more than tears. "Frankly, I'm amazed at how well you've both gotten along lately—for being such total opposites, I mean."

Darcy returned to her seat. She stirred the cooling liquid, wishing the sudden fire in her cheeks would cool as well. "He's a fine sort of fellow." She took a sip from her cup and began to peel her orange. "A good teacher."

"Yes, he is that," Charleigh agreed, her expression softly probing, as though she could sense more than Darcy was willing to reveal.

Darcy took her full cup to the basin. "Well, I'm a mite tired, and I have lessons to complete besides. You'd think Brent would ease up, what with the cabin fever everyone's had lately. . . ." Her words trailed off when she realized her slip. She'd never before used his Christian name in conversation. She only hoped Charleigh hadn't noticed. Hesitant, she turned.

Charleigh's smile was wide. "Yes, Brent can be rather dogmatic when it comes to schooling. He's just what those boys need. And what you need."

Darcy's ears grew hot. "He's helped quite a bit in teaching me to read and write; that's a fact."

Charleigh rose and looped an arm around Darcy's shoulders. "I know you like him, Darcy, and I think that's 'nifty,' as Tommy would say. So do stop trying to cover up. I'm one hundred percent in favor of you and Brent forming a more serious relationship, if that's what has you so flustered."

As she finished her last sentence, Brent strode into the kitchen. Darcy almost died from humiliation when she realized from the startled expression on his reddening face that he'd heard every word.

Chapter 5

Brent stopped, stared, and wondered what to do. Despite the chill in the house, his neck and face burned. He deliberated on the most appropriate way to extricate himself from this latest embarrassing predicament. That they knew he'd overheard Charleigh's shocking statement was obvious, judging from the way Darcy's face flamed poppy red.

"Excuse me," Darcy mumbled, hurrying past Brent. "I need to be about me business."

Relief mingled with an underlying sense of empathy. After all, the shocking words hadn't been Darcy's. He imagined she was as unnerved by them as he. Why Charleigh had even said such a thing was beyond Brent's reasoning. He swiveled to look at her.

Charleigh's gaze turned from the spot where Darcy had exited and met his own. She seemed ill at ease, repentant. "I should check on the boys." Before she moved through the doorway, she offered Brent an uncertain smile. "Good night."

Alone at last, Brent shook his head, let out a prolonged breath, and set his briefcase on the table. His disloyal mind replayed Charleigh's words, and he gave a short laugh. The idea of him and Darcy as a couple was so—so preposterous, so outlandish, so altogether incongruous that Brent didn't dwell on the picture overly long.

Instead, he moved to pour himself a cup of the strong coffee that good-hearted Irma had left on the stove. He needed something to help him keep alert while grading papers, and Brent didn't share Darcy's preference for tea.

Sitting at the table, he noticed her half-peeled orange and stared at it a few seconds—imagining her popping one of the segments into her mouth and then grinning at him. Abruptly he turned his attention to the first paper with a scowl. He must wrest his mind off Darcy Evans and apply it to the task at hand.

The short, quirky sentences and frequent blobs of ink testified to Joel's handiwork without Brent needing to look in the upper right-hand corner for the name. The boy was always trying to get away with the least amount of effort possible. The original poem was half the five stanzas of the story poem Brent had assigned, didn't rhyme, and glorified a runaway involved in a life of crime.

Sighing, Brent made corrections, took off a large percentage for not following directions, and gave Joel a 49. He picked up the next paper in the stack, a slight smile on his lips.

At least Tommy did try, as evidenced by his laborious efforts at doing a job well. Several half-written words over the page were crossed out and reattempted, some as many as four times until the word was spelled and written correctly. The paper was messy with its many alterations, but the lad had persistence; Brent would grant him that. The poem was unusual, about a toad eating a lame mouse, but Brent didn't like to tamper with his students' creative abilities. He was more concerned with grammar and sentence structure at this stage of their education. Giving Tommy a 70, he went on to the next paper. He picked it up and froze.

Darcy's large block letters stared up at him. She hadn't learned cursive writing, though Brent had attempted to teach her. But she often balked and demanded to know why a person had to learn to write in two different styles "when one way of writin' was all a body needed."

Familiar sounds in the room—the sporadic drip from the water pump hitting the basin, the creaking of the timbered house settling, the barely audible moan of wind outside—faded into the background as his gaze traveled over the neatly printed poem:

Let me tell you a story, a sad one, me friend,
About three young lads I knew in the East End,
Crackers was brite, often looking for a lark,
Hunstable was kwiet, but he had a certun spark,
Roger was gentel, a little lamb, and like no other,
And we all took good care of him as if he was our brother.

Most would call them feluns, for theevin' is what they done,
But the three of them became my friends when I had not a one.
For all his bluff and brashnuss, Crackers was a good leader of our gang,
'Til the day he was cot filchin' bread and was slammed in jail with a clang.

Hunstable changed once Crackers left, thoe he tried to take his place.
Once we were four, then we were three, 'til Hunstable vanisht with nary
*   a trace.*
And lastly there was dear Roger, a sweet angel in disgize,
Lame and sick, his stay weren't long, 'til one day he forever closed his eyes.

Yet the moral of me story, friend, has little to do with theevin',
Even those who don't know what the Good Book says know it's wrong to
*   make a life out of steelin'.*
Rather the message of me poem is this: Why did no one help us or care?
We was only children trying to servive in a world that was harsh and bare.

*Didn't peepul who read the Good Book see that it said to help the orfuns
     and needy?*
*Or did they just think us worthluss guttersnipes who was nothin' but dirty
     and greedy?*
I don't know the answer, friend, thoe I've long tried to find the reezin;
*But this I know, while I draw breath on this earth, I'll do what I can for
     those who be needin'.*
For each time I look on a poor child's face or that of a sad little orfun,
*I see me old friends, and remember our life, on the streets in the East End
     of London.*

Brent blinked away the unexpected moisture that had sprung to his eyes. Never mind the misspelled words—they were of little significance in relation to the gold mine he'd struck. Darcy had talent. Her prose was a bit rough, but the artistic content was very good for a beginner's first poem. It further shocked him to realize they shared a knack for writing poetry, though Brent could see from this first attempt that Darcy's skill might well exceed his someday. Mechanics could be taught. Talent could not.

He pondered the printed words, wondering what had happened to her friends. Reading over the poem again, he fiddled with the paper, considering. An idea came to mind that made him smile. He measured the possibility awhile longer, then swept the rest of the papers into his briefcase, placing Darcy's ungraded one on top. Closing his portfolio, he grabbed it and hurried to the parlor, hoping he could find the form he'd come across in last week's *Saturday Evening Post*.

❧

Darcy stood at the open attic window, inhaling the fresh, bracing air that heralded the coming of spring. Clumps of bright green broke through the melting snow, which lay in patches over the dark earth. She watched Joel and Chris, a quiet, skinny boy with an unruly shock of blond hair, as they made their way toward the barn with buckets, probably to milk the two cows.

Darcy wrinkled her brow in concern. Lately Joel seemed edgy, a container of pent-up energy waiting for a place to unleash. Of course, they all were anxious to spend time outside, having been holed up for most of the winter; but Joel seemed more volatile than the other boys.

Darcy smiled. Volatile. Her new word for the day. Every day she learned a different fancy word—one that Brent might use—in her efforts to increase her head knowledge. Maybe if she became more fancified, Brent might like her better.

The stray thought made her face go hot. Although behind his back the boys labeled Brent "a stick in the mud"—and rightly so—Darcy harbored a strong liking for the man ever since they'd talked last Christmas. She didn't care all that much if he was a bit stuffy and overly neat; yet Darcy knew he would never put up with the likes of her.

Sighing, she wished she could be more like Charleigh, who talked so proper-like and was genteel, a real lady. Darcy often found herself doing things and later finding out it wasn't considered appropriate. Nor had her rough, Cockney accent disappeared, though at least her words were more easily understood.

Determined to have a quick romp with the boys in the cheery spring day, Darcy headed for the door and down the stairs. She should help Irma with the bread pudding, but the weather was too fine to waste.

Before Darcy could reach the threshold, Charleigh came around the corner. Her eyes were dark in her strained, white face.

"Charleigh, luv, what's wrong?" Darcy gripped her friend's shoulders. She gave Charleigh a slight shake when she only stared. "Tell me! Ye look like ye've just seen a man leave his grave."

"A telegram came," Charleigh said, tears filling her eyes. "Stewart's father is deathly ill. . .something to do with his heart. Stewart is packing and leaving on the first train tomorrow."

"Oh, I am sorry!" Darcy pulled her friend into a hug.

"Oh, Darcy," Charleigh mumbled against the wide collar of Darcy's dress. "I'm trying to be brave, like a good wife should act. . .but. . .I just don't feel well."

Before Darcy could question her, Charleigh clutched Darcy's shoulder and collapsed in a faint against her.

🙥

Brent stood outside with Stewart and watched the boys do their chores. Stewart frowned on hiring guards, insisting that the unusual way he and Charleigh ran the institution was how they felt the Lord had instructed them to do it. Brent had to admit the experimental method worked well. Though some of the older families in Sothsby, whose generations dated back to the 1700s, still opposed having a reformatory there, the community as a whole hadn't outwardly rebelled.

Except for minor infractions, there had never been a need for corporal punishment. Once a new boy tried to run away, but he hadn't gotten far before Stewart found him. Now Lance seemed content at the reform. He never tried to escape again, and his tendency to withdraw from others had dissipated.

Brent watched Lance as he helped Samuel fix a broken porch rail. The weak sun shone over Lance's freckled face and strong body—worlds removed from the grubby, pale scarecrow who'd come to their doorstep years ago.

"I don't like leaving Charleigh," Stewart said, breaking into Brent's reverie. "But I have to do what I feel is right, just as she had to do years ago when she turned herself over to Scotland Yard."

"I agree."

Obviously still troubled, Stewart rotated the brim of his straw boater. "My family needs my legal counsel. Mother is helpless when it comes to dealing with business matters of any sort; and with Father bedridden, she's frightened they'll lose the store." He sounded as if he were trying hard to convince himself that he was doing the right thing. "Still, I'm worried about Charleigh. She had a fainting spell yesterday—which is so unlike her—though she didn't tell me a word about it. I had to hear the news from Darcy." Frowning, he looked off into the distance. "Charleigh's been under a great deal of strain, and I fear she's taken on too much with the boys and the upkeep of the house. She needs rest."

"I'll look after her welfare, as I'm sure Miss Evans will. Those two are close."

Stewart offered him a weak smile. "You don't know what a relief it is to hear you say that. And I'm doubly glad we sent for Charleigh's friend."

The front door opened and both women appeared. Brent noticed Charleigh slip her hand from Darcy's and straighten her shoulders. "The train will be leaving in a little over an hour," she said in a small brave voice. Her smile wavered. Darcy stepped up and said something close to her ear. Charleigh gave a brief nod and tacked a tight smile to her face. "Shall we go?"

❧❧

The ride to Ithaca was fraught with tension. False smiles were tossed about, and forced laughter crackled the air, feeling almost tangible and grating against raw nerves. Words of little import filled rare interludes of quiet.

As they neared town, Darcy noticed several people standing on the platform, waiting to say good-bye to loved ones and friends or to welcome those arriving. A small group of rowdy young men burst into raucous song that sounded better suited to a tavern.

Darcy stared at the trio, receiving a wink from a cheeky blond gent in return. Much to her shock, Brent grabbed her above the elbow once she alighted from the wagon and hurried her along after Stewart and Charleigh. What was even more of a surprise, he didn't release her once they came to the platform and stopped a short distance from the two, to give their friends a measure of privacy.

Darcy wasn't sure what to think. She wondered if it was wrong to enjoy him standing so close, his warm fingers wrapped around her sleeve, when Charleigh was depressed, uncertain if she'd ever see her husband again.

Darcy sobered. Charleigh had been quiet all afternoon, and Darcy knew that she and Stewart had argued last night. She'd heard them from her attic room.

Watching them now, Stewart seemed stiff, almost cold, and Charleigh appeared resigned. Darcy prayed that Stewart wouldn't leave Charleigh, as Darcy's own papa had left her mother when Darcy was all of five years. The war had obviously changed Stewart. Darcy was glad that Brent had been exempted, as Charleigh once informed her; and without meaning to, she voiced the thought aloud.

"What did you say?" Brent asked.

Darcy looked at him. "I was just sorry for them two and wishing they could make it right between them again," she blurted. "And I said I'm thankful, I am, that you weren't sent off to fight in the war—and aren't dealing with your own sufferings now because of it."

His eyes widened behind the spectacles. Darcy inwardly cringed. Would she ever learn to think before she spoke?

Brent's face went a shade darker. "Yes, well, thank you for the sentiment, Miss Evans." He cleared his throat, looking everywhere but at her.

Darcy's gaze slid down his long nose to his well-shaped lips. Idly, she wondered what it would feel like to kiss this man. Crackers sometimes kissed her on the forehead when she was sad, but that wasn't the same. They'd only been children.

Nearby, a couple locked in a farewell embrace. For a fleeting moment, Darcy considered throwing her arms around Brent and giving him a quick peck on the lips. Wouldn't that make his mouth drop open! The thought made her giggle.

Brent looked at her. "Something amuses you, Miss Evans?"

"Nothin', guv'ner. Nothin' ter squawk habout anyways," she deliberately replied in heavy Cockney, her smile wide.

His gaze softened, and Darcy was sure he was remembering their first meeting a little less than a year ago at this train station.

"I never told you," he said, his voice quiet, "how impressed I am with how far you've come in such a short time. You're a remarkable student."

Darcy managed not to let the smile slip from her face. Did he only approve of her now that she'd learned to talk right—well, almost right? The thought was disappointing. She wanted him to like her for the person she was on the inside. Not just for what she was being transformed into on the outside.

The train's warning whistle pierced the air, startling both Darcy and Brent. He stepped a few feet away, his actions almost self-conscious, and looked elsewhere. Darcy glanced toward Charleigh and Stewart and was relieved to see him draw his wife into his arms.

A tall, dark-haired young man in a drab uniform drew Darcy's attention as he stepped off the train. He returned her stare, then strode her way, a sly grin on his thin features. "Well, he-l-loo, sweet tomato. How's about a welcome-home hug for a returning doughboy?"

Darcy blinked. "Are ye talkin' to me?"

"I sure am, sugar—British sugar, unless I miss my guess." He rested his free hand on the post behind her, casually leaning her way. "So where do you hail from, sweet thing? I don't seem to remember seeing you in our small town."

"Sir, I shall have to ask you to leave the lady alone."

Brent's stern voice sounded from behind Darcy's right shoulder.

The man gave Brent a quick upward flick of his eyes. "This is between the lady and me," he said. He leaned closer to Darcy, eyeing her as if she were a choice cut of beefsteak. She smelled sour whiskey on his breath. "How's about you and me leaving this crummy dump and getting to know one another better?"

"Sir!" Brent protested.

"Aw, why don't you dry up," the stranger growled in disgust.

Before she could push him away, Darcy watched as the top half of a black umbrella whammed the man's shoulder from behind. He jumped and turned, fists raised. A short woman with white ringlets jiggling around her wrinkled face wagged a finger in his face, and he dropped his arms to his side in apparent shock.

"Clarence Lockhurst, you leave that poor young lady alone and apologize this instant," she said in a voice still strong for her advanced years. "You've been nothing but trouble since I had you as a student in my fourth-grade class. I had hoped that serving in the war might improve your disposition, if nothing else." Her strict countenance melted into a grudging smile. "Still, it's nice to see that the Germans didn't shoot you full of holes. Though you'll likely give your mother a case of the vapors, arriving like this without warning. But at least you made it home from that horrid hospital. Now come along. It's a good thing I came to see my niece off, or I might not have run into you."

"Yes, Miss Finnelton," the man muttered, and the woman walked away, obviously expecting him to follow. He seemed embarrassed, his gaze flitting to the platform before returning to Darcy again. He shrugged. "Sorry, miss. I was only trying to have a little fun. No harm intended."

"Clarence!" the woman called without slowing her pace.

Darcy watched in disbelief as the tall young man hurried after the diminutive old woman like a truant child. Somewhat amused by the spectacle, she turned to Brent. The words on her lips died when she saw anger flash in his eyes. Confused, she wondered if his ire was directed at her. Did he think she'd encouraged that man's advances? Did he care?

"Stewart is ready to board," he said through tight lips. "Charleigh needs us."

Darcy blinked in surprise. This was the first time she'd heard Brent use their Christian names. Likely because his emotions were running high, he hadn't been aware of the slip. Darcy just wished it could have been her name that rolled so easily off his tongue.

❧

The months seemed to fly by. Summer chased spring away, and the cool winds of autumn blew in early. Darcy had been at the refuge almost an entire year, and in that time she had learned much—especially the meaning of true Christianity. It was more than the prayer she'd spoken at Turreney Farm, accepting Jesus as her Savior. It was a walk she needed to take every day of her life.

She looked with concern to the closed schoolhouse door. Brent was late.

For the prompt schoolmaster to be tardy was tantamount to a major crisis. She wrinkled her brow as her thoughts drifted to Charleigh. These past months in Stewart's absence her friend had become a pale ghost, quiet, so much different from the Charleigh that Darcy had met years ago and come to love. Her faith in God was suffering, too, and Darcy didn't know how to help her, except to pray and be there for her when she could.

The boys' chatter and guffaws dwindled as the door opened, letting in pale September light—and Brent.

He carried a folded magazine and smiled, looking her way. Darcy's heart lurched in uncertainty mixed with an odd feeling of expectation.

Taking his place at the front of the room, Brent eyed the class. "I have an announcement, but first I want you to hear something."

He opened the magazine, whose cover bore a color illustration by Norman Rockwell. Then, to Darcy's astonishment, he read the poem she'd written months ago. Only the words sounded more proper, or maybe it was hearing them in Brent's polished Eastern accent that made the difference.

When he finished, he smiled at her. "Miss Evans, I suppose I should first ask your apology for submitting your poem without permission to a local contest the *Saturday Evening Post* was sponsoring this past spring. In defense of my decision, I didn't want to unnecessarily raise your hopes, and as your tutor I acted—perhaps rashly, but it is done. I also took the liberty of correcting misspelled words, as well as a few small grammatical errors, before sending in your poem. I hope you'll forgive me. Based on prior contests, I knew they would judge heavily on content, and on those grounds I decided to enter your poem."

Darcy blinked, trying to comprehend all he said. He was asking that she forgive him for correcting her assignment? And for sending it to a local magazine?

She watched Brent walk to the desk that had been specially made for her, while pulling an envelope from his pocket. His blue eyes sparkled as he set the envelope on her desktop.

"It's my pleasure to inform you that you've won second place in the beginner's category of the contest, the prize being eight dollars."

Gasps filtered through the room. Eight dollars? Whatever would she do with such wealth? She'd never had anything in her life, and now to be given this. . .

With saucerlike eyes, she stared at the envelope.

"What're ya gonna do with all that money, Darcy?" Tommy asked softly in wonder.

"I'll bet she's gonna buy them glad rags with all the bows and fripperies she was eyeing in that lady magazine the other day," another voice piped up. "So she can be all purty-fied for certain people."

Darcy ignored Joel's mocking words and the giggles that greeted his reply. Instead she looked up at Brent, still feeling as if she were in a dream. "May

I tell Charleigh?" she asked, her question coming out in a squeak. She cleared her throat and lowered her voice a notch. "It might cheer her to know her idea of me learning brought about some good."

Brent turned his stern countenance from Joel to her, and his expression softened. "Of course, Miss Evans. You may be excused."

Sliding from her seat, Darcy grasped the envelope as though it might evaporate into thin air. The smoothness of the fine-grained paper assured her it was indeed real, and her fingers clutched it more tightly. At the door she stopped and looked at Brent. His gaze still rested on her.

"Thank you, guv'ner, for sendin' in me poem. But most of all thank you for believin' in me," she managed before hurrying out the door.

Her mind played havoc with her heart. Why had he done it? Was there more to this gesture than a schoolmaster supporting a student? Could he, by chance, be starting to care for her?

Knowing she'd find Charleigh in her room this time of day, where she often sequestered herself now that Stewart was gone, Darcy sped up the stairs by twos. Whatever would she do with all this money? She hoped her good fortune would bring a smile to Charleigh's face. Should she also tell Charleigh how she felt about Brent, though her friend had already guessed? They'd never discussed him since the night he'd caught Charleigh and Darcy talking in the kitchen. All this time, Darcy felt she hadn't any chance with Brent. But after doing such a nice thing for her and after the way he'd looked at her when he gave her the envelope—maybe he did care.

Outside Charleigh's room, Darcy knocked. She didn't wait for an answer but opened the door and stepped inside, her mind so filled with conflicting thoughts that she didn't stop to consider that she was barging in without invitation.

Charleigh halted in the process of retrieving her dressing gown from the back of the chair. Her long nightgown detailed her rounded stomach.

Darcy inhaled swiftly, her gaze lifting to Charleigh's. "Whyever didn't you tell me?"

Charleigh released a weary breath and sank to the edge of the bed.

Her own news forgotten, Darcy closed the door, pocketed the envelope, and hurried to sit beside her friend. She looped an arm around her shoulders. "Does Stewart know?"

"I couldn't tell him. Not after losing the others. And with his father's recent death, he has so much on his mind as it is." Charleigh hesitated. "And I couldn't tell him before he left because I didn't want to use the baby as a means of keeping him here."

"You've known that long?"

"I suspected it."

"Oh, Charleigh, that's why you fainted that day, isn't it?" Darcy should have realized, though with Charleigh's plump form and roomy-waisted dresses it had been difficult to tell. "Have you been to see a doctor?"

"No. I suppose I should."

"Yes, you should," Darcy stated firmly. "And what's more, you should stay off your feet. I'll take over your duties until the babe comes." The prospect was daunting, but Darcy had observed Charleigh often in the year she'd been at Lyons' Refuge. With Irma and Brent's help, surely they could keep things running smoothly so Charleigh could get the rest she needed.

"I'm frightened." Charleigh turned wide green eyes her way. "I don't think I could stand to lose another child. To have a doctor tell me there's no hope for this one either. I–I've never been this far along—" Her voice broke.

Darcy grasped Charleigh's cold hand and squeezed it. "There, there, luv. That's no way to think. Between us, we'll pray that the good Lord protects the wee babe and brings it safely into the world in due time." She hesitated. "Do you know when that might be, by chance?"

Charleigh looked away. "In December, I think. Near Christmas."

"I'll have Irma call and see if the doctor can come today. You stay in bed and rest. You're looking a mite pale. I'll take care of everything."

"Oh, Darcy. I don't know what I'd do without you. You're so strong, and lately I feel as if my strength is seeping away. I've found it harder and harder to trust God." The admission was made with shame.

Darcy gave her friend an encouraging smile. "Well, then, we'll see what we can do to boost your faith again, shall we?" Like a mother hen, Darcy ushered Charleigh under the sheets and tucked her in. "But for now get some rest. And don't you worry about a thing, luv. Darcy has everything under control."

She almost believed her bold statement. Keeping the assured look on her face until she closed the door behind her, Darcy prayed, "Oh, Lord, I'm sure going to be needin' Your help. And help me friend, Charleigh; give her peace. Help her babe to grow strong—"

The front door banged open. "Where is everybody?" Herbert's voice sailed up the stairwell. Knowing Herbert, who got into more trouble than Darcy could have believed possible, she was sure some minor injury needed tending to.

Darcy closed her eyes. "About that peace, Lord," she muttered, "I sure could be usin' a dose of it, as well."

Chapter 6

The early October sun did what little it could to warm his back as Brent left the schoolroom. He had no idea what to do about Joel—about half the class, really. With Stewart's absence and Charleigh bedridden due to strict orders from the doctor, the boys took advantage of Brent. It seemed a day didn't pass that one of them wasn't disciplined for infractions inside and outside the classroom.

Brent rounded the schoolhouse, wondering how to handle the issue. Michael had moved to Lyons' Refuge with his wife to offer aid as well as reinforcement. Though Charleigh's father was tenderhearted to the lads, his massive size and gruff voice let them know he wasn't someone to cross. Yet Brent didn't want to run to Michael every time one of the boys misbehaved. Surely Brent was man enough to take on nine lads smaller than he?

Remembering the altercation at the train station with the man who'd accosted Darcy, Brent pressed his lips together. He hadn't been able to help her. The one brief look the loutish man had tossed his way made it clear he thought Brent lacking in the area of fisticuffs. Not that Brent had desired a fight—quite the opposite. But it stung that a stranger thought him unable to protect and that an elderly woman wielding an umbrella had exhibited more courage than Brent.

He halted suddenly, spotting Darcy and four boys across the expanse of yard, underneath the shedding oaks. The rakes they'd been using lay propped against the massive trunks, forgotten. All five were cavorting, chasing one another and dumping handfuls of brown, crimson, and yellow leaves on unsuspecting heads.

Brent sighed and crossed his arms over his chest. Why should it surprise him to see Darcy in such a role, rather than the one she should be adopting—that of overseeing the boys' chores? As Brent watched, Lance came at her from behind with a pail and showered her head with leaves at the same time Tommy bent to the ground and sprayed her with leaves from the front.

"Aaaeee," she squealed, her Cockney coming to the fore. "I'll see ever' one o' you scrubbin' floors, I will! And that'll be after ye rake the yard. So ye think ye can get the best o' Darcy Evans, do you?" Swiftly she changed direction, going after Lance. He shrieked and ran but didn't get far before she tackled him as if she were a football player and not a woman wearing a dress. They both went laughing and rolling into the only pile of raked leaves—scattering them. Red, yellow, and brown vegetation flew everywhere.

Shaking his head, Brent closed his eyes.

"Hey, guv'ner!" Darcy's cry sliced through the cool air. Brent grimaced at the annoying name she persisted in calling him but looked her way.

"Come join us!" She scooped up an armful of rich autumn colors and sent her bounty sailing into the air, with the abandonment of a gleeful child. "The leaves are fine. Crisp and crackly—perfect for rollin' about. So what say? Care to join in the tussle?"

"Join in the. . . ," he repeated quietly in shocked disbelief. With a shake of his head, he moved in the direction of the schoolroom. The four walls offered safety, sanity. He had enough troubles; no need to invite more.

Rapid crunching sounded behind him, growing louder. "Hey, guv'ner—don't leave yet!" Darcy's voice was breathless.

Knowing that the sensible thing would be to keep walking—before he was attacked from behind with a bucketful of leaves—Brent increased his pace, almost to a jog. She grabbed his sleeve and pulled. He whirled and hastily brought up a hand to block his eyes, expecting a smattering of leaves to dash him in the face. The action unbalanced them, and Darcy tumbled against his chest, almost sending them both to the ground.

In a reflexive act, Brent threw his arms around her at the same time she grabbed handfuls of his vest. An electrified moment elapsed before she lifted her stunned gaze. Equally shocked, he stared down at velvety eyes rimmed with black curly lashes. Eyes so dark, they held traces of deep, mesmerizing blue-purple.

"Hey! Look at Teacher and Miz Darcy," Ralph's voice piped up. "Reckon Joel was right and they'll be smoochin' in the cloakroom next?"

A chorus of chortles met his question.

Heat racing to his face, Brent dropped his arms from around Darcy's waist and stepped as far back as he could. She still clutched his vest, his shirt underneath, and one suspender.

"Miss Evans!" he exclaimed. "Would you mind releasing your hold?"

"What?" She blinked as if coming out of a stupor. "Oh, sorry!" She let go.

The suspender snapped back into place with a sting. By this time, the giggles from the boys had turned into rip-roaring laughter.

"Excuse me. I've business to attend." Brent turned and again headed for the safety of the schoolhouse.

"But, guv'ner. . ."

With his back to her, he hastily tucked in the few inches of shirt material that bagged loose above his high-waisted trousers. Once through the door, he sensed her presence behind him. He was sure of it when she barreled into him, stepping on his heels as he came to a stop.

Nowhere was safe any longer.

Letting out a slow breath for patience, he faced her. "Yes? You wish to speak with me?"

A sheepish expression crossed her pink face, now shiny from her exertions. With bits of colored leaves in her disheveled hair and clinging to her skirt, she looked little more than a girl. "I'm sorry, guv'ner. Really I ham. But you walk so fast!"

"Apology accepted," he said quickly. When she didn't move to go, he lifted his brow. "Was there something else?"

She crossed her arms and cocked her head to the side, all awkwardness leaving her as she observed him. "Tell me, guv'ner, why is it you don't like to have fun?"

"Excuse me?"

She rolled her eyes and shook her head. "Do I have to spell it out for you like I did last Christmas? Ever since I've known you, you do nothin' more than work, eat, and sleep. I've never seen you unbend—not once mind you—and have a good time."

Brent cleared his throat. "Perhaps your definition of fun doesn't coincide with mine."

"Okay, what's your definition?"

Brent opened his mouth to reply, then stopped to consider.

"Aha! See there? You don't even know what fun is!"

"I most certainly do." He removed his spectacles, grabbed his handkerchief from his pocket, and angrily swiped at the spotless lenses. "I just don't feel the need to reply to your query."

"And I'll bet my eyeteeth it's 'cause you don't know the answer."

"Miss Evans."

"Mr. Thomas."

Brent blinked, more stunned that she'd finally called him by his proper name than by her mimicking behavior.

She uncrossed her arms, a sly smile lifting her lips. "All right then. Prove it."

"Excuse me?"

"Prove to me that you can have fun."

Brent gave a curt shake of his head. "I hardly think a childish display of frolicking about in dead vegetation befits a schoolmaster of nine young boys."

She waved a dismissive hand. "I'm not talking about that. I have somethin' else in mind."

Unease crept up Brent's spine at the sudden speculating gleam in her eye. "Such as?"

"Two things really. Take part in the fence-paintin' contest we're havin' on Friday."

Brent considered. He could referee without actually having to be involved in what promised to be a messy undertaking. "Agreed. And the second?"

"I need your help with an idea for keepin' the boys in line. It's what I wanted to talk to you about in the first place." She swept past him toward the front of the schoolroom.

Puzzled, Brent turned and watched as she propped herself on the edge of his desk.

"Better take a seat, guv'ner. I have a feelin' this will do more than just make your mouth pop open."

&❧

Brent stared at her with uncertainty and approached slowly, his eyes wary. He still hadn't replaced his spectacles, and Darcy again thought what nice blue eyes he had. Instead of taking his usual place behind his desk, he walked to her small writing table six feet away, pulled out the chair, and sat down.

Darcy swiveled on his desk to face him.

"Well?" Brent asked.

"Just thinkin' how to put it best," she murmured. "All right, it's like this. When I was in town with Michael and Alice, gettin' supplies and such, I heard news of a carnival comin' to a neighborin' town next month. Now, bein' as I had no idea what a carnival was, mind you, I did some askin', and the storekeeper told me."

"A carnival?" Brent asked, already suspecting the worst.

Darcy shrugged one shoulder. "It's all on the up-and-up. I thought we could use the carnival as an incentive for the boys. A goal to help them show good behavior and keep up with their studies—that sort of thing."

Brent stared at her incredulously. "And just who do you propose to take nine miniature hooligans, still in the process of being reformed, out of the boundaries of Lyons' Refuge and to a frivolous function held in an unsuspecting town?"

"Why, you, of course. And me. And maybe Michael." She smiled as his eyes widened. "But it would just be three boys, not nine. The three who try the hardest and show the most progress. Like winnin' a contest, such as I did with that poetry one. That's where I got the idea."

Brent only stared. After several seconds elapsed, he shook his head. "That's the most preposterous idea I've heard! As I'm certain you know by now, there are those who are dead-set against having a reformatory in this town—though the community as a whole hasn't rebelled. That we take the boys outside Lyons' Refuge for church on Sundays is difficult for many to tolerate. But to take them to a carnival?"

Her mouth thinning, Darcy stood and faced him squarely, planting her hands on her hips. "They's just little boys, guv'ner. Little boys who had a hard lot in life and are payin' for their crimes. Why shouldn't they be allowed to 'ave a good time now and hagain, like other boys their age, 'specially if they be earnin' it?" Darcy forced herself to speak more slowly. When she was excited, she almost always slipped into her Cockney. "They'll be well supervised, one-on-one. So there'll be no shenanigans of any kind to worry about."

"But a *carnival*?" he stressed. "Now, I'll admit the fence-painting idea you devised is rather a good plan. It reminds me of a scene in a book by Mark Twain. However, a carnival is entirely out of the question. Not only would we most likely have to get permission from the judge who released the boys to our care, but there are other problems I foresee as well."

"Sure it isn't only 'cause you don't like ta have fun?" Darcy challenged.

He blew out a short breath. "Really, Miss Evans—"

"If I told you Charleigh was in favor of the idea, would that make you think twice?"

He halted whatever he was about to say. "You've talked to Mrs. Lyons about this?" At Darcy's abrupt nod, he lifted his brows in surprise. "And she agreed?"

"Most definitely. She said it was a smashing idea."

"And I thought she had more sense than that," Brent muttered, shaking his head and looking away. His gaze met hers again. "And Mr. Larkin? What does he say?"

"Michael was there when I talked to Charleigh. He thought the idea a grand one."

"He would." Brent slowly replaced his glasses. "It would appear that I'm outvoted by members of the board."

"Meaning?"

He looked at her, pained acceptance filling his eyes. "Meaning, Miss Evans, that in all likelihood we shall be attending a carnival."

❧

Late morning sunshine washed the grounds and the row of eager boys standing along the discolored wooden fence. Each lad held a paintbrush. Nine glowing, expectant faces turned toward Darcy, waiting for the signal. She eyed the row one more time to make certain everyone was in position, then cupped her hands around her mouth.

"Go!" she yelled.

Brushes plopped into pails of whitewash, and loud swishes of hard bristles on wood met her command. Gangly arms rapidly worked up and down as each boy painted his section of fence, striving to be the first to complete the contest. The winner would be awarded one of Darcy's famous blackberry pies all to himself. In addition, the winner would be given a free hour on Saturday while the other boys did their chores. Everyone who participated would receive a small prize—ribbons Darcy herself had made using Irma's box of sewing trinkets and scraps. Depending on how this first contest went, other contests might follow until all fences at Lyons' Refuge were whitewashed, a late task considering that freezing weather would soon be coming.

Darcy thought of something Charleigh said when Brent questioned her about the wisdom of issuing rewards for the contest. "All through the Bible the Lord blessed His children when they did what was right and good," Charleigh said. "And He still does today. Children need a goal to work toward. Everyone does."

As Darcy watched the boys work, she pondered Charleigh's words. Darcy supposed her goal was to work at bettering herself and talking right. Charleigh's goal was to have a healthy baby. Stewart's goal was obviously to help his family, since his father's death. And Brent?

Darcy cast her gaze to where he stood between two myrtle trees. With his hands behind his back, he watched the contest a safe distance from the boys. What goals did Brent have? Likely, if he did entertain goals, they revolved around teaching his students and keeping the peace at Lyons' Refuge in Stewart's absence. Certainly his goals could have nothing to do with fun. The boys had long ago dubbed him "Ole-Stick-in-the-Mud-Thomas." Darcy pondered the term. Although Brent wasn't old, being in his midtwenties if he were a day, seeing him standing there in his brown suit on the sodden ground, he did fit the adage well.

Darcy chuckled. The pleasant breeze must have carried the sound to Brent, for he turned his head to look. Seeing her gaze focused on him, he raised his brows suspiciously, which made her giggle again. She lifted her hands, palms up, in an innocent gesture, the grin growing wide on her face. Slowly, she shook her head, as if she had no idea why he stared so. His mouth twisted and he narrowed his eyes as if he knew exactly what she'd been thinking.

"Hey! You did that on purpose!"

The lighthearted moment broken, Darcy darted a glance along the fence. Herbert, his face tomato red, glowered at Joel. "You meant to sling whitewash on me." He used his sleeve to wipe the offending streak from his jaw.

"Did not!"

"Did so!"

"Boys!" Brent came up behind them. "What's going on here?"

"He meant to do it, Mr. Thomas."

Joel crossed his arms, apparently forgetting he still held a wet paintbrush. "You can't prove it," he said, a smirk on his face. "It was an accident, pure and simple."

Darcy wondered why a little more whitewash should matter to Herbert, who was already spattered with white, but she kept silent.

"It weren't no accident!" Herbert's eyes narrowed. "It was about as much an accident as you stopping up the stovepipe with—"

"Shut up!" Joel growled and uncrossed his arms, all indifference gone.

Herbert's expression was smug. "That's why the stove didn't work right last winter, Mr. Thomas. 'Cause Joel took some old rags and climbed the roof—"

With a ferocious yell, Joel barreled into Herbert, tackling him to the ground. "You squealer! I'll show you not to double-cross me. You're just as much to blame for holding the ladder."

Joel straddled Herbert and lifted the hand holding the paintbrush high. Before Brent could intervene, Joel gave the boy's face a few quick swipes with the brush, covering Herbert's red skin with white until he resembled a ghost. "There, have some more!"

"Aggghhh!" Herbert's hands went to his face. "He got it in my eyes! I can't see!"

"Mercy! What's going on now?" Irma screeched as she ran from the kitchen door, raising her skirts high. "Joel, you stop that this minute!"

Brent now had both arms around Joel, who still swung the paintbrush like a weapon, and pulled him back. Herbert lay on the ground, howling, hands over his eyes. Michael, his great size making him awkward, ran from overseeing the boys at the end of the row. He lifted the injured boy off the ground and jogged to the house.

"Irma, call Doc Sanderson," Brent ordered through clenched teeth as he restrained a struggling Joel. "Miss Evans, wash Herbert's eyes out." He looked at the other boys, and Darcy noticed his glasses were missing. "The contest is canceled."

Ignoring the cries of disappointment, Darcy ran after Michael, her heart beating with misgiving. Once inside the house, she pumped water into a basin. In the hallway, Irma cranked the telephone, trying to get the operator. She spoke into the mouthpiece on the wooden box attached to the wall. "Hello, Miranda? Miranda, can you hear me? Get Doc to the refuge as soon as possible. One of the boys is hurt."

Darcy stared into the filled basin. *Lord, help me. Don't let this poor boy go blind. Show me what to do.* She positioned the crying Herbert, placing his upper body over the table and turning his head sideways. Dipping a cup in the water, she saw she would need another pair of hands and glanced at Michael. "I could use assistance." Her voice wavered with the doubt she felt.

"Of course, lass." His expression grave, Michael took hold of Herbert's small wrists, forcing the boy's curled fingers from his face, and held them in one massive hand. With his other hand, Michael held the boy's head steady.

Using her thumb and forefinger, Darcy opened his tightly clenched eyelid and trickled water into the corner of his eye. Herbert howled in pain, but she didn't stop. Instead, she repeated the process several times with both eyes. Her heart wrenched at his pitiful sobs.

When the sound of horses' hooves and the jangle of harness finally came, Darcy felt a sudden relief, knowing someone more qualified would soon be taking over. Portly Doc Sanderson bustled into the kitchen. He quickly surveyed the scene, his full lips thinning. "Take the boy into the parlor, Michael. Put him on the sofa. I'll examine him there."

Michael carried Herbert into the next room, and Doc followed. Darcy collapsed onto the vacated chair and propped her elbows on the wet table. She dropped her forehead onto her palms. "Help him, Lord. Take care of his eyes."

"Amen," Irma murmured. "I'll make coffee." The clang of metal hitting metal rang through the air while she went about her task.

Darcy eyed the water that had run off the edge of the table to form a puddle on the planks. "I'll take care of this mess."

As she put away the mop, the back door opened and Brent walked inside. His suit jacket was covered with white smears and speckles, his hair was disheveled, and his glasses were missing. Never had Darcy seen the proper schoolmaster in such a state. She propped the mop against the wall. "What happened to your spectacles?"

Without a word, he fished them from his coat pocket. A wire earpiece had broken off, and a crack zigzagged over one lens.

Darcy peered up at him sheepishly. "Er, sorry, guv'ner. Why don't you sit down and rest a spell? Irma's makin' coffee."

His sober countenance melted into one of relief. "Coffee sounds superb." He took a seat opposite Darcy. "How is the boy?"

"Doc's with him in the parlor."

Brent nodded, his gaze pensive as he studied his hands clasped on the table. Irma set down two steaming cups of coffee and followed it with two plates, each containing a thick slice of blackberry pie. "No sense letting it go to waste," she muttered.

Darcy stared at the dessert she'd made only this morning. The purplish black berries and sauce oozed from beneath a thin, flaky crust. A prize for the winner. What a farce that had turned out to be!

Darcy pushed away her plate, unable to enjoy the treat. Brent, apparently, had no such compunction; and Darcy watched as he lifted a forkful of the fragrant pie to his mouth.

"Ah, Miss Evans, you've outdone yourself," he said after he chewed and swallowed the first bite. He drank the rest of his coffee. "Irma, may I have another cup?"

Irma let Darcy know from the start that she preferred to be known simply as "Irma," and Darcy assumed that was why Brent called the cook by her Christian name.

"It's a crying shame about your suit." Irma tsk-tsked. "Not sure I can get whitewash out, being how it's got lime and whiting in it, but I can give it a try."

"Thank you. I appreciate the offer. However, I think such an attempt would prove futile." Brent gave Irma a faded smile and held out a sleeve. "The paint appears to have absorbed into the wool and dried. I've needed to acquire a new suit for some time, and I suppose now is the time to do so."

"You can have what's left of my eight dollars," Darcy blurted. "I still have a little over four dollars left."

Brent's eyes widened. "I can't take your money, Miss Evans."

"Whyever not?"

The question seemed to baffle him. "Because it's yours."

"Well, now, I know that. I'm offering it. All, or as much as you need." She lowered her gaze to her untouched pie. "I'm feelin' a mite guilty—bein' as how the contest was my idea. And you'll need new glasses." Uncomfortable, she took a sip of the bitter black brew, trying not to scowl and hurt Irma's feelings. She really didn't like coffee.

"I appreciate your generous offer." Brent's voice came more quietly. "But I do have adequate funds to obtain a suit. I keep a spare pair of eyeglasses in my bureau drawer, as well."

Darcy gave a swift nod but didn't look up. She took another sip of coffee.

"Well, I need to be seeing what Charleigh wants for her lunch," Irma said, bustling from the room.

Brent picked up his cup. "Don't feel too badly, Miss Evans. Everyone is entitled to a substandard idea once in a lifetime. It's part of being human."

Her gaze shot upward. "Substandard?"

"A bad idea." When she shook her head in confusion, he added, "The contest."

"Oh, but I don't think my idea a bad one."

His sympathetic expression changed to one of incredulity. "Surely you must be jesting."

"No, guv'ner." Her voice came steady, and she carefully set her cup on the saucer. "Herbert and Joel are always bickering. Why should all the lads be punished for the mischief of two boys?"

His cup hit the saucer with a harsh clink. "Miss Evans—"

"Hear me out, guv'ner. What happened today isn't so unusual, though 'tis a pity the scuffle ended with Herbert injured." Concern washed over her again as she turned her gaze toward the closed door that led to the parlor. "But Herbert is always gettin' hurt, and Joel is always fighting—usually Herbert. You can hardly blame the contest for what happened today."

He released a weary sigh. "Granted, you may be right. Yet what do you propose we do to prevent this problem from resurfacing in the future?"

She shrugged one shoulder. "Simple. Because of their behavior, Joel and Herbert are excluded from the next contest. Tomorrow is Saturday. We'll try again then."

Exasperation filled Brent's eyes. "Miss Evans, did anyone ever tell you that you are one obdurate woman?"

"Obdurate?"

"Stubborn."

Darcy smiled. "And did anyone ever tell you, guv'ner, that you have the nicest blue eyes? Bright as robins' eggs they are, clear and shiny. You really should go without your glasses more often. It would be nice to see your eyes without them spectacles always in the way."

A flush of red swept up his neck to his face. Darcy thought it a good thing that his mouth wasn't full of dessert. She studied his face and form, thinking him to be quite attractive all the way around. *If only. . .*

"Eat your pie, guv'ner. Things are quite simpler than you're makin' 'em out to be. You'll see. One day, hopefully, you'll see everything that's sittin' in front of your face—with or without the aid of your spectacles."

Brent recovered enough to blot his mouth with a napkin. "And just what is that convoluted piece of logic supposed to mean?"

"Just this. Pigeons might not be as beautiful as peacocks, or as graceful as swans, or sing as pretty as larks—but they have their place in this world, too." She stood, braced her hands on the table, and leaned toward him. "And you know what, guv'ner? Some people prefer spendin' time with the likes o' them than with the other high falutin birds."

Darcy flounced from the room, leaving Brent gaping after her in bewilderment.

Chapter 7

After filling out quarterly progress reports, Brent decided it was time for a break. He stood, stretched the kinks out from between his shoulder blades, and glanced out the window overlooking the front yard. His brows rose in surprise.

Golden sunlight dappled bright circles through the sparsely leafed branches and onto Joel's white blond hair. He sat under an oak, his arms wrapped around his legs, his face on his knees. A trickle of red and gold fell around him as several leaves in the branches above surrendered their posts and wearily drifted to the ground.

Brent puzzled a moment and then headed for the door. Once outside, he made his way to where the boy sat, his crunching footsteps announcing his approach. Joel lifted his face, his tear-smudged cheeks evidence he'd been crying. His bright eyes were defiant. "What do you want?" His voice came out harsh.

Brent decided now was not the time to reprimand the boy for disrespect. Without being asked, he awkwardly sank to the leafy ground beside him and looped his arms around his bent knees, matching Joel's stance. Brent's everyday suit coat had been ruined from the whitewashing experience, so there was no need to protect it. He would replace it the next time he went into town.

He stared at the silvery blue horizon beyond the pasture, where two cows and four horses grazed on what was left of the grass. "Days like this often cause me to ponder former episodes of my life," Brent said quietly. From the corner of his eye, he could tell he'd won Joel's attention.

"Yeah. So?" Suspicion laced the boy's voice.

"Autumn is a season of change," Brent replied, still not looking at the lad. "A time when some things must die, so that they may be reborn."

"That's silly." Joel swiped a hand underneath his nose. "Why should something have to die so's it can be reborn? Why can't it just go on living forever?"

"Well, I believe that was the original plan, Joel." He plucked up a withered brown leaf. "Observe this leaf. Once it was green and soft and shiny. Now look at it." Brent crushed it in his hand. It crackled into small particles, showering like dust to the ground. "People can be like that. They can allow hatred and bitterness to make them hard and dry and brittle and age them before their time."

The boy said nothing, only stared at the brown fragments.

"What happens when spring comes, Joel?"

Indignant blue eyes snapped upward. "Any moron can tell you that, Mr. Thomas—and I ain't no moron."

Brent nodded. "Actually you're quite smart when you put your mind to it. Yet suppose you enlighten me in any case."

Joel rolled his eyes. "The trees get new leaves on 'em."

"Exactly! Brand-new leaves—shiny and green. But first the leaves start as tiny buds."

"So?" Joel shrugged, clearly bored.

"So, that's what happens when a person asks Jesus to be his Savior." Brent scooped up the brown fragments. "We're like this before having Jesus. Old, dry, dead in our sins. When we ask God to come inside our hearts, He gives us new life—and a new start. Like a bud in springtime. As we grow with Him, we bloom until we reach our full potential, though as long as we're on this earth, He constantly will be perfecting us."

Joel eyed the crisp foliage. "So what did these ole leaves do to deserve to die? Did they sin?"

Brent let out an exasperated breath. "You're missing the point, Joel. These are merely leaves. They don't have spirits like you and I do. Every person needs Jesus to be reborn. I was using the leaves to illustrate that."

Joel raised his chin. "My father never needed Jesus. So why should I?"

"And where is your father now?"

Joel's expression grew even more belligerent. "You know where he is. But he's only in jail 'cause someone double-crossed him!"

Brent paused before responding, not wanting to alienate the boy further. He knew Joel held his father in high regard, despite the man's lengthy criminal record. He was the boy's father, after all.

"The bad things we do have consequences, Joel; remember that. If you allow God into your life, He'll teach you a better way, a way without sin. Sin leads to prison. If not an actual prison with bars that you can see, then a prison of the heart that you can't see. People can have invisible bars across their heart without even realizing it. And that prison door keeps God out. They have to *choose* to let Jesus use the key and open the door to set them free. Yet many don't."

"That's silly." Joel scowled. "Why would anyone want to stay in some ole prison?"

"Perhaps due to fear of change?" Brent shrugged. "I really don't know if there's one particular answer to that question. There are probably many. Yet the most important question you need to consider, Joel, is this: What is your reason for staying in your heart prison?"

Joel's gaze lowered. The whir of insects seemed to grow louder as the quiet intensified between them. From across the pasture, a cow lowed. The boy continued to stare at the dead leaves, his mouth drawn into a tight line.

After minutes of silence, Brent stood, knowing he should return to the study and his unfinished work. He hoped he'd made some sort of impact but doubted it from the glower on Joel's face. He turned to go.

"Mr. Thomas?"

Brent looked back. The boy's eyes were again forlorn.

"I didn't mean to make Herbert go blind." Tears strained Joel's voice. "He shouldn't have squealed—but I never meant to hurt him. Not really."

"I realize that, Joel. We won't know if there's permanent damage to Herbert's vision until the doctor removes the bandages. Actually, Dr. Sanderson was quite optimistic of Herbert's prognosis, due to the eye rinses and salves that were administered."

Joel stared down at his shoes. "Do you think Herbert will ever talk to me again?" His lower teeth slid along his upper lip. "I mean, do you think he'll forgive me?"

"There's only one way to find out."

Joel looked up in surprise. "You mean ask him?"

"Yes."

"But what if he don't want nothin' to do with me no more? What if he hates me now?"

Brent regarded the boy. "Would you like to know what I really think?" At his slight nod, Brent continued. "I think the combination of the words *what* and *if* never should have been introduced to the English language. Those two words hold people back and often produce unnecessary fear. The past can't be altered, Joel, but the future can."

The boy pursed his lips in thought. "Meaning I should go and find out for myself, huh?"

"That would be a wise choice. I'll accompany you, if you'd prefer."

Joel hesitated another few seconds, then shook his head. "Thanks all the same, Mr. Thomas, but I best do this alone."

❧

Darcy sat in a chair next to the sofa and read to Herbert, who lay snug underneath a blanket. A long strip of cotton padding was wrapped around his head, over his eyes. For three days, the helpless patient had been pampered, read to, and waited on hand and foot.

Irma also felt sorry for the lad, worried he might be blinded for life, and constantly baked him goodies. From her room upstairs, Charleigh had ordered that Herbert not be moved from the parlor; and the sofa was loaded with blankets to make a comfortable bed, a fire ever-present in the grate to warm him.

A few of the boys had visited the patient, and Tommy gave Herbert half his winnings from the contest—a second blackberry pie Darcy had made. Though Tommy's walk was hampered because of his clubfoot, he made up for any lack with his strong arms, which had worked rapidly to paint the fence.

Darcy finished the third chapter from *Robinson Crusoe* and closed the book. "That's enough for today."

"Awww, don't quit. Read more, Miss Darcy."

"One chapter is enough. My voice is tired."

"But you left off right at the good part!"

Darcy ignored his plea, since he said that about every chapter she read. "How about some cider?" She rose and set the book on the table.

"Don't want no cider." Herbert pouted and crossed his arms. "Want *Robinson Crusoe*."

"Herbert," she said in warning, her hands going to her hips. A movement near the entryway caught her eye, and Joel walked into the room. Brent stood behind him, next to the wall.

The boy's eyes were uncertain as he stared at Herbert. At the hesitant shushing of footsteps on carpet, Herbert's head lifted higher. "Who's there, Miss Darcy?"

Darcy opened her mouth to answer but stopped when Brent shook his head and put a forefinger to his lips. He crooked his finger for her to join him and disappeared around the corner.

She turned to Herbert. "I'll be back with some tea and cheese sandwiches later."

"Don't want no cheese. Want thick slices of ham."

Darcy grimaced at Herbert's pigheadedness. She refused to explain to Herbert for the fifth time that they had run out of those items and needed to replenish the larder. He was set on being obstinate today, and the constant pampering he received did him no good, in her opinion. Yet she'd been just as much at fault.

Darcy strode from the room, watching curiously as Joel moved toward the sofa. When she came alongside Brent, Darcy turned in the direction of the kitchen. Surprise shot through her when he grasped her elbow to stop her. He gave a short shake of his head, pulling her awkwardly to stand in front of him. Her shoulder blades brushed his chest.

"I know it's wrong to eavesdrop," he whispered near her ear, "but in this case I'm making an exception. I'll explain later."

Darcy's heart somersaulted at the feel of his warm breath on her neck, stirring her hair. Afraid to move—even to breathe—for fear he would remove his hand from her arm and step away, she remained as motionless as a wooden hat tree while they peeked around the corner.

"Who's there, I said?" Herbert pushed himself to a sitting position on the couch.

"It's me. Joel."

Herbert didn't say a word.

"I, uh, just wanted to see how you're doing."

"Whadda you care?" Herbert sneered.

Brent tensed and his hold on Darcy's elbow tightened. He pressed closer to hear, his chest now flat against her back. She swallowed over a dry throat.

Joel seemed stymied for words. "I. . .uh. . ."

"Just get out." Herbert turned his bandaged head away.

Instead of being cowed by the harsh words, Joel stood taller. "You shoulda never double-crossed me, Herbert. I don't like squealers. That's why I painted your face. But I sure never meant to hurt your eyes none. I was just trying to shut up your mouth." His arms crossed in defiance. "And that's all I'm ever gonna say about it. So if it ain't good enough—well, that's just too bad!"

Darcy felt Brent's chest rise and fall and heard a weary sigh escape. Again his warm breath fanned her neck, sending her heart into another spasm. The steady crackle of fire in the grate filled the eternal moment of silence in the room.

Herbert's head turned Joel's way. "Ever read *Robinson Crusoe?*"

"No." Joel walked the few feet to the chair Darcy had vacated and picked up the book from the table, eyeing the cover. "Is it one of them sissified books of Miss Charleigh's?"

"Naw—I wouldn't have nothin' to do with them kinds of books—you know that. It's about a man who gets shipwrecked on a desert island," Herbert said, excitement tingeing his voice. "Miss Darcy's reading it to me, though she's sure takin' her sweet time about doin' it!"

Darcy heard Brent quietly chuckle, his chest vibrating with the motion.

"No foolin'? A desert island? With pirates and buried treasure and wild animals eating people?"

"Not exactly. Leastways nothin' like that's happened yet. But he's all alone, and it's an adventure just the same."

Brent moved away, gently pulling Darcy with him. He headed toward the kitchen, and she fell into step beside him. "What was that all about?" Darcy still felt a bit topsy-turvy from his recent closeness, and her voice came out funny.

"A successful lesson on the importance of contrition and forgiveness. Though the apology left much to be desired," Brent added wryly. "Still, I think it achieved its purpose."

He turned his head, smiling. "This calls for a victory celebration. Assuming they're still there, would you care to join me in partaking of the last two pieces of blackberry pie and coffee—or tea if you prefer?"

Darcy nodded, knowing she would join him for a trip around the world in a hot air balloon had he asked.

"Together, Miss Evans, I think we can do this." His words came out confident. Her breath caught in her throat at the word *together*. "Do what, guv'ner?"

"Steer the boys in Stewart and Charleigh's absence. I believe we finally have reached an understanding and will begin to see some positive results for all our hard labor." He paused. "Perhaps the time has come to present the plan."

"Plan?"

"The carnival. It might be just the incentive the boys need to continue along the road to improvement. The outing would be a desirable goal, one that will help them strive to succeed and recognize that life can bring rewards for making correct choices. . . ."

Darcy smiled as she listened to Brent talk as though he'd always approved of her plan.

There just might be hope for him yet.

&

"How are you feeling? Better?" Darcy plunked down on the chenille spread at the end of Charleigh's bed.

"Merely bored," Charleigh said. "You have no idea how difficult it is to stay in bed! And I still have two months to go."

Her gaze turned to the sepia photo of her husband in its silver frame. "But I'm thankful I've carried the baby this long, and I certainly don't mean to sound as if I'm complaining. Still, I wish I'd get another letter. I think he's avoiding me. His letters have been so impersonal lately. Though at least he's writing, so that's something. He never was much of a letter-writer, both during my last two years at Turreney Farm and during the war."

"Have you written him about the baby?"

Charleigh lowered her gaze to the blanket and shook her head.

"Honestly! Don't you think he might begin to wonder when he comes home and finds you with a child in your arms? Assuming he stays away that long, of course."

"It's not exactly something you can dash off in a letter, Darcy. 'Dear Stewart, everyone's fine. The school is running smoothly, the progress reports are in order—oh, and by the way, I'm seven months with child.' I just couldn't do it. Especially in something as impersonal as a letter. Besides, I don't want to get his hopes up if. . .if something should happen."

"Now, I'll hear no more of that kind of talk!"

Charleigh sobered. Penitent for her harsh words, Darcy leaned over to lay her hand on Charleigh's. "You have to hold on, luv. Even Doc Sanderson is optimistic with the way things are going."

"He did seem positive during his last visit, didn't he?" Charleigh asked, hope in her eyes.

"Yes, he did. And never you mind about Stewart. More the surprise for him—and another thing you can look forward to seeing. The look on his face when he finds out. Ought to be about as good as when Brent's mouth drops open after I say something shocking. Though I certainly don't do such a thing on purpose." Darcy winked, eliciting a giggle from Charleigh.

A short knock at the door was followed by Alice Larkin. "Hope I'm not intruding," she said uncertainly. Her salt-and-pepper hair had been swept under a kerchief. Obviously she'd been doing housework. A pair of silver-rimmed spectacles perched at the end of her thin nose. Darcy knew that Alice used to be Michael's housekeeper before they discovered a mutual respect and liking for one another, though Charleigh once mentioned that she suspected Alice had always loved her father.

Charleigh smiled at her stepmother. "Come in. We were just discussing how surprised Stewart will be when he learns he's a father."

Alice set a canvas bag on the foot of the bed. "That he will, make no mistake about it. I still can't understand why you didn't tell him before he left. Though it's none of my business, I suppose," she muttered. Her thin lips stretched into a smile. "And have you given any thought as to what the child will be wearing when he makes his entrance into the world?"

Charleigh's forehead creased. "Wearing?"

Alice shook her head. "If it wasn't for me, that poor babe would likely be stark naked throughout his entire infancy." She pulled a large skein of ivory-colored yarn from her bag, followed by a pair of bone knitting needles.

Charleigh looked at the materials, then up at her stepmother.

Alice lifted her brows. "Well, what are you gawking at, Charleigh?"

"I don't know how to knit."

"And what do you think I'm here for? I'm aiming to teach you. The good Lord knows you need something useful to do, stuck in this bed day in and day out."

Darcy could have hugged the old woman for her thoughtfulness. "What a wonderful idea!" Another thought occurred to her. "If it wouldn't be too much trouble, could you teach me, too?"

Alice smiled. "Got someone special in mind you want to make something for, missy?"

Heat rushed to Darcy's face at Alice's astute gaze. "Just wantin' to learn is all."

"Well, I expect it shouldn't be too hard coughing up another pair of knitting needles."

Charleigh leaned forward and fingered the ivory-colored yarn. For the first time since Alice came into the room, she gave a genuine smile.

A short knock sounded, and Irma poked her head inside. "Darcy? Sorry to interrupt, but I need to be talking tonight's menu over with you. What do you think of having baked salmon again, with cooked peas and carrots? I ran out of asparagus, though I'm sure the boys wouldn't mind hearing that piece o' news."

"That sounds fine, Irma. I'll be down to help in a little while." Darcy still worked as Cook's assistant; though since she'd taken over Charleigh's role of running things, Irma now often sought Darcy's approval on meals.

Once the cook left, Alice showed Charleigh and Darcy how to hold the needles. She pulled a long string of yarn from the skein, preparing to give the first lesson.

Uneven footsteps came along the hallway, followed by a hesitant knock.

"Yes?" Charleigh called.

The glass doorknob turned. "Miss Darcy?" Tommy said through the crack in the door. "Herbert wants to know if you'll read him another chapter from that island book."

Darcy rolled her eyes toward the ceiling. Every day Herbert asked the same thing. "Tell him he'll have to wait till tomorrow. Have ye finished your lessons?"

"Yes'm. I'll tell Herbert what you said." The door clicked closed, and awkward shuffling and clomping faded as Tommy limped away.

Darcy grinned. Since the boys had been in competition for the carnival this past week, no one had to push them to study.

"That Herbert is getting downright spoiled," Alice said to nobody in particular.

Darcy chose not to comment, especially since Alice was right.

"Now, as I was saying, you loop this piece around the tip of the needle, like so—"

A loud rap sounded on the door, shaking the wood in its casing.

Alice heaved a loud sigh. "It's getting to be about as popular in here as Grand Central!"

"Come in," Charleigh said, raising her voice.

Chris's head popped through this time. "Miss Darcy?"

"Yes, Chris, what is it?"

"Mr. Thomas wants to speak with you in the study."

Darcy rose from the bed. "I better go see what he wants."

Ignoring the shrewd gleam in Alice's eyes, Darcy swept past her and downstairs. She found Brent in Stewart's oak-paneled study. Brent sat in a chair behind the desk where he took care of the bookwork in Stewart's absence. He toyed with an envelope, staring at it as though his mind were a thousand miles away. His lips were turned down at the corners.

Darcy waited what seemed an interminable amount of time for him to notice her. She cleared her throat loudly.

"Hmmm?" Brent looked up, his eyes vacant. Seeing her on the threshold, he straightened. "Miss Evans—please, come in. Close the door and have a seat."

Curious, Darcy did as requested, then moved across the faded carpet to the chair across from Brent's. He regarded her soberly. "I must make a trip into town this weekend. I'll need you to take care of things in my absence." He didn't sound too happy about the prospect.

"Trouble?"

Brent's gaze shifted back to the envelope. He didn't answer right away. "My brother. He's coming to town and wishes to speak with me."

Darcy nodded as if she understood, though she was confused. Studying his unhappy expression, she ventured, "And is this a bad thing, guv'ner—him wishin' to speak with you?"

His gaze again lifted to hers, his expression weary. "With Bill, Miss Evans, it's always a bad thing."

Before she could think twice, she was out of her chair and around to his side of the desk. Kneeling in front of him, she put her hand over his in encouragement. "Well, then, guv'ner, I believe prayer is what's needed here, instead of you mopin' about the situation. Don't you? I'll pray with ye, if ye'd like."

Dumbly, he nodded, his eyes wide behind the spectacles. Bowing her head, her hand still cupped over his warm one, she murmured a heartfelt prayer for the brothers' reunion and God's leading in it all.

When Darcy finished, she looked up. Brent's eyes shimmered softly with something akin to amazement. Yet he said nothing. Was he so shocked by her behavior?

Suddenly uneasy, Darcy rose, made an excuse that she needed to help Irma with the meal, and left the room. She supposed she shouldn't have been so forward. Yet she hoped Brent didn't mind her praying with him. In fact, she hoped it was only the beginning of such occurrences.

Chapter 8

At half past two, Brent paced the station's loading area and peered off to the west. No pillar of gray smoke loomed above the trees nor marred the gray-blue sky to announce the train's arrival. No monstrous roar of clacking wheels shook the rails. No haunting blast of a sirenlike whistle pierced the still air. Again he glanced at his pocket watch. It wasn't usual for the train to arrive even a few minutes late. Unless it wasn't the train that was tardy, but his watch that was running slow. He lifted the timepiece to his ear. Not hearing any ticking, he shook it.

"Prompt as usual, little brother."

Almost dropping the watch, Brent tensed at the jocular words coming from behind him and pivoted to look. Bill stood only feet away, dapper in a silk suit with broad pinstripes. A matching gray felt fedora with a black band topped his hair, which was slicked down and looked a shade darker than its usual wheat blond color. No common bowler for his brother! Even his black Oxfords appeared shiny and new. Obviously life hadn't treated his brother too harshly, although the lines bracketing his mouth and the faint furrows between his brows testified that this wasn't entirely the case. Identical in features and coloring, the similarities between the brothers ended there.

"Bill." Brent nodded curtly, wishing he'd given in to the need to replace his suit coat. He pocketed his watch and cupped a hand over one elbow to hide an offending streak of dried whitewash. Such a gesture was futile when he thought about it. White speckles dotted the entire coat. "Where did you come from? The train hasn't arrived."

"I decided to take an earlier one. I came into town yesterday and stayed the night at the hotel."

"Yesterday? Why didn't you ring me at the reformatory?"

"Let's just say I thought the fewer people who knew my whereabouts, the better." Bill threw him one of his dashing smiles, one that Brent knew the women swooned over. "I decided a discreet and *expeditious* entrance into your small town would be the best plan for all concerned."

Brent ignored the mocking way Bill stressed the word. His brother always poked fun at Brent's thirst for knowledge and use of elaborate words. "So, what brings you to our unexciting little town? Are matters getting uncomfortable in the big city? Is the law too close for comfort?"

Bill chuckled. "You know, that's what I love about you, little brother. You always know how to make a guy feel welcome."

Brent refrained from answering. The last time Bill sought him out had been for monetary purposes. Judging from his brother's suave appearance, Brent didn't think that was the case this time.

The stationmaster ambled out onto the platform and gave them a cursory once-over before peering toward the west, where the faint roar of the oncoming train could now be heard.

"Let's take this elsewhere," Bill muttered, cocking the brim of his hat low over his forehead. "I don't have much time."

"I have a wagon parked around the side of the building."

"Doesn't surprise me. You never were one for progress."

Brent chose to ignore the barb and moved in the direction of the horse and cart, with Bill following. Once they'd taken their place on the long bench seat, Brent flicked the reins. Polly tossed her dark mane and plodded down the dirt road. Bill grew unusually quiet and stared at the long line of storefronts.

Brent cleared his throat. "Mind telling me where we're going?"

"Nowhere. Anywhere. Just drive."

Brent sighed, tamping down his irritation. When they reached the lane leading to the road out of town, Brent took it. Slender trees on both sides of the narrow path formed a brown latticework canopy of bare limbs above their heads. Winter's bite sharpened the chill air, and Brent was relieved that the contest winners for the carnival would be announced soon. On second thought, a good snowfall might prevent the event from taking place. So perhaps he should pray for snow instead.

It had been alarming to discover that Joel was tied with an intelligent but forgetful boy named Frank as one of the three who would achieve the right to attend the event. A week remained, and a major test involving geography still needed to be taken. Brent had to admit Darcy's plan was working well—all of the boys exhibited their best behavior. Still, the prospect of taking them to a carnival made him uneasy.

"I suppose you're wondering why I asked to see you." Bill's voice startled Brent from his reverie.

"The thought had crossed my mind."

"Okay, it's like this—I've decided to embark on a seagoing career. Ships are always in need of a few able-bodied sailors, and I've applied for the job."

Brent almost dropped the reins. "You're making sport of me again, aren't you?"

"Not this time."

Brent stared at his impeccably dressed brother, who'd always had a penchant for the finer things in life. He couldn't imagine this man in a drab, ill-fitting uniform, eating food of nondescriptive taste, while bouncing along five-foot waves. Certainly his brother was joshing him.

"You're right about there being trouble—only not with the law this time. That I could handle." Bill released a weary sigh. "Let's just say it's no longer safe to be connected with the men of my association, not after what I accidentally stumbled upon. And that's all I can tell you. It's for your own good, so don't look at me that way. I just thought you should know what's what, in case you don't hear from me for several years."

Several years? "I take it your acquaintances aren't aware of your plans?"

"I left without saying good-bye, if that's what you mean." Bill's mouth twisted into a wry grin. "I found it far safer for my continued health."

Brent mulled over his brother's words. He knew from previous newspaper accounts that the tough group of men Bill associated with wasn't above murder. "Do you plan to inform our parents of your decision?" Brent asked quietly.

"I thought I'd leave that up to you. They probably wouldn't care one way or the other what happens to me and would be relieved to hear they were rid of their black-hearted son."

Brent drew his brows together. Despite all the trouble Bill had caused, he was still family. As small boys, they had been inseparable. What had happened to change that?

Anxiety blurred Brent's focus of the surroundings but sharpened his imagination. "What if they discover your whereabouts? What happens then?" He wasn't sure why he voiced the questions since the answers were obvious, given Bill's previous statement.

"Let's just say I'd sink with the anchor—permanently."

"I don't find that amusing."

Bill looked at him, his mouth and eyes wide in feigned surprise. "Do I detect a note of concern, little brother?"

Brent's lips thinned. "Will you kindly desist with the sarcasm? For once, try to be serious when the situation warrants it."

Bill released a loud breath, discernible even over the clopping of horse's hooves on hard-packed soil. "Serious. All right. Frankly, I don't want to consider the possibility. My odds for staying alive are good, I think. There was another man once— Phil something or other. I can't remember his last name. He joined up with us years ago, but was only around a short time. . .Rawlins. Yes—Phil Rawlins. That was it. He was great in his line of work—a con man and safecracker—but untrustworthy as they come. When word leaked out that my former associates were planning to do him in, he slipped away and wasn't heard from again. I can do the same."

"How do you know they didn't find him and kill him?"

Bill smiled, though his eyes were deadly serious. "Believe me, Brent. If they'd rubbed him out, it wouldn't have been kept a secret. Not among those men."

Brent closed his eyes. "Bill, answer me this. Have you, yourself, ever killed anyone?"

A short silence ensued. "It might be best not to ask questions you really don't want the answers to, little brother." This time when Bill spoke, his voice was grave and not in any way amused.

Clenching his jaw, Brent gave a brisk nod.

"You better head back to the station. I've told you all you need to know, and I have a train to catch. The ship I've signed on with leaves at morning's tide." Bill threw Brent a crooked smile. "I sound like a sailor already, don't I?"

Hardly, Brent thought, but didn't say it.

"I've heard a bit of gambling goes on aboard ship—with or without the captain's knowledge. Lady Luck and I have always been soul mates. I doubt I'll have a problem finding my place with the boys." He winked.

The ride back was quiet, and Brent relived the conversation in his mind. Didn't even a morsel of decency remain in his brother? Was he truly a lost cause as their mother had once stated?

When they pulled up to the station, Brent faced Bill. "For what it's worth, I want you to know I'm praying for you. I have been for a long time. You're still my brother, regardless of everything. God keep you safe." He held out his hand.

Bill studied it a moment, then looked up at Brent in surprised confusion. After a short time, he took his brother's hand in a firm shake. "You know, Brent, sometimes I really do wish things could have turned out differently." He paused as if he wanted to say more, then seemed to change his mind and jumped down from the wagon.

His jovial manner returned. "You may have always been something of a fuddy-duddy, but you're an okay guy in my book, little brother." Tipping his hat, he offered Brent one last devil-may-care grin. "Don't take any wooden nickels!"

Brent shook his head as he watched him jog to the platform. Bill was the one running for his life due to wrong choices, and he was telling *Brent* not to do anything stupid? Deep concern for his brother's welfare engulfed him. The righteous anger and betrayal Brent felt when Bill's nefarious actions caused him to be ostracized as a schoolmaster had at some point melted away without his realizing it.

"Keep safe, big brother," Brent said under his breath as he watched Bill disappear around the corner. "Dear Lord, keep him safe. Help him to find You. Send perfect laborers into his path, people to whom he would listen. In fact, as muleheaded as he is, perhaps an episode with a burning bush might prove more beneficial."

He grinned at the thought of such a meeting.

❧

Darcy counted her remaining prize money from the poetry contest. Whatever should she do with it? She'd bought all she wanted. Charleigh didn't seem to need it or want it, for that matter. And Darcy didn't think she should single out any of the boys for fear of causing rivalries among them.

Hearing a horse, she moved to her attic window and looked down. Brent drove the wagon through the gates, along the lane toward the barn. Chickens squawked, scattering from the path. Darcy's first thought of why the chickens were running loose and not in their pen was followed by the shock of seeing Brent in a new suit—a warm golden brown one, classically styled.

She ran down the stairs and out the door. With lifted skirts, she ran to the barn. The chickens gave loud protests, skittering out of her way.

Brent climbed down from the wagon and faced her in the shade of the barn's overhang. The suit was good for his eyes and skin tone—much better than the drab color he'd worn before.

"You bought a new suit," Darcy blurted when she could catch her breath.

Brent cast a disparaging glance at his clothes. "The tailor made this two weeks ago. The previous customer was unable to pay for it after ordering alterations. Surprisingly, it fit, though it's not something I would have picked under normal circumstances. Yet I could no longer wear that paint-speckled suit. Here at the reform it wasn't so bad, but in town, to do so was embarrassing."

"Well, I like it," Darcy said with a decisive nod. "It does something for you. Makes you look less stuffy."

The corners of Brent's mouth turned down at the compliment-gone-wrong, and Darcy quickly changed the subject. "How did the chat with your brother go?"

"He's decided to become a sailor and is going to sea."

Darcy wasn't sure how to reply. She thought Brent should be pleased that his brother had left the criminal life. Yet he looked far from happy.

Brent stared at the black-feathered hen that strutted and pecked at the ground near his shoes. "Why are the chickens running loose? Who has the job of tending them this week?"

Darcy thought a moment. "Frank," she said hesitantly.

They stared somberly at one another. Frank was tied with Joel as the third boy to go to the carnival. Because of Frank's negligence, there was no longer a tie.

"Miss Evans, it wouldn't be wise to allow Joel to attend the carnival," Brent said as though reading her mind. "On the outside he's shown an aptitude to change. However, I don't think we're observing a genuine change of heart, as the other boys seem to have had. To put it bluntly, I don't trust Joel and don't want the responsibility involved in taking him away from the refuge."

Darcy chewed on her lower lip. She didn't trust the boy either. There was something about the look in his eyes when she would suddenly turn and catch him watching her. As if he were waiting for a certain moment—though to do what, Darcy had no idea.

"Then what'll we do, guv'ner? We can't change the rules this late in the game. We'd look dishonest—promising the boys one thing and then not living up to our part of the bargain."

"I didn't say that the decision would apply to all the boys. Only to Joel."

"I understand," Darcy said impatiently. "But if we did such a thing, the others would think we don't stand by our word. Maybe it wouldn't affect them directly this time, but they'd remember what we did, sure as I'm standin' here. And we may wind up with discipline problems because of it."

Obviously upset, Brent pulled off his glasses and cleaned the spotless lenses with his handkerchief. "Had I known Joel would catch up to the others, I might not have agreed to the idea. I sincerely didn't believe he would win. You and I both know that Joel is just waiting for an opportunity to run. He talks incessantly of finding his father. Suppose he decides to escape while we're at the carnival? What then?"

"Michael will be with us," Darcy countered. "The boys know better than to act up with him around."

"Yet suppose that doesn't prove to be the case when Joel's in a public, unrestricted area? Suppose the lure of freedom proves too powerful for him?"

Darcy put her fists on her hips. "As for supposin', suppose the sky falls down around our ears like it did for Chicken-Licken in that children's book I read last year? Suppose a felon ambushes the wagon on the way to the carnival and holds us up? Suppose a blizzard hits the county—in which case, this conversation is moot because there wouldn't be no carnival!" She shook her head. "You do too much supposin' and not enough trustin' in the Lord, guv'ner."

Brent held up his hands in a gesture of surrender, the temples of his glasses dangling from his fingers. "Very well, Miss Evans. If Charleigh and Michael agree, then obviously I'm outvoted. Still, I want you to know that I'm not in favor of taking Joel."

"You've made that clear as windowpane glass. But I think we should give him a chance."

Brent gave an abrupt nod. "I have a test to prepare. I'll see you at dinner."

❧❧

Days later, while Brent waited for Darcy and Michael to round up the three winners—Joel, Tommy, and Lance—he stared into the cloudless aquamarine sky and wondered again what he'd allowed himself to get into. He watched a formation of birds in their flight south. The scene reminded him of a postcard he'd seen recently detailing a fleet of ships in two neat rows, forming a V. He wondered about Bill and what he was doing. Had his desire to enter the seagoing life given him satisfaction? Or regret? Was he safe from the gangsters' clutches?

A door slammed, and Brent peered over his shoulder. Herbert leaned against the rail of the stoop, Lance next to him. Both redheads had their arms crossed while they talked. The resemblance between the two was striking. They could have been brothers, with their freckled faces and bright eyes full of mischief.

Herbert's expression was envious, but at the same time he seemed grateful. The dressing over his eyes had come off two days ago, and the doctor declared it a miracle that the boy suffered no permanent damage to his sight. He had commended Darcy for her quick thinking in rinsing Herbert's eyes. Darcy had looked uncomfortable at the praise but nodded, saying, "It was Mr. Thomas's idea. All the prayin' every one of us did sure must have helped some, too."

Brent thought about the young woman who'd come to the establishment a year ago. In fact, it seemed lately all he did was think about her. A truth that did little to please him. Twice in past months, he'd actually entertained the notion of courting her, then blinked at the absurdity of such an idea and quickly set his mind to the work at hand.

Even now he envisioned her, with her entrancing eyes—as dark blue as the sky sometimes appeared in late autumn after the sun had descended far below the horizon. She'd finally adopted the habit of wearing her dark tresses up, as propriety demanded; but wispy tendrils often trailed at her temples and neck, giving her a delightful air of femininity.

Again the door creaked open. Michael and the last two winners stepped outside. After several seconds elapsed, Darcy followed. Brent blinked, then blinked again, his heart skipping a beat.

Darcy had dressed for the occasion in a cobalt blue dress with a white ruffled inset—obviously an outfit of Charleigh's that had been altered to fit. Yet Brent couldn't imagine it on anyone else. The dress appeared as though it had been designed for Darcy, bringing out the rose of her cheeks and the shine of her hair. The blue hat she wore added to the stunning picture.

She stopped in front of him, offering him a puzzled stare. "Somethin' wrong, guv'ner?"

Her inquisitive words snapped Brent from his daze. He realized an audience of four watched with amusement and extreme interest. Joel snickered. Brent turned a formidable glance his way and, for good measure, cut it to the other two boys so they would realize from the start that Brent wasn't about to put up with any nonsense. He didn't dare look at Michael.

"Guv'ner?"

Darcy's soft query brought his attention her way. "No, Miss Evans, everything is splendid. Splendid. Allow me to help you to your seat."

Taking her soft, warm hand in his was a mistake, and Brent broke contact the second she was seated on the driver's bench. He felt her curious stare but concentrated on taking his seat and slapping the reins on Polly's back.

Despite Darcy's attempts at conversation, Brent continued to stare ahead, offering abrupt replies to any questions she presented. At last she gave up with a frustrated sigh and turned to watch the thick line of trees on her right while the wagon continued down the road.

Michael and the boys had entered into some sort of rapid word game. Brent shook his head in amusement at the sudden laughter that erupted from the back when Michael missed his cue—probably on purpose in order to gain the light-hearted response he had. He would make a superb grandfather.

Brent had never known his own grandparents. His only sister, Amy, older by eight years, once spoke about them from the little she remembered before they died. Yet they sounded too wonderful to be true; and as a child, Brent asked if Amy were inventing such paragons of benevolence. Whatever the truth, Brent wished he could have known them. Perhaps then he could better understand the concept of fun.

Much later, he pulled the wagon alongside a row of other wagons and several motorcars parked behind makeshift buildings and tents that were part of the carnival. The sun shone pale from a sky that had turned grayish blue, and the distinct smell of roasted peanuts and something sweet made Brent's mouth water.

Unexpectedly, he found himself actually beginning to look forward to the adventure ahead. He decided he would do his utmost to relax and have fun—without sacrificing his dignity or principles, of course. Moreover, he would endeavor to not be stuffy, as the women had dubbed him—first Charleigh, then Darcy.

"Well, my lads," he said, turning to look at the boys with a wide smile. He removed his glasses and placed them in his breast pocket. "Are you prepared to embark on an exciting escapade—one that in all likelihood you shall never forget for the rest of your days on this earth?"

The boys stared. Michael stared. Brent could feel Darcy's stare.

The smile slid from his face. Had he laid the ebullience on a little thick? Perhaps there was a proper way to relax and have fun—one of which he was unaware. Before the day was through, Brent determined to unveil the secret.

Chapter 9

Casting Brent a peculiar look, Darcy grabbed the picnic hamper.

"Leave it be, lass," Michael said. "We plan to return to the wagon at midday and eat our lunch."

"Of course." She'd already known that, but Brent's bizarre behavior had mystified her and made her act without thinking.

"Besides," Michael continued, "with five strong men to assist, you wouldn't be thinkin' we'd let a wee lass such as yourself carry even a small burden? Isn't that right, laddies?"

The boys responded with a loud chorus of "yessirs."

Darcy grinned. "Michael, you're a peach." She loved the old Irishman. He made her feel like somebody special, like his own daughter.

Brent cleared his throat and stepped down. "Ahem, yes. Shall we proceed?"

Darcy darted a somber glance his way, one he didn't see. Brent would never accept her as a lady, no matter what she did to improve herself. Tommy slipped his hand into hers while the other boys scampered ahead. "Somethin' the matter, Miss Darcy?"

His earnest brown eyes held concern, and she forced a smile. "Nothing for you to fret about. Now, as Mr. Thomas so aptly put it—let's have fun!" She squeezed his plump hand, and he grinned.

At the entrance, a wide banner billowed with the frequent gusts of wind that beat against it and proclaimed in large block letters: RENWALDI'S PREMIER CARNIVAL. Darcy took her first look at the fair. Twin rows of tents and buildings stretched into the distance, sitting closely side by side. The buildings bore elaborately carved and painted fronts. Jewel-colored pennants waved from the top of many. On closer inspection, Darcy saw that the makeshift buildings were narrow in size, and the fronts were false.

A wooden platform extended across the front of every building. One to three carnival workers—easy to recognize because of their outlandish dress—stood on each platform, facing the small crowds that gathered. From what Darcy could see of the aggressive barkers, they enticed anyone with "enough courage" to walk up the five steps and seek the mystery of what lay inside the buildings behind them.

Monstrous mechanical gadgets packed with people whirled round and round. From somewhere within the circular contraption that bore decorated wooden horses, lively organ music played. Laughter, screams, and the sounds of machinery clicking and clanging punctuated the air. Darcy's eyes widened when she noticed a machine built like a huge, spoked wheel. It slowly revolved and took people high—very high—to the top and then *whooshed* them to the ground again to repeat the process. Her stomach lurched just watching the spectacle.

As they moved farther into the noisy, exciting, and somewhat frightening world, the sudden amplified voice of a man captured Darcy's attention. She turned, and the boys followed, as curious as she. They made their way to the platform where a carnival worker stood and bent slightly toward the crowd of onlookers. In one hand he held a bamboo cane, which he waved about with a flourish while he spoke through a megaphone.

"Hurry, hurry—step right up and see Carelli's amazing freak show. The sights inside will astound you. The phenomenon within these four walls will mystify you. See Bruce, the strongest man in the world, lift five hundred pounds. That's right, folks, I said five hundred pounds."

A hairy, well-muscled bald man, wearing no more than a leopard-skin wrap around his thick middle, stepped from beyond the red curtain in the arched center of the false-fronted building. Teeth bared in an awful grimace, he took a stand at the opposite end of the platform. He bent at the waist, held his thick arms bowed out like a gorilla, and growled. A woman onlooker in front shrieked and clapped her hands to her mouth, taking a step back into the growing throng of people. Her companion put his arm around her shoulder in reassurance.

"See Lila, a true freak of nature, and only one of many abnormalities that lie beyond the crimson curtain," the hawker continued. Turning, he gestured with his cane toward the entrance. A young woman stepped from behind the drape to stand on the platform not far from where Darcy stood.

Darcy gasped, the rest of the hawker's speech wafting over her like so much nonsense. Lila's features were feminine, her ringed hands next to her full lilac skirts dainty, her body curved in all the right places. Yet she sported a full curly beard that matched her dark hair. For a moment, her thickly lashed brown eyes met Darcy's sympathetic ones; the bold, indifferent look flickered—but only for a moment. The young woman lifted her whiskered chin and stared Darcy down until she looked away uneasily.

"For only the price of a penny," the hawker continued, "you can witness these shocking freaks of nature and more. But only if you dare." At this, he flashed a wicked smile beneath his waxed handlebar mustache, revealing all his teeth. His last words were a certain lure to ignite every male's determination to prove his courage.

And the boys were no exception.

"Let's go in," Lance cried. "I ain't skeered!"

"I want to see the freaks," Joel said.

"Can we go in, please, Miss Darcy?" Tommy asked, tugging her sleeve.

"I, uh, don't know," she hedged, throwing a glance that cried "help" Brent's way. He looked just as perplexed.

"Perhaps we should find something else to do," he suggested quickly. "It appears that there are many activities to see and do at a carnival."

Obviously he felt as Darcy did. Curiosity had lured them to listen to the hawker. Shock kept them rooted to the ground through the spiel. But neither wanted to see what lay beyond the crimson curtain.

"Then again, it might do the lads some good," Michael deliberated. "And make them grateful for what they have. I say we take them inside."

Brent and Darcy stared at one another. Michael usually got the last word.

"If you'd rather not go, you can wait here," Brent said, his tone apologetic. "Mr. Larkin and I can oversee the boys in such a confined space."

Darcy gave a slight nod, her gaze traveling to the bearded lady. With a haughty lift of her chin, Lila stared at the crowd ogling her, then turned on her heel and marched back through the curtain. The strong man followed.

"No," Darcy murmured before she could think twice. Something about the bitter woman with the empty eyes caused her to state, "On second thought, I think I'll join you."

❧

Michael paid their admission, and they took the stairs up to the platform. The hawker held back the heavy velvet curtain as they stepped through the entrance.

Kerosene lamps lit the rectangular room, and swaths of crimson and black material were draped in front of the lanterns, giving off a subdued glow and adding to the mystery. A rough wooden stage with a black curtain that shielded what was beyond took up one entire side of the cramped room, which smelled of newly sawed wood. Wooden folding chairs sat lined up front, and many observers had already taken a seat. Brent motioned to six free chairs in the fourth of five rows.

Once seated, Darcy stared at the curtain. The hawker gave another spiel designed to get every heart pumping with fear of the unknown. Darcy almost changed her mind and left, but at that moment the curtain rose. She gasped, eyes wide. Seated on high stools for the people to gawk at were some of the most pitiful sights she'd ever seen.

Besides the bearded lady and the strong man, there was a man so thin one could see his blue veins, tendons, and bones through his translucent skin. Two young girls joined at the hip were propped against the same stool. A man with a head much too small for his body looked dully out at the audience. A woman so short she would likely come to Darcy's knees stood on one of the stools.

The hawker ordered them to the front, one by one, in order to perform some act that emphasized their deformity. Darcy wrinkled her brow, and fear melted into pity. She watched when a scoffing older boy was given the hawker's permission to pull on the bearded lady's chin to see if her whiskers were real. The woman flinched in pain at the cruel tug. Nervous laughter filtered through the room.

"I love every one of them, My daughter. And I want you to show them My love, as I have shown My love for you."

Darcy's eyes opened wide when she heard the gentle voice deep within her spirit—the voice she had come to know this past year through time spent with Him. "How, Lord?"

"Did you say something?" Brent whispered.

Darcy shook her head, not realizing she'd spoken aloud. Again she closed her eyes and concentrated, but she heard no reply to her question.

After the humiliating exhibit ended, the curtain lowered and the crowd was ushered outside. Annoyed, Darcy stood her ground. "May I speak with the others?" she asked the hawker.

"The freaks?" he said in surprise. "Why would you want to speak to them? You a reporter? News reporters are supposed to go through the general manager, Mr. Carson."

"No, I'm not a reporter." Darcy lifted her chin and stared him down, then reminded herself that ladies were supposed to be polite, as Charleigh had taught her. With difficulty, she forced her features into a pleasant expression. "I won't take up much of their time. I only want to talk with them for a few minutes. Perhaps I could just talk to Lila?"

"Sorry, Miss, but fraternizing with the freaks ain't allowed." He chewed on the stump of a cigar, giving her a level look. "But don't you go botherin' that pretty head o' yours about them. They's fed and well cared for, like all the other animals. So don't you worry none." With that, he strutted back to the entrance, twirling his cane as he did.

Darcy stuck out her tongue at his back. She couldn't help herself. When she realized she probably had an audience of three impressionable boys, she inwardly groaned and turned to face them, wondering how to explain her behavior. Thankfully their attention was engrossed in some dreadful ride on the midway.

Sometimes it was so hard acting respectable, like a Christian was supposed to act. Like a lady was required to act. Sighing noisily, she joined the others. She hoped this particular ride wasn't next on their agenda.

❧

As the day progressed, they visited a flea circus, a crazy house of mirrors, and a penny vaudeville featuring a pair of limber dancers. With his flat feet, Brent had never been able to dance well, but he enjoyed watching the spectacle, as he admired all things of beauty.

The boys looked on with bored expressions, obviously not sharing his sentiments. Lance began making rude noises with his hands and armpits, and Michael quickly escorted him outside. Only when a juggler took the stage did the other two boys perk up and strain on the edges of their seats in order to see better.

Throughout the afternoon Brent sent several worried stares Darcy's way. She'd been unusually quiet ever since the freak show. The event had disturbed him, as well. Not so much the physical imperfections and abnormalities, though Brent would be lying if he didn't admit to being a bit repulsed. Still, he felt sympathy for those people, who were forced to act like trained monkeys and entertain others.

Remembering the gasps of revulsion and the jeers from the so-called "normal" people in the audience, Brent was reminded of the games in the ancient Roman colosseum. The only difference he could see between the two was that the Romans had once held games of sport to kill the flesh. This sideshow had been designed to kill the spirit of those on exhibit. He frowned at the memory, wishing to put the event far behind him. Once the juggler exited the stage, he suggested they eat.

The huge lunch Irma had prepared didn't satisfy the boys, who insisted on roasted peanuts, candy apples, and other treats—all of which Michael readily supplied. Brent shook his head, thinking of the bicarbonate of soda that would likely be administered to three stomachaches tonight. Four, if Darcy kept at it. Her disturbance over the sideshow didn't seem to affect her appetite. Of course, he knew she was partial to fruit, but three candy apples and a small paper bag of sugared orange slices was taking it a bit far.

They passed a tall man in a clown suit handing out balloons to children. The man wore a green-and-white polka-dot shirt with a yellow bow tie, dark baggy pants, and a tiny hat on his head. His face was hidden behind layers of white and black paint, and a huge red frown replaced the usual clown smile.

"Would you like a balloon?" Michael asked the boys.

Joel and Lance both looked the clown's way but shook their heads. "Naw, them's for babies," Lance said. "Can we ride that?" He pointed to the upright circular monstrosity with seats resembling buckets.

"The Ferris wheel," Michael said, nodding. "I don't see why not."

Joel cocked his head. "You been to a carnival before, Mr. Larkin? You know the names of all the rides."

Michael smiled. "I've been to Coney Island's amusement park. It's a lot like this, only on a much grander scale."

As they drew closer to the Ferris wheel, Tommy's face blanched. "Do we have to ride on that if we don't want to?" he all but whispered.

Darcy gave his hand a reassuring squeeze. "Of course not. We can find something else to do while the others ride."

Michael nodded down the midway to the revolving ride with the painted wooden horses attached. "Why not take the lad on the carousel?"

Tommy nodded, smiling. "I do like horses, even if they ain't real."

Joel looked in that direction. "I'd like to go on that, too."

Brent stared at him skeptically. He would have figured Joel would be interested in the more thrilling ride.

"I'll take Lance," Michael said. "You two take the others. We'll meet at the hippodrome afterward."

"And see the Wild West show and the wild animals there?" Lance said hopefully, his eyes wide as he craned his head to look up at Michael.

The old Irishman grinned and ruffled his hair. "Aye. If we're in time for the next show. I t'ink it will be a lot like the circus I was telling you about."

Arrangements made, they went their separate ways.

"Mr. Thomas?"

Brent was only a few yards from the carousel when he heard his name called from behind. He turned to see a patriarch of their small town, one of those in strongest opposition to the reformatory. "Good afternoon, Mr. Forrester," Brent said courteously, though his stomach plummeted in dismay.

"Do my eyes deceive me?" The man's mouth turned down underneath his walruslike white mustache. He adjusted his monocle and gave the boys a scathing glance. "Have you taken these hooligans away from the reform to mix with members of decent society?"

Brent maintained his pleasant smile. "Mr. Forrester, I assure you, all precautions have been taken. These boys are being rewarded for their exemplary behavior—"

"Exemplary!" the old man scorned. "Since when is thievery, lying, and who knows what other fiendish acts cause for reward?"

"It is their changed behavior for which they're being rewarded." Briefly Brent described the contest.

Mr. Forrester's white brows knitted together. "I assume you cleared such a thing with Judge Markham?"

"Everything has been taken into account, Mr. Forrester. Now if you'll excuse me?" Brent tipped his hat, took Joel's hand, and moved away.

"Mark my words, Mr. Thomas, the town council will hear about this," Mr. Forrester called after him. "With criminal activity rampant in your own family, I find it shocking that Mr. Lyons would have left you in charge in the first place. A significant error on his part if this is how you choose to run the institution. . ."

Brent kept walking, though he felt the sharp stab of Mr. Forrester's words. Feelings of anger at Bill flared, and it was with difficulty that he pushed them away.

Darcy took a place beside Brent. "You're doin' a fine job, guv'ner—the boys are better behaved than I ever did see them. Why, even Charleigh was saying just yesterday how pleased she is with your work at the refuge."

Brent looked at her. Under the hat, her stormy eyes blazed.

"I cannot take full credit for that," he said. "The boys' improvement is due in part to your ministrations also. It's something we've accomplished together, with a significant amount of help from above."

Darcy stopped walking and stared at him in surprise. A soft smile tilted her lips. "Together. . .we do make a fine team, don't we, guv'ner?"

Her wistful-sounding words shook him. He couldn't look away from her shining face; and he suddenly longed to stroke her cheek, which appeared as soft as velvet.

A chuckle shook Brent from his trance. He blinked, noticing how people were walking around where he and Darcy stood and stared at each other in the middle of the midway.

"Daydreaming again, Mr. Thomas?" Joel inquired innocently. "Wonder what it's about this time." He snickered and elbowed Tommy in the ribs, earning an answering chuckle from the lad and a stern gaze from Brent.

"Come along," he snapped, his pace faster than before. "We haven't all day to waste at the fairgrounds."

❧

In a daze, Darcy stared at Brent's departing form then put a hand to the crown of her hat and hurried after him. For one breathless moment, she'd thought he might kiss her—there, in the midst of the crowd, with strains of calliope music coming from somewhere in the midway and mixing with the dreamy music from the carousel. His eyes had been so soft, so full of something that made Darcy's stomach whirl.

"Guv'ner?" she said as she came up behind him and put a hand to his shoulder.

Brent turned, his expression sober. The spark that lit his eyes when he stared at her earlier was gone. "Joel is complaining of a stomachache now and doesn't want to ride," he said, businesslike, his tone holding none of its former warmth. "With all the sweets he ate, I'm not surprised. We shall stand and watch while you take Tommy onto the carousel."

Lips compressed, she nodded curtly and took the boy's hand to lead him away, angry with herself for daring to hope. When would she learn? Brent thought of her—would always think of her—much as one of those poor freaks at the sideshow. It didn't matter how she improved herself; he most certainly would never see the change. She wondered why she bothered then shook away the thought.

She did it for herself. For Darcy Evans. She wanted to be everything God intended her to be. She enjoyed learning, both in her studies and on being a lady.

Her accomplishments made her feel good inside. Darcy lifted her chin with confidence as she stepped onto the stationary wooden disc with Tommy and located two painted horses side by side.

So much for Brent Thomas, she thought. She didn't need him or his stuffy ways.

At Tommy's timid request, Darcy took the life-sized horse closest to the outside rim after helping him up on his horse. Perching atop, she drew one leg under her long, full skirt, as though she were riding sidesaddle. With one hand she held onto the metal pole securing the horse to the wooden dais and canopy, while smiling at Tommy and assuring him that the ride wouldn't be a scary one. Pointing to the mirrored column in the middle, she got Tommy to laugh at the silly faces she made at her reflection. Darcy didn't even bother to cast a glance Brent's way, though she knew they were seated on the side where he and Joel stood.

The music of the carousel grew louder as the wheel slowly began to turn and then pick up speed. Darcy clutched her other hand around the pole, holding on for dear life. The cool breeze created by the wheel's movement brushed her face, and any apprehension she had fluttered away.

Suddenly carefree, she plucked off her wide-brimmed hat to let the wind cool her sweat-dampened hair. She laughed, trying to pick out the faces of those who stood watching the carousel spin. But the whole world was off balance, and such a feat proved impossible.

"Grab the ring, Miss Darcy!" Tommy squealed, pointing to a striped pole standing near the carousel. Several gold rings—a little larger than bracelets—hung from a protruding rod at the top. "If you get one, you win a free ride."

"How do you know?" Darcy asked.

"Mr. Larkin told me. Grab the ring!"

Spurred by the boy's excitement, Darcy nodded. With the next revolution, she spotted the candy-striped pole. However, stretching out to retrieve a ring seemed not only impossible but dangerous. Her gaze dropped to the unforgiving hard ground spinning crazily under the edge of the rotating platform. She tightened her grip on the pole. "Aaaee," she cried softly.

"You didn't try for the ring," Tommy said, a pout in his voice.

Darcy took a deep, steadying breath and straightened, waiting for the carousel to take them around again. This time she focused on the top of the pole, refusing to look at the ground. With the brim of her hat securely tucked beneath one knee, she kept her hand solidly fixed around the pole and leaned as far as she could toward the outside, stretching her other hand toward the ring.

"Miss Evans!" Brent's shocked voice came from somewhere within the revolving blur of faces. "What do you think you're doing?"

Her fingers just brushed the metal ring as the carousel took her out of its reach. Now determined, she tightened her grip on the pole and moved farther up on the horse, using her other leg to anchor her to a semikneeling position. The pole came in sight. She slid her hand farther up the slick rail, braced herself, and leaned as far over as she could, her upper body hovering above the ground. Her hat suddenly went sailing into the crowd of onlookers, but her fingers connected with cold metal. She locked her hand around the link and tugged, elated when she came away with the gold ring.

"You did it, Miss Darcy, you did it!" Tommy cried.

A burst of applause from behind almost unseated her. Once she'd settled onto the horse again, she looked over her shoulder. A man with a mustache and dark windblown hair leaned against one of the horses and smiled at her with amused approval in his eyes. Recognizing him as the carousel operator, Darcy hurriedly turned face front.

Her cheeks burned when she remembered the antics she'd gone through for the silly ring. Definitely not in any way ladylike—and what's more, Brent had witnessed the outrageous display. And her hat—her fashionable new blue hat that she'd paid seventy-five cents for! By now it was probably trodden underfoot.

This ride seemed to last longer than the ones she'd watched from afar; and when the carousel finally came to a stop, Darcy was sure the extra time had been deliberate. Especially when the carousel worker sauntered up to her painted horse with a sly smile and extended his hands.

"Need a lift, miss?"

"No, I'm fine—oh!" Her words shuddered to a stop when she felt his big hands clasp around her middle and swing her off the horse's painted back to settle her on the wooden planks.

His smile grew more personal. "That gold ring is worth a free ride, you know."

Irritated, Darcy awkwardly sidled past him, the ring clasped to her breast. "Yes, thank you. Another time. Come along, Tommy." She held out her hand to help him down.

"The ride isn't to be missed in the moonlight," the carousel operator called after her. "Come back after dark. There's a full moon out tonight."

Darcy ignored him, heat singeing her cheeks. She still felt a bit dizzy from the ride and clutched Tommy's hand hard as they made their way off the carousel. Tommy looked back at the man, then at her, but he didn't say a word.

Before she could find a familiar face in the crowd of onlookers, Darcy felt her arm clasped from behind.

Brent's eyes were stormy. "And just what was the meaning of that foolhardy exhibition?" He kept hold of her upper arm.

She held up the gold ring. "I won a free ride."

"And you decided to risk life and limb to do so?" he asked incredulously.

He shook his head. "Your behavior was appalling; the example you set for the boys atrocious."

Darcy wondered why he was so upset. True, she'd acted a little carelessly, but she'd done a lot worse in the past and never seen him so angry. She forced herself to remain calm. "You're absolutely right, guv'ner. I did act without thinking. I apologize."

He snorted, something out of place for the proper Brent, and stepped closer. "Who was that man ogling you? What was that all about?"

"Man ogling me?" Darcy uttered in surprise, marveling that he should care. "What man?"

"Don't play coy with me, Miss Evans. I distinctly saw him manhandle you and lift you off that horse."

"Oh, you must mean the carousel operator." She dismissed him with a toss of her hand, though the sudden pounding of her heart belied her indifferent attitude. Could Brent's uncharacteristic behavior actually mean he was jealous? The surprising thought greatly appealed to her womanly ego, and she couldn't help but stoke the fire a bit. "He was just a kindly gentleman helping a lady, is all, and trying to be friendly. Why, he even suggested I take a ride by moonlight," she couldn't resist adding when she saw his eyes narrow. "I have a free one coming, you know."

"Darcy Evans, you steer clear of that carousel worker. He is anything but a kindly gentleman. His kind is after one thing and one thing only. You must guard your reputation and be careful around these carnival workers—in light of your job at the refuge as a guardian of young boys, of course."

Darcy's eyes widened. Did Brent realize he'd said her first name? Offense quickly replaced wonder when she weighed his words. He must have very little faith in her judgment, telling her whom she wasn't to associate with—as if he had the right! Did he truly think she couldn't see beyond the carousel operator's wily charm and familiar ways? Daily, she had come up against much worse on the streets of East London and knew how to watch out for herself. Suddenly angry, she glared up at him.

"Mr. Thomas, I don't believe I care for your *supercilious* attitude. Now if you'll excuse me, I need to find me hat."

Brent didn't release his hold. Darcy turned, intending to break away, take Tommy, and stalk to the opposite side of the carousel. What did the boys think about their schoolmaster's bizarre display? And he had the audacity to complain about *her* behavior?

Her equilibrium still unsteady, Darcy teetered and suddenly found herself pressed against Brent's chest and in his arms. Staring up at him, she blinked in surprise. He looked down, evidently just as shocked as she.

"Miss Evans, I . . ." His hesitant words trailed off. His gaze magnetized hers and then lowered.

All anger dissolved. She parted her lips in expectation, her pulse rate quickening. His hold tightened, and his piercing blue gaze lifted from her mouth to roam her face. Electric seconds passed, the noise of the crowd vanishing to a muted roar in Darcy's ears. She felt suspended in a fantasy world where everything faded to the background—everything but she and Brent.

"I don't remember what it was that I wanted to say," he whispered, his absorbed expression proof that he was also caught up in whatever held her spellbound.

She lifted her hand to the back of his neck, exerting pressure downward while raising her face to his. Before their lips could touch, he straightened and released his hold on her.

"Miss Evans, you have my most sincere apology," he said, his voice sounding thick. "I don't know what came over me."

Darcy's heart teetered from the clouds and made a fast spiral to the bottom of her chest. Before she could recover, Tommy's high-pitched voice shattered the air, and his hand insistently tugged at her skirt.

"Miss Darcy! Where's Joel?"

Chapter 10

B rent and Darcy stared at one another in shock. Brent was the first to move. "He couldn't have gone far in such a short time."

However, a thorough search of the immediate area did nothing to produce the boy. "You take Tommy and tell Michael what happened. I'll start looking for Joel in that direction." Brent motioned beyond the carousel.

Darcy nodded and hurried toward the hippodrome with Tommy. Brent scanned the crowds in front of each makeshift building and tent. Where could the boy have gone? It had been a mistake to bring him, but of course that was all water under the bridge now. Joel's disappearance was Brent's fault, but he refused to visit that place in his mind. Refused to visit any thoughts that led him to Darcy Evans. He still felt rattled that he'd almost kissed her! Brent shook his head. They must find Joel before he escaped. Where would the boy go? Where would Brent run to if he were Joel?

Brent walked the crowded midway, making a careful scan of each face. Quite a number of boys was scattered throughout the horde, but none of them was Joel. Spotting a muscled, dark-haired man in a pin-striped shirt, he recognized him as the presumptuous carousel worker and frowned. He'd like to give the insolent fellow a piece of his mind.

Brent approached a large tent, eyeing the long row of people waiting to take a turn inside. He doubted Joel would be standing in any line, but it never hurt to be certain.

"Guv'ner!" He heard Darcy's breathless voice from behind him.

Brent quickly faced her. "Have you found him?"

She shook her head. "I only came ter offer me 'elp. Two pairs o' eyes is better than one, I expect. Michael's with Lance and Tommy, lookin' at that end." She pointed to the opposite side of the midway.

Brent would prefer not to be in her company after what happened—or almost happened—between them. Yet she was right: Two pairs of eyes were better than one. And he certainly wouldn't consider letting her go off by herself to search. Not when leeches such as that carousel worker abounded throughout the midway.

Together, Brent and Darcy scouted various attractions, inquiring of different vendors and carnival-goers if they'd seen a towheaded boy, about thirteen years of age, wearing a pair of brown knickers with suspenders and black stockings, a white shirt, and a battered tweed cap. A description that could apply to any number of lads visiting the carnival today, from what Brent could tell.

Twice they were directed to different areas by people who thought they'd seen Joel. Twice they came up empty.

After what must have amounted to half an hour of fruitless searching, Brent realized what had to be done. "I suppose it's time to contact the authorities."

"No," Darcy said. "Let's try a little while longer."

"The longer we wait, the greater a lead he has on us."

Darcy's eyes were troubled. "But if you call the bobbies—I mean, police— you could lose your position at the reform. Who's to say Mr. Forrester won't find out what happened and leak word to Judge Markham? Besides, I don't think Joel ran."

Brent stared at her in disbelief. "How can you say such a thing? It's apparent he did just that. He waited for his chance and took it."

"No." Darcy stubbornly shook her head. "This morning I heard him promise Herbert that he would bring him back a trinket from the carnival. Those two have become close since the fence-paintin' incident. If Joel were plannin' to run, he likely would've confided in Herbert—not led him to believe he would be back."

"Perhaps Joel knew the conversation was being overheard and only said that to waylay suspicion."

She shook her head again, her lips compressed. "I don't agree. One thing you don't know about criminals, guv'ner, is that they're a faithful lot—to one another. True, there are some that would betray a friend, but for the most part they's few and far between. Convicts are birds of a feather—an' usually don't keep secrets from one another, 'specially those they come to trust."

Brent considered her words. Darcy should know, having been a former convict. He remembered Bill's revelation concerning family secrets and something else that his brother had said years ago—about felons relying on a code of honor among themselves—as dishonorable and immoral as their actions were. Brent wavered in what steps to take—every second counted—but there was a chance she might be right.

"All right then, Miss Evans, what do you suggest we do?"

She looked at him in frank astonishment. "Why, guv'ner. I'm surprised you need to ask. We should pray for direction, like we should have done from the beginning. God knows where Joel is, don't He now?"

Darcy took his hand in hers and bowed her head. "Heavenly Father, point us the way to Joel. We ask this in Jesus' name. Amen."

When she looked up, Brent was staring at her in disbelief. A smile flickered on her lips. "Prayers don't need to be longwinded, guv'ner. Just sincere and from the heart. That's what God looks at," she couldn't resist adding. "The heart. Not what's on a person's outside."

Brent averted his gaze, slipping his hand from hers. "Of course. Shall we proceed?"

For the next several minutes, they searched the south end of the carnival grounds. "Let's try elsewhere." Brent touched her elbow to turn her in another direction, but she stopped and gripped his upper arm.

"Look there, guv'ner—beyond that sign advertising the fortune-teller. See the small man in the black suit and bowler? He looks mighty worried 'bout somethin'. He keeps peepin' over his shoulder—though he walks with purpose, as if he knows what he's about. There—see him? He's walking to the back of the tent."

Brent nodded. "It's worth looking into, I suppose."

They followed the short, skinny man around the side. The tents were close together, leaving a narrow walking space, like an alley, that took them to the back. They reached the end, and Brent grasped Darcy's arm when she would have boldly walked onward. Puzzled, she glanced at him.

"We don't know what we're getting into," he whispered. "It's best to proceed with caution."

She nodded, and they carefully looked around the edge of the tent.

Darcy spotted Joel's slim form immediately, and relief almost brought her to her knees. He stood in front of a little table with a man sitting behind it. A shell game was in progress. The man, Darcy noted with surprise, was the clown who had handed out balloons earlier. Some of his face paint was smudged, and his hat and bow tie were gone as well; but the loose polka dot shirt under the yellow suspenders was unmistakable. Both he and Joel were in deep conversation. The man stared intently at the boy, as if he'd found a gold mine. The short man in the bowler had halted his hurried approach and stood, as though uncertain.

Darcy watched while Joel deftly moved three inverted cups round and round on the table, interweaving them with each other. When he stopped, the man said something and pointed to the middle cup. Joel smirked and lifted it to show there was no red ball underneath. A predatory smile lifted the man's painted crimson mouth.

"Eric," the small man said in a surprisingly loud voice. "Carson will have your hide if he knows you're holding illegal shell games with minors. You're on probation now, as it is."

The man behind the table gave a careless wave of one hand, his eyes still on the boy. "Timmons, go back to your flea circus. Teach the mites to walk a tightrope or something spectacular of that nature." His sardonic voice held a faint European accent. He coughed a few times. "And send more customers my way while you're at it. With this lad's help, I have an idea that will rake in the dough."

The little man shook his head. "You're going to get us both kicked out of the carnival with these ideas of yours." He pointed a shaking finger at the clown. "Find your own customers from now on. I want no part of this any longer. I can't afford to lose this job, even if the pay is peanuts."

The clown looked steadily at Timmons. He rose from his chair in a threatening manner, both palms flat on the table.

Timmons backed down, his smile anxious. "Jewel will help you, Eric. She's sweet on you. And with her informing clients during the fortune-telling that money is soon to come their way from unexpected sources, they're bound to come in droves when she describes you to them."

The clown glared at the man, the frown on his face fiercer than the painted one. "I need no help from a woman!" he spat. "They cannot be trusted. And perhaps neither can you."

Timmons wiped his shining forehead with a kerchief. "I've never failed you, Eric, you know that. But my family needs to eat. Jewel means well. You can trust her."

"You can't trust any woman!" the clown shouted. As if remembering he had an audience, he visibly calmed and looked at the boy. "Timmons, allow me to introduce you to Joel. His talent is remarkable. I'm certain he could teach you a number of tricks as well. Where are you from, Lad?"

"The reformatory for boys in Sothsby. But I'm only there temporary-like, till my pop gets out of jail."

"The reformatory. Well, what do you know?" The clown continued to stare at Joel. A slow smile lifted his mouth. "I believe we have some business to discuss." He lowered his voice, making it impossible for Brent and Darcy to hear the rest of the conversation.

"Shouldn't we do something instead of just wastin' our time standin' here?" Darcy whispered.

Brent shook his head. "The man with whom Joel is consorting has a gun—I saw the strap of a shoulder holster in the opening of his shirt. I think our best course of action would be to wait until Joel removes himself from these unsavory characters and approach him then."

Darcy made a scoffing sound. "Don't be daft, guv'ner. We can't just stand here an' wait all day."

"Miss Evans, our best plan would be to delay until their conversation is finished—"

"I know his type, and if you aren't going to do anything about it, then I will!" So saying, she jerked her arm free of his light grasp and stepped forward, pasting a curious smile on her face.

"Joel, there you are! I been lookin' for you everywhere."

The two men started in surprise. Joel turned, his expression bordering between guilt and defiance. He stooped to pick up something from the ground, something she hadn't noticed before, and held out what was left of her blue bonnet.

"I found your hat, Miss Darcy," he explained. "I watched some girl pick it up, and I chased her down and made her give it back. I was lookin' to find you when I ran into him." He jerked a thumb toward the clown.

Darcy didn't look the man's way, nor did she ask Joel how he made the girl give him back the hat, deciding she'd rather not know. "Well, that's fine," she said, her tone purposely bright. "But it's time to meet the others now. We don't want to be late for the show. Come along." She held out her hand.

Joel hesitated, looking back at the man behind the table. With alarm, Darcy noticed some sort of understanding pass between them. The clown gave a short nod to the boy, then lifted his gaze to hers. Up close as she was now, Darcy was struck by the evil that radiated from the man's dark blue eyes.

"Come along, Joel," she said firmly. "It's time to go."

Joel grudgingly moved toward her. She grabbed his arm when he came near and walked with him to where Brent waited, concealed at the side of the tent. Brent didn't look at her, didn't say a word, just led them back to the midway. He seemed miffed—with her or Joel, Darcy couldn't tell.

Brent likely held her responsible for what had befallen them, since she had been the one to insist Joel be allowed to attend the carnival. *Some days it just don't pay to get out of bed,* Darcy thought. No matter how hard she tried, it seemed she wound up getting everything wrong.

🙢

Days later, Brent stood at the fence and glumly watched a spindly brown colt race toward its mother. His thoughts skittered back to the carnival, and he frowned. Hearing the crunch of footsteps on dry grass, he looked over his shoulder.

"Darcy asked me to fetch you," Michael said as he approached. "She would've come herself, but Herbert is keeping her busy winnowing out the splinter he managed to get into his finger."

Nodding, Brent looked at the horses.

"Somethin' troublin' you, lad?"

"I'm a failure, Mr. Larkin."

"Sure, and it can't be as bad as all that!" Michael clapped a friendly hand on Brent's shoulder. "You're too hard on yourself."

"No, I *am* a failure," Brent insisted. "At the carnival, I was petrified, afraid that man would pull his gun on us if we revealed ourselves to him. Miss Evans showed more courage than I could ever hope to have. And there have been other times I've proven my cowardice, as well."

"And you don't think it takes courage to teach a bunch of lads in trouble with the law? Aye, that it does," Michael said, answering his own question. "There are different types of courage, and you have plenty for the position you're in. When we feel that we're empty, the good Lord gives us what we need."

Brent experienced a sudden strong desire to confide in this man, as he might his father, though his father never had time for Brent's worries or confidences.

"Do you want to know a secret?" Brent lowered his head, ashamed. "Though I was humiliated when they rejected me from fighting in the Great War, I was secretly relieved—and not only because I'd promised Stewart to take charge of the reform. I've inwardly castigated myself for those despicable feelings ever since. What kind of man am I?" He gripped the fence and stared at his white knuckles.

"And do you think the men who fought carried no baggage of fear with them?" Michael asked. "I expect a great many of them did. No one is perfect, lad. We all have areas of our lives that need work. As you know, many years ago I, too, showed cowardice—the worst kind—in rejecting me own child."

Brent pondered Michael's sober words. He knew the story of how Charleigh had been born illegitimate, her mother becoming a prostitute in order to care for them. Eight years ago, through an act of God's mercy and grace, Michael was united with his only daughter—who had been under his roof for months, assuming the identity of his niece to escape the man who'd forced her into a life of crime. Brent knew the townspeople still talked of the miracle God had wrought in Michael and Charleigh's lives.

"Aye, Brent, I have a feeling deep in me bones," Michael went on to say, "that when it truly matters and when you desire it most, God will grant you all the courage you need. As He did with the boy David when he faced the mighty Goliath. David knew his source of strength was the Lord—and so will you."

Brent said nothing, only continued to stare at the colt frolicking about the pasture. He hoped Michael was right. Yet at the same time Brent would prefer never having to be in the position to find out.

Coward.

He closed his eyes as the word resonated through his mind.

Darcy sat on the edge of Charleigh's bed and related the recurring dream she'd had about Lila, the bearded lady. "I can't explain it, Charleigh. Except to say I know God wants to use me somehow, concerning her. I've had the feeling ever since the day of the carnival. But how?"

Charleigh looked tired but happy, her face flushed. She had only a little over a month until she was due, and the doctor had been very optimistic during his last visit. Not only that, but in spending hours of quiet time with the Lord while resting in her room, she had gained a measure of strength back—both physically and spiritually—and reminded Darcy of the old Charleigh.

"I believe you're right about God wanting to use you to help Lila," Charleigh agreed, leaning back against the propped-up pillows. Her hair was like fire, streaming around her shoulders. "You've been in situations, as I have, that help you to better understand people whom others discard as unworthy. With Stewart and me, God revealed our mission field was this reformatory and helping young criminals to find Him, through showing His love. I'm convinced God has a wondrous plan for your life as well and will reveal it to you as He sees fit."

Darcy nodded, encouraged by Charleigh's words. "By the way, I noticed a motorcar leave as Michael and I returned from town. Did someone come to visit?"

Charleigh's brows gathered into a frown. "Judge Markham came by to discuss the carnival outing with Brent. It seems Mr. Forrester complained, feeling it his duty. That man has been a thorn in our side for years and has tried to close us down every chance he gets."

"What did the judge say?" Darcy asked.

Charleigh shrugged. "Brent didn't tell me, but he didn't seem too upset. So I gather everything went well."

Darcy grew thoughtful. "I wonder if Brent told the judge of Joel's disappearance and how we found him. Likely not, since the boy was playing a shell game at the time."

Charleigh looked surprised. "A shell game?"

"Didn't I tell you? I thought I had. We found Joel behind a tent with a man dressed as a clown. The man was in deep conversation with Joel—apparently either givin' advice or receivin' it, concernin' the game." Darcy shivered, remembering the man's wicked eyes. "Definitely not someone we would want Joel to associate with."

"I should think not! Shell games are illegal." Charleigh grew sober, contemplative. "What did the man look like? We should report him to the authorities, especially if he's consorting with children."

"I think it's too late for that," Darcy mused, wondering why she hadn't thought of it before. "I heard in town today that the carnival pulls out tonight."

"Hmm. Perhaps. Still, it wouldn't hurt to report him."

Darcy thought a moment, then straightened. Charleigh's words suddenly made the clearest sense. "You're right!" She rose from the bed, knowing what the Lord would have her do. "Can you manage for a few hours without me or Brent at the reform?"

Charleigh looked curious, but nodded. "The boys are doing their chores. Father and Alice are here, so everything should be fine."

"Then I'll see you this evening."

"But where are you going?"

Darcy smiled. "I'll tell you about it later—if I'm successful. Right now, I have some convincin' to do on someone else." With a wide smile, she winked and hurried out the door. Before going downstairs, she went to her room and retrieved the purchase she'd made in town last week. At the time she didn't understand what led her to buy the book, since she had one similar. Now she did.

She found Brent in the parlor. "Good!" Darcy exclaimed. "Now I don't have to go in search of you."

He raised his brows. "You wish to speak with me?"

"Aye. That I do. Might as well grab your hat, guv'ner. We have somewhere to go." Darcy whisked toward the door and plucked her shawl from a wall peg.

"Somewhere to go?" Brent's confused voice echoed from behind.

Darcy lifted her battered blue bonnet from the hat tree and pulled the hatpin from the crown.

"Miss Evans, will you kindly inform me what this latest flurry of activity is all about?"

Darcy slapped the bonnet over her head, deciding to dispense with the pin this time, since her hair was braided to her waist. There hadn't been time to put it up this morning.

"*Miss Evans.*" His tone was impatient.

She turned. "It's quite simple, really. You're taking me to the carnival. We'd better get a move on, since they'll be leavin' soon."

His mouth dropped open. "I'm taking you to the. . ." He shook his head as though to clear it. "And do tell what has put such a preposterous notion into your head?"

She shrugged. "If you don't take me, then I'll go by meself—or ask Michael to drive me, though I'd rather not, since he took me to town once today. Oh, and Charleigh did give her approval. But not to worry, guv'ner. If you can't spare the time, I'm not afraid to go alone." Tapping her crown, she gave him a quirky smile and strolled outside.

Muttering under his breath, Brent grabbed his hat and hurried out the door after her.

Chapter 11

For the first mile of the ride, Brent remained quiet. Darcy didn't mind; she had enough to think about. Like how she would approach Lila and what she would say once she did. Darcy only hoped that the irritating barker wasn't around to thwart her plans. *Thwart*. Her new word for the day.

Darcy peered at her companion. Sitting rigid as ever, Brent held the reins in a strong grip, his jaw as tight as his fists. She shook her head.

"No need to look so dour, guv'ner. It's not like I kidnapped you or forced your hand in takin' me. I told you I was willin' to go alone. Anyway, Charleigh did say they can do without us for a few hours, and the day is quite lovely." She inhaled deeply, lifting her face to the cloudy sky and putting her hand to the crown of her hat. "Just smell that crisp air! It's a wonder you can actually smell cold weather, isn't it?"

Brent gave a curt nod, and Darcy looked away, resigned to enjoy the day alone.

"Perhaps you wouldn't mind telling me just why it is that we're embarking on this little outing," Brent said wryly after a few moments elapsed.

"Why, guv'ner—all you had to do was ask." At his startled glance, she threw him a saucy grin. "I need to talk to someone at the carnival, though I've no idea what I'll say. It's just something I feel the Lord's impressin' me to do."

Brent was silent, as though assimilating her words.

"And while I'm about me business, you should report the shell game incident."

"Pardon?"

"The clown who was with Joel—and from the looks of it, trying to get him to join his illegal activities. He should be reported, don't you think? So that he doesn't pollute another child's mind with his nefarious ways."

Brent stared at her, evidently surprised. He didn't remark on her fancy new word—by now she'd collected a hefty bundle of them—but rather arched his brow as if in thought.

"You're absolutely right, Miss Evans. I was so caught up in transporting the boys safely back to the reformatory that I didn't speculate on the matter. The man definitely should be reported, and I intend to do just that. How astute of you to think of it."

Darcy pulled off her hat and fiddled with the ribbon above the brim. "I can't take full credit. Charleigh is the one who suggested it." What was she doing? For once, Brent was offering her a sincere compliment not related to her education, and she was flinging it back in his face? Still, she didn't want praise if it wasn't rightly deserved.

He gave her an odd look, one that Darcy couldn't decipher, but he didn't reply.

Soon they arrived at the carnival grounds. In the soft gray light of overcast skies, Darcy saw the midway had taken on a dramatic transformation. Gone were the hordes of people, the barkers, the calliope music. The false fronts had been taken down, and the tents and makeshift buildings were being dismantled by workers too busy to notice Darcy and Brent's presence. The cool breeze picked up numerous leaflets, paper sacks, and other bits of discarded trash, sending them skidding over the ground as though they had a life of their own.

Darcy peered in the direction of the freak show. Her heart sank to see the building gone. Where would she find Lila?

Almost in answer to her mental question, the woman came walking around the corner of a tent and crossed the midway. In her arms she held a beautiful dark-haired child, possibly two years old. As she walked, Lila bounced the girl, who laughed with glee.

"Do 'gain!" the tot cried, clapping her hands. "Do 'gain!"

Lila caught sight of Darcy and halted in surprise. Wariness flitted through her eyes before she stiffly resumed walking, ignoring Brent and Darcy.

"Excuse me," Darcy said when the woman was only feet away. "I'd like to talk with you." She moved closer so she could be heard over the racket the workers made. "Me name's Darcy Evans."

Lila directed somber brown eyes at Darcy. "The freak show is over. Go home." She started to walk away.

Unfazed by the woman's abrupt words, Darcy hurried forward. "It isn't the show I've come to see you about."

"No?" The woman stopped and tilted her head in evident disinterest. "If you're a reporter, I'm not available for questioning, and I'm not interested in an interview." She clutched the child tighter to her breast. "I have nothing to say to the public."

"I'm not a reporter." When Lila remained unapproachable, Darcy deliberated, wondering how to convince her. She dropped her gaze to the wide-eyed child, who hooked one chubby arm around Lila's neck and stared at Darcy with uncertainty. "That's a gorgeous little girl you have there. Is she yours?"

Lila cocked a wry brow. "Surprised a freak can give birth to a normal child?"

"I didn't say that." Darcy gave an exasperated sigh. The woman was obviously bent on being difficult. "Can we go somewhere to talk? I mean no harm, and I won't take up much of your time."

Lila hesitated a long moment, eyeing Darcy, then gave a curt nod. "This way, then."

Darcy glanced at Brent before following Lila to a set of railroad tracks nearby, where the carnival train sat. On the side of each railcar were words painted in red, yellow, and blue, labeling the different attractions. Lila stepped up to one of the trailer cars and cast a brief glance back at Darcy before continuing into the car, which contained sleeping berths. She moved down the narrow aisle to one of the lower berths and gently deposited the child on a thin, dirty mattress.

"There now, Angel." Lila brushed the curly black locks from the girl's forehead and bent to kiss her pink cheek. "Time for all good girls to take a nap."

The girl pouted. "Don' want sweep. Want Mama an' Unka Buce."

"Mama has to take care of things so we can go bye-bye on the train tonight. And Uncle Bruce has to help the men take things down. But beautiful, bright-eyed girls named Angel must go to dreamland now." She tickled the girl's side, making her giggle, then grabbed a faded doll from the mattress and placed it in the girl's arms. "Sleep well, precious Angel. Mama will be back soon."

Lila stood, pulled the curtain that covered the berth closed, then looked at Darcy, her eyes cold again. "We can talk outside."

They exited the sleeping car, and immediately Lila faced Darcy, crossing her arms in a defensive gesture. "Just what do you want from me?"

Instead of answering, Darcy asked a question of her own. "Where is the child's father? Is he with the carnival, too?"

"Why do you want to know?"

"Just curious—it's a fault of mine. You don't have to tell me if you don't want to."

Lila paused, considering. Though her expression was indifferent, pain glimmered in her eyes. "I haven't the faintest idea where Angel's father is," she said at last. "Nor who he is. Late one night when we were at a small town in Jersey, I needed to make a quick trip into the nearby woods and was attacked in the dark. Angel was born nine months later. And though I'll always despise that lecher for what he did to me, I wouldn't trade anything for the joy that sweet child has brought these past two years."

Darcy nodded, unsure how to reply.

Lila's cold gaze traveled over Darcy's altered dress. "I suppose my story shocks you, since you come from a good home and have no concept of what pain or hardship means."

Darcy straightened to her full height and worked to keep her voice level. "A good home? Hardly. After me mum died, when I was ten, me stepfather came after me. I whacked him over the head with a frying pan and ran away. I lived on the streets of London and begged for me food. When the beggin' brought no pence, I stole what I could to feed me belly; and later, when I was older, I relied nightly on the numbing effect of ale. No, Lila, I didn't know any good thing except for the friendship of three other guttersnipes—who are now either dead or in jail and were as miserable as I."

Lila's cold disinterest melted as Darcy spoke. "Then you know how hard life can be."

"Aye, that I do. But I know somethin' else. Somethin' I never knew till someone told me. And though I'm not well educated in how to speak me mind, I came to share with you the truth I found. The truth a friend taught me. God loves you, Lila. He wants you to know it."

Lila stared in disbelief and gave a scoffing laugh. "You expect me to believe that? I suppose God loved me so much He decided to tack a beard and mustache to my face for good measure—making it impossible for any man to love me. Is that what you're saying?"

"All I know, Lila, is that God is not cruel and vindictive; He's lovin' and full of peace. He died on a cross so that ye could be with Him forever. All He asks is that ye accept His sacrifice and follow Him. He truly does love you. He sent me here to tell ye so."

"Did He now?" The words were mocking and harsh, but vulnerability flickered in Lila's brown eyes. "And just what else did He tell you?"

"He asked me to give you this." Darcy pulled the small book from the bag she carried.

Lila stared at it.

"It's a Bible."

"I know what it is," Lila snapped. Her gaze—cold again—lifted to Darcy's. "I know all about sacrifices, too. My father was a preacher. Surprised? I sensed how uncomfortable he was around me—how he couldn't stand to even look at me, and I overheard him tell my aunt one night of the sacrifice he'd made to raise me, of the burden God had given him. Knowing I wasn't wanted, I sneaked away from home four years ago when this carnival came to town, and I joined up with it."

Darcy didn't know what else to say or why the Lord had even directed her to come. Lila was hardened to hearing anything about the gospel. And she knew what was in the Good Book, if her father was a preacher. "Well, that's all I had to say, so I'll be leavin' now. I did so want to help you, but I can't force you to receive the message of God's love. Good-bye, Lila. I'll pray for ye tonight—and every night from here on out. You have me word on that." She tucked the Bible into Lila's crossed arms and moved away.

"Wait!"

Darcy turned in surprise.

Lila seemed uncertain. "Did you mean what you said? That you want to help?" Biting her lip, she uncrossed one arm, took the Bible in her hand, and moved a step toward Darcy. "This carnival is no place for Angel. I want her to live a normal life—or as normal as can be with a mother who's a freak. Do you think. . .can I come work for you? I'm a hard worker and am skilled in house-keeping, sewing, and cooking. I make all my own clothes and Angel's, too. My mother died when I was twelve, and I had to take over those duties while I lived with my father."

Seeing Darcy's eyes widen, she hastened to add, "I promise I'll stay out of your way and won't come anywhere near when your friends are around. I can shave off this beard, so I'd appear normal. The reason I haven't is a fear I've had since childhood—when I accidentally cut myself deep enough to produce a scar—and the idea of using a straight razor every day on my face is frightening. My hands aren't always steady, but I'll do it if I must. No one need know of my deformity. If I could bear to give up Angel, I'd ask you to take only her. But without her in my life, I'd surely die."

Darcy searched for something to say. "Lila, I can't hire you."

The woman's features hardened. "Never mind. It was foolish to ask. I suppose you're like those who have no problem speaking the gospel, but when it comes to living it, that's another matter altogether. I shouldn't be surprised. You might as well take this back. I've had enough of your kind to last me an eternity." Lila stuffed the Bible into Darcy's hand and moved away.

"Now you wait just one minute," Darcy snapped. "It has nothing to do with any such foolishness. I live at a boys' reformatory—a place for young criminals. The boys there can be cruel—believe me, I know—and bringing you home with me would be like bringing a lamb to wolves."

Lila shook her head, unconcerned. "I've heard every insult there is and am accustomed to being gawked at. I could handle any taunts and jeers. I'm only concerned about my Angel. Would she be unsafe there?"

"I've been there over a year, and while the boys are in definite need of refor-min', they would never hurt anyone. Of that I'm sure." Darcy blinked, realizing what she'd done. Instead of dissuading Lila, she'd given her reason to further plead her cause.

"I have no authority to hire you on, Lila. Neither does Brent Thomas, the schoolmaster there and the man I drove here with. All decisions are made by a small board of members at the reform. Brent is only one member of that board."

"The carnival doesn't leave until late tonight," Lila said quickly. "If your people disagree to the arrangement, I'll return here. I promise. And if that should happen, we'll find our own transport back so you won't be bothered with taking us."

Darcy hesitated. "What about Angel's uncle? Won't he miss her?"

"Angel's uncle? Oh, you must mean Bruce. He's the strong man in the freak show—no relation. Angel dotes on him and he on her. It would be hard for both

Angel and me to leave him—he's been a good friend—but as I said before, I only want what's best for my daughter. And I don't like some of the things that's been going on at this carnival lately." She quickly broke off as though she'd said too much. "Please, Miss Evans?"

Darcy studied the entreating, desperate eyes. She thought of Charleigh, of her kind and generous heart and tarnished past. She thought of Michael, who never condemned a soul and was always ready to help someone in need. She thought of Stewart, whose main objective in opening the reformatory was to help those nobody wanted. The hopeless cases. The outcasts.

Sighing, Darcy nodded. "Grab your daughter, and come along, then."

She didn't dare think of what Brent would say.

❧

"What in the name of all that is sane and normal were you thinking, Miss Evans?" Brent stared at Darcy, exasperation written on his face. "Have you lost all the good sense God gave you?"

They stood in a sheltered part of the woods near a creek. Lila was in the wagon changing Angel's diaper. This was their first moment alone since Darcy had returned to Brent with Lila and Angel in tow.

"I know Charleigh," Darcy insisted. "She would've done the same."

"Would she now?" Brent shook his head and started to pace again, threading his fingers through his hair—an uncustomary action for him. He'd left his hat in the wagon, and for a moment Darcy admired the way the sunlight through the trees picked out threads of bronze-gold in his tousled locks. "Yes, perhaps she might have, as it *is* her place to acquire any help needed at the reformatory. But *you* had no right to do so! There is already an efficient cook and housekeeper at Lyons' Refuge, and you were hired as the cook's assistant. What will that woman do at the institution?"

"That woman?" Darcy crossed her arms. "Tell me, guv'ner, this isn't about Lila's qualifications at all, is it? It's about her appearance."

Brent tensed and faced her. "What do you mean?"

"What do I mean?" Darcy scoffed. "Why, surely you could tell she sports a beard, couldn't you, guv'ner? But of course you could! Outside appearances are of great importance to you, aren't they now? Unfortunately, you can't see past them to the heart that beats inside. More's the pity."

A muscle twitched near his jaw as he approached. "Miss Evans, this conversation is highly irregular as well as being entirely preposterous—"

"Is it now?" she interrupted. "Preposterous, ye say? Then tell me why it is that ye've not noticed the changes I've made in the past year? Tell me why when you look at me you still see an uncouth, brash girl spoutin' Cockney. Well, all right, I may still be brash and slip into Cockney at times, but except for that poetry contest, ye've barely given me credit for any changes made! And I've tried—oh, how I've tried to win yer approval. I studied hard—harder than you know, harder than any o' the boys. I stayed up late night after night to learn how to be a better person—a lady you would admire, maybe even tyke a fancy to. But did it do any good, I ask you? No! Not that I care to impress you any longer. You're too busy judgin' on outward appearances and retainin' early impressions to give a person any room to change or see what lies on the inside—where God looks, I'll remind you again. And I pity you your ignorance and stony heart."

Darcy began to pace, then looked back and retraced her steps toward him, her annoyance not yet sated. "And with someone like Lila—who likely can never alter her appearance—you can't see beyond that to her heart, which is so pure and good and fine that the only thing she wants out of life is to do the best she can for her little girl. Well, Mr. Stuffed-Shirt Thomas, more's the pity for you!" She leaned forward and snapped her fingers beneath his nose. "And that's what I think o' that!"

Brent stood a moment, unblinking. Suddenly he grasped her upper arms, his eyes flaming. Her own eyes went wide in shock at his unexpected reaction.

"You think I don't care about people—that I don't have feelings? Oh, I have feelings, I assure you. I may not understand you, Darcy Evans, but I've definitely noticed you. I may not always commend you for your progress, but I've seen you excel in numerous areas and have been proud of your accomplishments. Keep in mind that I'm flesh and blood—not a 'stuffed shirt,' as you call it. Why, a few times this past week I almost kissed you—" Brent broke off, his face darkening in embarrassment. Hastily he lowered his hands to his sides. "Forgive me. That was uncalled for."

Before he could move away, Darcy spoke. "Well, why didn't you?"

He hesitated. "Why didn't I what?"

"Kiss me."

He looked uncomfortable. "Miss Evans, I strongly recommend that we cease this conversation."

"The name's Darcy, guv'ner. I've heard you use it before." She tilted her head. "I want to know what stopped you from kissing me—like ye said ye almost did."

Brent released an exasperated sigh. "We were in a public place. Such a display hardly would have been appropriate."

"This place seems private enough."

He blinked, his mouth dropping open as the meaning of her soft words hit him. "Miss Evans. . ." His voice cracked.

"Try again. It's Darcy."

"Darcy." He said the name tentatively. "Perhaps we should continue this conversation another time. I believe we should return to the wagon. Your friend will wonder what's happened to us." He turned to walk away.

Darcy acted, instinctively knowing that if she didn't do something, he never would. Hurrying up behind him, she put her hand to his shoulder and tugged. "Brent, wait."

He turned to face her, surprise on his features. Before she lost courage, she plucked off his spectacles, wrapped her arms around his neck, and planted a solid kiss on his mouth.

Warm tingles coursed through her, but he stood as stiff as one of the tree trunks surrounding them. Darcy was about to pull back in humiliated disappointment when suddenly his arms wrapped around her, pulling her close. His lips began to move over hers, sending her into a dreamlike trance from which she never wanted to emerge. After several seconds elapsed, Brent lifted his head and gazed at her, a heart-melting mixture of desire and surprise glimmering in his blue eyes.

Keeping her arms around his neck and grateful he hadn't removed his hands from the middle of her back, Darcy studied his face. "What now, guv'ner?" she asked quietly. "Where do we go from here?"

He shook his head. "I don't rightly know." His voice was hoarse.

"Well, then, may I make a suggestion until we arrive at a decision?" Putting her hand to the back of his head, she brought his face down to hers and kissed him again.

This time his response was nothing like that of a tree trunk.

Chapter 12

Hungry for something to tide him over until dinner, Brent rotated the knob of the back door leading to the kitchen. He stopped in surprise to see Lila sitting on a wooden chair, her back rigid, her eyes squeezed shut. A towel was draped under her chin. Alice stood next to her, gently sliding a straight razor over one cheek covered with white foam.

"Don't move, Lila," Alice gently warned. "There's nothing to be afraid of—nothing to this, really. I often give Michael a shave. And he's told me plenty a time I shoulda been a surgeon, what with my steady hands and all." She gave a self-conscious, almost girlish, giggle.

Uneasy at the sight of a woman being shaved, Brent closed the door with a quiet click and stepped off the porch. Two days had passed since Lila arrived at Lyons' Refuge. Darcy had been right. Charleigh and Michael welcomed her and her daughter with open arms, though some of the boys had been less than chivalrous. Lila stared at them while they spouted their malicious jibes and laughed sardonically after each one. Once the last verbal weapon was slung, she merely lifted an eyebrow and asked, "Are you finished yet? Because if that's all you can think of, let me tell you I've heard it all before. And, quite frankly, I'm bored with the sameness. Now, if you'll excuse me." With that she'd taken Angel in her arms and marched upstairs to her room—to the unease of six dazed boys, who'd been given extra work duties that evening for their cruelty.

Brent stared at the thick bank of murky clouds in the distance. The wind had picked up in the last hour, a herald of the coming storm. Brent hoped Michael would return to the refuge before the weather broke. He'd driven the wagon to his home, Larkin's Glen, to check on things there.

Brent watched the long, wheat-colored grasses bend underneath the weight of the chilling wind, as though bowing in submission to a force greater than they. Several bare branches of a nearby oak clattered against the fence at regular intervals when a sudden strong gust shook them. Brent's thoughts skittered to the accusation Darcy had hurled at him in the woods during their drive home from the carnival. Was she right? Was he judgmental, seeing people's appearances only and not their character within?

Since Lila had come to the refuge, Brent invented excuses to stay away from her, uncomfortable with her presence, even a trifle disgusted when looking at her—though she'd worn a dark blue veil as a harem girl might, to hide the beard.

He didn't admire his feelings, knew they were anything but charitable, but he couldn't seem to help them. He'd been appalled by Bill, not only with his choice of lifestyle but also with his preference for flamboyant clothing. He'd found fault with Darcy when she first came to the refuge—her Cockney, her clothing, her manner. . . .

Brent closed his eyes. Not only was he a coward, he *was* hypercritical of others.

"Heavenly Father," he muttered, "I don't desire to feel this way. I don't want to be judgmental and always finding fault. Help me, Lord, to love as You would love, no matter the outside appearances. Help me to see through to the heart as Darcy does, as Charleigh does—even as Michael does. To see true heart appearances and not merely the outward shell—"

"Guv'ner?"

Brent tensed at the suddenness of Darcy's voice behind him. The loud whisper of wind in the grasses had masked the sound of her approach. Had she heard his soft prayer? Slowly, he turned to face her.

Her hair hung in one braid to her waist, as she often wore it. Several long, dark tendrils had worked themselves loose around her face.

Unsettled with how close she stood, Brent took a hasty step backward, the recent memory of their kisses in the woods rushing to the forefront of his mind. He had enjoyed the feel of her in his arms that day—indeed, had allowed that last kiss to linger, even forgetting about Lila waiting in the wagon. Yet once he'd broken the embrace, the impropriety of the situation assaulted him; and he was thunderstruck by his unseemly behavior.

Cocking her head, Darcy looked at him with those smoky blue eyes. "Are you feeling all right? You look a mite pale."

"I'm well."

She frowned. "You don't look it." She pushed up one sleeve and lifted her forearm to his forehead, propelling him to take another step backward—a half step really, since his back came up against the wooden fence. "If you do have a fever, it's not high, though your face looks rather flushed now."

"I told you I'm fine," Brent snapped.

Her chin lifted. "Well, maybe your health is fine, but your disposition could sure use some improvin', and that's a fact! Ever since the day we brought Lila home, you've been snappin' like a turtle and avoidin' me like a turkey does a fox."

Brent chose not to answer. He took a deep breath and reached for his handkerchief to clean his glasses. The cloth wasn't there. He'd forgotten to tuck one into his pocket that morning. In fact, since their initial trip to the carnival, he found himself doing a lot of things out of character for him.

Feeling somewhat cornered, Brent took a sideways step, sliding along the fence and hoping he wasn't causing his new suit coat irreparable damage. He wanted to place himself in a more comfortable position with plenty of room between them. Nervously he cleared his throat. "About that day, Miss Evans—"

"So we're back to formal names, are we?"

"I owe you an apology," he continued as though she hadn't spoken. "My untoward behavior was totally uncalled-for, and I regret that you were a recipient."

❧

"Untoward behavior?"

His face darkened another shade. "The incident in the woods."

She scrunched her brows together. "Now let me get this straight. You're apologizin' for kissin' me?"

"Yes. My actions were reprehensible."

Darcy determined to look up that word the first chance she got. She had a feeling it wasn't good. "You're making much of nothin', Guv'ner. It was just a kiss."

"Be that as it may, in polite society such behavior isn't considered acceptable. If two people do choose to go courting, holding hands should be the limit of physical contact they share—weeks after the courtship commences, of course." Brent pulled at his collar as if it were too tight. "Although a chaste kiss on the cheek when parting is allowed, I do believe—"

"Sounds dull as salt what's lost its flavorin'."

He looked at her, stunned. "Pardon?"

"Who made such stuffy rules? You? And what does courtin' mean anyway?"

His mouth compressed into an offended line. "Courting is how things are done in a genteel society, Miss Evans."

"But there's no feeling to anything like that! It's like a rule book to follow instead of affection to share." She crossed her arms. "Oh, get that scandalized look out of your eye, guv'ner. I'm not suggesting anything improper. People aren't machines that ye wind a crank and out comes the same response. People have feelings, and they shouldn't have to bottle them up until a specific time states they're allowed to exhibit them."

Slowly uncrossing her arms, she stepped closer. "Why, if I wanted to put my hand to your cheek like this," she murmured, lightly cradling his jaw, "why shouldn't I be allowed to? I'm not hurtin' no one. And I'm showin' you what's in me heart."

"Rules are important," he stated, his voice coming out hoarse. "Guidelines are needed."

Darcy frowned, dropping her hand away. "Ye make it sound as if I'm suggestin' something illicit. I'm not, I told you. And I've given a black eye to those who've tried—and that's a fact!"

Brent didn't doubt it for a minute. He also didn't doubt that it was past time to end this conversation.

"Perhaps Mrs. Lyons could better instruct you on the topic of courting and all that it entails if you wish to know more. I have papers to grade. Good day, Miss Evans." He gave her a slight tip of his hat and hurried to the schoolhouse before she could say another word.

⁂

"That man is so irritating, Lord," Darcy grumbled as she stood at her window later that night, watching light sleet fall from a dark sky. "It's a wonder I feel the way I do about him. Just for a moment, there in the woods, I thought he'd unbent his stiff ways—just for a moment, mind You. Yet he hasn't changed one bit, has he? He's the same as always. Straitlaced, solemn, and oh, so noble—"

Darcy's words broke off as realization struck her a swift blow. Was she doing the same thing she'd accused Brent of? Judging merely on outward appearances and not seeing through to the heart of the man inside?

Her eyes fluttered closed. She was doing exactly that! And had been for quite a while. How many times had she labeled Brent proper, stuffy? She may have put on a good show of accepting others at face value, but in her heart she'd been as guilty as Brent. And just as judgmental.

"Oh, Jesus, I'm ever so sorry. Make me more tolerant of others, no matter what their shortcomings. Make me more sympathetic of things—and people—I don't understand."

All of a sudden Darcy caught the image of what looked like a slight form hunched over and running toward the barn. She pressed closer to the window. Positioning both hands around her eyes to block the light from the room's electric torch, she squinted through the blurred pane to try and see any kind of movement outside. She rubbed moisture away from the glass and watched as the dim form worked the barn door open.

So she hadn't been imagining things! From inside the barn, a lantern issued a feeble glow. The boy's cap fell off, revealing a thatch of hair, shining ivory in the pale light. He reclaimed his cap and entered the barn, shutting the door behind himself.

Joel! What mischief was he up to now—and in this kind of weather to boot?

Darcy rushed downstairs, grabbed her cloak, and threw it about her shoulders. Glancing at the parlor door, she considered telling Charleigh where she was going but dismissed the idea. Charleigh had overtaxed herself today, making a rare appearance downstairs to read to the boys, with the excuse that she was sick and tired of the four walls of her room. After the story, Alice had insisted Charleigh rest on the sofa, where she'd fallen asleep minutes later.

Darcy hurried through the front door, the pelting sleet harsher to her ears now that she stood in the midst of it. Before heading toward the barn, she glanced at the schoolhouse. Hazy light glowed in the window near Brent's desk. *He must be grading papers again.* Darcy considered acquiring his aid or at least informing him of the situation. Yet Brent was still angry with Joel for running off at the carnival—no matter that the boy said he'd only done so to rescue her hat. Darcy wasn't certain why Joel was skulking about; but if the boy had a plausible excuse for being in the barn when he should be in bed, Brent might be annoyed with her for bothering him. Or he might be unnecessarily harsh with Joel. Brent had been so unlike himself lately, and Darcy decided she would rather take care of this matter on her own.

With her decision made, she pulled the cloak's hood over her head and carefully made her way through the slippery grass toward the barn. The sleet fell heavier than before; and by the time she was halfway there, her thick stockings inside her shoes felt damp with icy water. Her irritation with Joel increased. He'd better have an awfully good reason for being in the barn this time of night!

At the old building, Darcy struggled to open the heavy wooden door enough to slip inside. She peered around the dimly lit barn and up to the loft on the other side, near where the horses and cows were penned in their stalls.

"Joel?" Her voice wavered in the chill air, which smelled of manure and wet hay. "I know you're here. I saw you from my window."

A horse's soft whinny and snort was the only reply.

Swallowing her irritation, Darcy stepped toward the lantern light flickering on the crude board walls.

"Joel, talk to me," she said, her eyes trained on the pale yellow light. "You know you're not supposed to be outside the house after dark. Is something upsetting you? Maybe I can help." She stopped suddenly. The light. She had seen the lantern before Joel entered the barn. Which meant—

"Joel, who's here with you? Herbert? Lance?" When eerie silence met her demands, she frowned. "Very well, Joel. If you—and whoever else is here—don't come out this minute and tell me what this is about, then you leave me no alternative but to enlist the aid of the substitute headmaster. And you'll receive a much harsher discipline than ye normally would have for breaking curfew, of that I can assure you."

Before she could say more, a man's arm clapped across her chest, followed by the ominous click of metal near her ear—the sound of a gun's hammer being cocked.

Darcy struggled for balance as her shoulder blades pressed against the man's heaving chest. The cold steel barrel of the pistol bit into her scalp, and fear swallowed her whole.

"I hardly think that will be necessary," the man rasped close to her ear. "*Now* you play by my rules."

❧

Brent set down his pen and rotated his shoulders, trying to work out the kinks from sitting in one position too long. His mind traveled to Darcy, as it frequently had since he started grading today's tests. In fact, it would be wise to go over the marks he'd made a second time, since his mind hadn't been entirely on his job.

He sighed and looked out the sleet-spattered window. This afternoon's conversation with her had been uncomfortable, to say the least; still, he was unable to cease thinking of it.

Did he wish to court her? They were so dissimilar to one another, yet there was something about being in her presence that made him feel whole. As though she contained an element missing in his nature. Brave, loyal, fun-loving—Darcy was all those things and more. Yet, what did he have to offer in return?

He was a reject. A failure. How could he promise protection in the possible role of her husband when courage for him was as unreachable as the moon? Michael's words floated to his memory. "When it truly matters and when you need it most, God will give you the courage you need."

Brent removed his spectacles and closed his eyes. He wished he could be certain. He had faith in God; that wasn't the problem. Rather, he entertained little faith in his own ability to carry through if the situation should warrant it.

Sighing, he folded the temples of his spectacles, opened his desk drawer, and laid them inside. He purposely had not attended dinner at the main house that evening, wanting to avoid Darcy, but he was hungry now. Knowing Darcy, she likely had put something aside for him.

After grabbing his overcoat and hat, Brent turned down the kerosene lamp and moved toward the door.

❧

"Be still!"

Darcy recognized the faintly accented voice of the man holding the gun to her head. It was the clown from the carnival.

"What do you want with me?" she asked, maintaining a show of bravado though her heart beat with the fury of a panicked bird. "Why are you here?"

He chuckled then coughed. Darcy could feel his body tremble and noticed how heat seemed to radiate from him. He was obviously quite ill.

"You cost me my job," he growled through his teeth. "Word spread of how one of the freaks left with a lady Brit to work at a boys' reformatory." He coughed, the sound raspier. "When I was fired after a stranger informed my boss of my 'illegal activities'—only minutes after you and your boyfriend left with Lila—it wasn't hard to figure out. Especially after making your acquaintance behind the fortune-teller's tent last week." A severe bout of coughing shook him.

Darcy swallowed. "You're ill. You need care."

"The only thing I need now is vengeance!" he growled in a low voice, pressing the barrel harder to her head. "This day was long in coming. I've waited for it for years, and neither you nor anyone else is going to rob me of my satisfaction."

Darcy furrowed her brow. "Long in coming? What do you mean? You're not making sense." The fever must be giving him delusions.

"Shut up!" he ordered. "We three are going to the main house now, and you're going to lead the way. But I warn you. One false move, and I'll blow you to kingdom come. I'm an expert marksman."

Darcy turned to face her attacker. She'd been right in her assumption regarding his identity. In the lamp's glow, she could see his aristocratic features were sickly pale, almost gaunt, with shadows under his eyes. He wore no overcoat, only a pair of trousers with a shirt and suspenders and a shoulder holster under one arm. He was thin, his body shivering. Sweat-dampened hair clung to his head. In his hand he held a gun—now trained at her heart.

"We haven't any money if that's what you're after." Immediately Darcy thought about her remaining three and a half dollars and flinched, but he seemed not to notice.

"That's not what I'm after," he said. "It's a simple matter of justice. And revenge."

Darcy said nothing, wondering how someone of his caliber could equate the word *justice* with his dark motives.

"Mister, you said no one was going to get hurt." Joel's uncertain voice came from somewhere behind Darcy. "I told you I'd go with you. Just leave her and the others alone."

Rage ignited in the man's eyes as they snapped toward the boy. "Joel, as my new associate, you must learn never to talk back to your superior." His low words were smooth but full of undisguised venom. "I'll not have it."

"Yes, sir," the boy whispered, his voice barely audible above the sound of sleet falling on the roof.

The man returned his gaze to Darcy, a smile lifting the corners of his cracked lips. "Actually, Joel, you're about to learn an important lesson in the art of seeking justice from those who've wronged you. Keep your eyes and ears open. There may be a test afterwards." He chuckled, then coughed and motioned with his gun toward the door. "After you, miss. And, remember, if you want your friends to remain alive, I'd advise you not to do anything foolish."

Keeping her expression blank, Darcy moved in the direction he indicated, trying not to let him see her fear.

Chapter 13

Brent let himself in through the kitchen door and lit a nearby lamp, preferring its soft glow to the harsh glare of the electric light. He felt like a boy sneaking into the kitchen after hours for a late-night snack. He opened the icebox and crouched to peer inside. Hmmm. Interesting. The bowl there appeared to contain a vegetable mix with strips of chicken. He wondered if Darcy had made it. She was a wonderful cook.

The unmistakable sound of the front door flying open, then slamming shut, broke the silence. Brent shot to a standing position and faced the hallway entrance. Who would be up this time of the night? Darcy? Samuel? Or had Michael returned?

About to call out, he changed his mind. The household was surely asleep; and if the sound of the front door hadn't awakened anyone, Brent certainly didn't want to. Nine boys were difficult to get back to bed.

Curious, he shut the icebox and crept along the hallway. He heard a man's low voice—not Michael's or Samuel's—in the parlor. Suddenly Charleigh gave a soft cry of fright.

"Eric!" she exclaimed as though she'd seen a ghost.

Alarmed, but instinctively knowing he must remain silent, Brent peered around the corner. In the light of a lantern Joel held, Darcy sat wide-eyed next to a pale Charleigh on the sofa. All three were staring at a tall man who pointed a gun at the two women. Brent's mouth went dry.

The man chuckled. "*Bonsoir*, dear Charlotte, or should I say Charleigh? That is the name you're going by now, isn't it? Destiny brings us together yet again. I've waited for this day a long time, and the Fates were kind enough to drop the opportunity into my lap."

Shaking her head in shocked denial, Charleigh pulled the blanket closer around her shoulders. "But—but Stewart told me years ago that he'd read an account of your death in the paper!"

"Yet, as you can see, I'm not dead," Eric said with a slight wave of his gun.

"A dockworker identified your body!" Charleigh insisted, as though by saying it, she could make it true.

"Men will do anything for money. And his price wasn't so steep." Eric coughed. "I found the need to, shall we say, disappear. Some of my former associates in Manhattan were out to kill me."

"Imagine that," Charleigh muttered sarcastically. "So you murdered another poor soul to lose your identity?"

Eric shrugged. "Actually, no. Someone had already done the deed. I stumbled across his corpse one night on the docks, saw my chance, and took it. The dockworker fixed his face so no one would recognize him."

During the conversation, Darcy repeatedly looked in confusion from Eric to Charleigh. She spoke for the first time. "You know this man?"

"Yes," Charleigh said bitterly. "This is the man who was with me on the *Titanic*. The man I assisted for three years in a life of crime. Darcy Evans, meet Eric Fontaneau—the cruelest man alive."

"Fontaine, now," Eric said, his manner almost glib. "After disposing of my alias, Philip Rawlins, with the dead man, I took back my real name—only changed the surname to sound more American. And I tried to lose the French accent, though a trace has quite obviously remained." Again he coughed.

Brent grasped the edge of the wall, remembering the despicable things Stewart had told him about this man. And he was here now with Darcy and Charleigh, his intentions boding evil. Brent couldn't simply stand by and allow these women to remain in danger. He couldn't! Yet what could he do? The man was armed. Brent knew Stewart kept several guns locked in his study, but he didn't know where the key to the glass case was—and even if he did, he didn't know how to fire a weapon. The phone was too close to use. Even if he whispered, he would be overheard.

"What do you intend to do with us?" Charleigh asked. "Why are you here?"

"Why am I here?" Eric repeated, almost cordially. He moved, and Brent zipped back around the corner to avoid detection, waited a moment, then looked again. Eric was now seated in the rocking chair facing the sofa, his gun still trained on the women.

"Well, dear Charleigh, since you ask, originally I planned to take both you and Joel from this place and resume our 'life of crime'—isn't that how you put it?" He chuckled, then coughed again, harsher this time. When the spell ended, he waved the gun toward Charleigh. His gaze lowered to her rounded belly. "Yet, in your present condition, my plan to use you as bait will no longer work."

"I did my time, Eric," Charleigh seethed. "I went to a reformatory and paid for my crimes. And I will not return to that life again!" She straightened, lifting her chin. "I want you out of my house—now."

"I hardly think you're in a position to make demands," Eric said. He leaned toward her, his jaw rigid. "I told you once before that I don't like my women to talk back. You would do well to remember that."

Darcy put a protective arm across Charleigh's chest. "She's not your woman. She never was."

"Indeed?" Eric sounded amused. "I beg to differ, Miss Evans. She has always belonged to me."

"Stewart paid you—" Charleigh began.

Eric waved his gun to silence her. "Did you honestly think I would agree to his stipulations? You're mine, Charleigh. I'll admit, when you foolishly turned yourself over to Scotland Yard and were sentenced to the reformatory, that little setback altered my plans for us. And your present condition certainly isn't going to help matters. Regardless, you're coming with me."

"No!"

To Brent's horror, Darcy rocketed up from the couch, her hands flying to her hips, her face flushed with anger. She seemed suddenly oblivious to the gun Eric turned her way.

"Sit down," he ordered impatiently.

"Ye won't harm a hair on her head, ye won't," Darcy bit out. Instead of sitting down, she took another step forward, making Brent's heart lurch in fear. "I heard about what you done to her—how you made her think she was married to you all those years when she wasn't, how you beat her and ended up killin' the baby she carried—"

"Darcy, no!" Charleigh whispered.

Eric swung his shocked gaze toward Charleigh. "Baby? You were carrying my child and didn't tell me?"

Charleigh's expression grew bitter. "It doesn't matter any longer. I'm another man's wife, and I carry his child. I'm also a Christian and have repented of the former life I led."

"How touching," Eric said in disdain.

Brent surveyed the room, knowing he must do something soon. Suddenly Joel turned his head and met his gaze. Brent tensed. The boy studied him for a few eternal seconds. "Mr. Fontaine?" Joel asked, gaining the man's attention.

Brent frantically considered what to do if the boy should reveal his presence. Should he run up and surprise Eric before Joel could speak? And do. . .what? He ran a hand through his damp hair. How could he stop Eric?

"What is it, Joel?" Eric asked impatiently.

"We can make it fine—just us. I'm a fast learner, and I'll show you everything my pop taught me, if you want to know. We don't need no skirt along. My pop once said that womenfolk just get in the way of a man's business. . . ."

Brent listened in amazement, realizing what Joel was doing. He was diverting Eric's attention so that Brent could act. Again, Brent's gaze swept the room—and landed on Michael's pipe, which sat on its stand on a nearby piecrust table. An idea struck. A rather lame idea, but it was an idea.

God, help me.

Moving from behind the wall, Brent crept toward the stand, the carpet underneath his feet muffling his footsteps. He grabbed the pipe and slowly made his way toward Eric.

❧

Darcy watched, baffled, as Brent crept up behind Eric holding a pipe. A pipe? Had he gone daft? What was he doing? Was he going to suggest they smoke a peace pipe and have a powwow like her history book said the Indians once did?

Brent caught her eye and shook his head. Immediately Darcy looked away.

"In most cases, I would agree with you, Joel," Eric replied. "Women cannot be trusted. Yet when someone takes what's yours—as Mr. Lyons did to me—justice must be met. He won't have her again; of that I'll make certain."

"You're not going to kill her, are you?" the boy asked fearfully, eyes wide.

"No," Eric said, "but I'll kill anyone who stands in my way this time." He cocked the hammer of his gun and stared at Darcy. "Anyone."

From the corner of her eye, Darcy saw Brent falter. She swallowed hard, silently begging God to shield his presence. He advanced the last few feet to Eric's chair. Lifting his arm, he pushed the stem of the pipe against Eric's upper back. The man gave a startled jump.

"No," Brent said, his voice surprisingly calm. "I don't imagine you'll harm anyone, Mr. Fontaine. Now be so good as to drop the gun."

Eric moved to turn, but Brent jabbed the pipe stem harder against his shirt. "*Now*, if you please."

Eric complied, and Brent looked at the boy. "Joel, please retrieve the weapon and bring it to me."

Joel looked uncertainly between the two men for an excruciating moment, then nodded and picked up the gun from the carpet, handing it to Brent. Brent pocketed the pipe and held the gun.

"Now, put your hands in the air and slowly turn around," Brent said.

Eric did so, his eyes widening. "Bill? What are you doing here?"

Brent looked confused for a moment, then said, "If the man to whom you're referring is Bill Thomas, he's my brother."

Eric looked taken aback. "Except for your clothing, you could be twins."

"So I've been told." Brent glanced at Darcy. "Please, Miss Evans, retrieve some rope to tie up our guest."

Eric's gaze grew calculating. "Actually, I remember Bill talking quite a bit about you. Brent is your name. He mentioned you were the timid sort. Afraid of your own shadow, he said. Certainly not the type to use a gun on anyone."

Darcy wrinkled her brow. This wasn't going well.

"Get the rope," Brent ordered again, his voice wavering.

Before Darcy could move to comply, Eric lunged at Brent, and both men fell to the ground. Darcy stared in horror as Eric pulled back his fist and hit Brent in the jaw twice, then reached for the gun. Brent held his own, throwing a few surprisingly well-placed punches. Eric's weakness worked against him, and soon Brent had the upper hand as both men fought for possession of the gun.

A deafening shot cracked the air.

Both men fell slack.

Darcy screamed.

Chapter 14

Surprise covered Eric's face as he put a hand to his side. A spot of crimson quickly spread across his shirt. "I've been shot."

Brent stared at the gun in his hand. He looked at the two women, his eyes disbelieving. "I didn't mean to shoot. The gun went off without me realizing it—"

"Mercy! What's going on in this place now?" Irma cried as she rounded the corner in her nightcap and robe. She gasped when she saw Eric lying prone on the floor.

"Irma, ring for the police," Darcy said, taking charge. "And get some hot water and bandages."

Irma hustled off, and Darcy stared down at Eric, tilting her head and crossing her arms. "Though we should just dump you outside in the sleet or maybe put you in the barn with the other animals, my Christian training won't allow that." She turned to Charleigh, who still looked pale. "Where should we put him?"

"Here," Charleigh said, rising from the sofa and protectively clutching her middle.

Irma hustled back in. "The phone's not working. I'll get the bandages and water."

With Darcy's help, Brent lifted Eric onto the couch. The wounded man moaned, closing his eyes. Alice and Lila soon joined them, demanding to know what the ruckus was about. Several boys plodded downstairs in their nightshirts and bare feet.

"What's going on?" Lance asked, curiously peering around the corner into the parlor.

"Nothing that concerns you." Lila moved to block their vision and shooed them away. "Back to bed, all of you."

Darcy turned to the spot where she'd last seen Brent, but he was gone.

❦

Brent stroked his throbbing jaw and stared out the kitchen window at the sleet, which had turned to snow a few minutes ago. Though the hour was late, the household was awake. All were too nervous to retire to their quarters with a murderer under their roof, even if the man was seriously injured. Brent's thoughts went to Bill, and he shook his head. Obviously Eric knew his brother well.

"Brent?" Darcy's low voice came from behind him.

He tensed but didn't look at her. She touched his sleeve and came around to stand in front of him. "Thank you for saving our lives," she said. "You're a hero."

Brent shook his head. "I almost killed a man."

"Before he had a chance to kill us," she shot back softly. Her fingertips stroked his cheek, and he flinched. "Does it hurt?"

"No," he lied, enjoying her touch too much.

She smiled. "Aren't you the one who's taught me and the boys to always speak the truth?"

"You're right," he amended. "I apologize."

"I can chip off some ice from the block in the icebox. That should take the swelling down."

Swelling? That would explain why the lower part of his face felt as if it were on fire.

"You look like a squirrel hoarding nuts in its cheeks," she added. "Your lip is bleeding, too."

Brent felt for his handkerchief. Realizing he didn't have it, he gingerly wiped the corner of his mouth with his knuckles.

Darcy fetched a dishcloth and wet it with water from the pump. "Joel confessed that at the carnival Eric promised he would help the boy find his father if Joel would join up with him. But when Joel heard Eric and Charleigh talk tonight, he decided Eric was bad news." She returned to Brent and dabbed gently at his lip with the wet cloth. "He could've gone with Eric and left us all to whatever fate Eric had planned. Perhaps this is the heart change we've been looking for in Joel."

"Perhaps." Brent was mesmerized by her liquid dark eyes, as deep and mysterious as an indigo sky.

"Charleigh won't sleep. She's edgy and upset. She won't confide in me, and I don't know what to say to her. But it can't be a good thing for the baby, her staying up all night and pacing the floor like she's doing." Her gaze lifted to his. "Alice said Eric was only nicked, though with all the blood he lost I'm amazed. She mentioned his illness might be what's made his blood thinner—though of course she's no doctor. Still, I think she stitched him up well."

"I have faith in her abilities," Brent said quietly.

Darcy pulled the cloth from his mouth but didn't move away. "Irma said the roads are probably icy. We might not get help for some time."

"I'll stay in the main house until help arrives."

"That would be nice."

He fidgeted, nervous, yet unable to look away from her. "I'm relieved that you survived the ordeal."

She smiled. "I feel the same about you."

He cleared his throat. "Well, I must check on our prisoner."

Releasing a frustrated breath, Darcy grasped his coat lapels before he could leave. "Can't you forget about etiquette for once? I almost lost you in there—you could have been killed. I could have been killed! If it's wrong for me to break society's courtin' rules and express me feelings, then so be it, but express me feelin's I will!"

She wrapped her arms around his neck in a hug and kissed him gently. At first Brent tensed, not so much from shock but from pain. Even her soft lips caused him agony. She pulled away with a sad sigh.

"You know, guv'ner, you could easily discourage a girl. If I didn't suspect you liked me, too, I'd give up. I just might at that. One too many rejections, and a girl soon gets the message." Shaking her head in disappointment, she gave him one last look before leaving the kitchen.

Brent made an effort to gather his wits about him. He would analyze her words another time. Right now, there was something he must know.

Determined, he headed for the parlor and stared at the wounded man on the sofa. A lantern burned on the table beside Eric. He opened his eyes and stared up at Brent, his expression wary.

Brent came straight to the point. "How do you know my brother?"

Eric paused a long moment. "He was with a gang I joined up with in Manhattan," he said at last. "He warned me that my life was in danger and put his own life on the line to do it. He was like that, always trying to prevent someone from getting hurt."

Brent stared, taken aback. Bill had saved this man? Is that what had put Bill's life in jeopardy? Perhaps Brent had judged his brother too harshly. He didn't understand what made Bill do the things he did, but Brent was relieved to hear that his brother wasn't as black as he'd painted him, even if the life he saved was that of a criminal's.

"Thank you for telling me." Brent moved away.

"Bill was wrong about you," Eric said, his raspy voice filled with grudging respect. "You're no coward. In fact, you're alike in many ways."

Brent smiled, though it made his jaw ache. Any credit for courage he owed to God.

❧

The phone lines were still down the following day, with more snow falling. Darcy looked toward Eric, who lay on the sofa and stared up at the ceiling, his expression sullen. He'd barely spoken a word all afternoon, though he'd eaten the stew Irma brought him.

Darcy stretched in the rocker and set down her book. It was agreed that every adult take a watch over the prisoner, and Darcy's vigil was almost over. Any moment now Brent would walk in for the night shift. Since Darcy's kiss in the kitchen last night, he'd become more distant; and Darcy resolutely made up her mind that she would leave him be from now on. If he wanted a relationship, he would have to be the one to make the first move.

Footsteps sounded in the hall. Expecting to see Brent, Darcy was surprised when Charleigh rounded the corner.

"Charleigh? Shouldn't you be in bed?" she asked.

"There's something I must do," Charleigh said, determined. She glanced toward Eric. At her entrance he had peered her way, then quickly looked back to the ceiling. Charleigh waddled toward him, her hands clenched into fists at her sides.

"Eric, I have something to say to you." When he didn't respond, she stepped closer. "Look at me!"

At her demanding words, his gaze narrowed on her.

"You made my life miserable and taught me the meaning of true fear. And though I've every reason to despise you for all you've done—" She took a deep breath. "I choose to forgive you. I know it's what God wants, because He's been dealing with me ever since you got here. He forgave all my sins, and I can do no less when it comes to you."

His expression remained unchanged, but he didn't look away.

"I don't expect you to understand." She hesitated. "Anyway, that's all I have to say." She turned to go.

"Charleigh, wait," he whispered, wincing and clutching his side. "You've gained courage since we were together. How did this come about?"

"If I have courage, it's because of God. I know He'll stand up for me, so I'm not afraid to speak. Nor am I afraid of you anymore."

He studied her in silence, then turned his sober gaze to the ceiling again. Charleigh left the room.

When Brent came to relieve Darcy, she gave him a polite smile—no more—and went to her room to lie down. Yet she couldn't rest. Charleigh's act of forgiveness stirred something deep within her, bringing to the surface something she knew the Lord was telling her to do.

"Oh, Lord, no. Please. Not him." She sat at her bureau, her gaze lifted to the mirror. In her dark, beseeching eyes, she recognized the truth.

❧

The next morning the phone was working, and Irma called the police. Michael arrived at the same time they did. "What's going on?" he asked as he walked through the door behind one of the officers. "Did one of the boys get into trouble? The weather kept me stranded at home, or I would have come sooner."

Alice grabbed his arm with an affectionate squeeze, pulling him past the parlor entrance. "Everything's fine now. I'll tell you all about it over a cup of coffee. I'm just so glad to have you with me again." She moved with him in the direction of the kitchen. Obviously she was concerned about Michael's reaction when he learned of Eric's presence, considering what the Frenchman had once done to Charleigh.

Frowning, Brent watched as Darcy swept past without looking at him. She'd been avoiding him since yesterday. Clutching something tightly in her hand, she walked toward the sofa. Two policemen helped Eric to stand, one on each side of him. Though he was still weak and shaky, handcuffs circled his wrists in front. Darcy stopped close to Eric.

When she said nothing, he raised a mocking eyebrow. "Well?"

"Right," she said and stuffed a few crumpled bills into his hand. "For you to buy an overcoat. You're in desperate need of one."

The bills fluttered to the carpet. Darcy picked them up and tucked them back between his fingers.

"You're giving me money to buy a coat?" he asked incredulously.

"That's right. Three dollars. It should be enough. If there's any left over, you can buy a pair of gloves, too."

"Why? Why are you doing this?"

"Because you need a coat. You're ill. And, well, I felt the Lord tell me to give you the money."

Disbelief filled Eric's eyes as he stared down at the three crumpled bills. "I could have robbed you," he said quietly. "I held a gun to your head and might have killed you. And you're giving me money to buy a coat?"

Darcy smiled brightly. "Life sure is strange, isn't it? But then Christians are often called a peculiar people." She sobered. "I once promised God I would do all I could for the needy, having come from just such a situation. I even wrote a poem about it—that's where the money came from. I won it because of me poem. And last night the Lord reminded me of my vow and told me to give you the money."

Several seconds of quiet elapsed.

"No one's ever given me anything," Eric murmured as he stared at the bills in his clasped hands. Moisture glistened in his eyes when he looked up. "Not even my father, except for the nightly beatings when he'd had too much wine. My mother left him when I was too small to remember. I had to fight, tooth and nail, for everything I had. . . ." He looked away, embarrassed for disclosing a part of his past. Glancing at Darcy once more, he offered a swift nod. The policemen on either side grabbed his upper arms and escorted him to the door.

"I shall pray for you, Eric," Charleigh said before they stepped outside. "That you find the Truth that will set you free."

He halted, the policemen also stopping, and looked her way. There was no malice in his eyes, only bewilderment. "Why? Why would you pray for me after all I've done to you?"

"Because I've learned that true forgiveness means not only forgetting the past. It also means refusing to punish the person who's wronged you, while holding their best interests at heart."

Eric shook his head. "I don't understand."

Charleigh smiled. "Perhaps not now. But I feel strongly in my heart that one day you will. God go with you, Eric."

Brent stood in the entrance and watched while the two policemen slowly escorted the shaky man to their motorcar. Darcy came to stand beside him.

"That was a noble gesture, giving him that money," he said, relieved she was no longer avoiding him.

Darcy offered a faint smile, then moved away without a word. Frustrated, Brent watched her go.

❧

Darcy stood in the loft and used a pitchfork to toss hay below. Months had passed since the night Eric disrupted their lives, at the same time bringing all of them into a closer understanding of true Christianity. Spring had come and with it a sense of release for Darcy.

Throughout the long winter, Brent remained distant, though often Darcy would catch him watching her. Yet she kept her vow not to push herself on him. She still cared for Brent; in fact, her feelings had deepened despite the distance between them. Still, Darcy had learned something. It wasn't all that important if Brent accepted her or if anyone else did, for that matter. As Alice often told her, she couldn't please everyone. God loved her for who she was, and she liked herself. That was all that truly mattered.

She straightened to wipe perspiration from her brow and then bent to shovel another forkful of hay and toss it onto the growing mound. She needed to hurry. She had promised to help with Charleigh's new baby, Clementine, while Alice and Irma went to town and Charleigh got some much-needed rest. Clementine had been born the day after Christmas, healthy and beautiful, bringing joy to all their lives.

"Miss Evans!"

Startled to hear Brent's voice directly below, Darcy peered over the loft. He stared up at her, his hair and suit sprinkled with the hay she'd just tossed.

"Oh, sorry, guv'ner!" she apologized, giggling.

"If you're sorry, why are you laughing?"

She grinned. "It's just that you look so funny!"

"Hmmm. Be that as it may, I have something I wish to discuss with you."

His sober tone sent warning bells ringing inside Darcy. "Not now. I'm finishing up Tommy's job—since he's been sick with those awful stomach cramps." She turned to shovel up another forkful.

"If that's for the animals, you could feed the town's livestock on what you have down here."

Wrinkling her brow, she stared at the towering mound. Had she pitched too much hay? She wasn't familiar with the chore.

"Very well," Brent said. "I'll come up there."

Darcy blinked. "You'll come up here?" she said, watching as he climbed the ladder. He reached the top rung and she backed up, made uneasy by the determined look in his bright blue eyes. She noticed he wasn't wearing his spectacles.

"Really, guv'ner, I'll be down in a jiffy. There's no need for you to come up."

"Too late," he said as he stepped onto the loft's wooden floor.

She clutched the handle of the pitchfork, uncertain. His strange, intense behavior rattled her. Before she could think about what she was doing, Darcy tossed the pitchfork aside and jumped onto the high mound below. She landed with a loud rustle, the lumpy hay prickling her through her dress.

"Wait, don't go!" Brent called. To her surprise, another rustle filled her ears as he landed on the mound beside her. He grabbed her arm before she could scramble away. "Why did you jump?" he asked.

"Because you're actin' so peculiar!"

He shook his head in exasperation, giving her a wry grin. "You know, Darcy Evans, you make it extremely difficult for a man to make the first move."

Her mouth dropped open. "Guv'ner?"

"Brent," he corrected, drawing her close. "The name is Brent." And with that, he kissed her like he'd never kissed her before.

When he pulled away, Darcy stared, dazed and breathless. "Did you really kiss me?" she whispered, still not believing it.

"Yes, I did. And I intend to do so every day we have left together on this earth. That is, if you'll have me."

"You're askin' me to marry you?"

"I am. Frankly, I don't know how I existed this long without you." His gaze softened. "You taught me to enjoy life and to look beyond outward appearances— to the heart. And, Darcy, your heart is so selfless and pure and beautiful, always wanting to do good—a man would have to be a fool not to love you."

She smiled, hardly daring to believe what she was hearing. "You love me?"

"I denied it for a long time, but, yes, I love you dearly."

"Oh—and I love you dearly, too!" She hugged him hard, but her joy flickered as a thought came to her. "Does this mean we'll be courting the full year?" Alice had informed Darcy about courting, also telling her that many considered it outdated.

Disappointment glimmered in Brent's eyes. "If you would prefer to, we can. Yet, due to our long association, I don't feel a short engagement would be inappropriate."

"Good! But keep in mind, I'll likely always be brash and speak me mind. Often the Cockney slips out despite my best efforts to speak right."

"And I shall likely oftentimes be stuffy." A pained look crossed his face.

Darcy laughed. She couldn't help herself. She loved this man so much—especially covered with hay as he was now. He looked anything but stuffy!

He plucked a piece of straw from her hair. "Something amuses you, Miss Evans?"

"Nothing, guv'ner," she said, her smile wide. "Nothing ter squawk habout anyways."

Brent laughed at the familiar phrase.

"And the answer is yes—I'll marry you as soon as you like. In fact, the sooner the better, as far as I'm concerned! Does tomorrow sound all right with you?"

He shook his head, his eyes dancing. "Oh, Darcy. However did I survive my bleak life until you came along?"

Before she could think of a response, he pulled her close and kissed her again.

Epilogue

Darcy stood beside her husband of seven weeks and stared at the magnificent sunset. "I'm going to miss Lila and Angel," she murmured. Brent slipped a comforting arm around her waist, and she settled her head on his shoulder. Her fingertips brushed the edge of her jacket. A gift from Lila.

Yesterday, while trying to decide what to pack, Lila had thrown her colorful garments into a heap on the floor, stating she wanted no reminders of her carnival days and intended to burn them. Darcy had been horrified to see the gorgeous red jacket with Chinese embroidery and gold buttons cast onto the pile. Seeing Darcy longingly eye the crimson satin, Lila lifted it from the heap and placed it around her shoulders, rendering Darcy speechless. Not only was the jacket a perfect fit, it was ten times prettier than the jacket the organ grinder's monkey wore all those years ago, when she was a child.

Joy over the long-desired treasure mixed with sadness upon losing a friend. Lila and Angel were leaving the refuge tomorrow. It had been a shock when Bruce, the strong man from the carnival, showed up at the door last week, begging to see Lila. Concerned, Darcy eavesdropped and heard Bruce vow his love, telling Lila she was the sole reason he'd stayed with the carnival. Judging from the shy smile Lila offered when she later informed Charleigh and Darcy of her impending marriage, Darcy knew Bruce's feelings were returned; and she was happy for her friend. One thing was certain: Lila and Angel would always be in her prayers.

"I'm amazed at how well Joel has taken to Lila," Brent said thoughtfully. "Especially since he was her worst tormentor those first few weeks she was here."

"It is amazing, isn't it?" Darcy asked. To everyone's shock, the two had grown close. After his experience with Eric, Joel changed. He still talked incessantly of finding his father one day, but he wasn't as volatile as before. He'd grown considerate of others, conscientious in his studies, and rarely started a fight with any of the boys.

"Well, I best be seeing to the baby," Charleigh said from her post by the porch rail. She moved to go, then stopped. "Oh dear, isn't that Mr. Forrester's car? What does he want now?"

Darcy peered up the lane toward the gate. Sure enough, a black motorcar with a bent fender chugged their way.

"He's probably found something else to bicker about." Charleigh blew out a frustrated breath. "Honestly! It seems that man has nothing better to do than meddle in our affairs and try to find a reason for closing us down."

A sudden wail reached them from inside.

"Clemmie," Darcy said to Charleigh. "Go. I'll take care of Mr. Forrester."

With a grateful nod, Charleigh hurried inside.

"Darcy," Brent warned.

She flashed him a smile. "In a nice way, of course."

"Perhaps you'd better let me handle this," Brent suggested as the car rolled to a stop. "Especially after the way you lit into that peddler last week for his derogatory comments about Lila when he spotted Alice shaving her—" His words broke off as he stared at the vehicle.

Looking thinner and tired, Stewart patted the side of the car and motioned a farewell to the driver. A scrawny young boy in ill-fitting clothes stood off to the side. Mr. Forrester offered a feeble smile and drove away while Stewart hurried up the steps. He clasped Brent's hand in a heartfelt shake and accepted Darcy's welcoming hug.

"Delighted to have you back," Brent said.

"You could have told Charleigh your plans," Darcy lightly admonished. "I do believe she was beginning to wonder if you were ever coming home."

"Darcy," Brent said.

"No, she's right," Stewart replied, his voice hoarse. "Things have been rough. Mother almost lost her home, and I had to intervene. Then I got sick, and there were other problems, too."

"Stewart." Charleigh's disbelieving whisper reached them.

His gaze whipped past Darcy's shoulder, and he moved the few yards toward his wife, though he didn't take her in his arms as Darcy thought he might. He looked awkward, standing there, and Darcy's heart went out to him.

"Forgive me, Charleigh. Forgive me for staying away." His voice came low. Brent averted his gaze, but Darcy watched the reunion out of concern for her friend. Charleigh nodded but looked as uneasy as Stewart did.

"I need to tell you something. Something that might help you understand why I had to go." Stewart hesitated. "Since the war's end, I've dealt with some tough issues. You were depressed about losing the babies, and I didn't feel I should burden you, but now you need to know. Two days before the fighting ended, a good friend of mine, a lieutenant, died in my arms in the trenches because he obeyed my orders."

"Oh, Stewart." Charleigh clasped her hands in her skirt, seeming at a loss.

"I won a medal for saving others, but I couldn't save Rudy," he continued, as though he had to get the words out quickly before he lost courage to say them.

"I failed him. A good man depended on me and died. Eventually I convinced myself that you'd be better off without me, too—that I'd brought you nothing but heartache—"

"No, that's not true."

"Please, Charleigh, let me finish. I'm telling you this now because in mending the breach with my family and helping them, I began to heal. But it wasn't until I was laid up with the flu and had idle time that I saw how unfair I was being to you, by not sharing what I was going through. And by staying away. I was wrong. I decided that as soon as I recovered, I'd come home and somehow make it up to you. So here I am." He lifted his hands upward. "That is, if I'm still welcome."

"Of course you're welcome," Charleigh whispered. "But you're not the only one at fault, Stewart. I was wrong, too. I was so absorbed in self-pity, thinking only of myself at the time, that I wasn't even aware you were hurting and needed me."

Unmoving, they stared at one another, then closed the short distance between them until they were in each other's arms, murmuring words of love and forgiveness. "I'll never stay away again, Charleigh," Stewart said. "You're all the world to me."

Tears stung Darcy's eyes, and Brent drew her close. "Perhaps we should go inside," he whispered. Darcy nodded, and they moved to go.

Stewart pulled away from his wife, keeping her within the circle of his arms. "Please, wait—both of you. There's someone I want you to meet." He looked toward the child still standing where the car had left him off. "Clint, come here."

The scruffy-looking boy hesitated, then, hands in his pockets, shuffled toward them and halted at the foot of the steps. Darcy figured he was ten. His wheat-colored hair hung in clumps around his ears, and he looked and smelled as if he hadn't had a bath in weeks.

"This is Clint. I met him at the station in Raleigh—after I chased him down when he picked my pocket. He's an orphan and was sleeping in some crates in an alley. I told him he has a home here at the refuge from now on."

"Of course he does," Charleigh said, brushing a tear from her eye. "Hello, Clint."

Darcy moved down the three steps and put out her hand. "Welcome to Lyons' Refuge."

The boy only stared back.

Darcy lowered her arm. "That's all right. You'll get used to us soon enough, I expect. Lyons' Refuge is a place like no other, you'll soon find." She laughed and looked toward the porch. "That's the schoolmaster, Mr. Thomas, and I'm the cook's assistant. You can call me Darcy. Do you like apple cake? I baked one this morning."

The boy shrugged. "Don't know. Ain't never et no cake before."

"Suh-fee!" a child's voice suddenly cried out. "Hi, Suh-fee!"

Everyone turned to look at the toddler in the open doorway. In her yellow frock, with her shiny, dark curls and big brown eyes, Angel looked as sweet as her name. Staring at Brent, she clapped her hands and jumped up and down, then fell to her frilled bottom.

From within the house an infant cried, the sound growing stronger. Alice walked out, a baby in her arms. "I think she wants you, Charleigh." Seeing Stewart, she stopped in surprise.

Stewart stared at the infant with bright red hair, then looked at his wife.

"Um, I also have someone I'd like for you to meet." Charleigh cleared her throat. "This is Clementine Marielle Lyons. Your daughter."

Stewart remained motionless, as though in a trance.

"Here now—would you like to hold her?" Alice asked. Before he could reply, she placed the baby in his arms.

Clemmie stopped crying and stared up at him, wide-eyed. Tears rolled down Stewart's cheeks. After a moment, he looked at Charleigh, his expression pained. "Why didn't you tell me? I never would've stayed away—"

Shaking her head, Charleigh pressed her fingers to his lips to stop his strangled words. "You're home now. That's all that matters. Let's put the past where it belongs—behind us."

Stewart gave a short nod and with his free arm drew her tightly to his side.

Angel toddled over to Brent and tugged on his jacket. "Suh-fee?"

"What *is* that child saying?" Stewart asked. "And who is she? Do we take in small girls now?"

Darcy laughed, returning to the porch, and scooped Angel up in her arms. "She's a friend's daughter, and she's saying Stuffy." She grinned up at her husband. "Somehow she got hold of that name for Brent and won't let go."

"Stuffy?" Stewart repeated.

"Suh-fee!" Angel squealed. She leaned over and threw her chubby arms around Brent's neck in a tight hug. They all laughed.

Stewart glanced at Brent. "Everything went well? No problems to report?"

Brent and Darcy shared a look. "Nothing we couldn't handle together," Brent said.

"Glad to hear it. You can fill me in on everything that's happened later. Right now I just want to relax and spend some time with my family. It's good to be home." With one arm around Charleigh and the other cradling his daughter, Stewart went inside. Angel kicked her legs to get down, and Darcy set her on the porch. She ran into the house, and Darcy and Brent moved to follow.

"Hey, lady!" Clint yelled after them. "What about me?"

Darcy turned her head and grinned. "Well, what are you just standing there for? This is your home now, too. Come on inside, and I'll get you a nice, thick slice of that cake."

This time the boy didn't hesitate. Wearing a bright smile, he was through the door faster than Darcy would have imagined it possible.

"He seems to have taken a liking to you," Brent said. "But then that comes as no surprise."

She grabbed his sleeve to stop him before he could follow the others. "Brent, about what you told Stewart—we do make a fine team, don't we?"

"Indubitably!"

Darcy arched her brow, determined to look up that word as soon as she could.

Brent laughed and tilted her chin up with his forefinger and thumb. "Most certainly," he clarified. "The very best." Bending down, he gave her a gentle kiss.

"Well then," she whispered once he lifted his head, "would ye care to make it a threesome?"

"A threesome?" He looked puzzled.

Darcy smiled. "In eight months, I expect. Sometime around Clemmie's first birthday. How do ye feel about the name Beatrice? 'Course if it's a boy, he'd have to be Brent."

His eyes widened behind the spectacles, and his mouth dropped open. "Darcy, you don't mean. . ."

"I most certainly do! As long as everyone else is makin' introductions tonight, I might as well be makin' one of me own!"

She looped her arms around Brent's neck and kissed him soundly. From the side of the house, boys' snickering could be heard, but Darcy didn't mind.

Neither, it seemed, did Brent.

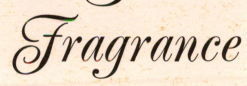

A Gentle Fragrance

Dedication

A huge thanks to Tamela Hancock Murray and Jill Stengl,
for staying near their computers during the onslaught of chapters
and for getting back critiques to me in record time.
Your faithfulness overwhelms me, ladies.
Also, another huge thanks to my mom,
whose loving help has pulled me through more than once.
Thanks to all who helped with this project.
As always, dedicated to my Lord and Savior,
who does not look upon the former things,
but creates a new beginning for all who come to Him.

Chapter 1

The South Pacific, 1921

I f he ever returned to New York, he was a dead man.

Bill Thomas stood at the stern of the ship, his pensive gaze sweeping the deep blue ocean and the globe of an orange sun setting beyond a distant island. Here at sea, they would never find him. Yet this time, that reminder did little to steady his nerves.

As he stood watch, the fire of the sky faded to dull blue and violet. The sea grew ever darker, save for two ripples of crimson forming a trail of light toward the horizon. His mind traveled a course all its own, reliving the peril of two years ago.

Somehow, he'd succeeded in escaping Manhattan and gaining employment as a sailor on this vessel. New York remained a distant memory. But even after sailing the high seas for fourteen months, he couldn't shake the fear of reprisal that often had him looking over his shoulder. His brother, Brent, would say the hounds of heaven were giving chase and the guilt for Bill's past crimes was finally catching up to him. Maybe Brent was right, though ironically this time Bill's escape had nothing to do with his own folly.

With his hands spaced wide apart and gripping the rail, he leaned forward. In the last glimmer of evening light, he noticed the water break and white spray shoot upward. Within seconds, a dolphin arced above the surface, outlined for a moment against the horizon, then disappeared back into the water to repeat the process. The antics of the playful water animal brought a faint smile to Bill's face.

Yes, he was a fugitive, but he couldn't have picked a better spot in which to find sanctuary. This chain of South Sea Islands held a mystery that intrigued Bill each time the ship anchored near them to deliver and collect goods. The expansive sea offered secrets of continual interest. Life could be worse.

A thud struck the deck behind him, louder than the creaks of timbers and slap of waves hitting the hull. Bill sharply pivoted to look. In the shadowy twilight, he couldn't make out any sign of life on board. Only the usual ropes, barrels, and crates. A full moon rose above the waters, and faint stars dotted the sky, but he wished for more light.

"Ahoy, who goes there?" Slowly he headed in the direction he'd heard the noise.

No response.

Hair bristled at the back of his neck, but he continued forward as duty demanded.

After investigating the area to find it empty, he scolded himself for allowing old fears to harass him once again. He was free of all that had happened in New York. There was no reason to keep dwelling on those days.

Returning his attention to the dolphin, he squinted to see the sea creature and noted that it now jumped closer to the ship, its splashes easily heard. The sun was only a memory; the sky the color of faded ink.

A thick arm grabbed Bill around his upper chest from behind while something razor-sharp sliced into his ribs. Vision clouding from pain, Bill barely made out the terse words whispered in his ear, "Sleep with the fish. Compliments of Vittorio."

Nausea rose to his throat as his attacker pushed him over the rail. The sea rose up to meet him as his wounded body splashed into the ocean. Thrashing his arms to keep afloat despite the searing pain, Bill spat out salty water. "Help!" His plea came faint. He choked down a breath, certain it would be his last. His blurry focus latched onto the bright moon shining like a beacon.

"Dear God, save me!" he cried through water that invaded his mouth and nose and strangled his words.

The ship sailed farther away. He struggled to stay conscious, to stay afloat, but he could feel his body weaken and his mind fade with every slosh of the waves against his face.

He was going to die.

❧

Sarah opened her eyes and sat straight up in her rope hammock. It rocked back and forth with the motion, and she caught a startled breath. What had awakened her? A sense of foreboding, as if something had happened or was about to happen, plagued her mind and spirit.

She swung her legs over the side, gripping the hammock to steady herself. The moon's glow washed the inside of the thatched hut with brilliant white light. Her father's form lay inert in the hammock across the room. His loud snores proved he was breathing and well, so the danger didn't lie there. She looked out the square hole of the window, her focus going to the moon etched on a blue-black canvas of sky spangled with stars.

The urgency to go outside overwhelmed her, and she walked out the door.

A warm scented breeze caressed her face and body and stirred the coconut palm fronds as she took the familiar pathway. She could walk it even if there were no moon by which to see. The village path was to her right, but she felt the strong impression to go left. Standing high upon a cliff, she surveyed this edge of her island world and noticed movement in the ocean near the beach. Moonlight illumined the waters.

A villager's boat? At night? All the fishermen returned with their catch hours ago. While she watched, her eyes widened. That was no boat!

She raced down the path leading to the empty beach, not stopping when her feet reached the sea's warm, foamy waters. Splashing through, she continued as fast as her legs could move against the press of hindering water. When it surrounded her waist, she dove into the next shallow wave and began swimming with skill, matching that of the dolphin to which someone clung—a man, she could see as she swam nearer.

"I will help you," she called in her native tongue, but he didn't respond. Grabbing his arm in order to shift his inert body toward her, she was surprised when he weakly struggled to be free.

"I mean no harm," she tried again.

His eyes closed. He began sliding off the dolphin. She grabbed him before his head went under and wrapped her arm beneath his limp shoulders around the broad expanse of his chest. Awkwardly she swam with her burden, grateful for the waves that helped push her toward land until her feet could again touch the ocean floor. She considered it a blessing that he'd not been near the coral reef farther down the island, for surely if he had, he would have been cut to ribbons. With difficulty, Sarah dragged him, pulling under his arms, onto the packed wet sand of the beach, until she felt sure the ocean wouldn't carry him away again.

From where had he come? His fair features gave testimony to the fact that this was no islander. For the first time she saw a dark stain at the bottom of his striped shirt.

The man was injured!

She dropped to her knees beside him and pushed the material up so she could see. The surf rushed against them, water washing the blood away from a deep wound that marred his side. Once the wave receded, the wound began to flow again, worrying her. If she didn't do something soon, he could bleed to death.

Using what was on hand, Sarah struggled to rip away his shirt from his body to make a bandage, pulling at the tear at the side. He regained consciousness and open dulled eyes. Again he weakly struck out, attempting to fight her off. Surprised, Sarah drew back.

"No," he groaned in the English tongue of her father. "Leave me alone! I didn't kill Marco." He weakened, arms dropping to the sand. His eyes flickered shut. "Didn't. . . double-cross. . .no one." These last words were faint, and Sarah had to bend her ear to his mouth to hear.

Seeing he was again unconscious, she hurried to resume her task and tied the torn material in a knot around his torso. Sarah studied his ashen face, praying he wasn't dead. She pressed her palm against his chest. Relief washed through her when she felt a faint heartbeat.

Knowing she'd done all she could and must now get help, she pushed herself to her feet and sped up the path to her father's hut.

Chapter 2

Bill opened his eyes. Brightness seared them, and he raised a hand to shield his face, then cried out as fire ripped through his gut. Within seconds, a vision blocked the sun. He wondered if he had died. For surely the form of the woman who'd come to stand near him was that of an angel.

She wore her black hair loose, past her hips. A breeze from somewhere ruffled wisps of it over bare shoulders and arms. Her feet were also bare, and she wore a bright red sarong covered with white flowers. Did angels wear such finery?

He shifted and gave another muffled cry. The vision knelt and laid her slender hand against his shoulder. "You must lie still. You were wounded and feverish, but my father and I are taking care of you. You have been with us three days."

Her husky-soft voice soothed, and he relaxed back onto what he now realized was a straw mat. His throat felt dry. "Water," he rasped.

She left and soon returned with a wooden dipper. Slipping her hand behind his neck, she helped him raise his head. Cool and pure, the water slid down his throat.

"Where am I?" he asked when he could talk.

"On our island in my father's hut. He's a missionary to the people here."

He took note of her clear skin, a pale pecan-brown. Her almond eyes were brown also, but with golden lights in them, and her lashes were thick and black. Her delicate bone structure, lush thick hair, and slender carriage reminded him of the many beautiful island women he'd seen, but her coloring was too fair to be a native's.

"What's your name?" he whispered.

"Sarah."

The door to the hut opened. A tall, thin man walked inside, his scraggly beard, mustache, and hair salt-and-pepper gray. His swarthy skin was almost as tanned as Bill's arms and torso. Like the woman, he wore no shoes, though his trousers and shirt looked American.

"Ah, good," he said. "Our patient is awake." Green eyes twinkled in a weathered face. He set a straw basket onto a carved oak desk, oddly out of place in this primitive hut.

Sarah gracefully rose to her feet. "Father." She kissed his cheek and took the basket to a table. He walked closer to Bill and squatted beside his mat.

"Welcome to our modest home. I am Josiah LaRue, sent as a missionary from America to this island more than twenty years ago. And you are?"

"Bill." Uncertain of whom to trust, he didn't give his last name.

"Well, Bill, consider yourself fortunate. If that dolphin hadn't brought you here and my daughter hadn't been at the beach to bring you to land, you would be a dead man. If not by drowning, then by sharks. The Lord must have a great mission in mind for you."

Josiah's mention of God made Bill uneasy. Why should God save him? He'd done nothing right in his sorry existence. The man's words fully sank in.

"A dolphin brought me?"

"Yes. Queerest thing I ever heard of, but Sarah was a witness. The dolphin carried you to the island. I imagine it's the same one that's become something of a pet of hers. In my forty-eight years on this earth, I've learned the Almighty can and will use anything to achieve His purposes. Once He caused a donkey to speak to a man named Balaam, so I suppose He could and would use a friendly dolphin to help rescue a lost seafarer."

Bill remembered. He had cried out to God to save him. Just as he thought he would sink to the ocean floor, the dolphin he'd been watching from the ship glided near him, slowly circling. Desperate, he'd grabbed its dorsal fin. The dolphin had nosed under, lifting Bill partly out of the water, and he'd held on. Bill remembered little of what happened next.

"Did you fall overboard?" Josiah asked. "I assume from your clothing that you're a sailor."

"Yes. I fell overboard." Bill left it at that. The less these people knew, the better.

The man was quiet a moment, his intent gaze causing Bill discomfort.

"You must have hit something sharp on your way down," Josiah said. "The gash in your side was deep, but with my daughter's knowledge in healing herbs and the little suturing I've learned, it's on the mend now." He straightened to a stand. "You're welcome to stay with us as long as you like."

"I appreciate that."

Josiah gave a nod. "You must be hungry. Sarah, fix our guest a meal."

"Yes, Father."

Bill looked past Josiah to Sarah. Unsmiling, she steadily regarded Bill. The way she stared made him look away, uneasy. How could she know he was holding back the truth?

❧

Sarah sliced the white meat of a coconut. Each chop of the knife punctuated the truth ringing in her mind. The man called Bill had lied to them. Why? And whom had he thought he'd addressed when he fought her help that night on the beach?

As it had many times, her gaze went to his slumbering form. Never had she seen eyes so light in color, reminding her of shallow turquoise waters, or hair so pale. It grew past his ears and resembled the shade of yellow grasses near the center of the island when the noonday sun hit them. When she'd first seen his hair wet that night on the beach, it had been dark, and she'd been surprised to see the color lighten once it dried. She'd never seen hair do that. Curious, she further studied his face. His profile resembled the picture of an aristocratic prince in a history book of her father's. Yet this man was no prince.

He lay there, frail as a newborn. Bruises marred his stomach and arms, but his muscular torso gave testimony to untold strength. He must be strong to endure what he had. She'd been amazed she was able to drag him from the sea, and he'd survived the stabbing, though certainly that must be in part due to their many petitions to God. Sarah was certain it was a stab wound Bill had suffered, not a "gash" he'd received during his fall into the ocean, as Father suggested.

Two years ago, a boy had been attacked with a knife after a village ceremony. Sarah's father had attended the boy. His wound resembled Bill's, though sadly it was closer to the heart, and the boy died.

"Sarah?"

Her father's muted voice caught her attention. Abandoning the preparation of their meal, she moved to join him where he stood by the open door. He led her a short distance from the hut, into the shade of a coconut palm.

"You are so like your mother, quiet and still, but your eyes reveal your secrets. You're not happy Bill is staying with us."

"I do not trust him." Sarah lifted her palms in a delicate shrug. "Yet what else is to be done? He needs our help. You're a missionary; you cannot turn him out."

"You're right, Sarah. I can't." Her father lifted his gaze to the white clouds in an azure sky, a gesture used when he had something of merit to say. "I sense his wound is not merely of a physical nature. The fearful words he yelled to you that night prove that. After talking with him, I sense a spiritual struggle similar to what I endured after your mother died. It's my duty as God's chosen servant to help this young man in whatever way possible, in the nurture of both his body and his spirit. Perhaps he was sent to us for that purpose, Sarah."

For a time, neither spoke. Sarah waited until he again looked in her direction.

"If it is your will to have him here, Father, then I will make him feel welcome."

"That's my beautiful girl." He hugged her close with one arm.

Still, unease twined around Sarah when she thought about the man called Bill.

❧

Bill surveyed the round hut for what must have been the hundredth time. Never one for inactivity, he was about to go mad from lying flat. According to his mental time track, two days had passed since he'd woken from the fever. A total of five days on this island. The girl and her father treated him well enough and saw to his every need, but he almost wished they'd been cruel to help ease his guilt for withholding the truth and for invading their home. True, the man was a missionary, accustomed to lending aid. But that fact strangely doubled Bill's guilt.

His stoic brother had tried to get him to see the light of Christianity, a light from which Bill had always run fast and run hard. Now he lay stranded, physically helpless, in a missionary's hut. How disgustingly ironic.

Bill looked out the window at a pale square of blue. Palm fronds edged it, and he heard the ocean's surf nearby. Again his mind went to that night aboard ship. Weeks ago, they'd left port with a batch of new sailors, and Bill had been nervous, plagued by the past. One sailor, Guido, used his work as an excuse not to look at Bill, even when Bill addressed the man directly. Had Guido been Bill's assailant?

The crisp sound of a page turning had him shift his focus to the girl. She sat relaxed in her hammock, reading a book.

"What is there to do on this godforsaken island anyway?" he grumbled.

"You are bored?" she inquired, not looking up from the page. "Would you like one of my father's books to read?"

"No, I would not like one of your father's books to read," he clipped, frustrated. "I want to get outside this hut!"

"Soon, you will heal." She turned another page. "Your wound is better with each day."

He snorted. "That's what you said yesterday. And the day before that."

"Instead of being angry, you should thank God that in His great wisdom He has seen fit to keep you alive."

Bill knew that, but her offhand reminder didn't improve his attitude. "Will you please look at me and at least acknowledge my existence? If I'm to be stuck here, the least you could do is talk to me."

She closed the book, her golden-brown eyes focusing on him. "Very well. What is it you wish to discuss?"

Unnerved by her unruffled manner and steady gaze, Bill averted his attention to the thatched roof. "Tell me about this island. How long have you lived here?"

"I was born here."

"What about the village? Why don't you live there instead?"

He heard her slow intake of breath. "After my mother and her unborn child perished, my father moved from the village to build this hut."

Bill looked her way. "How old were you?"

"Seven."

"You've lived here alone all this time? Why?"

She stood up from the hammock and laid the book on the desk. "My father should be better able to answer your questions when he returns. I must tend to chores."

"Wait!" Bill didn't want to have the hut all to himself again. "Don't go. I promise to keep my inquiries less personal if you'll stay. And I'll try to be nicer."

She hesitated.

"Cross my heart," Bill said, making the motion with his right hand.

"Cross your. . . ?" Her words trailed off, confused.

"Never mind. Really, I'd like to hear more about your island, so I'll know what to expect once I'm on my feet."

She tilted her head as if considering his request. "I will tell you what you wish to know. On one condition."

"Condition?" This couldn't be good.

"You are recovered enough to sit at our table. Tonight, instead of sleeping, you will listen to my father read the words from the Holy Book. It would please him. On this condition only will I remain and tell you about our island."

Bill grimaced. What she asked wasn't so much, he supposed, though he didn't look forward to the prospect. Agreeing to commit to an hour or more of sure drudgery might be worth it to spend time in her company and learn about this place that would be home until the next ship arrived.

"All right, doll. You got yourself a deal."

"A deal?" Her brows lifted. "This is a yes?"

"Yeah."

She nodded once, as graceful as a princess acknowledging one of her subjects. Pulling her thigh-length hair over one shoulder, she took a seat near his mat. All her movements were graceful, fluid. Again he became entranced by her beauty, then by her words as time slipped into some invisible slot and she opened up to him the mysteries of her island.

Chapter 3

Sarah was confused. Naturally, it pleased her that Bill had agreed to take part in hearing her father read from the Bible, but she couldn't help feeling his motives were suspect. Perhaps it was the look in his eyes when she caught him watching her, as if he lay in wait like one of the sharks who prowled the waters. Uneasy around him, she looked for excuses to be absent. Conversely, she felt a pull toward him she couldn't explain.

By the light of the candles, Sarah sneaked glances Bill's way. The first two nights he'd listened to the gospel, he'd seemed indifferent, enduring the hour. But tonight, his eyes were alert, his expression tense as he watched her father.

After the book closed, a crackling silence reigned.

"I don't understand," Bill said at last. "Paul helped capture and kill Christians, and God chose him?"

"Yes, another wonderful example of God's saving grace. We're all sinners; all of us deserve hell and damnation. But because of a loving Father, we have assurance of salvation through our Lord and Savior, Jesus Christ."

Frowning, Bill looked out the window. After a moment, he stood. "I need air." He walked through the door, moving more easily than before, yet his actions were slow, stilted.

"You should go to him."

Stunned, Sarah regarded her father. "I? Why should I go to him?"

"Because he'll listen to you."

Amazement gave way to incredulity.

"Speak with him," her father urged. "He turns a deaf ear toward me, and I've noticed he listens to you."

She didn't know where her father had gotten that impression. If anything, Bill argued with her on a continual basis.

"I'll do as you ask," she said, rising from her mat. *But I'll not like it.*

"You're a true credit to a missionary, Sarah."

Sarah pondered his words. She'd been trained to be subservient to her father as her authority. At the same time, her mother's sister taught her to rely solely on an inner source for strength. Her father called the strength Jehovah. Aunt Lefu called the strength many gods. Sarah did not know what to call it. She believed in the Almighty God, of whom her father preached. Likewise her aunt spoke of the island gods. Sarah had attended village rituals, seen the people's devotion.

Was their homage and commitment without basis? Did only one God exist?

She found Bill standing on the cliff where she'd stood seven nights ago, looking out to sea. As on that night, the moon hung low, and a hibiscus-scented breeze stirred the warm air.

Hearing her approach, he glanced over his shoulder, then back out to sea.

"You believe in all your father says?" Bill's question was abrupt, his voice taut.

"I believe there's a God, and Jesus is His Son."

He turned fully to look at her. "From the way you said that, I sense some hesitance on your part."

"There is much yet I don't understand."

"And here I thought you and your kind had all the answers."

When she didn't respond to his caustic remark, he stepped closer. She tensed, again reminded of the shark. The look in his eyes seemed dangerous.

"What's the matter, pretty Sarah? Do I frighten you?" He slowly brushed his fingertips along her hair, down to her shoulder. Shivers of uncertainty and pleasure raced along her spine.

"No man frightens me." She kept her face expressionless as he baited her.

His brows arched in mockery, even as his mouth quirked, as though not entirely pleased with her answer. "What does frighten you?" He traced his fingertips down her shoulder to her elbow. "Monsters in the night? Headhunters? The bogeyman?"

"I've learned to contain my fears, to not let them conquer me."

"Have you? How admirable. Just as a good Christian girl should do." His fingers and thumb went to her chin, and he lifted it high as though inspecting something. "Ah, yes. There *is* the sign of victory in those eyes! And yet, every champion has his weakness. What's your weakness, Sarah?"

Before she could answer, his lips were on hers in a kiss meant both to seduce and possess. Almost immediately it turned gentle, tender. Taken by surprise, she didn't fight him. A floodgate of emotions raged through her soul. As abruptly as the kiss came, he ended it. Released his hold on her chin. Stepped back.

Offense gave way to compassion when Sarah saw remorse infuse his eyes.

"Forgive me." His plea was no more than a croak.

Before she could respond, he turned on his heel and left her. Sarah watched him go, thrashing the bushes out of his way, his step heavy and swift as he headed for the beach as though he were the one now being hunted.

Thoughts in a whirlwind, she returned to her father's hut. Of all the emotions Bill's unexpected kiss evoked, the one that alarmed her most was the longing she'd felt for it never to end.

❧

Bill stared at the crested waves sweeping the barren beach, his eyes seeing little. Annoyed frustration with himself and with these religious-minded people had goaded him to move forward, to break through Sarah's aloof barrier with an earth-shaking kiss. But he was the one who'd felt the earth move beneath his feet. And he didn't like what was happening to him.

When his lips pressed against her soft ones, the desire to strike out instantly vanished. As quickly as the kiss altered something indefinable inside Bill, so also came the realization that he didn't want to change Sarah. At that split second the kiss became genuine, no longer a trap he'd designed to cause her to fall off her throne of cool detachment.

He released a breath fraught with aggravation. He had to get off this island. What kind of man was he that he would try to seduce the chaste daughter of the holy man who'd opened his home to him, cared for him, shown him nothing but graciousness?

The worst kind of man.

That kiss not only opened his eyes to the discovery that he preferred Sarah just as she was, but it unearthed the realization that he didn't like himself. And he wasn't the type comfortable with inward examination. Only since he'd come to the island had he analyzed his motives.

Bill wasn't sure what he believed about God, but each day that passed in the missionary's presence brought Bill closer to the plateau to which both the missionary and his daughter were trying to take him. If Bill did accept what they told him, how could he then face himself? His sins were too great and too dark to count. To acknowledge a God and to believe in His Son would push Bill to a point from which there was no return and from where there was no escape. No more running.

The thought was almost more terrifying than being hunted by criminals.

❧

Finished with the wash, Sarah cradled the basket of wet linens under her arm and retraced her steps uphill. The sand burned her feet, and she carried a great banana leaf above her head as a sunshade to block out the sun. The air seemed sleepy as it always did this time of day, any sound unusually loud and misplaced. Many villagers had retreated into the shade of their homes to sleep, but Sarah felt restless.

Catching sight of Bill ahead, standing between two palms and staring out to sea, she hesitated. For the past week he'd steered clear of her, and while his erratic behavior confused, oddly it also disappointed. In the nighttime, she lay awake in her hammock and relived his kiss; in the mornings, she pushed it from her mind.

He turned upon hearing her footsteps rustle in the grass but didn't move away as he'd done every other day this week when he caught sight of her. Instead, he waited until she drew near. Without a word, he took the basket from her, and together they continued up the path. Silence thickened between them, broken only by the sound of the surf upon the beach and the gulls' mewling cries.

He glanced at her, then back up the path. "I'm not a decent man, Sarah. Where I come from, I'm not even considered a good man."

She gave time for his heavy words to settle before she spoke. "There is no one who's truly good, according to Father. All men are evil or have evil thoughts. The goodness must come from without, from relying on God. No one owns true goodness unless they know its Source."

He released a pent-up breath. "You make it sound so simple."

"It is. Father says the problem with many accepting salvation lies in the fact that people want to complicate what should be kept simple. Logic and intelligence confuse, and it is only with the mind and heart of a child one can understand."

He halted, turning on her. "*You* confuse me, Sarah. You speak with such conviction, even if you are only parroting your father. But I've watched you. I followed you last evening."

Sarah's face flushed hot. Bill had spied on her? Her father would be grieved to learn she'd accompanied Aunt Lefu to the temple, something she'd done under great pressure.

"You shouldn't have followed me," she said gravely. "There are dangers of which you know nothing. Things considered taboo to those not of our island."

"Then tell me so I can understand."

His blue-eyed gaze drilled into her, and she looked sideways, to the churning sea. How could she tell him when she herself didn't understand the pull that drew her to her mother's people? During the years her father was ill in spirit, she had drawn close to her aunt, attended tribal rituals. Though she rarely partook of them, she'd opened her ears and mind to the beliefs they reflected.

"How can you expect me to understand, when you yourself seem so lost?" he asked quietly.

She was saved a reply when she heard clicks and squeals and caught sight of a familiar shape breaking above the water. Smiling, she put her hand to his arm. He drew back a little in surprise.

"Come, you must meet Maliu."

"Maliu?"

"Come," she said pulling on his arm that was not holding the basket. "You will see."

❧

Like a child, Sarah almost dragged Bill down the sandy slope and toward the expansive sea, where a rock basin formed a pool. He worked to keep a good hold on the basket. The stab wound had healed over, and her father had removed the thread from the stitching yesterday, but now his side ached due to the fast pace at which she led him.

"Sarah, what's this all about?"

"You'll see." A glint colored her eyes, but it was her mysterious smile that captured his breath. She turned toward the water. "Maliu! Come!"

To his surprise, a blue dolphin broke the ocean's surface, jumping high into the air. The sun glinted off its sleek back as it completed its arc and dove head-first into the water.

Understanding dawned. "The dolphin that saved my life."

She nodded and took hold of his hand. "Come."

Weary of struggling with the slipping basket, he dropped it to the sand before moving with her toward the rock basin.

He watched as she waded into the water, but he held back. She looked at him.

"Our clothes'll get wet." The explanation sounded lame even to his ears.

She giggled, as if wading into the water fully clothed was an everyday occurrence for her. "They will dry," she teased, pulling him with her.

Bill allowed her to lead him into the frothy, warm water, which lapped at his ankles, then at the knees of his trousers. He'd never seen her like this, so carefree, so happy. The transformation amazed him, and rather than watch the dolphin, which swam closer to receive her friendly pats and soft words, he watched her.

"You can pet him." She looked up. "He won't bite."

Bill patted the area close to the blowhole on the mammal's head, more to please her than the dolphin. Its skin was rubbery and cold. Through intelligent, friendly black eyes it viewed Bill and let out a series of whistles and clicks.

"Maliu likes you," Sarah said in approval.

Bill wondered how she had arrived at such a conclusion. Before he could ask, she swung her legs over the rock and mounted the dolphin as one would a horse. Her frame was slight and the dolphin was long, but her unexpected action put Bill at a loss for words.

As if it had taken this course many times, the dolphin swam with Sarah, circling the shallow waters as she held to its dorsal fin. Her hair hung in a silky curtain, its ends trailing the water. Her face and arms glistened with droplets, and Bill thought he'd never seen a more breathtaking sight as Sarah enjoying a ride on her pet.

She continued laughing as the dolphin neared him. Instead of reentering the pool where he still stood with water past his knees, she slid off the dolphin's back until she was immersed neck-deep in the sea.

"Swim with me?" she asked, treading the water.

The appeal of Sarah almost had him diving in to frolic in the sea beside her. "Too much physical activity isn't good for me right now."

Concern covered her face, and her gaze lowered to his shirt. "You are in pain?"

"Not much. I think I'd rather just sit and watch you." He took a seat on the lumpy lavalike rock shelf that rose inches above the water.

Her smile seemed uncertain, but she gracefully turned her back to him. Her head dipped beneath the water to reappear yards farther out. The loose, knee-length flowered dress she wore didn't impede her movements, and he watched her swim through the water as if she were a mermaid born to it. With every ounce of restraint he held back, though he wished to be there with her, to capture her in his embrace, to hold her, to touch her, and yes, to kiss her again.

He inhaled a shaky breath.

Sarah, Sarah. . .what are you doing to me?

Chapter 4

I would like more coconut milk." Josiah leaned back in his chair and held out his cup to Sarah. "Please."

Brows gathered in evident confusion, she looked into the empty container, then at her father. "I will need to gather them. We finished the last with our meal."

"Take your time."

Alert, Bill watched Sarah leave the hut, then turned to look at the missionary. He'd never noticed Josiah had a particular fondness for the ultra sweet, watery milk and suspected a deeper reason hid within the man's directive to his daughter.

Josiah closed his Bible, laid it with infinite care upon the desk, then turned his attention toward Bill. "I have long considered what I'm about to say, and I have a favor to ask."

Bill tensed. Gravity steeled the man's quiet words, putting Bill on the immediate defensive. "I can't promise anything."

"Nor should you without knowing the circumstances." Josiah shifted his gaze to the window and the sea beyond. "When you are ready to leave our island, when a ship comes to take you back to the States, I want you to take Sarah with you."

Bill stared. Surely he couldn't have heard right.

Josiah looked at him, his eyes deadly serious. "This is the only home she's known, and it's time she discovered where my roots lie. I want her to be among other God-fearing Christians, and though there are those here who have come to know Christ, she isn't finding what she needs on this island. I blame myself. Had I been more attentive after my wife died, she might not have sought wisdom from her aunt, who deplores my faith. I only pray any damage done is reversible. You can help me, Bill. You can help me make my peace with God by doing what's best for Sarah."

Bill shot up from his chair and paced to the window. He plowed a hand through his hair. "You don't know what you're asking. You don't know the man I am."

"I've watched you these past weeks. You have a hunger for God, a sincere thirst for knowledge of the truth, and I haven't seen that desire exhibited in many young men. What are you, thirty?"

"Twenty-seven." The reply came automatically, his mind still in conflict with Josiah's request.

Josiah nodded. "God's called you, Bill. You can't escape Him, though you've tried. He saved your life and has chosen you. You're the one holding back, but from your avid questions lately, I don't think it will be much longer until you reach the place of acceptance in Christ."

Bill swung around. "You don't get it—I killed a man. Several men."

Josiah calmly regarded Bill as if he'd just told him he'd swatted a fly.

"Don't you understand?" Bill swung his hands out to the sides. "I'm not worth the trouble."

"Whatever sins lay in your past, God has knowledge of every one of them. Still, He desires you to come to Him, just as He called Saul and gave him a new name and a new mission. He brought you to this island, carried on the back of a dolphin, to recover in a missionary's hut. Do you not see the irony of that?" He chuckled, but Bill didn't feel like laughing. "Would it ease your mind to talk of it?"

Bill closed his eyes. He'd pushed the killings to a far corner of his mind, hoping the memory would rot and disintegrate there. But bad memories never died. "It was either be gunned down or pull the trigger. When someone points a gun at your heart, you don't ask questions."

"I understand."

"Do you?" Bill turned on him. "How can you? Have you ever killed a man in cold blood? Watched as the life seeped from him, as his eyes filled with fear? As he reached up as though begging you somehow to save him, to turn back time—when only seconds before he was the enemy?" He clutched handfuls of his hair. Tore at it while stalking away.

"Yes."

The word came so soft at first Bill didn't think he'd heard correctly.

"Years before I became a missionary, I was a violent young man accustomed to barroom brawling."

Bill swung around to face Josiah.

"During one such brawl, I confronted a peer who'd proven to be an enemy to my selfish desires. I was drunk. I was angry. I knew when to quit but didn't. He kept coming at me, giving punch for punch. I hit him over the head with a chair. He crumpled at my feet. Yet even then, Bill, even then I drew back my fist to finish him off. It was the look in his eyes that stopped me. I'd never seen such fear, such knowing. He reached up—not with his fist—but with his hand out-stretched, and clasped my shoulder as if to hold on, as if he were drowning and I was his rope. Something inside me broke. Instead of punching him, I cradled him against me as if he were a child. He died that night. So you see, Bill, I do know."

Gripping silence filled the air. Throat working hard against emotion, Bill swallowed and stared into the cheerless face of the calm man before him. Then without another word, he turned and left the hut.

Twilight's indigo darkness colored the warm air as Sarah returned, her arms laden with coconuts. She couldn't help but feel her father had pushed her out. That he wanted to talk to Bill alone was patently obvious. She had obeyed, yes, but at the same time she'd shielded her true feelings of hurt confusion.

The sound of gasping, as though someone were struggling for air to breathe, made her stop in alarm. Quickly she moved through the trees, her steps silent. She spotted Bill standing at the edge of the cliff, his back to her, the moon silvering his fair hair. The peaceful thunder of the reef echoed beyond. His shoulders shook.

"I'll never understand," he rasped. "Not in a million years. It makes no sense. But who am I to talk about sense? An ex-mobster. A chiseler, a racketeer, and God knows what else. . . ." His chuckle was dry. "Yeah, I guess You do know, don't You? I guess there's no hiding anything from You, though I certainly never tried. Lay all one's cards out on the table—that was always Lucky Bill's motto. So here I am, laying out every filthy card in my deck."

Sarah struggled to hear his next words.

"I have no idea why You'd want the likes of me, but after hearing Josiah's story, I've got no more excuses to run. I've heard what's been read every night for the past two weeks—all about You and what You've done—and I recognize truth for what it is. You got my attention with the dolphin, but being forced to listen really opened my eyes." He let out a self-derisive laugh. "I think I might've recognized the truth when Brent was always preaching it, but I was too much of a tough guy to admit it. I always felt my luck would carry me through, that I didn't need You. But those days are gone. I don't feel so tough or so lucky anymore."

As Sarah watched, Bill dropped to his knees. Her arms tightened around the coconuts. Compassion knotted her throat.

"Josiah said all I had to do was ask You to take over, Jesus. So that's what I'm doing. I've made a huge mess of things, and I have no idea where I'm going. But one thing I'm sure of is that I need You at the helm." He let out a thundering breath in a humorless laugh. "Not sure how that'll work since I've been captain of my ship for so long, doing things my way. But I'm willing to turn the wheel over now. You sure couldn't make things any worse than they already are."

His last words were hoarse, and he bowed his head. Deep sobs shook his body.

Her heart twisted at his brokenness. Something inside whispered for Sarah to go forward, to lay her hand against his shoulder, but she held back, thinking he might not welcome her eavesdropping.

She should have made her presence known, but she hadn't wanted to disturb him. Nor had she wanted to slip away. To secretly share in Bill's decision pleased her. She couldn't recall a time in which a villager's decision for Christ gave her such joy as did Bill's soul-stirring, heart-to-heart talk with God.

Teary-eyed, she watched him several seconds longer, then silently retraced her steps to her father's hut.

🕮

"Now that I've told you about my home, will you show me your island, Sarah?"

The question startled her, and she turned to study Bill.

"I need the exercise after lying around like a vegetable for so long."

Of its own accord, her gaze flicked down his trim physique; she couldn't see that his convalescence had caused him to suffer in that regard. Embarrassed by the thought, she looked up into his eyes, which regarded her steadily but with none of the predatory animal look that had been in them during his first two weeks on the island.

She glanced away, stacking the last of her father's books on the shelf above his desk. "If you would like."

"I would like very much."

Tenderness laced his voice, making her warm all over. "Then we should go now before the hour comes that I must prepare dinner."

"I'm ready as a rooster."

She looked at him, confused by the terminology as she often was when he used what he called "slang."

He smiled and motioned for her to precede him. "Lead the way."

She cast him an uncertain smile before walking out of the hut. He soon joined her on the path. Why she should feel so awkward, she didn't understand, and she fished for something to say.

"It is difficult for me to see in my mind this Manhattan of which you speak. I cannot imagine buildings so tall they reach to the clouds, nor the absence of so many trees." She looked at the wild panorama of greenery and color all around her. In the boughs of the breadfruit trees, birds let loose shrill cries, and geckos sought their shade. "What do the lizards climb if there are no trees? Where do the birds build their nests?"

Bill laughed and the sound stirred her heart. "Sarah, you're a delight. New York has no lizards, at least not giant ones that run amok like they do here. We have birds, though, and a park in the middle of the city. I guess they make their home there."

"No lizards?" She thought about that. "What about snakes or sharks?"

"Not snakes like here. And the real sharks wear three-piece suits with felt fedoras and carry guns." The smile left his face, and Sarah wished to bring it back.

"Today, I will show you my favorite place on the island." She smiled wide, attempting to rekindle his happiness. "It is where I go when circumstances lie heavy on my heart and I must think."

A Gentle Fragrance

They walked deeper into the forest while she answered Bill's frequent questions about the flora, the fauna, and the village. Sarah carefully avoided areas she knew presented dangers, both on the paths over which they walked and in the answers she gave about the people and their customs.

"I can see why you love this island. Do you think you'll ever want to leave?"

His low words made Sarah stare. "I cannot think of leaving, it is all I know. . . and yet. . ."

"Yes?" he prompted when she remained silent.

"I've wondered what lies beyond the sea. My father's books show me much, but they cannot tell me all I wish to know." His question made her uneasy, as did the steady look he gave, and she moved ahead. "It's up here, this place I wish to show you."

As they neared the area, Sarah heard the running of water rushing upon itself and quickened her pace. She rounded the corner and parted the bushes for Bill, watching his expression. His eyes brightened, and he smiled.

"This is great, Sarah. I can see why you'd want to come here."

Pleased with his response, she viewed the lofty wall of bushes that surrounded the clearing, as though nurturing the waterfall and pool nestled within, secreting it away for her sole pleasure. Exotic flowers of ruby, violet, and gold bloomed from the bushes, and the grass lay soft beneath her feet. A natural rockslide stood at the edge, connected to the pool, something she'd enjoyed many times in her girlhood.

"So quiet all of a sudden?" Bill prodded.

"At times, I wish for my childhood back. Things were so uncomplicated then."

"And what's to complicate your life now?" He plucked a red hibiscus from a bush and slid it behind her ear. "There. That's what was missing."

The touch of his fingers on her hair, at her ear, made her breath catch.

"Sarah?" His smile faded, and his eyes grew serious.

She turned away, looking at the pool. She did want him to kiss her; she didn't want him to kiss her. Never had she been so confused. But she didn't want him to think her weak, and she masked her expression before facing him.

"You are right. There is little to complicate my life; I am blessed."

He narrowed his eyes, studying her, when suddenly an ear-splitting screech split the air.

❧

Alarmed, Bill looked up, just as a furry animal jumped down on him from the trees, its legs and arms spread wide. "Agh!" He slapped at the creature hanging on to him from behind, trying to wrest its hairy arms from around his shoulders, and was surprised to hear Sarah laughing.

"Mutu, you naughty boy," she said between chortles.

The thing had a hand and began thumping Bill on the head with the flat of it.

"Get it off me!" he demanded.

"Mutu will harm no one. He only wants to be friends."

"This is friendly?" Bill grimaced as the monkey poked its finger into his ear. "Since you appear to be on good terms with the creatures of the animal kingdom, will you please tell it to get off?"

"Mutu, come. You mustn't treat our guest in such a way."

The animal didn't budge, letting out a few *ha-hoo, ha-hoo*s as though arguing with her.

"Perhaps if we walk back to the hut, Mutu will lose interest."

"I've never seen him before," Bill said, striving for patience as he walked with her. "I didn't know the island had monkeys." Now he could feel the inquisitive beast pulling up strands of his hair to study it. At least he hoped that's all it was doing and that it didn't have an appetite for hair.

"Mutu was a freewill gift from a sea captain to my father. But Father will not let him into the hut. He does not like Mutu."

Bill had no problem understanding that viewpoint.

"He sometimes visits me outside when I do chores. And he walks with me over the island when I visit my aunt."

"Do you go to the vill-age arfen?" Bill tried to talk around the monkey's fingers, which now pulled at his lower lip.

"Mutu, stop that." Her voice rang with quiet authority. To Bill's relief, the monkey unlooped its arms from around him and fastened them around her neck, jumping to her side and wrapping its legs around her. Not pausing in her steps, she looped her arm around its back. "I go as often as necessary."

"Do you act as a nurse there? A teacher?"

She hesitated. "My aunt teaches me many things. I go to learn from her."

Remembering what Josiah said, Bill looked at her. "The beliefs of your mother's people?"

"Do not judge what you do not understand."

"How can I learn the truth if I don't raise questions?" When she didn't respond, he persisted. "Last night, your father read that the Almighty God is a jealous God and there should be no others before Him. Yet isn't that what your relatives do? Put other gods before Him? Even ancestor worship? So why do you take part in it?"

Her step faltered. Bill reached out to grab her, but she quickly regained ground. The monkey chattered at him.

"I do not take part. I go to learn the ancient beliefs and stories of my mother's people. That is all."

"Why? Your father told me that the Bible forbids us to conform to the world's ideals. Wouldn't that same rule apply to life on this island? Tell me. I wish to know, Sarah. How can what your aunt teaches you and what your father teaches you be in any way related?"

She frowned, drawing her brows together. "You must speak of this with my father. I'm not well versed enough in the Word to give you an answer."

Silence settled between them, broken only by the monkey's chattering and the myriad calls of birds in the trees. Once they reached the hut, Sarah made her excuses that she must see to the meal and left with the monkey still riding her hip. Bill watched her go, then turned his attention to her father, who sat about fifty feet away, whittling on something, with his back against the trunk of a palm. Bill moved toward him.

"Did you have a pleasant walk?" Josiah asked, never taking his eyes from the knife he used to cut grooves onto the stick he held.

"You realize that to take Sarah off this island and onto a ship of rowdy sailors for weeks on end is dangerous, don't you?" Bill greeted him. "Have you thought that through? She's beautiful and intelligent, but she's also naive."

"So, you've decided to return and stop running. I'm glad. You'll never be free until you face your fears."

Bill shrugged, as if it were of little consequence, when in reality he'd thought of little else since the night he'd turned to God. The idea of returning had nagged at him until he could no longer push it away. He could lose himself in New York at the reform school where his brother taught. The sea, the islands, they were wild and beautiful, but he missed home.

"I sense you're the type of man to protect others." Josiah's response came lazily. "You'll see to it that no harm comes to Sarah."

"But I can't be with her all the time!" Bill shook his head in frustration. "The vessel on which we sail will probably be a merchant mariner, like the one I was employed on—not a luxury passenger liner with a wide choice of rooms. And those sleeping berths don't have locks on the doors!"

"Well, then. . ." With unhurried ease, Josiah put his handiwork aside, also laying down his knife. He looked up, regarding Bill steadily. "There appears to be only one recourse."

Bill snorted. "And what's that?"

"Marry my daughter."

Chapter 5

Marry Sarah? *Marry Sarah?*

Bill struggled with the idea from the moment he had blinked at Josiah after the man had calmly uttered those profound words. Bill then spun on his heel—away from the absurd suggestion—running from it, right up until now, as he sat on the empty beach and stared at the moon. They would probably wonder why he hadn't returned for dinner, but at this moment, Bill didn't care. He had no desire to face either of them.

Yes, she was a beauty, and he was, without a doubt, attracted to her. The thought of holding Sarah in his arms—as his wife—sent warmth soaring through his veins. Her purity, her sweetness drew him. Her intelligence amazed him and at other times needled him. Though he'd never submitted to any authority, he respected the gentle obedience she exhibited toward her father and the loyalty she showed her aunt, even if he didn't understand her reasons for doing what he'd heard was wrong.

But Bill wasn't the marrying type. Never had been. Never would be. That sort of thing was for men like his brother, Brent.

Bill released a pent-up breath and rose from the sand, dusting off his trousers. He picked up a shell and pitched it toward the colorless sea. It disappeared in the silvery blackness.

That's what he'd attempted to do. Disappear. But it was time to resurface. He'd known it, even before Josiah broached the subject weeks ago. New York shouldn't hold any dangers since Vittorio thought him dead. And Sarah would enjoy discovering the countryside. . . .

No. Bill clenched his jaw. He may be a "new man," as Josiah had told him, but marriage didn't fit in with his plans for a new life, either. Josiah would just have to understand.

Guilt swamped Bill. The missionary had done so much for him: opened his home and ministered to his needs both physical and spiritual, saved his life. Bill now looked forward to his nightly talks with Josiah and realized how heavily he relied on the man's insights and wisdom. His own father had never had time for him, never approved of him, and Josiah had filled the father role in Bill's life.

But marry Sarah? Asking him to link his life to another person's for all his natural-born days? Well, that was just asking too much.

❧

Sarah sat on the floor of her aunt's hut. While Aunt Lefu prepared octopus for the evening meal, Sarah continued to weave the golden-white thin strands from the pandanus tree for the fine mat she had worked on for two years, as was custom for her dowry.

"The time has come that you should marry, Sarah. I do not understand your father in this matter of choice he's given you." Aunt Lefu raised her hands in irritation and shook her head of thick black hair. "I was told whom I would marry."

"But you were born to *taupo*. As a chief's daughter, more was expected of you."

Lefu's mouth thinned. "Your father's way will see you old and unmarried. Are there no boys in the village to interest you?"

Sarah wove the fronds. She didn't want a boy. She wanted a man. A man such as Bill.

Heat seared her cool cheeks, and Lefu's eyes narrowed.

"So, you have interest in a bridegroom! Is it Nua? He stares at you often with moon eyes."

Sarah ignored that. She didn't think much of Ono's young son, who exhibited as much intelligence as a land crab and proved to be about as agile.

Lefu grunted. "Very well. It is time we speak of what will be required of you."

Sarah briefly looked up, uncertain of what was coming.

"Your husband you must serve, and you must be submissive to him. But never let him see what lies within your heart. That shows weakness, Sarah. You must guard your emotions well, for that is your strength. I have taught you this since you were young, but still you forget. Do not be like the weak or simpering—like the silly women of this village, Meta and others. You are the granddaughter of a chieftain. Because of this, do not go with a suitor if he asks you on a nighttime tryst. You must show no eagerness, another failing you have. And it is not wise to walk around the island without a chaperone."

Sarah couldn't imagine always being guarded as many of the young, unmarried daughters of higher rank were. "I'm careful. I talk to no one."

"And what of this man Bill?"

Sarah's eyes snapped up from her task.

"You look at me in surprise. Did you think I would not learn of him and your walks over the island? Meta does not know how to control her tongue."

Sarah swallowed hard. "My father approves."

"Your father does not understand the ways of our people. If the village men thought you were violated, there might be no offers of marriage. It is bad enough you are a missionary's daughter. Do not add to those sins."

Uneasy, Sarah's glance went to the sun, lowering beyond the mountain. "It is late. I need to prepare the fish." At least, she hoped Bill and her father had caught fish. A second night of bananas, yams, and taro didn't appeal.

"Guard my words well, Sarah."

Her aunt's parting admonition followed Sarah the entire walk home. Bill approached her from the path to the beach, his face animated, so unlike the distance he'd shown since their return from the waterfall. Often these days she would catch him staring at her, but rarely did he speak.

"I caught a fish!" Bill announced. "With a spear!"

"That is good." Remembering her aunt's words, she tempered her happy smile at seeing him until her face was a mask of indifference. "I will go and prepare it. And you, Father?" She turned to watch as he came up behind Bill.

"Two small ones. His catch should adequately feed all of us. How is Lefu?"

"She is well." She hesitated. "She thinks it is time I seek a husband. Perhaps she is right." Without looking at Bill, Sarah walked to the hut to start a fire for the fish.

❧

Unable to relax, Bill took the path to the beach after his nightly talk with Josiah. His mind went to the meeting he'd had yesterday when several men had returned from their day of fishing, pulling their canoe up to the beach, and Josiah had made introductions.

A few of those men had been loudly teasing a skinny boy named Nua of his love for a young woman and a poem he'd written but never given her. Nua had cast quick glances to Josiah as he approached with Bill, as if nervous the older man should hear, and the others quieted upon seeing the missionary.

Surely such talk had not been a cause for shame. . .unless the reason for their sudden silence had to do with Sarah. Had she been the woman discussed?

She thinks it is time I seek a husband. Perhaps she is right.

Sarah's earlier parting words left an indelible imprint on Bill's brain. So what if Sarah married one of the villagers? That certainly would solve his problem. If she gained interest in one of the island men, then Bill could depart to America in peace, freed from any guilt and matrimonial ties.

A woman's lilting laugh cornered his mind. Curious, he walked along the path to the beach, staying hidden beyond a fringe of palms.

Against the flame of sky that stretched over the waters, Sarah played with a boy and girl who'd wandered far from the village. They chased Sarah, all of them giggling, through the surf. Sarah visibly slowed her pace so they could catch her, and both children threw their arms around her waist, all three of them falling into the water, laughing harder. Pensive, Bill watched the gaiety a while longer before he turned and headed back up the path and into the hut.

Josiah sat at his desk and looked up from the letter he was writing.

"All right," Bill said without preamble. "I'll marry Sarah."

152

Sarah stood and listened to the waterfall whisper to her one last time.

When Bill had approached her two nights ago and asked to speak to her alone, she wasn't prepared for the shock when he said her father wanted him to take her back with him to America on a ship that had recently arrived. But when Bill further explained that it would be to Sarah's benefit if she married him first, an arrangement to which her father also agreed, she'd only stared, speechless.

A loveless proposal for a marriage. An arrangement of convenience.

Her father later affirmed Bill's words, and they'd talked long into the night while Bill slept. She'd been curious about the world beyond her little island, and Father wanted her to learn of the customs and the land from which he came, though he'd assured her the decision to marry Bill would be hers alone. One day soon, according to Aunt Lefu, she must wed, and no villager attracted her as a potential bridegroom. As such, she'd thought she would spend her life serving her father, taking care of him, and that idea had been satisfactory.

Until Bill had washed up on shore.

"Sarah?"

She turned, startled to hear his voice. He appeared through the bushes.

"I thought I'd find you here. It's time. The ship leaves in an hour."

Nodding mutely, she kept her expression blank. She wouldn't let him know how terrified she was at this moment.

"Wait," he said before she could precede him onto the path.

She turned to look and felt the stem of a hibiscus slide into her hair above her ear.

"That's better. You should always wear flowers. They look good on you." His voice was as taut as his smile.

The next hour went by in a haze for Sarah. Standing beside Bill as her father read from the book he used for Christian ceremonies of this nature. . .her soft answers to his questions to love, honor, and obey mirroring the gravity of Bill's responses. . .the stiff kiss Bill imparted to her lips once her father pronounced them man and wife. . .the villagers' hugs and well wishes for a safe journey.

Only Aunt Lefu held herself aloof, distant from the others, though her parting hug to Sarah was warm. "I do not understand your choice, Sarah, or your wish to leave us. But I will always carry you in my heart. Remember all I have taught you."

"I will."

Her father hugged her long and hard, and she couldn't stem the tears that streamed down her cheeks.

"I shall miss you; I cannot imagine what life will be like without you." Sarah pulled back and memorized the lines of his dear, craggy face.

"I knew this day must come, long before you did." His own eyes were watery.

"It's as it should be. Bill's a good man; he'll make you a fine husband." He put into her hands the cross on which he'd been whittling for weeks. Onto the wooden stick as long as her forearm and half its thickness, he'd carved beautiful wavy marks and pictures.

"It's a piece of our life. Each symbol represents a monumental event that took place, and each groove represents the love and prayers I continually have for you. The shape is in a cross to remind you that our Savior has been and always will be in control of your life and holds us together in spirit. Guard it well, Sarah."

Moved beyond words, she nodded, kissed his cheek, then turned to walk with her new husband toward the small ship that would carry her away to an indistinct world. Behind, the villagers lifted their voices in a song of farewell. Her hold on the cross tightened. Bleak uncertainty threatened her resolve not to cry.

Bill touched her arm. "It'll be all right."

She looked at him, then back at the ship, and continued her course.

Chapter 6

Days later, Bill gripped the ship's rail. How much longer he could keep up this distance, he didn't know. Just to be with Sarah in close quarters, to smell her sweet fragrance, to look into her fathomless eyes, to hear the melody of her words was almost more than he could bear. And those times she inadvertently brushed against him sent fire surging through his veins. Purposely he stayed away, waiting until the early morning hours when he was physically exhausted and she was sound asleep before allowing himself to lie down, his back to her.

He'd half convinced himself that he married Sarah to repay the man who'd saved his life and in gratitude to Sarah for all she'd done—to help her find a good life in America as her father wished. Honorable intentions. All lies.

Now that he was being honest with himself, Bill knew his true reason for marrying Sarah was entirely selfish. He didn't want Sarah to come to him in submission; he wanted her to come to him in love. Nothing else would do.

He loved her and wanted her for his wife. She *was* his wife. And somehow, he would make her love a blackguard like himself. She'd only married him in compliance with her father's wishes. Bill had seen her daughterly obedience in every regard, and if she *did* have feelings for him, why then did she never show it? Her expression was always so placid. She'd rarely smiled since they married. The only time he'd seen Sarah display any emotion, besides her frolicking with the animals and children, was when she'd parted with her father. Then the tears had fallen in earnest, and he'd seen the emptiness that hollowed her eyes.

Bill felt like a criminal, taking Sarah away from all she loved, even if it was at the request of her father. Somehow, he would get through these days at sea. Once they were in New York at his brother's home, the situation was bound to be easier than it was with them both being so confined.

At least the captain's orders made Bill's life a little easier.

❧

Her father's stories of what to expect couldn't prepare Sarah for life aboard a ship, especially one filled with sailors who spent their lives at sea. The shipping vessel on which they journeyed wasn't supplied with suitable quarters for a woman. However, when a few men showed immediate interest in Sarah within an hour after they'd boarded and set sail, and it almost led to a fistfight with Bill and the rowdy sailors, the captain informed them both that she and Bill would be given his quarters for the duration of the voyage. The captain asked Sarah to stay within the cabin to avoid further conflicts. She knew he wasn't pleased to have her aboard, being the superstitious sort who didn't cater to a woman being on his ship, but at both Bill's and her father's persuasion, he had allowed her passage.

The first few days, she'd been seasick and hadn't minded staying inside, but after a week, she recovered enough that if she didn't leave the cabin, she would go mad. Her father at some point had secreted his small Bible, filled with his handwritten notes, into the canvas bag containing all her worldly possessions from the island. And that thoughtful gift helped to fill many empty hours.

Bill, for the most part, stayed absent. In fact, he hadn't touched her since they'd boarded ship, and that confused her greatly. She knew little of what went on in a marriage; her aunt had left her ignorant in that regard. Perhaps he'd made no move toward her because he regretted taking her as his wife.

The torturing thought plagued Sarah's heart.

Nighttime had come, and the lure of fresh air, the need to leave such confining quarters, brought her out of the cabin. This late, it surely couldn't hurt to seize several minutes alone on deck.

She climbed the narrow stairs, alert to every sound and grateful for no sign of humanity. The salty air breezed across her face, and she inhaled a deep, cleansing breath before walking farther. To feel the coolness against her skin was sheer bliss after the imprisonment of the cabin. The sound of men's faint voices rolled from the front of the ship. She caught sight of Bill standing alone at the side.

Grabbing the rail, he looked out over the black water, where a shimmer of moonlight formed an obscure path. He stood as if a weight burdened his soul. All at once he straightened, turned.

"Sarah? What are you doing up here?"

Closing the distance, she noted he didn't seem pleased to see her. "No one is nearby. Why should I not be allowed to partake of fresh air as everyone else on board does? As you do?"

Her words made him flinch. "Those were the captain's orders, not mine."

Resigned, she gave a nod. "I will return."

"Wait." He blew out a breath. "A few more minutes won't hurt. And it *is* quiet."

She watched him, not understanding his odd behavior. One minute he seemed angry with her; the next, he coveted her company. All week, it had been like this.

He solemnly studied her face. His gaze went to her hair, and he gathered a thick strand of it. "Pretty Sarah. . .how it shines in the moonlight," he whispered. "Like rich black satin."

Stunned, Sarah didn't move, didn't speak. Bill continued to slowly rub the lock of hair between his fingers, staring at it as if he'd never seen it before, letting it fall bit by bit to her shoulder. When he returned his gaze to hers, she inhaled an inaudible, expectant breath at the intense look in his eyes, thinking he might kiss her.

Instead, he took in a deep lungful of air and let it out slowly through his mouth. "You should return to the cabin—before the captain sees us, and we're both in trouble."

"Will you come also?"

His glance toward her came quick, and she read surprise there before he averted his gaze to some point mid-deck.

"I'll be along later, long after you're asleep. Don't wait up." He turned his attention to the sea.

Now that he couldn't see her, Sarah allowed her mask of detachment to fall away at his rejection. Hurt drew her brows together, and the sting of tears came as she swiftly retraced her steps.

The crash of thunder awoke Sarah. Heart beating fast, she jumped to a sitting position, clutching the blanket. Another deafening crash made her whimper and recoil, hitting against Bill, who lay beside her. On the island, she'd hated the rainy season with its never-ending storms, but on a rocking ship, the sound seemed magnified. She felt vulnerable, alone, abandoned. Would they all die?

"Sarah?" Bill asked groggily. She felt him sit up. "What's wrong?"

She couldn't answer, couldn't stop trembling.

"Sarah?" His voice was curious, soft. "Is it the storm?"

She gave an abrupt nod, squeezing her eyes shut when a white flash lit the entire cabin and thunder seemed to crack against the side of the ship.

His arms closed around her, drawing her close. "Shhh, it's all right. This isn't so bad. I've seen worse. There's no reason to fear, pretty Sarah. The ship appears to be a seaworthy vessel."

He smoothed his hand over her hair, kissed her temple, held her more tightly. His strength, his warmth helped to soothe her. She relaxed, resting her head against his shoulder. He stiffened.

"Don't let me go," she whispered, alarmed he might draw away.

And he didn't. All through the violent storm, he held her close to his heart. Even after the thunder abated, his arms remained around her. Now that the danger had passed, her senses became fully attuned to the man who held her. Her husband, and her mind wrapped around a night on the island. . .and a kiss.

Her heartbeat quickened, matching his.

"Sarah. . .?"

His voice was hoarse, full of an emotion she couldn't discern, but one that had her lifting her face to his in entreaty. A flash of delayed lightning revealed his searching expression, but a flame kindled in his eyes, taking Sarah's breath away.

Their kiss was both tender and consuming. A give and take that shook Sarah to her core, while reassuring her heart that at last all would be well between them.

Chapter 7

New York was more than Sarah could have imagined and nothing close to what she had dreamed. Accustomed to life on her quiet island with only bird cries and the ocean's surf to sing to her, she was unprepared for the raucous dissonance of sound that was Manhattan.

Noisy automobiles chugged and roared and popped. Hordes of people walked the sidewalks, a far greater number than were in her village, and they spoke and shouted and laughed. Everywhere there was motion; everywhere confusion.

Unconsciously, she drew closer to Bill, clutching his sleeve, then scolded herself for doing so and released it. After that wondrous night they'd shared in one another's arms, Sarah had awoken to find Bill gone. Memory of her childish fear of the storm then broke through the cloud of sweet contentment and twined itself around her mind. She now regretted that she'd let him observe such weakness in her. Aunt Lefu would have been displeased. Sarah assumed that at some point later in the night, Bill had recalled her shortcomings, her panicked tears, her clutching tightly to him like a child, and had been disappointed in her weakness. No other explanation presented itself as to why he would leave her before daybreak and again put emotional distance between them—as he had put distance between them throughout the following weeks, though he'd been polite, even charming. She could not fault him for that. Yet after the intimacy they'd shared, he now seemed as if he were attempting to be a stranger.

Women dressed in boyish, drab dresses with their hair cut in bobs or piled in strange shapes on their heads and wearing outlandish hats, eyed Sarah with looks ranging from horror to curiosity to outrage. Sarah looked down at her sarong and unadorned loose hair. She did not fit in with these people.

Bill must have arrived at the same conclusion, for he immediately herded her to one of many similar buildings that lined the streets, putting her under the care of an elderly lady who hemmed and hawed throughout most of what she called a fitting. Within hours, Sarah was outfitted in a shapeless dress as drab as the rest of them she'd seen. She endured the changes for Bill, hoping he would then look at her with approval, hoping he would look at her at all.

He did look at her, but not in delight. Rather his eyes were sad. Trying to see what he did, she lowered her gaze to the calf-length, gray-checked chemise with its low waistline, and the thick braid hanging past her stomach that she'd allowed the lady to weave when Sarah would not let her pile it atop her head.

"We need to catch the train in an hour. Are you ready?" Bill's voice was somber, distant.

Sarah inwardly sighed. "Yes." Was she? If he did not accept her or approve of her appearance, how then did she expect his people to?

The huge expanse of Pennsylvania Station with its many levels of stairs overwhelmed Sarah. She did not resist clutching Bill's arm this time, fearing she might lose him in the crowds of people swarming all around her.

Only when they were safely sheltered within a compartment on a train did Sarah allow herself the pleasure of relaxing. She had never been on a train either, but she was so tired, and she closed her eyes.

❧

Bill watched Sarah as she slept. Her face lacked the color it had held on the island, her posture was weary, and Bill's heart constricted that he'd had to bow to the dictates of society and clothe her in a dress that seemed entirely inappropriate for his free-spirited Sarah. He'd been annoyed by the looks cast her way from snobbish women who'd crossed their path and had hoped to alleviate the problem with a portion of the money Josiah had given him for the journey. Yet the obnoxious ogling continued, and he knew Sarah must have felt their silent barbs. For himself, he didn't care. He'd had worse stares thrown his way. But for Sarah, he desired her happiness and comfort.

Since that night of heaven, when he and Sarah had become one, Bill had run the gamut of emotions. His love and desire to protect had intensified, but at the same time, when he'd awoken to see his beautiful Sarah lying beside him, oppressive anguish tore at his soul. Self-bitterness raged through him that he'd taken advantage of her vulnerability and allowed his own weakness, his strong desire to be with her, to overtake his objective.

Bill had never known love. Not from his parents, not from his associates, not from former girlfriends, of which there'd been a number. Yet those painted floozies with their selfish ambitions couldn't hold a candle to Sarah. For the first time, Bill knew what it was to love, and he desperately wanted her love in return.

Maybe if Sarah had told him she loved him after he'd whispered to her his own adoration as she lay within his arms, he'd feel differently. Maybe if she'd shown any emotion on her face the next morning when he'd bolstered enough courage to reenter their cabin. But she hadn't. Instead she regarded him, her face as placid as always, her eyes blank.

And that look had blasted his heart as surely as if she'd pulled the trigger of a gun.

Closing his eyes, he tried to rest. The next few hours of their uncertain future were trying enough without dredging up the recent past. That Brent would be surprised to see his long-lost brother was a given. Hopefully surprise would

160

be the only negative reaction, and there would be a welcome. Bill had been given no opportunity to write a letter announcing their arrival, no method by which to send it, and even if he had, he didn't know the address of the reform school.

Reform school. He let out a derisive chuckle. For the past twelve years, he'd done his best to evade the police, and now he was bringing his new wife with him to a place that most likely contained bars on the windows.

But Vittorio was still out there, he and the rest of his mobsters. And until Bill was far away from Manhattan, he wouldn't feel safe. A small town near Ithaca seemed like the perfect solution.

❧

Once they exited the train, Sarah stood with Bill on the wooden platform. He carried her canvas bag and looked around the area, his features rigid. Clutching her father's cross to her heart for reassurance, she also studied the town. Here the buildings were much smaller, not so tall, and she counted only one automobile puttering along the street. A red- and white-striped pole stood nearby. On the window next to it, the words BARBER SHOP were painted in white.

Bill also stared in that direction and swept a hand over the back of his hair. "I guess if I want to make a good impression with my brother, I'd better get a trim. I let it grow good and wild on the island." He looked at Sarah, as if suddenly unsure what to do with her. "There's a shop you can visit next door. Why don't you wait for me there? A barber shop isn't a place for ladies."

Sarah nodded, taking comfort in the fact that he would be in the building beside her. This place was much quieter than the city in which the ship had docked, but she still felt in limbo in this strange new world.

They parted at the doorway. Sarah's heart went weak when the expression in Bill's eyes softened for an instant, and he smiled. "I'll only be next door."

She watched as he disappeared into the barbershop. Her interest to explore revived, and she turned to see what this building contained. The room into which Sarah walked seemed dark after just coming out of bright sunlight. The area smelled of coffee and tobacco. Other scents tantalized—unusual but appealing scents—and she approached the wooden counter. An array of jars filled with mixtures of all shapes and colors heightened her curiosity.

"That horehound candy is especially nice, though I prefer fresh peaches and plums meself," a friendly but strange-sounding voice observed from behind her. The accent was unusual, unlike any Sarah had heard. She turned around to see a woman of about the same height as herself, with a flowered hat rakishly perched atop her piled-up hair. Her eyes, the color of indigo blue waters, sparkled with mischief and fun. Sarah felt a pang of homesickness as she was reminded of her father and his penchant for joviality. A baby lay nestled against the woman's shoulder.

The woman held out a hand. "Me name's Darcy. And you are?"

"Sarah." She could barely speak, for as the child yawned and opened his eyes, she saw the same turquoise blue as her husband's. A closer examination of the little round face made her catch a swift breath. This child could be her husband's! He looked like a small copy of Bill.

"Are you all right, luv?" Darcy asked in concern. Her dark brows raised in confusion, she looked at the golden-haired boy then at Sarah again.

Sarah strived for composure. "Yes. It's just that—"

The door suddenly opened, and in walked Bill. Sarah blinked. No, not Bill. This man wore different clothing, and he held a child of the same age. . .identical to the one the woman Darcy held. The same in age and size, at least, though the child he held was a girl. Sarah looked back and forth between the two, then up into the man's face. The same turquoise-colored eyes, same long nose and high cheekbones. Only upon looking more intently could she tell his unshaven jaw wasn't quite as strong and defined as Bill's without his beard, his brows weren't as thick, his hair wasn't as long. Except for those small differences, they could be the same person.

Sarah swallowed and clutched the cross more tightly, feeling dizzy. For as she looked from face to face, she realized this must be her husband's family. Remembering snippets of conversation Bill had shared with her, she knew this must be the brother with whom Bill had been estranged for quite some time.

The door opened again. Bill stepped inside. "Barbershop's full. Too many people in line for me to wait around, and—" He cut off abruptly, halting his advance, as his image holding the child swung to face him.

Stunned silence crackled the air between them.

"Brent." Bill's word came out taut as he gave a slight nod.

"Bill. . ." The man holding the child blinked, then shook his head. "I don't believe it. Though the fact that you still exhibit a tendency for impatience doesn't surprise me in the slightest."

"Yeah, well, you know I never was one to bide my time well." Bill's words were casual, but Sarah could tell he was nervous. He looked at her, then moved her way. "And this is Sarah. My wife." His hand went to her back, and she was grateful for his support. Without it, she might have fallen in a dead faint. The blood seemed to surge from her head.

Bill's brother stared at her, his eyes wide in shock. After another set of tense seconds elapsed, Darcy glanced at him curiously, then stepped forward with a smile. "I knew the moment I laid eyes on you I'd like you, Sarah. You're an odd duck like meself, so we're a matched set. Welcome to the family." She gave her a quick one-armed embrace.

Sarah blinked. Bill stared. Brent gawked.

"Well now!" Darcy spoke again, her voice high and chipper as if to lighten the situation. She shifted the child to her other shoulder. "I think we should move this little reunion to Lyons' Refuge where it belongs. What d'ye say, guv'ner?" She looped her hand around Brent's forearm, moving closer to him.

He visibly relaxed, glanced at her, then back at Bill. "Before I agree, I feel it my duty to ask: Will we be expecting only the two of you? Or will the cops and robbers be beating a path to our door, as well?"

Darcy laughed nervously. Sarah could see a bald little man had taken a stand behind the counter and listened with rapt attention. He slowly rubbed a cloth over some tins on a shelf, his widened eyes fixed on the group in front of him.

Bill's mouth quirked in a parody of a smile. "Well, little brother, I see you've found the quality of humor somewhere inside that intelligent brain of yours, after all." He softly snorted and gave a faint shake of his head as if in self-mockery. "And yes, it will be just the two of us."

Brent gave a curt nod. "In that case, you're welcome to visit. The wagon is outside. Come along, Darcy." He turned without waiting for Bill's reply.

Darcy gave an uncertain smile and followed. Sarah threw a sharp glance at Bill. His answering nod reassured, but now she wondered if these people would ever accept them as members of their household.

Chapter 8

That had not gone well.

Blowing out a heavy breath, Bill sat with Sarah in the back of the wagon that took them to Lyons' Refuge. All his plans to confidently approach Brent—clean-shaven, hair neatly trimmed, and clad in a decent suit of clothes—had failed. The shirt he wore was Josiah's, given to him after the remnants of his own shirt were thrown out. He had needed to wear it unbuttoned on the island since the man was slighter in build. But once they reached New York, Bill had forced the buttons through the holes, though the material strained across his shoulders and made movement difficult. And his trousers were frayed at the ends.

He supposed he should have purchased a suit of clothes while he waited on Sarah, but he didn't feel confident showing his face around the area on the chance someone might recognize him. On second thought, that chance was slim. A growth of beard covered his face, and his hair hung almost to his shoulders. He looked like what he was—a former castaway of a Pacific island. *Not* the impression he'd wanted to make on his brother as a man who'd renounced his corrupt behavior.

Sarah, on the other hand, looked wonderful. She may not completely have conformed to protocol concerning dress, but Bill wouldn't have her any other way. He loved her long hair and was glad she hadn't cut it in a bob or stuck it up in some ridiculous bouffant that some women seemed to favor nowadays. And those hats were absurd. His gaze went to the bobbing flower on top of Darcy's wide-brimmed number. He couldn't say much for his sister-in-law's taste in clothing, but he liked the character she'd shown, more so when she made Sarah feel so welcome. And Brent was a father, too! Amazing. . .

Glimpses of the fair-headed twins on either side of Darcy's lap put a lump in his throat. For the first time in his life, Bill wondered what it would be like to be a father.

His gaze went to Sarah, and his heart lurched. She stared at him, anxiety in her eyes. He gave her a faint smile, but instead of responding, she looked down at her lap as though ashamed. Or disappointed. In him?

Bill flicked his eyes closed and averted his gaze to the back of the wagon and the rows of trees in full summer bloom on each side of the dirt lane. Somehow, he would capture her love and respect; there must be a way.

When the wagon reached Lyons' Refuge, as the sign outside the gate said, Bill stared in shock. No bars blocked the windows. No policemen strolled the grounds. What kind of place was this?

A large stone-and-wood house, simple and homey, stood on several acres of well-kept lawn. Beyond that stretched open land, and the only fences in evidence appeared to be those that kept livestock without and not criminals within. Bill spotted a few horses and cows. He could actually get to like it here. . . .

A chorus of boys' cries disrupted the peace as a small mob of miniature hooligans descended upon the wagon. Bill counted eight of them. Sarah's eyes widened.

"Master Brent, Master Brent," one of the smallest cried. "Herbert set a fire in the schoolroom and burneded the papers."

"Didn't mean to!" A redheaded, freckle-faced boy shot back. "It was an accident when I lit the stove."

"Unh-uh. You was mad."

"Boys!" Brent's roar silenced them. "That's better. We shall discuss this further when we meet in an hour at the schoolroom, which I assume is still standing."

"Mr. Lyons put the fire out like this." The first boy clutched the wagon and stamped his foot up and down. "He had to stomp on it like an Injun."

"I am pleased to hear of the rescue of the schoolhouse, Jimmy. Now, you boys may resume your chores."

By this time, most of them had taken notice of Sarah and Bill in the back of the wagon. Their eyes grew so large that Bill could see the whites of them.

"Go on with you," Darcy said. "You heard Mr. Thomas."

They scattered like field mice.

Inside the large house, a second round of people, mostly adults, converged upon the newcomers. Bill felt overwhelmed; he could well imagine how Sarah must be feeling.

"Is there somewhere my wife could rest?" he asked in an aside to Charleigh Lyons, a plump redhead with a benevolent smile. "We've traveled a long way, and I know she's tired."

"Of course. Please, follow me," she replied with a British accent much like Darcy's.

She led them upstairs to a bedroom containing a four-poster bed. Bill's gaze traveled to the right and the horsehair sofa sitting alongside one wall.

"When we bought new furniture for the parlor, we brought that up here. I suppose one day we'll get rid of it, but for now this was the only place to store it and keep it safe from rowdy boys. Though my husband does have plans for building a storehouse soon."

A baby suddenly shrieked, then began bawling as if the world had ended.

"Oh, my. That's Clementine. I'm sorry." She turned to look at Sarah. "Please feel free to lie down. And welcome to our home."

Charleigh directed a quick smile to both of them before bustling out of the room, leaving Bill alone with Sarah. She looked at him as if waiting for him to instruct her on what to do. He set her canvas bag on the sofa.

"I need to go speak with my brother. You should get some rest."

"They did not expect us. They do not know we intend to stay."

He winced at what he felt was quiet accusation. "There was no way to get a letter here from the island, and before I could find a telephone and get their number, we ran into them." He brushed his knuckles against her cheek. "Don't worry, pretty Sarah. I'll straighten it all out."

After he'd closed the door, Sarah put her hand to the cheek Bill had just touched. His unexpected caress had done more to soothe her turmoil than any words spoken.

Quietly, she moved toward the bed and lay upon it, still clutching her cross to her chest. The events of this day and the past weeks converged upon her, and she closed her eyes, squeezing away a tear. Homesick for her island, she tried to imagine her father's steady, quiet voice speaking to her on the morning of her wedding.

"Courage, my beautiful girl. All will be well. I'm convinced that God had this planned from the beginning."

She only wished she could believe it were so.

After they retreated to the study, Bill eased into the chair his brother motioned toward, unable to quench an ironic amusement. Once Bill had been the dapper young man in glad rags, dressed in expensive suits. Now Brent looked the well-dressed—if austere—gentleman, and Bill resembled a ragamuffin from the docks. He watched as Brent pulled some round spectacles from his pocket and slid them over his ears.

"Why are you here?" Brent came straight to the point.

Bill crossed his ankle over his leg, his wrists dangling over the chair arms with ease. "Ah, dear brother. You always did know how to make a man feel welcome." Brent's face reddened, and Bill's mocking smile slipped from his face. What was he doing? This was no way to earn sympathy. Nor did the usual sarcasm he'd shown Brent in the past feel like a secure fit anymore.

He sighed, wiped a hand over his beard. "My wife and I need a place to stay."

"A place to stay?"

"That's right. I'm not asking for charity; I'm good with my hands. I can take a gander at anything that needs fixing or building—"

Brent held up his hand, cutting his brother off. "We seem to be passing over a rather important issue in regard to our last meeting that took place at the train depot more than a year ago. If memory serves me correctly, you're a wanted man."

"The police aren't looking for me if that's what you're worried about. And neither is Vittorio." Too late, he wondered if he should have added the last. He had planned to tell him one day, yes, but after they'd settled in and the waters had smoothed over a bit.

"Vittorio?"

"The man I worked for. He thought it was curtains for me." Bill squirmed the slightest bit when Brent only stared. "He, uh, sent someone to rub me out."

"Rub you out? You mean he tried to kill you."

Bill's nod was short as he pulled up his shirt a fraction, showing the scar. "Knifed in the gut."

Brent stared at Bill's bronzed stomach with its white scar, then back into his eyes. "And you want to make your home here, and in so doing, bring imminent trouble upon the heads of all those staying at the refuge?" His words were incredulous.

"I told you. They think I'm dead. I was pushed overboard." Bill hesitated before saying the rest. "A dolphin saved me and took me to an island. Sarah found me and dragged me to the beach."

Brent's mouth dropped partly open, his stare one of speculative disbelief.

"I'm not making any of this up. I know it sounds far-fetched, but it's the truth, so help me."

"You've been on this island this entire time?"

"Only for the past two months. I, uh. . ." The shirt Bill wore felt incredibly tight, and he shifted. "I recovered from my wound in the home of a missionary. Sarah's father." It was time to tell the rest, come what may. "Fact is, I found Christ there."

Brent's mouth dropped down farther, his eyes widening. "By Christ, I assume you mean—"

"Jesus Christ, God's Son." Bill gave a soft snort. "Is the concept so hard for you to believe? That your black-hearted brother can find salvation, too?"

Brent shook his head in wonder. "Well, it wasn't a burning bush, after all, but a dolphin."

"Excuse me?" Bill drew his brows together at his brother's faint remark.

"Never mind." Brent gave Bill the first real smile he had seen, though uncertainty tinged it. "I can't tell you how happy I am to hear that you changed your course in life. You have changed your course?" Brent added.

"I wouldn't be here if I hadn't. I figured a place that gives young criminals a second chance might be willing to give an old criminal one, too." His words came sincerely from a heart that he now laid bare before his brother. "I'm not happy about the past, Brent. If I could turn back the clock, I would, and I'd do things differently. But I can't. So I'll just have to muddle through somehow and hope something right comes of it."

"We all have that problem, wishing we'd done things differently. Yet God can steer you in the right direction if you ask Him."

"I have."

Brent stared at his clasped hands a taut moment, then rose from the chair. "I'll have to take this up with the board. I don't have the authority to make such weighty decisions without approval."

"That's all I ask." Bill stood, considered, then held out his hand.

Brent started, obviously taken aback, but reached across the desk and accepted Bill's hand in a shake. They stood that way for a moment, tears welling in their eyes.

Except for a brief farewell handshake at the train station almost two years before, this was the first physical contact the two brothers had shared since Bill ran away from home twelve years ago. Yet this felt like a handshake of welcome and, Bill hoped, the start of a new beginning.

Chapter 9

Sarah often felt adrift in an ocean whose wild waves splashed all around her. Since Stewart Lyons and the rest of the board had approved her and Bill living at the refuge, life had taken on a surreal quality. On the island, she had pored endless hours through her father's many books, greedily soaking up every word about the world far from which she lived. But nothing could have prepared her for life at Lyons' Refuge.

Fifteen boisterous boys made their home there, ranging in ages from six to sixteen. All of them formerly in trouble with the law, they had been sent or brought to the refuge by Stewart Lyons, the headmaster of the reform school. Among those helping him with the massive task of improving the boys' minds and hearts was his wife, Charleigh.

Charleigh and Darcy, the cook, were an entity unto themselves. Full of fun and wit, Darcy thought nothing of speaking her mind, surprising Sarah, who'd always been taught restraint. It amazed Sarah to learn that both women had met in a London jail cell. She listened with rapt attention to their personal stories and to how they founded the school when Stewart, a former attorney, had built the place while Charleigh served her sentence in London.

Always quiet, Sarah didn't mind sitting on the fringes of the women's conversations, absorbing all they said. Yet one afternoon, as the women discussed the daily details of the household, Sarah spoke.

"What can I do for the refuge? I want to help, as well."

Both women looked at her, taken aback by her sudden entry into the conversation.

"I could always use help in the kitchen," Darcy said. "Since Irma moved away to her sister's, I'm the only cook here now."

"Can you cook?" Charleigh's eyes were kind.

"Yes. I know how to prepare fish, octopus, eel. . ." Sarah ended her list when the women gave her blank stares. She looked down. "But not the food you have here in America, no."

"Say. . ." Darcy's voice sparkled. "I have an idea, but I'll need to speak with Brent first. Have you ever taught children?"

"In the village, I helped my father with his missionary efforts."

"How lovely. Would you be willin' to speak with the boys about life on your island? It might do them a world of good, opening up their minds to new

169

adventures and the like. Let them see how the other part of the world lives. They certainly seemed to like that book *Robinson Crusoe*."

"I agree," Charleigh said. "That's a splendid idea, Darcy."

Sarah willed her heart to stop beating so fast. Teach a roomful of fifteen boys, some of them young men? The children she'd ministered to had been small. She kept her face a mask and nodded. "If my husband approves, I can do this."

"Wonderful. I'll speak with Brent tonight."

Feeling suddenly unable to breathe, wondering if she'd spoken too soon, Sarah excused herself and went outside. She strolled along the grounds, taking in the scenery.

Here in New York the trees didn't have fronds or fruit and coconuts growing from within their boughs as they did on the island. These trees were covered in a mixture of greens, from light to dark, with smaller leaves of serrated or round shapes, different from the palms. But they stood taller and gave much shade. And though here the air was cooler than the sultry heat of her island at noonday, the shade was welcome since the sun shone brightly.

In the distance she could see Bill on a ladder as he stood near the roof of the barn and pounded with a hammer. She drew closer.

His shirt and hair were damp from perspiration. After a time, he stopped, as though sensing her silent presence, and looked over his shoulder. He no longer wore a beard, though he'd kept a faint mustache and had trimmed his hair. The effect was pleasing but made him seem different from the man she'd learned to know on the island. It almost seemed as if he had wrought the physical changes to underscore the distance that remained between them.

"Sarah. Is everything all right?"

"I would like to speak with you if I may."

Bill glanced at the roof, as if he'd really rather pound on it some more, then looked back at her and gave a swift nod. He climbed down the ladder and faced her.

"Okay. You've got my undivided attention."

As he had hers. She could feel his warmth, his nearness, and something went weak inside her. His blue eyes were piercing, though they contained gentleness and not anger, touching her very soul. With a sad little inward sigh, she wondered what had gone wrong between them, so much so that he no longer wanted her.

She told him about Charleigh and Darcy's proposal, and he smiled. "That sounds like a great idea."

"You approve?"

"Of course. I think it might be good for you, Sarah. You have such circles under your eyes lately." He gently brushed his fingertip underneath her eye as he spoke, so lightly, it almost wasn't a touch at all.

A GENTLE FRAGRANCE

Yet Sarah felt the caress down to her very soul. She held her breath.

"But are you sure you can handle the task?" He lowered his hand to his side. "I realize it's been difficult for you to learn a new manner of living, and this place isn't your usual sort. I know you've been homesick."

Sarah swallowed back the emotion that rose to her throat. Missing her father and the island had been expected. Missing her husband's touch and presence had not.

"I believe I can do this."

"Then you should." He looked at her seconds longer, then glanced away. "I have to get back to work. That roof needs repairing before any more rain falls."

Sarah didn't want to go. "Is there anything I can do to help, Bill? Perhaps you would like a glass of water?" She wished she'd thought to bring some with her.

"That would be swell."

"Swell?" A vision of water ballooning into a huge bubble formed in her mind.

He grinned. "Meaning I'd like some very much, thanks. I think it's time I teach you slang, though Brent would have a conniption. He's very proper, in case you hadn't noticed." He winked slightly as if sharing a joke.

Again her heart felt as though it no longer belonged to her. The thought of spending time with her husband in any capacity birthed new hope within. "I should like to learn this slang if it would please you." *I should like to learn everything there is to know about you,* she silently added.

He looked at her a long moment. His smile faded, and a tender expression entered his eyes, reminding her of that long-ago night.

"Sarah?"

"Yes, Bill?"

"Let's skip out on the noonday meal and go have ourselves a picnic. There's a lake not too far from here, I'm told. We could go there."

His words slowly brought to life a part of her that had started to die.

❧

Excited at the prospect of spending time alone with his wife in the pleasurable atmosphere of a picnic, Bill hurried through his task of fixing the roof. When he entered the main house, however, Sarah was nowhere to be found.

"I believe she went upstairs to lie down," Charleigh offered as she set one of the two dining-room tables. "She wasn't feeling well, poor thing."

Worried, Bill took the stairs by twos. "Sarah?" he asked as he opened their bedroom door.

She lay upon the bed, still. Her eyes remained closed.

He hurried to the bedside and knelt down, putting a gentle hand to her shoulder. "Sarah, are you all right?"

Her eyes opened. "Bill?" she asked, as though coming out of a fog. Her eyes

171

grew more alert. "Is it time for our picnic?"

"Never mind about that." He gently pushed her back down when she started to rise. "We can do it another day. You look tired, and maybe you should just rest this afternoon." He didn't like how pale her face appeared, and her mouth seemed strained.

"I would like to go with you on this picnic."

"Another time, Sarah. This whole journey to America has taken quite a toll on you. You've hardly had any rest since we got here. Not that I've seen, anyway." He attempted a smile, though concern pounded through his brain. "Your father wouldn't be at all happy with me if I didn't take the best care of you. I promised him I would, and I don't intend to let him down." By referring to her father, he hoped she would see reason, since she respected the man so.

Sarah's eyes grew sad for an instant, before the emotionless mask again slipped into place. Bill scolded himself for an unwise decision. Broaching the subject of her father had only served to increase her loneliness and homesickness.

"Very well, Bill. I will do as you wish." She turned from him, curling up on her side.

He stood looking down at her forlorn form for the longest time, strongly wanting to lie down beside her, to take her in his arms and comfort her.

Instead, he turned and left the room.

Chapter 10

Sarah heard the door close. Only then did she open her eyes. Heaviness threatened to weigh her spirit down, and she felt like she might retch. Bill had so quickly found an excuse to cancel their picnic, as if he'd regretted his impulsive invitation. His comment about her father had merely served to emphasize what she already knew. Bill married her at her father's request, to please him. Perhaps in gratitude for saving Bill's life.

Again, she asked herself the question she'd posed since the first night on the ship: Was there hope for their marriage? If only she had someone to confide in, someone who could point out to her what she was doing wrong. She loved Bill, if love meant that every ounce of who she was desired to be with him, to know him, to share in his every success, and to comfort him in his defeats. If only Aunt Lefu were here to guide her and give her advice She tried to show strength and not weakness, but as her aunt had often scolded her, she still had much to learn. Too often, Sarah revealed what lay enclosed within her heart. Through her eyes, which her father told her were a mirror to her soul. And through her expressions that she knew were the windows of her emotions. Perhaps the fact that her father was the type of man to exhibit his feelings made it more difficult for Sarah not to do the same.

With a sigh, Sarah rose to a sitting position and swung her feet to the floor. She still felt dizzy but desired no further sleep. Her gaze went to the cross on the bed-stand table, and she reached for it. Gently she ran her fingers over the grooves and the wavy lines in the smooth wood.

"Pray for me, Father. For both of us. Bill and I are in great need of your prayers."

Though she had looked at the cross many times, she had never actually studied it. Now her gaze went to the symbol carved at the top. A sun and moon, with the crescent of the moon inside the sun. From conversations with her father, she knew what that meant. The sun was her father, the moon her mother. The two were combined to show unity. Their marriage.

She looked at the next symbol, lower down, a crown next to the same sun bearing the moon, and smiled. Her father had once told her that her name meant *princess*. A fitting choice, since her grandfather had been a chieftain, but perhaps there was more to it than that. She pondered the thought, then looked still lower.

Here the crown lay next to a waterfall, with the sun-moon in the background hovering over it. Her mother and father protectively watching over her as a child while she played near her favorite spot, no doubt. She pressed her fingertips atop the symbol, memories of happier times swimming to her mind. After a while, she looked down at the next symbol.

A weaker sun had been carved to the left and a heavy line separated it from the crescent moon, which had a tiny moon inside it. Tears welled in Sarah's eyes. The death of her mother and stillborn child. A girl, her father once told her.

Unable to complete her study of the cross, Sarah brought it to her heart and held it there.

❧

Disappointed about the canceled picnic, Bill didn't feel like joining the throng at the dinner table and instead slipped into the kitchen to grab a sandwich. Darcy stood at the counter, humming and slicing bread, which she piled onto a platter.

"Mind if I help myself?" Bill motioned to the bread.

"You're not eating with the rest of us?"

"Not much up to it. Thought I'd just grab a bite in here and then head back to work." He eyed the platter of sliced roast beef. "Mind if I have some of that, too?"

"Help yourself. Is Sarah not coming down either?"

"She wasn't feeling well." He studied Darcy's kind eyes that never seemed to snub anyone. "Would you mind too much going up and looking in on her after the meal? I think she's homesick, and a women's chat-to-chat might perk her up."

"Sure thing, guv. I'm always ready for a friendly chat."

She offered him a smile, allowing him to fork hefty amounts of roast beef on his bread before she grabbed the two platters and left the kitchen. Bill pumped water into a glass, then headed for the small table in the corner. Before he could take a bite, Brent strode into the room.

"It has come to my attention that you plan to dine in the kitchen instead of partaking of the meal with the rest of us."

Bill gave a curt nod.

"May I ask why?"

"I just don't feel up to all the lively chatter right now." Bill hoped he would get the point.

Instead, Brent pulled a chair out and sat down across from him. "You never were the type of man to be labeled as an introvert. Is there a problem?"

Bill stared at the sandwich he held before lowering it to his plate. It might help to get it off his chest, and Brent was his brother. What a switch, though! Bill had always been the one to steer Brent when they were boys, and he'd never thought of him as anything but a kid brother, someone who needed to be taught, not a teacher. Yet Brent was a teacher, come to think of it, and a good one according to what Bill had heard.

"It's about me and Sarah." And with that opening line, the entire story of their meeting on the island up through the arranged marriage came gushing forth. However, he didn't tell Brent about the one night he had shared with Sarah on the ship; that was too personal, too special.

Brent removed his spectacles and polished them. Bill relied on every store of patience he possessed as he waited.

"One tidbit of information I've learned throughout my courtship and marriage to Darcy is the importance of acting upon how you feel. If you love your wife, do not only tell her so, but show it in your actions." Brent replaced his spectacles over his ears.

Tell her? Bill shied from the idea, picturing Sarah's bland, expressionless reaction. He couldn't take that again. "Exactly how do you recommend I show her? I've tried by dressing her like the other women so she wouldn't feel like an outsider. I've tried by suggesting a picnic, though we have yet to go on it. I've tried by giving her time alone to adjust to this new life."

"Those things are all well and good, but I meant to show her in a more personal manner. A poem, a touch, a kiss." Brent reddened. "Surely I don't need to go into detail. I know you were quite the ladies' man. Women like romance. Be a romantic, but most importantly be considerate of her feelings and put her best interests before your own."

Bill wondered how Sarah would respond to such overtures. With acceptance and joy, or with no expression whatsoever? He sighed, then directed his thoughts to his brother. "You've changed a lot in fourteen months. There was a day when you would never speak so openly about personal matters."

"Being married to Darcy does that to a person." Brent smiled. "I fear her spontaneity and proclivity to speak her mind have rubbed off on me somewhat."

"There you go with those big fancy words again," Bill mocked, more in amusement than ridicule. "You know, I used to envy you all your knowledge and your ability to make something worthwhile of yourself. Someone people could look up to and admire."

Brent's face went slack in shock, and his mouth fell open. "You admired me?"

"Still do."

"I always assumed you thought little of me."

Bill could understand why, recalling past unkind remarks to Brent. "I think part of why I talked the way I did had to do with your Christianity. I didn't understand it, and in a bizarre way that you probably wouldn't understand, it threatened me. My words to you were more of a defense, but yeah, Brent, I've always thought you were quite a whiz, the best brother a guy could have. You always had the smarts up here." Bill tapped the side of his head. "Ever since we were kids."

Brent removed his spectacles, foggy with what looked suspiciously like tears, and cleared his throat. "In those days, I thought you were a really swell guy, too."

Bill stared, this time the one to let his mouth hang open.

Brent chuckled. "Surely you must realize that, being a schoolmaster to fifteen boys from all walks of life, I've heard my share of slang."

"Well, yeah, I know you've heard it. But I never thought I'd hear you say it."

Polishing the mist from his spectacles, Brent again replaced them on his head and leveled a steady look at Bill. "Should you make mention of the fact, I will aggressively deny it. After all, I have a reputation as a stuffy schoolmaster to uphold." His light tone belied his grim words.

Bill chuckled, liking this change in his brother. Mentally, he took off his hat to Darcy, certain her love had been the needed factor to get Brent to lose some of his somberness.

Brent rose from the table. "Now, why don't you come and join the rest of the family for luncheon? Unless you truly would prefer to eat your sandwich in here?"

The invitation and inclusion of Bill in the word *family* had been the first sign of acceptance on Brent's part since Bill arrived at the refuge almost a week ago.

Feeling hopeful again, Bill nodded. "Thanks. Maybe I will join you guys after all."

He walked around the table to his brother, warmly clapping a hand to his shoulder for an instant, and followed Brent to one of the dining tables.

Fifteen hungry, impatient, lively boys waited. Bill noticed his chair wasn't the only one vacant.

"Where's Darcy?" Brent asked, taking his chair.

"She went up to take a plate to Sarah." Charleigh tied a napkin around her small daughter's chin. Clementine sat in a highchair, banging on the table with her palm, as if picking up on the boys' impatience. "Hush, Clemmie, that's no way to act."

"She's been gone for ages," Joel, a blond scamp said. "I think she musta got lost."

"I'm sure she wouldn't mind if we began the meal without her." Charleigh took the plump hand of her little girl and of the boy to her right. Her husband, Stewart, sitting at the opposite end of the table, did the same to the boys on either side of him. Bill likewise took the hands of the little boys put on either side of him, reaching across Sarah's empty chair to take Joel's hand. The older boys at the other table did the same. As they all said grace, Bill wondered about Sarah, and silently added a prayer that God would help her. Help both of them.

Chapter 11

Sarah bent over the chamber pot in misery. She heard a light knock on the door, but before she could answer, her stomach released its contents again. She was barely aware of anyone entering the room.

"Oh, my." Darcy's voice oozed compassion as the woman knelt beside Sarah and laid her palm against her back. "You poor lamb."

Spent, Sarah crawled back on her hands and knees and sat against the wall for support. She closed her eyes and heard Darcy rise. The clink of the pitcher and water pouring into the basin filled the quiet, and she sensed Darcy in front of her again. A cool, wet cloth was pressed to her forehead.

"Thank you." Sarah opened her eyes.

Darcy regarded her, sympathy etched on her face. "Have you been this way long, luv?"

"Three days. I cannot remember being sick a day in my life. The journey must have been too taxing, as Bill said. These past weeks, I've also been dizzy at times and must need more rest."

"In this matter, I think Bill is wrong. Not about the rest though."

She looked at Darcy in confusion, noticing the light dancing in her eyes.

"Sarah." Darcy pressed her hand against Sarah's forearm, her action eager. "Unless I miss me guess—and I don't think I do since I've seen the same before in Charleigh and meself—you are with child!"

Sarah blinked, stunned by the words, though they rang true through her mind and settled deep within her heart. She had always been regular with her cycles and assumed the stressful journey had delayed it. A baby. . .Bill's baby.

A wondering smile lifted her lips. "A baby."

Darcy chuckled. "Seems to me you've recovered somewhat. I doubt you'd want the meal I brought up for you, so I'll just take it away, shall I?"

A stab of fear tore through the gilded dream, and Sarah grabbed Darcy's arm. "What will I do? I know nothing of being a mother. I've helped to bring a child into the world in the village of my mother's people, but that is all. I had no mother to teach me, and my aunt did not speak of such things."

Darcy patted her hand. "You'll do fine. Something is inborn in a woman that God put there. I can't explain it meself, but when the time comes that the babe is laid in your arms, you'll know what to do. And I had twins my first experience!" She laughed.

Even physically exhausted, Sarah caught onto Darcy's words. "Your first. . ."

Darcy nodded, her grin widening. "Aye, luv. I be in the same position as you. So what say we help one another and support each other when our times arrive?"

Sarah felt reassured in knowing that they shared this bond. Another thought invaded, making her tremble.

"Sarah?" Darcy's brows pulled together in worry.

"Don't tell Bill. He must not know."

Darcy's eyes widened in incredulous surprise. "And how do you plan on keepin' it from him? When your stomach starts balloonin' out, he'll be bound to wonder."

Sarah averted her gaze, sliding her teeth over the edge of her upper lip. "There has been. . .difficulty between us."

"News of a babe coming into the world might help matters," Darcy softly suggested.

Or they might make things worse, and Bill might turn completely away from her.

"Please, Darcy. I will tell Bill when I feel it is the proper time."

"It's not me place to give such news to your husband, luv. Only, Sarah, a word of caution. Charleigh did the same with Stewart, and I know she'll not mind me tellin' you, but it caused nothin' but pain for the both of them. What she feared wasn't true, and they could have both been saved a great deal of worryin' if she'd been up-front about it. Don't wait too long."

Sarah closed her eyes, knowing Darcy was right, but at the same time, fearing she might be wrong.

❧

To Bill, Sunday morning at Lyons' Refuge could best be described as well-ordered chaos. The entire household was swept into a whirlwind as Stewart, Charleigh, Brent, and Darcy rounded up all fifteen boys, saw to it they were clean and in their best clothes, fed them, hurried them, and then herded them into two Tin Lizzies and one horse-driven wagon for the mile-long ride to church.

Lyons' Refuge was a complete anomaly to Bill. He chuckled to himself at how quickly he'd picked up on Brent's vocabulary to think of such a word. Little like a reformatory and more like a boys' school, the motto at the refuge was: "Love tempered with discipline." Bill saw evidence of that every day. Stewart and Charleigh, Brent and Darcy, never failed to listen to the young scamps, never failed to give a needed hug, but at the same time they meted out any deserved discipline. The punishment always fit the crime yet was constructive.

When Clint wrote on the barnyard wall words and pictures of a crass nature, he was given the disciplinary action of painting the entire barn. Last evening after two boys, Joel and Herbert, got into a fight, they were made to sit on the same stair step and told they must remain there and would not receive supper until they worked out their differences in a mature fashion. When everyone gathered around the tables, Bill noticed the two boys were there, joshing each other and laughing, obviously the best of friends again.

Sarah came downstairs. Bill pushed away further musings of the refuge and approached his wife. "Are you feeling better today?"

"Yes, Bill. Thank you." Her smile was faint. "I look forward to visiting an American church."

"Well, then. . ." He slipped his arm through hers. "Let's not keep the others waiting." She seemed improved, though he detected her slight trembling. "Did you eat breakfast?"

She seemed to blanch. "I had a muffin and some berries. It was all I wanted."

Bill didn't argue, but he didn't like the fact that her appetite had diminished since they'd arrived in New York. The thought again brought guilt, since he knew her condition stemmed from her missing her father and her island.

Angry with himself, though he'd only done what her father wanted by bringing Sarah to America, he gave a stiff nod and escorted her to one of the automobiles.

At the little white church, the members of the refuge filled up three entire pews. Bill listened to the minister preach about deceit and was reminded of Josiah in that the preacher had the same quiet fervor as the missionary. Sarah, too, sat alert beside Bill, her attention riveted to the pastor, whether it was because of the message or the likeness to her father, Bill wondered.

After the service, many came forward to greet the newcomers to Lyons' Refuge. Bill was maddened at the haughty stares from two old crones directed to Sarah from across the room, likely because of her desire to wear her hair in one long braid and keep it uncovered. Or perhaps the women's censure stemmed from the fact that Sarah was half Polynesian.

He glared at the women who had the effrontery to think themselves superior to his wife and was satisfied when they grew flustered and averted their attention. No doubt they'd heard about Brent's murdering mobster brother and feared what he might do to them. Not that Bill would hurt any woman, then or now. But it satisfied him to know he'd made an impact, which he hoped would mean an end to further hostilities directed toward Sarah. She seemed not to notice, but then her expression rarely gave away her feelings.

The pastor welcomed both Bill and Sarah with sincere warmth, and shook Bill's hand with gusto. "I'm Pastor Wilkins. I've heard so much about you."

"I'm afraid to ask what, though I can imagine. Let me just state from the start, I'm not the same man I was."

"I'm relieved to know it." The pastor's eyes sparkled.

"And this is my wife, Sarah."

"Hello, Sarah." His smile was genuine. "It's a pleasure to have you and your husband join our little community. You must meet my wife. She loves stories of adventure, and I'm certain she'd enjoy hearing about your island."

Bill looked around expectantly.

"Sadly, she's not here today. Her mother took ill, and she's gone to visit her."

"I'm sorry to hear that." Sarah looked at Bill, then back to the pastor. "May I ask a question?"

"Certainly."

"You spoke of Moses and Aaron and the golden calf. I have never heard this story. My father spoke mainly of the teachings in the New Testament. Is it truly a sin to pay homage to other gods? If one worships Jehovah as the main God, is it wrong to visit the temples of other idols?"

Astounded at Sarah's forthrightness, Bill realized she must have been accustomed to approaching her father with spiritual questions. The pastor didn't seem one bit fazed by her candor, though a woman within hearing distance turned to look sharply at her, caught sight of Bill, and looked away again.

"My first question to one who does these things is why visit the temples?"

"Where I come from, the bond of family is strong."

"So it is to please family?"

"In part. Also the curiosity to know and understand."

"I see." The pastor's expression became grave. He looked up, seeming to just notice they were drawing unwanted attention from a few women who had edged closer, though they appeared to be in quiet conversation with one another.

He shook his head with an expression of frustrated tolerance, then returned his gaze to Sarah. "I should like to talk with you on this matter further. I'm sorry to say, this is not the time to do so. Perhaps later this week you can come by for a visit? I live in the brown house, farther down the road. My wife should have returned by Wednesday."

Sarah looked up at Bill. He nodded. "I'll drive her here myself."

❧

The changes that took over her body confused and amazed Sarah but also stressed to her the truth of the matter. She was indeed with child. Most confusing to her was her wide range of emotions and how she could travel from joy and smiles to despair and tears within moments. Since the day they'd arrived at the refuge, every night Bill remained downstairs long after the household went to sleep. When he did come up, he slept on the sofa, though it looked uncomfortable despite the blanket he'd thrown over it. He had not touched Sarah or shared her bed since that night on the ship, and because of this, Sarah was able to hide her condition from him. When her stomach became queasy, it was an easy matter to slip from the room as Bill lay sleeping far on the other side, against the wall.

Tonight as she quickly padded to the door, Bill stirred and rolled over onto his back. "Sarah?"

Her heart jumped, and she willed it to be still. "I'm fine. I will be back in a moment." Quickly she hurried out before he could stop her, afraid she would not make it in time. When she returned, shaky but relieved, Bill again lay sound asleep. Light snores whispered past his lips.

The moon washed through the window, spilling onto the sofa. She went to stand before him, admiring his handsome face, which looked so like a little boy's in slumber. No worry lines or tension marred his features in sleep. Unable to resist, she braced her hand against the sofa arm and bent to brush her fingertips against his smooth cheek.

Would their son look like Bill?

Would Bill welcome a child into his life?

A swift rush of fearful uncertainty made her draw her hand away and return to her lonely bed. Their own troubles aside, Sarah knew Bill despised his father and had run away from home to escape the man's severity. According to Bill, his father had loathed and ridiculed him, and his mother had shown no love either. Both brothers endured a childhood of sorrows, and Sarah wondered if Bill might now resent the babe that lay within her belly. Resent her for carrying this child.

Torn by the thought, Sarah clutched the pillow and squeezed her eyes shut to try to thwart the hot tears that threatened. However could she bear it if Bill came to despise her? His apathy was hard enough to endure, though at times he exhibited politeness or even gentle regard. Yet he acted nothing like he did on the island or during that one incredible night on the ship.

Sarah curled on her side into a ball, fearful she had already lost him and not understanding the reason for it. If he did turn completely away from her, her heart would surely wither and die.

Chapter 12

Bill awoke from a dream, heart beating fast. Chased by Vittorio's mobsters, he'd been cornered and had looked down the barrels of eighteen guns before their silent explosions shook him from sleep. He swallowed hard, wiping the sweat from his face. A woman's muffled sobs startled him.

Sarah?

He sat up and looked toward the four-poster. In the moon's glow, he could see that she lay on her stomach, her face buried in the pillow, shoulders shaking. Grief tore through his heart to witness her pain. Would this intense homesickness ever subside or, better yet, depart from her?

He didn't stop to consider his actions. His wife, who rarely showed emotion, was hurting deeply. Even if it was in part due to his action of bringing her here, Bill could not resist going to her. Approaching the bed, he felt a tug pull at his heart at how forlorn she looked among the expanse of white sheeting.

He settled himself beside her and laid his hand on her back. "Sarah?"

She stiffened, tried to capture her sobs.

The pain in Bill intensified. *No, Sarah, no. Don't pull away from me again. Don't retreat behind a mask of indifference, even if it's all you feel toward me. Even if you can't bring yourself to love me as I love you.* These words he whispered in his heart; he didn't dare air them aloud when he knew that to do so might again give her the power to wound him if she could not or would not reassure him his fears were in vain. If she didn't respond.

He moved closer and gathered her into his arms. Thankfully, she didn't resist.

Another torrent of tears soaked his nightshirt, which she clutched in one small hand. Closing his eyes, he held her tightly until the moon shifted and white light covered the counterpane. Even after she cried herself to sleep, Bill didn't let go. Enjoying the feel of his wife in his arms, he also closed his eyes and slept.

❧

Sarah awoke with the sense of something being different. Curious, she opened her eyes. She lay alone in her bed; a glance around the room showed Bill wasn't anywhere in sight. Then she remembered. He had been there with her. He had held her the entire time she cried, and that was the last she remembered.

Heat suffused her face. Her aunt Lefu would have been appalled to learn of Sarah's weakness. "Never let your husband see you cry," she had told Sarah

182

one day. "It is a grave mistake, for then he will look upon you with contempt." Though Sarah noticed not all of her aunt's admonishments related to the way other village women acted, Aunt Lefu was highly respected by her husband and by all those in the village. She was a strong woman.

For a moment, Sarah allowed herself to treasure the memory of being held against Bill's warmth, feeling protected, his arms firmly around her. She sighed, wondering if he had pitied her weakness and that was why he'd come to her. Yet pity was just as bad as contempt. Sarah desperately wanted Bill's respect, for him to think of her as strong. And she wanted his love.

With a hopeless sigh, she pulled off the voluminous bed gown Charleigh had given her. Before dressing, she laid a hand against her bare stomach, thinking of the life inside her. Soon this child would grow, and her stomach would expand. She would have to tell Bill, but she could not bring herself to do so yet. She must find clothes to hide her condition.

While she made her own sarongs on the island, she wasn't familiar with the fashion of this drab-colored American dress that hung so slack, making her form almost boyish. Yet that was how Bill wanted her, so that is how she would be. She desperately wished to please her husband. It wasn't so much a matter of subservience, though Sarah had been taught that, but the desire to do all she could to make Bill happy.

Deciding she would speak to Darcy, Sarah washed her face of the dried tearstains, dressed, and went downstairs. As she reached the foyer, Bill walked in from the parlor.

They both stopped, staring at one another.

Smoothing her expression into blandness, Sarah waited. A barrage of thoughts volleyed against her mind. Pleasure at the memory of being held in his arms; fear that he now thought her weak and pitied her, or worse still, regarded her with contempt; apprehension at the somber look on his face. His eyes that she had thought gleamed upon seeing her now looked shuttered, closing her out.

"Good morning, Sarah. You're feeling better today I trust?"

His cold, polite words struck her as surely as if he'd slapped her. She struggled to maintain her placid expression. "Yes, thank you. I feel as if I could eat breakfast."

"I'm glad to hear it." He looked at her a moment longer, then gave a tight nod and left.

At the click of the front door, all Sarah's resolve to remain strong threatened to lift from her heart. But she firmed her shoulders and headed for the kitchen, while within, her world crumbled down around her feet.

❧

Bill stared across the grounds, idly watching the boys do their chores. He had hoped that things would be different between them after last night. But again,

Sarah had shunned him with her cool regard, blasted him with another of her well-aimed bullets to his seeking heart. If there had been the slightest flicker of expression on her face, the slightest amount of joy upon seeing him. . .

He closed his eyes and swallowed hard. He would earn Sarah's respect and love or die trying. He'd never treated her like other women he'd known—except for that one predatory kiss on the island that shamed him to this day—and he had no idea how to gain her love. His hopeless thoughts moved into a hopeful prayer, and that brought the memory of the pastor's invitation three days ago.

Today he would take her to see Pastor Wilkins, to talk with him and his wife. They needed time alone, away from the constant chaos of the refuge. Always someone stood nearby or walked into the room, interrupting them whenever he did try to talk with Sarah. Maybe he'd even take her on that promised picnic. Show her that hidden spot by the lake, which he'd found last week and knew she would enjoy. Sarah had said she was feeling better today, even talked about eating a meal.

He would talk to Darcy, ask her to pack them a lunch, and surprise Sarah with his plan.

⁂

"What's botherin' you, luv?" Darcy asked as Sarah helped prepare breakfast by scrambling the eggs into a creamy batter so Darcy could cook them. "A sour stomach again?"

"No, last night was bad. But today is better. The tea with mint helped."

"I'm glad to hear it. I imagine you'll want to be puttin' off teachin' the boys until this stage passes?"

"Then it will pass?" The news relieved her. She was weary of feeling this way.

"It did for me and Charleigh, when she carried Clemmie. I'm sure it will for you, too." Darcy regarded her with compassion, then quit her task to put a motherly arm around Sarah. "You're such a tiny thing, little more than a babe yourself."

Sarah might be young, but with all she'd endured, she felt as old as the wife of Tua, the chieftain of her mother's tribe. True, she had turned seventeen only months ago, but a few girls on her island had already nursed their first babies at Sarah's age.

Still, Darcy's gesture kindled a great need in Sarah, one missing ever since her mother died. The desperate urge to confide in someone overwhelmed her, and Darcy had been such a friend.

Quietly, Sarah spoke, admitting her weakness, telling her of all the lessons her aunt had taught and how horribly she'd failed. How she did not know how to be strong. How she knew Bill must resent her or pity her.

Darcy shook her head, her eyes wide in incredulity. "I 'ave never heard such a heap of horse rubbish in all me born days."

184

Wounded by the unexpected attack, Sarah began to withdraw.

Darcy's arm tightened. "No, no, not you, luv. As you know by now, I'm one t' speak me mind and often blurt things out without thinkin'. But I'm here to tell you, those teachings of your aunt's are pure rubbish. A man don't think less kindly of his wife just because he sees her cry. Well, most men don't, anyways, and I feel Bill is most men. If anything, it makes a man feel stronger, more of a protector—as a man needs to feel. And Bill surely doesn't look at you with pity or contempt! Not from what I've seen, he doesn't."

Recalling the stiffness on his face a moment ago, the ice frosting his blue eyes, Sarah shook her head. Darcy had not seen what she had seen.

"There now, never mind. I think your aunt misled you into believin' something that just isn't so. The strength that you need for the bad days you can't just pull up from inside you, Sarah. The strength has to come from somewhere on the outside. It doesn't just grow inside your belly, like the babe you carry. That strength is God, and it's Him you need to look to for help when times are hard."

Sarah vaguely nodded. "My father said that strength was Jehovah, and *Jehovah Rapha* means *the God who heals*."

"There now, you see!" Darcy pulled away, her eyes triumphant.

"But my aunt said that strength came from many gods. And she is a very strong woman. Cannot both my father and my aunt be right?"

Such a look of concerned pity filled Darcy's eyes that Sarah looked away, almost ashamed to air such a question. She felt so confused.

"I think Pastor Wilkins can better answer your questions and help you to understand more than I ever could, Sarah." Darcy gave a faint smile. "Say, why don't you come to Manhattan with Charleigh and meself? Stewart is taking us there next week. He needs to talk with a judge, and we women need to shop for trifles our small town doesn't carry. It might do you good to get away for a spell."

Sarah thought the matter over. "I'll talk with Bill."

"Good. Now I best be finishin' these eggs before I have fifteen hungry boys stampeding me kitchen! Be a love, and set the table, would you?"

Sarah nodded and set about the task, taking plates from the sideboard into the large dining room and laying them out on the two tables. She wished she could feel comforted, but it was hard for her to reconcile herself to the fact that Aunt Lefu could be mistaken when her aunt was so strong—harsh, many called it. For the past ten years, her aunt had taught her. Sarah wasn't sure if she could just throw all those teachings away.

Chapter 13

As he drove toward the pastor's home, Bill darted a glance to Sarah every now and then. Tendrils of black hair had come loose from her thick braid, stirred by the air from the open window. Her expression was serene; her face glowed as though she were imbued with life. He wondered if his mention of the picnic had brought that flush of color to her cheeks, that luminescence to her face. Earlier, she had caught him putting the hamper in the back of the Tin Lizzie, so he'd admitted his plan. For the first time, her eyes had sparkled with what looked like joy, and that gave Bill hope. Maybe he could win her heart sooner than he'd thought.

At the pastor's home a short and plump, gray-haired woman opened the door. She smiled effusively and greeted Sarah with open eagerness. "My husband told me all about meeting the two of you last Sunday. I'm so excited to know you, Sarah, and I look forward to long talks with you about your island." Her green eyes sparkled. "As I'm sure my husband told you, I thrive on adventure. My great-grandfather was a sea captain. My grandfather was a general in the War Between the States. My father was a hot-air balloon enthusiast. And I married a preacher." She laughed delightedly. "Believe me when I tell you, *that* is an adventure of and unto itself."

Pastor Wilkins cleared his throat from the opposite side of the room. "I see you've all met." He gave a tolerant but loving look to his wife. "My dear, would you bring us some tea?"

"Of course, dear." Her look was just as affectionate as she whisked away.

Something twisted inside Bill, making him hungry for such camaraderie between himself and Sarah. On the island, they'd come midway to that point. He hoped that today would be the start of reaching it in full.

Several chairs stood close in the small parlor, where Pastor Wilkins had laid out his notes and a Bible. Once settled, he went over the notes of Sunday's meeting, also bringing up the first commandment: "Thou shalt have no other gods before me."

Bill listened, as interested as Sarah. He noticed that at times her brow clouded, as if she were confused or uncertain. Pastor Wilkins patiently answered her many questions and took her still further through the Bible, showing her in 1 Kings how those kings who did evil in the sight of the Lord and who worshipped idols were punished. But those who did good and worshipped only the

Lord God were blessed. His wife brought tea and swept quietly out again. While they drank the hot beverage, Pastor Wilkins clarified and taught and listened. Bill was impressed with the man. He was as new to this as Sarah, but after an hour in the pastor's company, he didn't see how she could question any longer.

"If what you say is truly wrong. . ." Sarah's eyes clouded. "Why then do my people take part in such things? They are good men and women; they seek only to do what is right."

Bill felt a stab of apprehension. This was the first he'd ever heard her refer to them as her people and not as her mother's people. In an instant, he realized just how strong the connection was to her aunt and why this was so difficult for her.

"Didn't you tell me that your father is a missionary?" The pastor looked confused.

"Yes, but many of the villagers do as he tells them with their lips and actions only; they do not believe in the Christian God with their hearts—though there are some who do."

"And what do you believe, Sarah?"

"I believe in Jesus, the Christ, and in all He did. I believe He is God."

"Well, that's the first step." The pastor looked relieved. "But anyone can believe. You have to receive Him into your heart and life."

"I believe I have done this. I have accepted Jesus as my own. But for years, my aunt has taught me another way, and I have visited her temple."

"And your father allowed this?" There was no mistaking the pastor's shock.

Sarah briefly looked down at her lap, her brows sadly drawn together. "For a long time, my father turned away from God after my mother died. He allowed me to go where I wished and took little notice of me. His sorrow was very great. After he returned to God, at times he tried to tell me what you speak now. But I didn't understand and told him so, since in the time of his great sorrow he never denied me attending the ceremonies or learning from my aunt."

Sarah remembered the look of agony that had crossed her father's face at her quiet words of confusion. The tears that had filled his eyes. He had hugged her close, then swiftly turned and left the hut.

The pastor thought a long moment. "Sarah, do you have access to a Bible?"

"My father sent his Bible with me, and I read some on the ship. I have not finished it."

At this, the pastor's lips quirked at the corners. "Yes, it does take some time to reach that point. I have written down some scriptures and would like you to study them. I could read them to you, but I've found it helps when one looks at the passages for oneself. My methods might seem odd to some of my calling, but this is what I've determined works best."

Sarah took the paper. "I will do as you ask."

The pastor talked with them a while longer; then his wife popped in to bring cookies and more tea. Sarah barely nibbled at her shortbread wafer. Suddenly she looked up, her eyes hopeful.

"May I have a pickle?"

All of them stared at her—whether for her lack of social decorum or her odd request Bill didn't know. He supposed he shouldn't be too surprised. For a woman whose daily diet had often included octopus and eel, a sour pickle with tea wasn't so unusual. Feeling Sarah withdraw just by noting the way her body slightly recoiled and her chin lowered, as if embarrassed, Bill spoke up. "If it wouldn't be too much trouble, I'd like a pickle, too."

❧❧

Once they left the pastor's home, Sarah let out a relieved sigh. The woman didn't have any pickles, unlike Darcy, who bought them from the grocer on a regular basis, and Sarah wished now she hadn't given in to this strange craving of the dills and asked for one. Although the pastor's wife didn't say a word and treated her just as kindly as when Sarah had walked through the front door, questioning her about the island, Sarah realized she'd committed a social error.

Bill was quieter, directing a sort of sad smile her way now and again. She buried a sigh, knowing she must have disappointed him.

At her first view of the lake, Sarah exhaled softly. It wasn't home, with its breadfruits and palms, its tropical flowers, and waterfall, but this place contained a beauty and peace all its own that soothed Sarah's soul. Trees of lush green surrounded a shimmering body of water. Sunlight pushed through leafy boughs and glanced off the water, gilding it in ripples. Quiet birdsong filled the trees.

Bill led the way to a grassy area and laid a blanket on the ground. Sarah ignored the blanket and moved to the edge of the lake. The call of the water, which she had so missed, enticed her, and she sat down to pull off the uncomfortable narrow pumps that all the women in New York wore.

"Sarah?"

Next came off her stockings.

"What are you doing?" His voice was dazed. "That water must be near freezing. I wouldn't try it if I were you. The lake could be deep."

She hesitated, torn between his words and the desire to feel moving water around her again. She gave him a hopeful smile. "Surely it is not as deep as an ocean?"

He stared at her several more seconds, then gave a slight permissive nod.

Sarah tested the waters. Bill was right; it chilled her senses but at the same time revived them. To feel the water lap over her bare foot freed something inside her. Seeing that the edge was shallow and allowed for her to wade in, she bunched up her dress around her hips and did so.

"Sarah. . ." His voice held a note of caution. "Be careful."

The clear water rushed gently past her legs as if welcoming her, and she almost wept with how good it felt. She waded out farther until the hem of her dress absorbed the water. What she would give to swim again, though in this long dress such a feat was unlikely.

She stood awhile longer, then, with a sigh, retraced her steps to Bill, who'd not altered from his position or from staring at her. She sensed pain in his eyes before he turned his attention to the picnic hamper.

"Let's see what Darcy packed for us, shall we?" His tone came light, though his shoulders looked heavy.

Sarah collected her stockings and shoes and joined him on the blanket, hoping she had not upset him. His stance seemed distant, though his words welcomed her.

"Sandwiches—ham, by the looks of it. Fruit—knowing Darcy, that's no surprise." He pulled out a container. "And here are your pickles!"

"Thank you." Sarah smiled as she took the container and the sandwich he offered.

Bill opened the wrapper and picked up his own sandwich, opening his mouth in readiness for a bite, then glanced at Sarah, who sat still, calmly waiting.

"What?" he asked.

"Should we not offer thanks?"

"Zowie! You're right. I'm still new at this." He set down his sandwich and bowed his head as Sarah did, offering a short prayer.

"Tell me," she asked as she ate her sandwich, glad her stomach didn't rebel and she could eat again. "Is *zowie* slang?"

"Sure is. Means full of zip." At her blank look, he added, "Energy."

"Will you teach me more of this slang, Bill? I should like to know it."

The conversation between them lightened considerably as Bill did just that, making Sarah laugh at the slang words and their meanings. He taught her slang phrases for any person who was remarkable, comically pantomiming "the bee's knees," "the elephant's eyebrows," "the snake's hips," and more, until she was laughing so hard tears rolled from her eyes.

When he got down on all fours and pantomimed "the cat's meow," and actually sidled near her, purring, she had the craziest urge to pet him and did lift her hand. Before she went through with it, however, she realized what she was doing and slowly withdrew it. He seemed not to notice and went on to show her "the gnat's elbow" and "the cat's pajamas."

Thoroughly entertained by her husband's silly antics, Sarah felt the first stirrings of hope that their marriage could flourish, based on friendship alone, if not love.

Though on her part, she would always love Bill.

Chapter 14

Three days later, Bill stood on the porch and thought a lot about that picnic. It was the first time he'd seen and heard Sarah laugh again, really laugh. Like she had during her ride on her pet dolphin. And he'd purposely striven for humor, acting like a sap, just to hear her delight. The ring of her laughter made him feel good inside.

The screen door creaked open, and he turned his head. Brent joined him on the porch, coming to stand beside him. Both men stared straight ahead.

"I came to inquire as to whether you're feeling well," Brent said. "You were quiet at dinner."

Bill chuckled. "I'm surprised you noticed. With fifteen boys chattering away, dinnertime can't exactly be described as silent in this place."

"Yes, that is one area on which we still have improvements to make. The newest additions to the refuge instigate questions and incite the others to trouble."

"Chad and Roland?"

Brent nodded. "They do more than instigate questions, I'm sorry to say. Being brothers, they often urge one another to dissension."

"They play off one another." Bill thought about that. "I've noticed Chad tends to be more of a leader. They seem very close. I rarely see them apart."

"They are close."

The words Brent spoke didn't seem to be all about Chad and Roland, and Bill felt his brother nurtured the same thoughts he did. In speaking of the two boys, Bill couldn't help but be reminded of how close he and Brent once were, Brent always playing follower to Bill's leader.

"We did have some good times, didn't we?" Bill let out a sigh of reminiscence.

Brent's expression became nostalgic. "We did."

The desire to rectify past mistakes spurred Bill to speak. "But we can never go back, can we?"

Brent hesitated. "It's not always wise to revisit the past, no."

Bill closed his eyes, the crushing blow of defeat bowing his shoulders. He had so wanted not only to make amends with his brother and ask for his forgiveness, but also he'd hoped to rekindle the strong friendship they'd once shared. Though his brother had accepted him back, had even been friendly, he maintained a wary distance.

Again, Bill wondered if he would always be chained to his past sins. God had forgiven him and accepted him, though he was in no way as good a Christian as his brother and Stewart were, and he doubted he would ever be considered worthy enough to have the town regard him with respect. Still, he had hoped that at some point Brent could move beyond the past and give Bill another chance to be his brother, as close as they'd once been.

Before Bill could retreat to the house, Brent spoke. "Perhaps it's not my place to ask this, but given the fact you did come to me for advice, I don't feel as if I'm treading on forbidden ground." He cleared his throat. "I trust matters have improved between you and your wife?"

Bill wished he could give him a positive response, but the truth was he just didn't know. "She seemed to enjoy the picnic and the lake."

"Yes, so I've heard. Darcy tells me she has visited the lake every day since you took her there."

Bill eyed him in shock. "She has? How did she get there? She doesn't know how to drive a car or wagon."

"Apparently, she walked. As the lake is off the road, it's not difficult to find."

Bill shouldn't have been surprised Sarah went on foot those two miles, since she'd engaged in more walking than that every day when on her island. But the impulsive, unpredictable actions of his young wife never failed to astonish him. Part woman, part child, Sarah excited and delighted him. *I'd do anything if I could have her love. I just don't know what to do anymore to get it.*

"Perhaps you're trying too hard?"

Bill hadn't realized he'd spoken, and he looked at Brent in surprise.

"Love is a gentle fragrance, Bill. As delicate as the sweet scent of a rose. It cannot be forced, nor can it be captured. It blossoms when it's ready, and when that day arrives, the fragrance stirs the senses in ways that cannot be expressed or imagined."

Brent's words moved him. "You always were such a poet." His remark was not unkind. "Yet what if that rose never blossoms. Then what?"

Brent actually grinned. His eyes seemed to sparkle behind his spectacles. "Somehow, Bill, I don't think you have cause for concern in that regard."

Bill realized his brother had no idea of the truth, since he didn't know all the facts, including that his and Sarah's marital relations were nonexistent. And he felt it was time to change the subject. "Can I ask a question?"

Brent inclined his head in an inviting manner.

"What's the story behind the spectacles? Sometimes you have them on, sometimes you carry them in your pocket."

"The twins have a tendency to grab for them."

Brent's face flushed, and Bill grinned, suddenly realizing the true reason Brent went without them far more than he wore them. He'd overheard Darcy comment to Brent how much she liked his eyes, and Bill felt the absence of the spectacles must have something to do with that.

Bill looked out over the yard. A few of the boys who'd been working there now stared toward the thicket that led to the road. Their mouths hung open as they gawked, standing as though turned into living statues.

Bill looked that way. His heart jumped, then dropped.

Sarah came walking toward them, barefoot, her long hair damp, loose, and hanging to her thighs. Instead of the gray dress she usually wore, she had reverted to her islandwear and wore her red, knee-length sarong.

"Hello." Her smile was uncertain as she reached them.

Brent turned. His eyes went wide in shock before he hurriedly looked away. "I should go grade some essays. Good day, Sarah. Bill." Quickly he escaped into the house.

Sarah halted. "I have done something wrong?" The worry on her face did not escape Bill's notice.

He should explain to his wife about conventions concerning dress and what was considered appropriate. Her father had let her run too wild on that island. Noticing that the boys continued to gawk, he called out to them. "Don't you have chores that need tending to?"

A few looked away and resumed their work. But the rest continued to stare.

He took hold of Sarah's arm, pulling her with him into the house. "You should change clothes. You must be cold."

"I'm not cold."

"Well, you should change clothes anyway."

"I have done something to displease you?"

Her soft anxious words gave Bill pause, and he forced himself to calm. "Don't you like the dress I bought you?" He continued walking with her up the stairs.

"I cannot swim in it."

"Swim?" He looked at her, though he shouldn't be surprised. They reached their bedroom, and he brought her with him inside, away from the prying ears of anyone curious enough to listen.

"You do not approve?"

He felt her withdrawal, saw the hurt disappointment in her eyes. When had her eyes ever been so revealing? Her face was awash with emotion, showing her feelings as she never had before except on the day she left her father. And he realized this must be very important to her. How could he deny her this one request when she'd given up so much by leaving her island and those she loved?

"I suppose it's all right for you to visit the lake and swim. I know how much you love the water." He sighed, leaned against the door. "But from now on, I want you to take the other dress with you and change into it before you return to the refuge."

She looked down at her sarong, then up at him again. "Does the dress displease you, Bill?"

The dress definitely did not displease him. Forcing himself to look away from her slender curves and shapely calves, he stared into her eyes. They held such a look of distressed confusion, and he knew he wasn't going about this at all well. Maybe Darcy or Charleigh could explain about social propriety if he asked. He was sure they wouldn't mind.

"Please, just change into the dress I bought you, Sarah."

He managed a stiff smile before leaving the room. As he strode downstairs, a sense of irony struck him. He had never conformed to strict conventions or society's stiff rules. Yet those ideas altered the moment he saw those boys gawking at his wife. Even though he knew she'd been blameless in her actions, he hadn't liked the attention she received. Not one bit. Odd that he, who'd once snubbed his nose at the law and everything about it, was now all in favor of protocol. Bill shook his head in stupefied amusement at the changed man he'd become.

Life, indeed, was an irony.

※

With no one to see her, Sarah let the tears run down her cheeks as she changed into the ugly gray dress. Never had she imagined her simple sarong would cause such a stir. Bill never said anything about it on the island. But then, New York was so different from her island.

She sighed and picked up the cross, again looking at its symbols. Under the one showing her mother's death had been carved another one—the sun, weak and far to the corner. The crown at the opposite corner showed the distance that had come between her and her father, no doubt. But between them was what looked like a snake.

She frowned. A snake?

Snakes symbolized evil, according to her father. She wondered why he would show evil had come between them.

A knock at the door broke her from her musings. "Yes?"

Charleigh entered, smiling. "I hope you don't mind if I visit for a bit. Bill thought you might like to talk."

"Of course." Sarah laid down the cross and watched as Charleigh came to sit beside her on the bed. Her bright red hair shone as the sun hit it, reminding Sarah of one of the beautiful tropical flowers on her island. The woman was so beautiful in both features and spirit. Since the day Sarah had come here, Charleigh had shown her nothing but kindness.

"I heard about what happened." Charleigh's green eyes conveyed sympathy. "I know things are difficult for you, adapting to a new way of life, but I want you to know I'm here to help you as you learn. And I'd like to explain how things are here in America, so it will help you understand what just happened and why everyone acted so strangely."

She went on to explain about conventions and that hemlines to the knees were looked upon with horror—protocol stated they must remain below the calves, though some people didn't even approve of that and were horrified by the rising hemlines. As she spoke, her gaze went to both the drab dress Sarah wore and the colorful one she'd laid across a chair. "It's very pretty."

"Thank you. I made it myself. On the island, many of the women wear clothes of such color, of many different hues." Sarah sighed.

Charleigh fingered the cloth. She looked back at the gray-checked dress, then to the sarong, her gaze thoughtful. "As the months progress, you'll need new clothing at any rate. Darcy told me about your condition, and I'm so happy for you. She also mentioned that she invited you to join us when we go to Manhattan next week." She brightened. "We could visit the boutique and buy you a lovely dress, Sarah. You would look pretty in green or blue."

Sarah lowered her head. "I am not certain Bill would approve."

"I think he would adore you in those colors."

"No, I mean about going to Manhattan. When I have spoken of the city in the past, he became very quiet. I think he has bad memories there."

"Would you like Stewart to talk with him?"

Sarah considered the offer. "If he wouldn't mind, yes. I should like to go with you to the city." Charleigh and Darcy had become such good friends. To be in their close company for a day might take some of the burden of loneliness off Sarah's heart caused by her husband's distance.

❧

"No." Bill's reply came swift and forceful.

Stewart's eyes flashed in surprise. But then, Bill reasoned, the man couldn't know the dangers of what he asked. The two sat on chairs on the porch. Bill often came here to relax, yet the suddenness of Stewart's question caused him to tense.

Stewart was silent a moment. "Perhaps you might think it over? The women really enjoy a day of shopping in Manhattan. I try to bring them with me whenever business takes me there, and I must meet with a judge about an important matter concerning one of the boys he put in my care."

Bill admired this man who had done so much for so many child delinquents. "You take from all the courts then?"

"My former position as a lawyer puts me in contact with many from that establishment." He looked straight at Bill. "I take those no one wants, those the court has given up on, and I try to give them a home, hope, and a second chance."

"Your place reminds me of another charity I've heard about. Boys Town. Ever hear of it?"

"In Omaha." Stewart nodded. "A worthy institution. My desire is to one day provide even more room to house the children who need help. There are so many wandering souls out there." He looked out over the trees, his expression distant.

"You do a good job with what you have."

Another stretch of silence came between them.

"If you're worried that the women will be unaccompanied, I assure you, you have no cause for concern." Stewart glanced at Bill. "Except for the short time I leave them under the care of the boutique's manager, I'm with them at all times."

Bill carefully considered his next words. He'd been at the refuge almost two months, had hoped to put more time behind him before touching on those days, but maybe the moment had come for him to share a snippet of his dark past that refused to remain buried in his mind. With Stewart, who'd become an acquaintance but still considered Bill a stranger, he could. With Brent, who'd once been a close brother but still considered Bill a traitor, he could not. He still felt the distance between him and his brother.

"When I left Manhattan more than a year ago, I left in a hurry." He collected his thoughts, realizing Stewart already knew this. "I worked for a family involved in the underworld. Never mind what I did; I'm sure you can fill in the blanks, and you'd be right no matter what you put in them."

Stewart gave a short, comprehending nod.

"There was trouble within the family. One of the sons was doing a double-cross—er, betraying his father. He wanted all the power—something you often find in that kind of racket. Thirst for power." Bill stared out across the lawn, finding it easier to look at the trees ahead than at Stewart. "I was what you would call stuck in the middle. I'd saved the man's son once, and well, even though an outsider never becomes part of the family, that doesn't mean they still don't work for them."

"I do understand, Bill. I was a Manhattan lawyer, remember."

"Right." Bill blew out a breath. "Okay, well, it's like this. I drove Vittorio's son to a meeting place. He was involved in some underhanded dealings with the enemy—another crime family—and, things went bad. Real bad. Vittorio's son got shot, and someone on the outside saw me with a gun. The real killers vamoosed before they were seen, and I was left holding the bag. Word leaked back to Vittorio that I'd been the one to shoot his son. Thing is, he never would have believed Marco was anything but loyal. Marco was a convincing liar. But one doesn't go up to the crime boss and say, "Sorry, you got the wrong fellow"—one runs. Because if you don't, you're a dead man. When you hurt one of the family, you have just nailed your own coffin shut."

Stewart remained silent a moment. "I understand your reason for leaving the country. But I don't understand why you're concerned about Sarah visiting Manhattan with us. You told Brent that Vittorio's family thinks you're dead."

Stewart's reasoning was sound, yet Bill couldn't help feel a niggling fear.

"No one from Vittorio's family knows Sarah is your wife. I shall take the women into Manhattan and be with them almost continually, and I do know how to protect if confronted, Bill. However, I sincerely doubt that even if a member of Vittorio's crime family were to see Sarah, they would make the connection that she was your wife. They don't know us, either. We'll just be another group of people among the thousands there."

"May I ask why you're so strongly in favor of taking Sarah?"

Grinning, Stewart gave a helpless shrug. "It's important to Charleigh, and what's important to her is important to me. I want to do whatever is in my power to see her happy. She and Darcy enjoy shopping in the boutiques, and since I take them no more than twice a year, it's a special event."

A sense of sadness swept into Bill's heart. Stewart and Charleigh. Brent and Darcy. Obviously two couples so much in love. He wanted the same with Sarah. He could feel that vacancy in his life that much more strongly when he stood in the others' presence and witnessed their adoring glances, the small touches they gave to one another. A loving hand on the back, a gentle touch on the arm.

Bill sighed. "Do you think I don't care about Sarah's happiness?"

"Not at all. I know you do. But at the same time, I think you're being over-protective, which is natural, considering what you went through. But that was over a year ago, Bill, and they assume you're dead. This is one day in Manhattan."

Stewart's tall muscular frame and no-nonsense attitude helped to relieve any doubts about his ability to protect the women. But a man's build or size didn't factor in when talking about guns. A bullet could down the strongest man alive.

Yet Bill knew Vittorio's family wouldn't gun them down in the street. That wasn't how the family operated. Their ways were more underhanded and sneaky, less public.

"Give me a few days to think it over," Bill amended. "I just can't give you an answer right now."

"Fair enough." Stewart rose to his feet. "I had better get back to the book work."

Bill said nothing, his mind active as it visited the past once again.

Chapter 15

Sarah was excited to visit the church again, her embarrassment over her social error no longer disturbing. After Darcy had shared some mistakes she'd made when she'd first arrived at the refuge, Sarah laughed and felt much better about her own awkward moments.

As she and Bill approached the church, a sudden faint yipping sound came from behind her. She turned at the same moment a brown puppy scampered up to her on awkward legs. It jumped against her ankles. The little animal was so tiny, so cute, she had no fear of it and bent to gather the warm furry bundle into her hands.

"Why, hello!" She brought it closer to her. Its pink tongue began bathing her face. There had been dogs of a type on her island but none as cute as this little fellow.

"Uh, Sarah. . ." At Bill's low words, she looked up. He stared at someone beyond her, then turned his attention to her. "Maybe we should go inside?"

Sarah glanced in the direction Bill had been looking. An elderly woman Sarah remembered as Mrs. Cosgrove stared at Sarah in shocked disdain, then lifted her head high and entered the church.

Heart deflated, Sarah looked back at Bill. "Playing with dogs before a church meeting is not allowed in society's rules?"

A tender expression crossed his face. "No, you go ahead and enjoy that pup. I think his owner is coming this way."

Sarah held onto the wriggling bundle, smiling down into his affectionate brown eyes, but a morsel of the joy had been lost. Bill was being kind; she had obviously embarrassed him again. The pup licked her face, bringing back her smile. She watched as Bill walked over to a young boy and talked with him. The child made a lot of motions with his hands, pointing behind him, pointing toward her and the pup. Bill soon returned with the boy in tow.

"Sorry about that, ma'am." The boy held his hands out for the pup. "Little guy gets loose a lot when my brother leaves the barn door open. He was the runt of the litter, though as fast as he runs now, you'd never believe it."

Sarah smiled acknowledgment to the child as Bill led her into church, and they slipped into a pew. The service was as stimulating as the last one she'd attended. The hymns of worship blessed her soul, especially the song "All Hail the Power of Jesus' Name," and she longed to learn the music so she could sing along, as well. The pastor's message from 1 Corinthians dealt with unconditional love and spoke to her heart. She was again reminded of her father both in the way the pastor delivered the sermon and by his friendly attitude.

Afterward, the pastor's wife and the organist sought Sarah out to speak with her while Bill excused himself. Curious about what was so important that it couldn't wait until they reached the refuge, Sarah watched as he talked to his brother and Stewart. Perhaps Bill felt uncomfortable being the sole male in a group of women now clustered around her. Though these women were kind, Sarah couldn't help but notice the snubs she received from other parishioners, women and men alike. She kept the mask of cool detachment on her features, but the slights wounded, and she wondered if they had listened to today's message.

Darcy came up to the group, nodded a greeting to the others, then looked at Sarah. "Bill asked that we take you home with us. One of the boys is sick and we need to return. Sorry, luv."

"Bill's not coming?"

"He said he'll meet us at the refuge."

"Oh." Sarah wasn't sure what to think or why Bill would simply vanish like that, but she accompanied Darcy to the waiting car and was silent the entire ride home.

Once at the refuge, she went to her room, restless, and picked up the cross. She looked at the symbol below the last one—the crown seemed to hang in limbo and at a titled angle, the sun much smaller and far away, the snake larger— then she again set it on the table. She didn't want to think what it meant, though she suspected she knew. Her aunt had brought darkness into her life, according to what her father and those at Lyons' Refuge thought. And after reading all of 1 Kings and other passages in the Bible that Pastor Wilkins had recommended, Sarah was beginning to feel as if her father was right.

She loved her aunt; that would never change. But as she'd read the words of life, the conviction deep within her spirit could not be ignored. She recognized truth in them and now felt cheated. Sarah had needed guidance. Her father had been unable to give it. Her aunt had provided it, and now Sarah realized all that she'd been taught was wrong. Much of it was considered wicked, and she felt as if a rift had been ripped open inside her. A part of her childhood and young girl-hood must be torn away from her in order for her to please the Lord. Though she desired to serve Christ, she couldn't help but feel bitter tears well up for all she'd learned and lost.

It did no good to question why these events happened. She didn't blame her father for his lack of fatherly wisdom or withdrawal during those two years; she knew his love for her mother had been immense. As a child, she'd felt such reassurance, such happiness to see them together. Her mother had been a soft-spoken woman, but she, too, spoke of faith in the Lord to Sarah. At the memory,

Sarah wondered what had drawn her to listen to her aunt, when her own mother had been a Christian convert.

The rattling sound of an automobile coming up the path drew her to the window. She frowned when she saw the Tin Lizzie swerve from side to side a couple of times, as though Bill worked to keep it on the dirt path.

She hurried downstairs, wondering if he was ill. As she walked out the door, Bill exited the vehicle, his smile so wide it captured her heart and her breath, and then her gaze lowered to the wriggling brown ball of fur in his hands.

"He's for you, Sarah." Bill held out the puppy to her. "Your new pet."

She gasped. Stunned at his thoughtfulness, she felt tears glaze her eyes. Her heart felt so full she thought she might float away. Without thought, without hesitation, she went to him, rose up on her toes, and, laying one hand on his shoulder, gently kissed his cheek.

❧

Bill stood on the porch hours later, touching the cheek that Sarah had kissed. He still could hardly believe she'd done that. Afterward she'd seemed embarrassed and had drawn back, though her smile was genuine as she took the squirming pup who'd been christened with the name Sasi. All through the drive from the previous owner's, Bill had worked to hold onto the writhing ball of fur, almost driving off the road a few times as the Tin Lizzie chugged along. The animal had even wet on his trousers in its excitement, but the ordeal had been worth it to see the look in Sarah's eyes. And to receive the gift of her kiss.

He inhaled deeply, then headed inside. Charleigh sat in a rocker with Clementine, humming a song to her.

"Any idea where Sarah is?"

"I think she went to the lake."

"This late?" Bill didn't like the sound of that. Only a few hours remained until sunset. "Mind if I borrow the car?"

"Oh, I'm sorry, Bill. Stewart took it into town. And Samuel and Greg are working on the other one. The brake sticks."

"Okay. Thanks." He headed out the door, wondering what to do. Well, his wife made the walk every day. He didn't suppose it would hurt him, and hopefully he would run into her coming back.

The summer day was mild, but by the time he got to the lake, the water looked inviting. More so, with his wife in it. Unnoticed, Bill stood beneath the trees and watched.

She laughed and played with the puppy as it waded near her, slowly dog-paddling in circles before it moved to shore. The pup padded out and shook itself briskly before scampering to the gray dress to sniff it. Seeing Bill, it ran at an angle toward him and jumped about his ankles a few times. Absently he reached down to pet it, while keeping his eye out for his wife, who had immediately dived under the water once her pet left her. The pup went to make a bed in the gray dress.

Sarah broke the surface, and Bill watched her swim in her sarong, her movements graceful, alluring. Once he'd resisted the pull to join her in the water, at the island, but now he accepted the push that sent him wanting to rush to her. Heart beating fast, he bent to pull off his shoes.

❧

Reveling in the feel of the silky water around her skin, Sarah swam with delight. After a while, the water no longer felt cold, and she loved to spend her afternoons here. She glided underneath and resurfaced to swim on her back. The top of her head hit something solid. More than curious, she swirled around and came face-to-face with Bill!

She blinked, a short pause ensued, and then he grinned.

"Ever had a water fight?" His tone came out boyish, innocent, as he sprayed her with water.

Laughing, she threw her hands up to cover her eyes. "Bill!"

He didn't relent in his playful attack, and she squealed, ducked, then came up with a spray of her own and splashed him with it. Thoroughly enjoying herself, she laid back and kicked the water so it showered in his face.

"All right, you. . ." His look of mock retribution as he steadily advanced had her squealing again, and she tried to swim away. He slid underneath the water and grabbed her legs, pulling her down and dunking her beneath with him.

They came up for air, Sarah laughing. They were close, closer than before. Her heart thudded with expectation at the look that suddenly entered his eyes, and the mood between them changed, going from playful to electric.

"Sarah," he whispered before his lips touched hers.

She felt as if she were floating and falling at the same time and wrapped her arms around his neck, both to anchor herself and keep from sinking. His arms drew her closer. Their kisses took her heart to a place she'd known only one other night. . . .

" 'Won't you come home, Bill Bailey, won't you come home—she cried the whole night lo-ong.' "

The sudden sound of two boys singing at the top of their lungs, and badly, startled them and broke them apart. They turned to the bushes to see Joel and Herbert, their hands pressed to their hearts in mock-dramatic flair as they belted out the tune. The pup woke up from its nap and began barking.

" 'I'll do the cookin' darlin','" Joel sang in high falsetto, turning to Herbert.

" 'I'll pay the rent,'" Herbert answered back in a deeper voice than normal.

" 'I knows I done you wrong,'" they both crooned, clasping both hands and holding them to their hearts as they each put their weight on one leg and leaned toward the other, heads held high, while facing Sarah and Bill.

Bill closed his eyes and groaned. Sarah couldn't help but giggle.

" 'Remember, that rainy evening I threw you out, with nothin' but a fine-toothed comb,'" Joel sang. Then together they gave their finale, " 'I know I'se to blame, well, ain't that a shame—Bill Bailey won't you please, Bill Bailey won't you please, Bill Bailey won't you pleeease come hooome!'" Joel swept off his cap from his fair hair, and both boys bowed deeply from the waist.

Bill shook his head. "Don't you kids have anything better to do than to spy on your elders?" Tenseness edged the humor of his words, and Sarah looked at him.

"Aw, we weren't doing no spying," Herbert said. "Honest. Ain't that right, Joel?"

"That's right. Mr. Lyons asked where you were, and since we were out berry-picking anyways for Miss Darcy so she can make her pies, we told him we'd look for you." He picked up a pail that was at his feet. "See?" Herbert picked up his, too.

"Well, you found me. Your message is delivered, so you can both skedaddle now."

"Didn't know we'd find you in the middle of the lake though." Joel's angelic face couldn't hide his mischief. Herbert sniggered.

"Yeah, yeah." Bill let go of Sarah and made as if he was coming their way. "Don't make me have to tell you twice."

Joel's grin was wide. "Come on, Herbert. We know when we're not wanted." The boys took off, laughing and singing another round of the same song.

Bill shook his head. "Young scamps."

Sarah's heart settled back in her chest, lower than before. "You don't like children, Bill?"

"Never been around that many to know." He looked back at her, a look of resigned disappointment on his face. "Come on. We should be getting back anyway. The sun will soon set, and I don't like the idea of you walking home alone in the dark. I'd rather from now on you didn't come out here this late." He waded out of the water to the shore.

She watched him a few seconds, then followed. The beautiful moment between them had been shattered, but not just because of the boys' sudden entrance. She would do anything to recapture what she and Bill had just shared. He turned his back to her as she changed into the dry dress, then he took the wet one from her and they set out for the refuge. Yet even though they walked side by side, Bill seemed distant once again.

❧

"Bill, I'd like you to meet Charleigh's father. This is Michael Larkin. He's a strong supporter of the refuge."

" 'Tis a pleasure to meet with ye, Bill."

Bill shook the man's hand, admiring his strong grasp. An Irishman by the sound of his voice, his obvious strength belied his years. And his tact was commendable, as well.

When Bill and Sarah returned from the lake, Bill in wet clothes and Sarah with her hair wet around her hips, the husky, gray-haired man who'd been sitting on the porch hadn't batted an eyelid. Of course, considering the craziness that went on at the refuge on a continual basis, maybe a grown man in dripping trousers and shirt wasn't all that odd to see.

"He's coming to Manhattan with us in a few days," Stewart went on to explain. "We've decided to stay overnight. Michael wants to treat us to a Broadway show. I think Sarah would enjoy that, as well as seeing some of the sights. And while I'm talking to Judge Markston, Michael will be staying with the ladies so they'll never be alone."

Bill directed a sharp glance at Stewart, to which the man shook his head. "No, I didn't tell him your story. But I don't think he'll be too shocked. Charleigh served a term in prison, remember, and at one time she also had a killer after her. Your brother saved both Darcy and Charleigh from his vengeful agenda."

"My brother?" Bill's eyes grew wide.

"Yes. In a most ingenious way, too. Got a swollen jaw and split lip for his efforts. As a matter of fact, I think the killer was a former associate of yours—Philip Rawlins, though we knew him as Eric."

Bill stood rooted to the spot. "Phil came here?"

"It's a long story. One day I'll have to tell you about it."

A wash of emotions swept over Bill. Disbelief that his brother could find the courage needed to face a killer and save the women. Shock that the killer was the man Bill had once saved. Vittorio had marked Philip as a dead man, and Bill had warned him in advance. He shook his head, trying to get a grip on reality. It all seemed so bizarre.

"I also had a run-in with Eric years ago, and saved Charleigh from his clutches before you knew him. He's in jail last I heard. And while Brent won't be coming with us since he has to teach the boys, I want to assure you again that Sarah will be safe. We won't let her out of our sight."

Bill felt his defenses weakening. Stewart knew how to make a convincing argument. If Brent could and did protect the women, Bill certainly knew these men could.

"I'll think more on it." It was the best he could do.

Chapter 16

With her hair again braided into a more acceptable style, Sarah left the bedroom. She stopped upon hearing Charleigh's beautiful voice wafting down the corridor in a soothing tune.

" 'Too-ra-loo-ra-loo-ral...too-ra-loo-ra-li...Too-ra-loo-ra-loo-ral...Hush now, don't you cry....' "

Sarah came to the threshold of Charleigh and Stewart's bedroom and peeked in, not wanting to disrupt the poignant moment. Charleigh sat in a rocker, smiling down at Clementine, who lay in her arms. The child's wide eyes looked up at her. Her hair, a shade lighter than her mother's, shone copper red.

" 'Too-ra-loo-ra-loo-ral. . .too-ra-loo-ra-li. . . Too-ra-loo-ra-loo-ral. . . That's an Irish lullaby. . . .' "

Tears came to Sarah's eyes as the haunting melody reached down deep to touch her soul, and she placed her hand to her stomach, hopeful for the day she would sing her own little one to sleep.

Charleigh looked up. Sarah, now embarrassed, turned away.

"Please don't go. Clemmie isn't being cooperative anyway. No lullaby created is going to put this one to sleep for her nap." Charleigh laid a fingertip to the child's nose, and she giggled.

Clementine twisted in her mother's lap and looked toward the doorway. She smiled, and Sarah's heart was touched. "May I hold her?"

Charleigh seemed surprised, but it was no wonder. Sarah had never offered to hold a child during all her weeks at the refuge. "Certainly. Maybe she just needs a change of hands to help her settle down." Charleigh rose from the rocker and handed the girl to her.

"Sa-rah," Clementine said with a smile, putting her little fingers on Sarah's cheek.

At that moment, something inside Sarah changed. Gone was the fear of impending motherhood and the fear of Bill's rejection of their child, while the entrance of motherly love captured her heart and soul. She desperately wanted her own baby to hold in her arms and almost wept with the release of the bonds that had constricted her from admitting that.

Searching for something to say to quell the rise of tears, she took the seat Charleigh had vacated and looked up at her. "This place, Lyons' Refuge, is such a place of song. Always I hear humming or singing from you or Darcy or even

Stewart. And the boys shared a song with me and Bill today, as well."

She told her of it, and Charleigh laughed. "Not much of a surprise. That tune was a favorite years ago. We often play the phonograph of a Sunday or after the boys are bedded for the night."

"I come from an island of song," Sarah said wistfully as she began slowly rocking. "We are taught to dance with the song, to show its meaning. The boys' song reminded me of that, though at the same time it was nothing like it."

A sympathetic look crossed Charleigh's face. "Do you miss home very much, Sarah?"

"I do miss it; I miss my father most. But since I've come here, I feel a bond also to you at the refuge. The continual song, the Bible readings you hold every night, the openness and acceptance you have toward one another as family, all are so much of how my life was like on the island."

"I hope you know that we consider you family, too, Sarah. You're a part of us."

The words, soft and sincere, caressed Sarah. They gave her comfort that helped to heal the breach caused by her husband's frequent distance.

"How do I cause my husband to care for me?" Sarah stopped rocking, shocked that her deepest concern had come tumbling from her mouth.

Charleigh regarded her with some surprise. "I wouldn't think that was a problem where you and Bill are concerned."

Sarah shrugged one shoulder and started rocking again. "He is often distant. I fear it is because of my wea—because of something I may have done." She had almost spoken of her weakness. Remembering Darcy's reaction, she didn't want to invite further censure regarding her aunt. Sarah now understood that much of what Aunt Lefu taught had been wrong, but she did not wish to speak of it. The subject still distressed her.

Charleigh's smile was sad. "You two have been through a great deal these past months. Bill's escape from death, your swift marriage, and then leaving your home and father to come to a new land that holds bad memories for Bill. Hmm. . .I think what you two need is a little good old-fashioned romance. Take some time alone together, which is difficult to find at this place—how well I know! Perhaps tonight is a good time to bring out the phonograph. The moon seen from the porch is very conducive to romance. Stewart and I take advantage of it whenever we can find the opportunity." Charleigh grinned. "And tonight's moon should be full, which is even more romantic."

The thought of being in Bill's arms again sent Sarah's heart beating a little faster. She made an effort to slow her rocking, so as not to disturb Clementine, whose small head now rested against her shoulder, her eyes closed.

❦

Once the table had been cleared, the dishes washed, and the boys and other children had been sent to or tucked into their beds, Charleigh pulled a record from its sleeve and glanced toward Sarah and Bill. "I hear there's a gorgeous full moon outside this evening. Huge and bright."

Bill hadn't missed the loving smile Darcy and his brother had shared earlier, nor their quiet exit from the room. And now he didn't miss the way Stewart came up behind Charleigh and lowered his head to whisper something in her ear. She giggled like a schoolgirl, but her gaze remained fixed on Sarah and Bill.

"Air is nice and warm, too. A perfect night to take in the stars."

Bill looked at Sarah, his pulse going a bit unsteady both at the idea of having her to himself and the fear that she might refuse. "Would you like to step outside and take a look?"

"Yes, Bill."

His heart lurched at the shy, soft glow in her dark eyes, the hint of a smile on her upturned face. He swallowed, hardly daring to believe what he was seeing, feeling almost like a schoolboy again and not like a man courting his wife. "Okay." He grinned.

"That moon isn't getting any brighter," Stewart teased, and Charleigh playfully slapped his arm, which had snaked around her waist, though she was smiling.

Bill needed no further encouragement. He slipped his hand inside Sarah's and walked with her outside to the porch, then closed the door behind them.

He turned to look at her, but suddenly didn't know what to say. From inside, the scratchy sound of a record being played on the phonograph caught his attention. He watched Sarah as she glanced toward the sheer curtains. He cast a glance that way too. Stewart and Charleigh were dancing cheek to cheek.

Sarah turned her wide eyes upon him. He swallowed hard. "Would you care to dance, Sarah?"

"Yes, Bill." She held her hands out toward him, and he clasped one in his, slipping his other arm around her tiny waist. Slowly he danced with his wife, the porch too small for anything other than making tight circles. All the while they looked into one another's eyes.

"By the light of the silvery moon, I want to spoon, to my honey I'll croon love's tune. . . ." The music played on.

"Bill?"

"Yes, Sarah." His voice came soft.

"What is *spoon*? Is it slang, too?"

Her innocent question caused his heart to race, contrary to the slow movements they made as they danced. "Allow me to show you."

Bending down, he pressed his lips to hers in a kiss that revealed his heart. Sweet and passionate, tender and warm, the kiss continued until the end of the song. When Bill lifted his head, Sarah's eyes shone brightly.

"I like this word *spoon*."

He chuckled. "So do I."

When the record restarted, the two danced on. Bill pressed his cheek against her temple and her sleek hair, closing his eyes, inhaling the sweet fragrance of her.

"Sarah?"

"Yes, Bill?"

"I love you."

The words slipped out, begging for release. When only silence answered, Bill pushed down his disappointment, squeezing his eyes shut.

"I love you, too."

The words were as gentle as a whisper, but they triumphantly sounded a herald inside his mind. Clasping her upper arms, he pulled away to look at her.

"You love me?"

Her look was slightly puzzled. "Of course. I have loved you since we were on the island. Since I chose you for my husband."

Since I chose you. Bill blinked, astounded by the revelation. He had not taken Sarah from her island. . .she had chosen to come with him. She had chosen *him*.

"You never said it before, never told me." Emotion made his voice rough. "That night on the ship, I told you I loved you then, but you didn't answer."

Her lips parted in amazement. "I never heard you." Her lashes swept down as though to conceal embarrassment, before looking up at him again. "But I was taught I should not express my feelings, that it was considered weak for a woman to do so. My aunt Lefu told me this."

"Well, your aunt was wrong." Bill could hardly believe what he was hearing. She loved him! All this time she had loved him. "Never think that you can't express your feelings to me, Sarah. Never. I want to know what you think and feel every moment. When you hurt, I want to know so I can share your pain; when you're happy, I want to know so I can share your joy. When you shut me out, it makes me feel as if I'm not important to you."

Her eyes widened at this, and he could tell such a thing had never occurred to her.

The irony of the moment—that all this time they'd each loved the other and neither had known it—struck him in the midst of the awe, and he gave a chuckle of disbelief. "It seems we've both been foolish. Maybe I was the real sap for not saying anything. You only did what you were taught; I should have known better. I've also loved you, maybe as far back as the day you made that deal with me to listen to the Bible, then told me about your island."

Such joy shone in her eyes, it took Bill's breath away. "Sarah. . ." Unable to hold back any longer, he kissed her again with tender passion.

"Your silvery beams will bring love dreams, we'll be cuddling soon, by the silvery moon. . ."

And as the song played on, they did just that.

Sarah hummed as she went about her task. Morning sunlight streamed through the windows. As she made the bed, she looked at the two pillows close together and smiled. Since the night of the silvery moon, three evenings ago, life had changed. If she had ever doubted Bill's love for her, Sarah could do so no longer. Every action, every word, he gave from his heart, and Sarah blossomed. Even when he just looked at her from across the room, Sarah felt wrapped up in his embrace. And Sarah abandoned her aunt Lefu's teachings, instead showing her love for Bill. Yet for all their newfound delight in one another, a tremor of fear still plagued Sarah.

She still had not told him about the baby. Their shared love was too new, too fragile. If she told him and he retreated from her again, unhappy or upset about the news, she would wither like a rose without the nurturing water to keep it alive. She knew she must tell him soon, but each day that passed, she put it off. Her mind went to last night, as they had sat on the porch alone, together on the glider, and he had held her within the circle of his arms.

"Sarah?" he'd asked. "Do you really want to go to Manhattan?"

Her heart jumped at the thought. "I would like to see more of it, to see a Broadway show, and to shop with Charleigh and Darcy, yes. I enjoy their company." She hesitated. "But I wish also that you would come."

He released a heavy sigh. "You know why I can't."

"I know." Sarah nestled her head against his shoulder. Last night, he had told her all about Vittorio and his former association with the mobster.

He let out another long, weighty breath. "If I allow you to go with them tomorrow, promise me you'll be very careful? That you'll stay close to Stewart or Michael at all times?"

She had looked up at him with surprise and reassurance. "I will do what you ask."

As Sarah stood by the bed and remembered, she felt Bill's presence behind her. His arm slid around her waist, gently drawing her back to him. She sighed in love's sweet contentment. She didn't want to be separated from her husband, even though she would soon be with him again. Yet as the baby grew within her, she would need new clothes. For that reason alone, she must go, if for no other.

"What are you thinking about, pretty Sarah, to look so sad?"

She moved her hand to cover his. "That I do not look forward to being apart from you. Even for one night."

"Believe me. I don't relish the thought, either. But I've heard reunions can be wonderful." He nibbled at her ear.

She giggled, pleasure trickling through her at his touch.

He held her more tightly for a long moment, then let out a sigh and broke away. "I imagine they're waiting for you. I know Stewart wanted to get an early start to the station. Is your valise packed?"

She looked at the borrowed reticule that contained only a few items. "Yes."

"Sarah." When she didn't answer, he put his fingers to her chin and directed her gaze to his face. "I want you to have a good time. I want you to enjoy yourself. This is something your father wanted, for you to see how this culture lives, to take in the sights. He told me so."

Smiling, she nodded, yet she couldn't help but feel the distance even though they weren't parted yet. A premonition of fear took her by such force that the sudden desire to throw herself into his arms, crush him tightly to her, keep him with her forever washed over her. She swallowed hard and looked into his eyes.

Bill bent to kiss her, and the oddest feeling that it was a kiss of farewell—and not just for this moment—hit her. Sarah pushed aside her fears, refusing to give in to the weakness, but she did give in to the desire to embrace him more tightly, to kiss him with all the fervor she felt for him. His arms tightened around her, drawing her closer. After a while, he broke away from her lips and brought her head to rest against his chest and his wildly beating heart.

"If you keep that up, pretty Sarah, I might change my mind about letting you go." His voice was hoarse, half teasing. "Tomorrow evening, we'll be together again. You'll be back before you know it."

However, for all his best intentions, his words did nothing to reassure.

Chapter 17

Please, sit down." Brent's voice was calm. "You make me uneasy just to watch you. You put me in mind of a prowling wildcat."

"Maybe it was a mistake letting her go." Bill plowed a hand through his hair and held the nape of his neck. "She's new to this kind of world, this kind of life. And Manhattan is so crowded."

"Sarah seems to be a woman of remarkable strength of character and high intelligence. I'm certain she'll do well."

"That city can be a zoo. I know. I lived there." Bill paced to the other end of the porch, then spun to face his brother. "The sharks she's accustomed to from her island are tame in comparison to the ones I ran into in that city. Though, granted, with the kind of company I kept, that was to be expected." He gave a mock-amused shake of his head.

"If you're so concerned, why did you change your mind and allow her to go?"

Bill expelled a long breath. "Just because I'm on a chain doesn't mean I want to keep her on a leash. I knew she wanted to go, and I knew she'd be safe in the men's care."

Brent sat back and took a drink of the lemonade beside him. "I must admit, the first time Darcy left with Charleigh to visit the city, I wasn't in complete favor of her going. Due to the fact that someone must remain behind with the boys, I haven't been able to partake of this particular event on any of the occasions they've visited the city, which amounts to three. Yet we've both found that the short absence from each other worked well for our marriage. It's helped us to appreciate each other that much more."

Bill couldn't even begin to relate. Six hours had elapsed since Sarah had left. They felt more like six weeks.

"However, you being so newly married, I imagine that what I said makes no sense to you at this moment."

Bill gave an amused snort. "You've got that right."

"Then neither do I need to ask if you've worked out your difficulties." Brent settled back in his chair. "Never mind. I've heard you whistling while you've been finishing work on the storehouse this past week, exactly as you did when we were boys. You only did that when everything was going well for you."

Needing to get his mind off of missing his wife, Bill looked out over the wooded horizon then back to his brother. "I noticed a chess set in the study.

Would you be interested in a game after dinner? I imagine it's going to be awfully lonely around here without everyone." Without Sarah.

Brent laughed. "With fifteen boys for company? That's not likely."

"Yeah, you're probably right about that."

"A game does sound like a fine idea though." Brent stood. "But at this moment, I need to see about grading papers. And then I suppose I should check into what Darcy left us to eat. I know she made three roasts and four pies. Hopefully it will be enough to feed our army and provide sandwiches for lunch tomorrow."

Bill nodded, his appetite not that sharp. Once his brother retreated indoors, Bill took a seat on the top step of the porch. He'd worked harder than usual all day, trying to get his mind off the fact that his wife wasn't on the premises. The storehouse on which he, Samuel, and a few of the older boys were working was nearing completion.

Noticing that Sasi lay nearby, head on his paws in a dejected manner, his brown eyes sad, Bill reached over to scratch the pup between his ears.

"I know, little fella. I miss her, too."

🙢

Sarah's eyes went wide as she surveyed the island of Manhattan. When she had first arrived with Bill to New York, she had been exhausted, and the explosion of sight and sound had been too much to comprehend. Fully rested, it was still much to bear.

Building after building lined both sides of the street on which they stood, all of them tall, almost seeming to soar to the clouds. Horses and carriages intermingled with noisy automobiles. Hordes of people were everywhere—standing, walking, hurrying to catch a train.

Michael must have sensed her hesitation, for he patted her hand that she'd linked through his arm upon entering Pennsylvania Station. "There now, lass. 'Tis a sight to behold, to be sure. But there's no reason to fear. Stewart and I will be takin' good care of you, and that's the truth."

Sarah gave the old Irishman a grateful smile. Since they'd boarded the train hours ago and departed it, he had taken her under his wing, acting as a father toward her.

"Well, now that we're here, what shall we do first?" Ever the boisterous one, Darcy looked to and fro along the street, her eyes bright with excitement. The flower on her hat swung with the motions.

"Shall we get something to eat?" Charleigh asked Stewart.

"Now if you don't be mindin' it, I found a grand restaurant near the Italian district, serves the finest food in all the city." Michael's blue eyes twinkled. "That is, if ye don't mind the wait. I'd like to treat you."

"That sounds fine. But I need to speak with the judge before we do too much," Stewart said.

Darcy gave an affirmative nod. "After the apples I ate on the train, I can stand the wait."

"Don't forget the plums and peaches," Charleigh said with a wink.

"Can I help it if me appetite's increased now that I'm carryin' another wee babe?"

Charleigh grinned, though Sarah noticed the men looked uncomfortable with Darcy's reply. She assumed Darcy had spoken out of turn and said something she shouldn't, but then, "that was Darcy" as everyone was wont to say.

"I only hope the twins will be all right while I'm gone." Darcy looked pensive.

Charleigh squeezed her arm. "Brent has taken care of them on his own before. They'll be fine."

"Aye, but Beatrice is teething, and likely Robert Brent will be soon enough." She glanced at Clementine, who had looped one arm around her father's neck. "Perhaps I should 'ave brought both of 'em along."

Sarah listened to the two women, hoping she would be as good a mother as they were. Sometimes she had her qualms, but with each day, what Darcy called the mothering instinct grew more firmly planted within her.

"I suggest I drop you ladies off at the boutique, along with Michael; you do your shopping, make your orders; and we get something to eat then."

"Well, now, guv, I do like the sound of that," Darcy agreed.

"So do I." Charleigh nodded.

"Then it's settled." Stewart looked relieved

Sarah bustled along with the rest of them, and she couldn't help but notice, the men flanked either side of her, as if protecting her. She wondered if it was due to their promise to Bill to see to her care. The kindness all of them had shown her, "another odd egg," as Darcy liked to say, moved Sarah beyond words. She now felt as if she fit in with them, but she missed Bill. Tomorrow evening couldn't come soon enough.

An hour later at the boutique, she was shown a dress similar to the one she wore, though of a much darker color. Darcy must have sensed her disappointment, for she turned to Mrs. Dempsey and shook her head.

"Nothin' doin'. This isn't for a funeral, after all. 'Aven't you got anything that doesn't look like it's the color of ashes from a pyre?"

The woman looked taken aback. "I had thought, what with Mrs. Thomas's condition, she would prefer something more sedate."

"She's carryin' a child, not a coffin."

"Co-ffin!" Clemmie squealed and clapped her hands.

Obviously flustered, the tall, rail-thin woman blinked and looked as if she might hyperventilate or pass out.

They had attracted the attention of another patron, a blond lady dressed in a beige chemise in the latest style. She wore a cloche hat snug to her head. A string of golden-orange beads circled her neck, reminding Sarah of the Pandanus seed necklaces she had made on the island. The woman looked at Sarah, then quickly averted her gaze.

Charleigh stepped in. "Perhaps something in a midnight blue?"

"Still too dark," Darcy insisted. "She needs somethin' bright and cheery. Like that lovely island dress she wore."

While Sarah left the women to decide the fate of her new dress, she watched the other woman, who edged closer to hear, though she kept her focus on the decor on the wall.

"The color red won't work, Darcy. All of Ithaca is bound to shun her then. You know that red is considered loose."

"I'm not sayin' to dress her as a floozy, Charleigh. I'm sayin' we might as well put her in somethin' Bill would like. What husband wants to see his wife in somethin' drab like that?" She nodded to the dress in question. "Might as well smear ashes on her forehead to give it the full effect.

"Bring us something yellow. Or pink," Darcy added to the boutique owner.

"Perhaps something in a muted shade of blue or green?" Charleigh suggested.

Mrs. Dempsey looked from one to the other throughout the entire exchange. She gave an uncertain vague smile and nodded before hurrying to disappear into a back room.

"Perhaps I was a mite hard on her?" Darcy asked.

"Perhaps just a bit." Charleigh grinned at Darcy's sheepish expression.

Sarah noticed the expensively dressed woman walk out the door of the boutique without having tried anything on. As she walked, she looked once through the window, meeting Sarah's stare, then hurried her pace until she was gone.

Chapter 18

A loud squalling from the blanket on the grass made both Bill and Brent jump.

"Here." Brent's tone was almost frantic as he thrust little Robert into Bill's hands. "You hold him. I need to see what's wrong with Beatrice."

"Wha—I can't. . ." But it was too late, and Bill sat holding his nephew like a sack of potatoes. He stared into the child's eyes. The boy looked at him a few seconds, then scrunched up his round face as if he was about to let loose with a bellow to match his sister's.

"Oh, no you don't." Feeling like a fish suddenly tossed onto dry land, Bill shot up from the chair, jiggling the baby up and down. Robert sniffled a bit, then opened his mouth wide and began to bawl.

"Hey, little fella." Desperate, Bill held the boy on his back, lying against one arm, as he'd seen Brent do. "You got a raw deal being stuck with me, didn't you?" He jiggled him again, only softer this time, and walked with him up and down the porch. Robert's cries lessened to a faint wail.

"Tell you what, you tell me your sob story, and one day your uncle Bill will tell you his. When you're much older, that is." The boy fully quieted. He hiccupped a couple of times and looked up at Bill, his sky-blue eyes wide as if he could understand.

"What, clamming up already?" Bill chuckled and lifted his hand to the side of Robert's head, stroking the baby fine hair with one finger for an instant. How did babies get to be so soft? "A little young to be worrying about spilling the beans, aren't you?"

"You do that well."

Bill looked at Brent in surprise. His brother walked up the porch stairs, Beatrice in his arms. The girl looked at Bill, then swung her tearstained face away, burying it into Brent's neck.

"You would make a good father."

Brent's unexpected words of praise settled inside Bill and shook him at the same time. "Me? A good father?"

"Yes, you."

Bill considered Brent's words. The thought of creating a child with Sarah, of becoming a father to a helpless baby, boggled his mind. What kid would want to get stuck with him?

As though Brent could read his mind, he shook his head. "You don't give yourself enough credit, though in that regard I doubt I've been much aid to you. I was leery of you when you first came here; I admit it. Because of your criminal associations, a number of desirable positions in the teaching field were formerly closed to me. Stewart gave me an opportunity, and now looking back, I can see God's hand was upon that path of my life. Yet once I was bitter because you and I bore the same name and blood."

Uncertain of how to respond, Bill stared. This was the first he'd heard any of it. Shame caused him to lower his gaze to the porch, and he looked at the cracks there.

"Yet I would be remiss not to note that a different man came home than the one who left here almost two years ago. I've seen the changes; you're not the same person."

Bill looked up. The boy in his arms started to sniffle and shudder again, and Bill absently jiggled him.

"The truth of the matter is—and I say this with all sincerity—I'm happy to have you with us at the refuge. I'm relieved you came home." Brent's expression was earnest.

Tears stung Bill's eyes, and he had trouble swallowing over the lump in his throat. "Thanks for telling me."

As they stared at one another, the years, the obstacles, all fell away. Both men walked toward one another at the same time, closing the distance, and with their free arms, they embraced as brothers at long last.

☙

After being fitted in a dress that was a pleasant shade of blue and receiving two other dresses, one a fine dress of yellow linen for church meetings, and another in a rich shade of green with cream lace, Sarah felt speechless at the women's generosity.

"Posh," Darcy said. "You need it. And family takes care of family. Isn't that right, Charleigh?"

"Darcy's right." Charleigh gave Sarah a one-armed hug. "We may not be blood-related, but that doesn't make you any less family. Bill works for the refuge now, and you both live in our home. We take care of our own."

Afterward, Michael, who'd been waiting on a sofa provided for members of the male gender while their women tried on garments, rose to greet them. "Did ye find all ye needed?"

"Yes, Papa." Charleigh smiled at Sarah. "We chose some lovely dresses, and the seamstress assured us they would be ready to collect in the morning before our train leaves."

"Splendid. Then I suppose we should go meet Stewart. I imagine his meeting is long over."

They found Stewart at the aforementioned meeting place in Central Park, which to Sarah was like a haven of trees and grass in the midst of a stone and wood jungle. He looked at Charleigh, his manner somewhat tense. Without asking why, all eyes were drawn to the small child who sat on the bench beside him. Her face dirty, her brown hair in pigtails, she glared up at them. The apprehension that marked her face belied her tough exterior.

"Stewart?" Charleigh's eyes were wide as she turned to him.

He cleared his throat. "This is Miranda. She'll be joining us at the refuge."

Stunned silence met his announcement.

"A girl?" Charleigh blinked, looked back at the child, then at Stewart.

"See, I told ya they wouldn' want me." Miranda scowled and shot off the bench.

Still looking at Charleigh, Stewart caught the girl by the sleeve before she could go anywhere.

"Let me go! Get your stinkin' hands off me!"

"Judge Markston has handed Miranda over to my care," he explained, not looking at the girl. "Bill's almost finished with the storehouse. Perhaps it's time to make it official and take in girls as we talked about months ago. We could use the storehouse to house the older boys and give Miranda their room."

Charleigh shared a long look with him, then smiled. "Perhaps it is time at that. But oh, what will the townspeople say when they find out?" Her words were spoken lightly, and he chuckled. She looked at Miranda. "And we do want you. You are welcome."

Darcy moved forward and held out her hand. "Hello, Miranda. Me name's Darcy. I'm the cook there."

Miranda just glared.

"Well, I think I be hearing my stomach a-growlin'," Michael inserted. "Am I the only one ready to enjoy a meal?"

All in agreement, they hailed a cab, and soon the horse-drawn carriage brought them to their destination. They settled behind the red- and white-checked tablecloth of a fine-looking establishment. Sweet strains of music came from a far corner, and Sarah looked to see a dark-haired gentleman playing an instrument at one of the tables. Delicious aromas, such as she had never known, made Sarah's mouth water. Everyone at the table engaged in pleasant conversation. All except for the newcomer, Miranda. She sat in her chair, arms crossed over her chest, and pouted as if she were being jailed. However, when a plate of what Darcy called spaghetti was placed before her, the child's eyes widened, and she leaned forward to practically inhale the long noodles and meatballs without waiting for the blessing Stewart gave.

Once they finished their meal, with Sarah now labeling Italian food a new favorite, a lovely young girl, not quite a woman, came to the table. Sarah stared at her curiously. This girl, with her long fair hair held back with a blue ribbon that matched her bright eyes, seemed different from the dark-haired workers Sarah had seen, among them the exotically beautiful older woman who'd served them their meal.

"Hello. My name is Melissa. My aunt Maria was called away suddenly, and she asked me to come and see if there's anything else you need. My aunt Maria and uncle Tony own this restaurant," she added proudly.

"It's a lovely place," Charleigh said. "I can't help but think that your aunt looks familiar, yet I've never been here before."

The girl gave a delicate shrug. "She rarely leaves the restaurant, so I don't know where you two might have met."

"Perhaps at the boutique?"

"It's a possibility." She looked toward the door as it opened and frowned. When she looked at them again, her smile had returned. "I need to go back to the kitchen now. On behalf of my uncle and my aunt, I want to thank you for visiting our establishment."

"It was a delight," Stewart assured. "The food was superb."

Melissa gave a faint smile and nod, again casting a distant glance toward the door before she hurried away.

Sarah turned to see what had captured the young girl's interest. A black-haired man in a sharp-looking three-piece suit with padded shoulders and wearing a fedora sauntered to a nearby table. A waiter suddenly appeared at his elbow, effusively greeting him.

Stewart also looked that way and frowned. "I think it's best we leave. I'm certain the women will want to freshen up at the hotel before the show tonight."

Charleigh looked his way, her brows drawn up in curiosity, to which Stewart only gave a slight quelling shake of his head. His eyes flicked to the man at the table, and Charleigh followed his gaze. She looked back at him, her eyes widening, and he gravely nodded.

Sarah didn't miss the signals between them. As they left, she directed a stare toward the mysterious man seated at the table. As if he felt her curiosity, he looked up at her. Sarah's heart iced over at the evil she sensed behind the man's dark eyes before he lowered his gaze back to the wine the waiter had brought him.

No one had to tell her why Stewart was suddenly so anxious to leave. Sarah had no doubt that she was staring at one of Vittorio's henchmen.

An uneasy pall covered the group, but the men later decided to go ahead and take the women to see the Ziegfeld Follies. Sarah enjoyed the music, the costumes, and the dancing considerably, no longer worried about Vittorio or his family. The restaurant was located on the other side of the city; the chances of them running into any of the men in this theater were slim. And as Michael and Stewart had reassured her earlier, the man didn't even know she was Bill's wife, so there was no reason for alarm.

All through the spectacular presentation, Darcy excitedly spoke under her breath to Sarah, who sat in the aisle seat. Charleigh had opted out, staying behind at the hotel with Clementine and Miranda, saying she'd seen plenty of Broadway shows and wanted Sarah to go and enjoy herself.

And she did. She enjoyed the colorful costumes, the pageantry, the music, but when she returned to her hotel room, it was with a sense of relief. Unaccustomed to the business and night life of such a bustling city, she looked forward to returning home to the countryside of the refuge tomorrow. And to Bill. She missed him so.

Clutching a second pillow to her chest, she lay on her side to sleep.

Chapter 19

I don't like the looks of that sky." Bill stood on the porch late in the afternoon, hands on his hips as he stared at the dark cloud bank. "Soon it'll be raining pitchforks, unless I miss my guess."

"It certainly will make traveling to the station difficult, since I'll need to take the wagon as the automobile will not hold everyone." Brent surveyed him from the chair where he sat, holding both twins on his lap. "We still have only the one; the brake on the other vehicle isn't yet fixed."

Bill nodded. "It's an old hay-burner if you ask me. Too expensive to run," he clarified for Brent.

"I hope that the rain doesn't interfere with the picnic this coming weekend."

"Picnic?"

"Didn't I mention it earlier this week?" Brent shook his head. "Perhaps father-hood makes one forgetful."

"You always did have your head in the clouds." Bill's comment lacked the mockery of old times but still bore a wealth of teasing. "Seriously, you're a good father, Brent. I've watched you these past two days, and it's been nothing short of amazing how you take care of those two. I don't know how you've managed as well as you have without Darcy here."

"The first occasion was difficult," Brent admitted as he rescued his spectacles from Robert's seeking hands, which had found Brent's pocket. "However, I learned by both experience and mistake. Darcy almost single-handedly tends to the children approximately 363 days of the year. Giving her a few days' reprieve to enjoy Manhattan twice in that same year wasn't so much to offer. Though I must admit, had I known that both Beatrice and Robert were teething, I might not have been so eager to enlist my aid. I hope she didn't keep you awake all night?"

"Between her and Sasi's howling, it was an experience." Bill chuckled. The truth was that without Sarah beside him, he'd found it difficult to sleep, no matter the situation. "About the picnic. . . ?"

"Ah, yes, the picnic. There will be a church picnic by the lake after the meeting this Sunday. It's an annual event before we must bid the summer farewell."

Robert suddenly began wailing. Bill moved toward his brother. "I'll take her if you need to see to Robert."

"Yes, thank you." Once Bill took Beatrice, Brent went with the boy into the house. He was back a few minutes later. "I don't like this. Robert seems to be running a temperature, likely due to teething, but I certainly don't want to take him outdoors due to the possibility of rain. Darcy would have my head if I exposed him. Would you mind terribly going to the station alone to collect them? You do remember how to get there?"

"After the turnoff, there's only one road to follow, Brent." Bill shook his head, amused. "I think I can find the place."

"Splendid."

Bill swiped his jaw, noticing the rough whiskers. "Maybe I'll head out early and get a trim and a shave while I'm at it."

"Ah, yes. You do want to get dolled up and look spiffy for Sarah. Of course, I do believe she already thinks you're the bee's knees." Brent's eyes twinkled.

Bill stared at his brother. "I don't believe it. Twice in almost two weeks with the slang. Be on the level with me. Are you an imposter? Have you kidnapped my brother?"

"I do believe it was bound to happen one day. I'm surrounded by slang, no matter what efforts I employ to try to train the boys to speak properly. And then, there's my wife." He grinned. "It's difficult to maintain the quality of stuffiness in such exacting situations."

Bill laughed. It felt like old times again, when they were kids and used to josh each other and horse around. Since yesterday, Brent had completely let down his guard around Bill, bantering with him like he used to do when they were young boys, when Brent had looked up to Bill while Bill regarded him as his kid brother. Bill missed Sarah tremendously, yes, but at the same time he was thankful for this opportunity he'd had to share with Brent and really talk. The occasions had been rare in the past weeks, but once the boys were in bed last night, the two had found one another out on the porch and breached the chasm in their relationship.

"Well, I'm off. Toodle-oo!" Bill lifted a hand in a wave as he stepped off the stairs.

"Cheerio!" came the good-natured reply.

Bill shook his head in amusement without looking back. That one had to be Darcy's doing. Once again, he mentally tipped his hat toward her for teaching his brother to relax and enjoy life.

The drive into town went well—no rain. He headed to the barber shop, glad to see only one other customer there. A towel lay over his face, and his head rested back against the chair he sat in.

The barber, a plump man in his fifties, looked Bill's way. "I know you. You're Brent's brother—Bill Thomas. Right?"

"Yeah?" Bill waited.

"A man was in here an hour or so ago, looking for you. Seemed to think you would be at the station, waiting for a train."

"A man?" Bill thought a moment. Maybe the train was early, though that would be odd. Train schedules were very strict. "Did he give his name? Was it Stewart Lyons? Or Michael Larkin?"

"No, no. I know both of those gentlemen." As he spoke, he moved a straight razor up and down a strop. "This was a stranger."

A stranger. Fear locked down hard on Bill. "What did he look like?"

"Blond gent. Medium height—about as tall as you. Blue eyes." His own eyes brightened. "He talked with a funny accent."

"It was French," came from behind the cloth of the man waiting for his shave.

"Yeah. That was it—French. Had that smooth ooh-la-la sound to it."

Bill stared. The man he described sounded just like Philip Rawlins, only he knew his old associate didn't work for Vittorio any longer. "Did he leave any kind of message?"

"No. Said he was just passing through town and heard you were here."

"Thanks." Forgetting all about his shave and haircut, Bill left the shop in a daze.

Why would Phil Rawlins search him out? Unless it wasn't Phil Rawlins at all, but one of Vittorio's hatchet men. . .no, that made no sense. The killers Vittorio had working for him in the family were mostly Italian; not blond with French accents. He and Phil had been the exception as far as coloring went.

Bill walked down the street, the minutes rambling by without order, while he tried to unscramble the situation in his mind. As he walked past the postal office, he noticed a dark-haired middle-aged woman who sat on a bench outside and fanned herself with a newspaper. She looked up at him as if she knew him.

"You're Bill Thomas? From Lyons' Refuge?"

"Yes."

"I thought so. I've seen you in church. I have something for you. A man came by and dropped it off. I'd put it with the other mail for the refuge, but as long as you're here, I'll go and get it. And you can have the rest of the mail, too."

This day was taking on a surreal aspect. "Thanks, I'd appreciate it."

Soon she waddled back out to the porch, a sheaf of envelopes and magazines in her hands. Bill took the bundle with another word of thanks and began walking away as he shuffled through the correspondence, a *Saturday Evening Post*, another few envelopes, a circular—until he found what he was looking for.

He stared hard at the plain envelope that bore his name and the name of the refuge underneath. Knowing he couldn't read it and juggle the rest of the items, he returned to the wagon, set the rest of the mail on the bench, and tore into the letter:

Bill,

> *Don't ask why I'm doing this or even how I know. Call it payback for saving my life like you did that time I put the bite on V and he planned to*

bump me off. For reasons I don't want to touch on here, I can't visit you at Lyons' Refuge, so I wrote this note instead. V knows you didn't die. A life for a life—that's always been his motto, and he won't stop until he finds you and makes that happen. You're no chump; take this as a warning. Keep your back covered. If I were you, I'd pack a rod at all times.

P. R.

So, it was Phil. The warning from his old associate wove deep down into Bill's mind, making him both angry and tense. He had gotten his life in order, was finally trying to stay on the up and up and do what was right. He'd brought God into his life—so why was this happening to him? Why now, when his relationship with Sarah was working out so well and they'd discovered mutual love? Sarah. . .

Horror swept through him.

A life for a life.

Closing his eyes, Bill felt the warning scream down into his very soul.

❧

Confused, Sarah studied her husband all through dinner. Since he had collected them at the station, she had sensed his unease. When he'd embraced her at the depot, he'd held her tightly for several seconds, almost as if he were afraid to let her go, then gave a faint, flippant smile when he pulled away. Even Stewart asked if anything was the matter, a question which Bill carelessly shrugged off with the comment that he'd missed his wife.

Sarah had missed him, too, but that didn't account for Bill's strange behavior. The troubled look she'd seen in his eyes all night. The heavy set to his shoulders as if they carried an unseen weight.

"Bill?" She came up to him where he sat on the porch, staring blankly at the stars. No one was with them, and he pulled her onto his lap. "What's biting you? You seem so worried." She pushed at a lock of his hair.

Despite his tense expression, he quietly chuckled. "If you're going to speak slang, pretty Sarah, you need to get it right. It's 'what's eating you?'" His words were gentle, teasing, but she didn't want to be put off.

"Please tell me," she quietly insisted.

He looked at her a long time, his eyes roving to each part of her face as though memorizing it.

"Bill?"

"Let's go away, Sarah. Just the two of us. We can find somewhere nice, somewhere quiet, safe. Build a life there."

"Go away?" Her brows pulled together in confusion. "Don't you like it here at the refuge? Now that you and your brother are getting along so well, I should think you would want to stay."

"It's all right here, I guess." He grew somber and looked into the distance. "There sure are a lot of kids around, though. And that new one has a mouth on her that won't quit. She'd shame a sailor."

Something twisted inside her heart. "You don't like kids, Bill?"

"Oh, I don't know." He seemed frustrated as he shook his head. "They're all right, I guess. But I think maybe we should head off somewhere else for a while. I hear Connecticut is nice. That's where your father is from if I remember right."

"Yes, he told me this. But why Connecticut? I have no relatives there any longer."

He blew out a heavy breath. "I don't know, Sarah. If you don't want to go there, that's fine. We can go somewhere else. I just want to get out of New York for a while."

She remained quiet as she observed him. She loved the refuge and all the people in it, who'd become her family. But she loved Bill more. "If you want to go to Connecticut, then we shall go. I only want for us to be together."

"Doll, you can't get rid of me."

The hoarseness in his voice confused her. He swallowed hard, and Sarah wondered in shock at the tears she saw glazing his eyes. But she had no time to think of his unpredictable behavior as his hand went to the back of her head and he swiftly pulled her toward him.

His mouth on hers both thrilled her and frightened her. He kissed her urgently, passionately, as if it were the last time he might ever do so. A maelstrom of emotion swept through Sarah at his kiss, and she kept her arms around his neck as if to hold on. With her answering kiss, she tried to show him her reassurance and her devotion, tried to comfort him and not be frightened.

But later that night, as Bill lay trembling in her arms, again holding her so very tightly, Sarah knew something was definitely wrong.

Chapter 20

I shall miss you." Charleigh helped Darcy with the dishes and looked toward Sarah. "At least you'll be coming with us on the picnic this weekend."

"Yes. Bill wanted to attend the church meeting once more and spend one last day with everyone here in a leisurely atmosphere." Sarah laid the plate she'd just dried onto a shelf. Feeling a fluttering inside, she put a hand to her stomach.

Darcy took her hands out of the dishwater and glanced Sarah's way, her expression concerned. "How are you feelin', luv? Is the sickness any better?"

"I'm doing much better. Only. . ." She hesitated, wondering if she should speak. Seeing only kindness in the women's eyes, feeling a closeness to them she'd never had with any other woman, including her aunt, she decided to share. "I have not yet told Bill about the baby. I fear he doesn't like children and I may lose him if he knows." Without warning, the tears came, and she buried her face in the dish towel. She had been so emotional lately and couldn't seem to quench this latest outburst. Her shoulders shook as she tried.

She felt Darcy's arm slip around her waist as she drew her close. "There, there. Don't cry so." She smoothed her hair. "Bill loves you—even a blind man could see that. And I don't think he dislikes children neither. Brent told me he took quite a shine to Robert Brent. Held both babies in his arms and helped Brent take care of 'em while we was away. Poor dears. That's sayin' a lot for two teethin' babies!"

Sarah hiccupped softly and looked up. "Really?"

"Most certainly." Darcy nodded emphatically as if to prove her point.

Charleigh dried her hands. "Sarah, I understand your fears, but like Darcy, I agree that they aren't warranted. Any day you'll be showing, and I really think you need to tell Bill soon. I know Darcy told you of my experience in keeping news of Clementine from Stewart when I carried her, and let me assure you, if I could go back and redo the past, I would have told him the moment I knew. It could have saved us so much heartache and pain."

"If only we could go back and redo the past." Sarah sighed as another thought took hold. "I've made a great many mistakes; the greatest I believe was to cleave to the pagan teachings of my aunt. Something deep inside me felt uneasy even as I listened and attended the ceremonies, but when my father distanced himself from me after my mother died, I was lonely. I relied on my aunt to show me love and attention. I believed what she said, and even later, after my father told me differently, I would not listen."

"You were a small child when that happened." Shaking her head, Charleigh laid a comforting hand against Sarah's shoulder. "It wasn't your fault. Now that you've matured into an adult and have learned and know the truth, you're making a wise decision to abstain from island beliefs."

Sarah nodded, deciding she must also make another decision. "You are right in what you advise concerning Bill. Already I have felt life within my belly, and I know I cannot hide it from him any longer. I will tell him about the babe at the picnic." In a relaxed setting—surely this would be the best place to reveal such news.

"I'm tickled pink to hear it," Darcy said with a grin. "And I'm sure your pot and pan will be just as pleased." At Sarah's blank stare, Darcy added, "Your husband, luv. That's me Cockney slipping in, as you no doubt have heard many times before." She let out a delighted laugh.

Sarah grinned. Between Bill's American slang and Darcy's British Cockney, her vocabulary had increased immensely over the past weeks.

A baby started crying, and another one soon joined in.

"Poor lambs. I best go see what's troublin' 'em now." Darcy left the kitchen. Charleigh and Sarah resumed their task of washing the dishes.

"In a pig's eye! And I don't have to tell you nothin'."

Both women jumped upon hearing Miranda's shout from outside. They hurried to the door.

Miranda stood, fists on her hips, leaning toward two boys Sarah recognized as Petey and Clint. Her braids were askew as always; her reddened face smudged with dirt.

"You're just a dumb girl," Petey shot back. "You don't know nothin' nohow."

"Says you! I'm smarter than all of you put together."

"If you're such a smarty-pants, whatcha doin' here?" Clint taunted. "You musta got caught to end up in this place. Watcha do—snitch a lollipop off a baby?"

The boys snickered.

"None of your beeswax!" Miranda said hotly. "You're both just a bunch of bozos!"

"Oh, yeah—well, so's your old man," Clint shot back.

Miranda flew at him, knocking him to the ground. She straddled him, her fist flying, but Charleigh flew off the porch and caught her arm before the girl could punch him in the nose. Sarah followed but stayed a distance behind.

"Stop it!" Charleigh commanded. "All of you. Clint and Petey, march right to Mr. Lyons' office—now! Miranda, you come with me."

"Whatcha gonna do? Beat me to a pulp?" The girl glared at both women. "I ain't afraid of any of you."

Charleigh maintained calm. "Miranda, we would never strike a child in anger; that's simply not right, nor is it how we do things here at the refuge. But you will be disciplined. I cannot allow fighting to go unpunished. For now, I want you to sit on the porch. Do not move from that spot. I need to talk this over with Mr. Lyons."

Miranda wrenched her arm away from Charleigh and marched to the porch. With a huff, she flopped onto it, her skirts ruffling with the action. Sarah was surprised the girl had given in so quickly. Over the past several days at the refuge, she had rejected authority, though the second time she'd been sent to her room without supper. Perhaps that had helped to curb her rebellion.

Charleigh shook her head, the look she gave Sarah filled with concerned exasperation. "Would you mind keeping an eye on her while I talk with Stewart? She appears to have settled down some, but I'd prefer it if she wasn't alone."

"Of course."

Charleigh left for the house. Sasi, who'd awoken from his nap, came to sniff Miranda. The girl put out her hand and tentatively petted the pup. Seeing Sarah approach, she quickly withdrew her hand.

"You may pet Sasi if you like." Sarah smiled, but the girl looked away. She hesitated, then sat on the porch, keeping Sasi between them. Sasi moved to lick Sarah's hand, and she absently petted the puppy. He playfully nipped at her, and Sarah chuckled.

"Is he yours?" Miranda asked, still staring straight ahead.

Sarah sensed a strange longing in the child's voice. "Yes. My husband gave him to me. I've always had a great fondness for animals. On the island where I was born, I had a pet monkey and a dolphin."

Miranda turned wide eyes to Sarah. "No foolin'? I seed pictures of 'em in books before, but never seen one in real life. My pa wouldn't let me have a dog. Wouldn't let me have nothin'. Exceptin' the back of his belt." The girl turned sullen again.

Wanting to bring back the shine she'd seen in Miranda's eyes, Sarah spoke. "I suppose I truly did not own either of them. They were wild and only came to visit me when they were ready. I miss them, but now I have Sasi." She reached down to rub his belly, and Sasi's tail thumped the porch. "The monkey was actually a gift to my father, but he did not like Mutu. He would often steal his bananas or other fruit from him when my father was not looking. He never did so to me, though. We had an understanding. I carried him through the forest, and he did not steal from my plate." Sarah grinned and was pleased when Miranda smiled. But again it faded.

"Sometimes if you wanna eat ya gotta steal," the girl countered in sad resignation. "Ain't nothin' you can do about that."

Sarah thought a moment. "You should talk to Darcy. When she was a girl, she lived in the streets of London and stole food to eat. She was also a pickpocket. She stole money from gentlemen's pockets."

Miranda's eyes widened. "Really? I figured she was just a goody-goody like the rest of 'em."

"Goody-goody? I have not heard this term."

Miranda gave a scornful half laugh. "Lady, you are way behind the times. A goody-goody is someone who's too good to be true. Like this place." She shook her head. "Ain't no way these people here are real. One day I'm gonna wake up and they'll be just as mean as my pa was."

Sarah felt saddened by the girl's pain. "And your mother?"

"She ran off long ago. Who needs her anyway?" Scowling, Miranda picked up a pebble lying nearby and threw it far across the lawn.

"I also had no mother. I lost her when I was seven."

Miranda looked at Sarah. "That's when my old lady ran out on me. Two years ago. Pa's been meaner than a hornet ever since, though he took off, too. Took his money and gambled it all away."

Sarah stared out over the lawn as silence settled between them. Something inside urged her to speak. "This term, *goody-goody*. It makes me think of God, and how He is all that is good. My father taught me that no one is truly good, and that is so. Everyone at one time or another does what is wrong when they wish to do what is right. The people here at the refuge have God living inside their hearts; that is the goodness you see. They want to reach out and share this goodness with others. Everyone here has been through many difficulties, as you have. Charleigh served a term in a British prison for her crimes, as did Darcy. That is where they met."

Shock covered Miranda's face. "No foolin'?"

Sarah nodded. "They would not mind me speaking of this, since everyone here knows of their story. Do not be afraid of this goodness you see, Miranda. It is real and will not be taken from you."

Miranda looked away and didn't answer. Seconds elapsed before she turned to Sarah again. Her eyes seemed hopeful, though hesitant. "Will you tell me more about your dolphin and your monkey?"

Sarah laughed, grateful that Miranda had finally reached out. "I would be most honored to."

❧❧

Stewart's eyes were grave as he set the letter on the desk. He looked up at Bill. "Why should Eric do this, is what I want to know? What kind of hidden motive does he have?"

A tap sounded on the door, and Charleigh walked inside. "Oh, sorry to interrupt. I'll come back later."

"No, wait." Stewart looked at Bill then back to his wife. "You need to hear this, too."

Curiosity lifting her brows, Charleigh approached the desk. Stewart handed her the letter. She read over it, then looked up, her eyes even more confused.

"P. R. is Philip Rawlins. . .Eric."

Her face blanched. Stewart rose from his chair to put an arm around her shoulders. "Don't worry, sweetheart. I won't let him near you again."

She nodded faintly, then looked at Bill. "Is this why you feel you must leave the refuge?"

The refuge. An odd choice of words. Was anywhere really safe?

"It would be best for everyone here if we did leave. And please, I don't want Sarah to know about that letter."

"You don't want your wife to know a killer might be after you?" Stewart shook his head. "Is that fair to her? Don't you think she should be told?"

Bill wondered about that. If he thought that it was only about him, he might be able to handle the prospect of Vittorio's henchmen lurking somewhere close by far better. But the fear that Sarah was the target had him literally trembling. Ever since he'd received the missive, Bill was frantic, his emotions so near the surface he'd been unable to control them or hide them from his wife. That had been the motivation for him bringing the letter to Stewart. He hoped somehow Stewart could help him.

"You can't run all your life, Bill." Stewart's words were calm. "After Connecticut, then where? There will always be some place else you'll feel the need to run. The offer to stay here with Sarah still stands."

Frustrated, Bill shook his head, rubbed a hand along his nape. "You don't know these people like I do. What Phil wrote—a life for a life—is exactly how Vittorio thinks. He won't stop until he achieves his purpose. Phil knows that, too."

He noticed the look they shared.

"Look, I know you don't think much of Phil—or Eric, as you knew him," Bill corrected. "But he was my friend; I saved his life once, and that means something in the underworld where I come from. I don't think he's playing me for a sap. This is on the level. And I also think if he meant you guys harm, he wouldn't have written that letter. He would have come here. He didn't try to disguise the fact that it was from him."

"You could be right about that." Stewart's answer was grim. "Still, I'd find it hard to believe that there was any morsel of good in the man."

Charleigh put a gentling hand to Stewart's tense arm, and he relaxed, again glancing at her. His gaze softened.

Bill could understand their dilemma. He'd heard everything his former associate had done to this poor woman. Deceiving her into believing they were married, using her as his fellow con artist, and then, after the *Titanic* sank, searching her out and threatening her again. His own brother had saved everyone at the refuge on the night Phil had arrived to wreak his revenge. But Bill would be a sorry soul if he were to judge Phil for his past sins when his own were just as bad.

"If I were packing heat, I'd feel safer, but I no longer have a gun."

"I'm sorry. I have no gun to give you. Here at the refuge, especially considering some of the situations these children come from, we find it safer not to have firearms on the premises. I no longer keep guns here. But I do understand your dilemma, and I'm not suggesting that it isn't real. I believe it's very real."

"The only protection I can offer you is my prayers," Charleigh said earnestly. "You and Sarah will always have those."

"Yeah, thanks." Bill tightened inside. If God really cared about his life, would He have allowed this to happen? He'd asked God to take over, but Bill figured somewhere along the line, God must have gotten lost, too. He didn't understand this alarming course on which he was being taken.

As if he'd read his mind, Stewart eyed him somberly. "Sometimes, even after we become Christians, we end up having to suffer the consequences for past mistakes. Maybe it doesn't seem fair, and maybe it doesn't seem like God really cares. But He does. And we just have to keep trusting Him to work out our lives, even when it seems like everything is falling apart."

Bill nodded, knowing Stewart was just trying to help, though he wasn't sure he bought all of what the man said. He'd be happy when he and Sarah were out of New York.

Chapter 21

W e'll be leaving for the picnic as soon as the twins are up from their nap."

Sitting on the edge of the bed, Sarah nodded and continued staring at the object in her hand. As she studied the last few engraved symbols, Bill came to sit beside her.

"Your father's cross?" he asked, and again she nodded. "Do you understand what all those symbols mean?"

"Most of them." She explained to him that the wavy lines meant the prayers of her father, and then enlightened him to the other symbols she'd figured out. Afterward she motioned to the top of the last two. "This, I think, means you." She pointed to a symbol next to the crown. "When Maliu brought you to the island and I found you."

Bill leaned forward to see, then snorted. "Please tell me that's not what I think it is."

Sarah's smile grew wide. "Yes, it is an angel. My father was very fond of the meanings of symbols and names and studied them. The night before we married, he told me that your true name—William—means *determined guardian*. Like an angel, perhaps?" Her heart fairly danced as he shook his head in embarrassed agitation.

"Why is it carrying that crown?"

"The crown is me. The name Sarah means *princess*. You, my guardian, carried the princess away from the island."

His eyes clouded over. "Do you regret that, Sarah? I've sometimes wondered if you held it against me."

"No, Bill. I have found much happiness with you here in New York. More than I ever dreamed possible. I wouldn't have left the island with you had I not wanted to."

They shared a tender look, and he pointed to the bottom symbol. "What's that last one mean?"

Sarah again studied the symbol that had given her so much confusion. The crown was closed off inside a thick circle and separate from the symbols on the outside, which were at opposite angles. A snake. A cross. "This one I do not know. I have studied it and studied it. The snake, I think, means evil, and the cross is good. Perhaps showing that Aunt Lefu's way was evil and Father's way was good?" She shook her head. "But why it shows at the bottom is what I don't understand."

Bill intently looked at the carving a long moment. "Sarah, what if this was your father's way of showing you that you had closed yourself within two worlds and must make a choice? That you can't serve more than one God?"

At his quiet words, a flash of blinding clarity streamed through her mind. Her father had tried to talk to her several times after his great sorrow when he had returned to God to point out that Sarah shouldn't attend the pagan ceremonies or cleave to the words of her aunt. But she hadn't understood since he'd never stopped her before. And so he had discontinued his counsel. Was this his last way of reaching out to her, to try and get her to realize the truth?

Tears swam to her eyes as she looked at Bill. "I think you may be right. I think that must have been the message that Father was trying to tell me. If only he could know that I've learned the truth and now in my heart serve only one God. The true God."

With his index finger, Bill traced one of the wavy lines. "I think he probably does know, Sarah."

❧

A balmy breeze heightened the summer day, making it comfortable. Bill joined Sarah on the blanket for their picnic. With them, Darcy and Brent, Charleigh and Stewart, all enjoyed sandwiches while the children played, having already engulfed their food. Their excitement over running through the grass or wading in the lake nearby made everyone smile. Even Miranda seemed to be enjoying herself and didn't pick fights with the boys as she often did.

Robert Brent crawled over to Bill, grabbed his index finger, and put it in his mouth, gumming down on it.

Darcy tugged on his diaper, pulling the boy back. "Now then, you'll not be usin' people for teethers, young man."

"That's all right." Bill gave a smile of consent, then looked down at the kid. "Me and Robert have an understanding, don't we, little fella?"

Robert made gurgling noises as he continued to gum Bill's finger. Bill looked up at Sarah and was stunned by the glow of happiness in her eyes. "Sarah?" he breathed in confusion.

She looked down at her lap, but he couldn't miss the shyness that swept over her face. Darcy and Charleigh exchanged a grin.

"Well now, as much as we'd love to keep your company, bein' as how ye will soon be leavin' the refuge, I think it's a splendid day for young lovers to take a walk." When neither Bill nor Sarah made a move, Darcy shooed them. "Do I need to set a fire underneath you? Well then, off with ye both."

Brent chuckled. "Trust me, Bill. You'd be wise to just do as she suggests."

"I like the idea." Stewart rose and held his hand out to Charleigh. "Shall we?"

She nodded, her eyes bright as she stood to take his arm, and the two began to walk. Bill and Sarah did the same, taking the opposite direction.

They hadn't gone far, when they heard the unmistakable sound of Sasi's yipping. Bill turned to look, and noticed Miranda following them and carrying the pup.

"Don't you have anything better to do?" Bill pointedly asked. "I hear the children are going to have a potato-sack race soon."

"Don't like races."

"Well, then go take a swim."

"Can't. Don't know how."

Bill let out a frustrated breath. "Well, I'm sure you can find something to do rather than spy on your elders. In other words—scram!"

"Aw, no need to get in a lather, mister." Miranda scowled. "I know when I ain't wanted." She turned on her heel in a huff.

"Bill." Sarah put a hand to his sleeve.

"Can't a man spend time alone with his wife?" he implored, half amused, half frustrated.

"Yes, of course. But I think you were too hard on her. She has been through so much, and we have talked. I think she is starting to open up with me."

Bill looked into Sarah's gentle eyes, which always seemed to have the power to transform him from a growling bear to a bear cub within seconds. He blew out a resigned breath. "Yeah, maybe you're right. I was too hard on the kid. I'm just not used to them is all. Never been around any before I came to the refuge."

They continued walking and entered a shady area where the trees blocked them from view of the rest of the picnickers. Holding her hand, Bill led Sarah farther into the woods, then turned with a smile and pulled her into his arms for a long, tender kiss.

Caught up in the delight of Sarah, he heard the rustle of the grass only when it was too late.

"Well, now. Looks to me like Lucky Bill ain't so lucky after all."

An ominous click sounded.

Bill tensed and hurriedly pulled away from Sarah, setting her behind him so that he mostly stood in front of her.

In pinstriped suits and wearing fedoras, two men Bill recognized as Alfonzo and Lucio both pointed guns at Bill's heart.

❧

Fear tore into Sarah's mind. Dread ripped away her composure.

"Good thing Vonnie was at the boutique the day your little wife was," the darker of the two said.

Sarah recognized him as the stranger from the restaurant, and she clutched the sleeve of Bill's suit coat, her eyes wide. She realized these must be the mobsters

Bill had been running from.

"You got what you want." Bill's voice was tight but calm. "Let her go."

His words of defeat terrified Sarah. She shot a glance to her husband, her grip on his arm tightening as if by force of will she could protect him from these men's evil intentions with her touch alone.

"Well now," the first man responded, "we can't do that, Bill. We don't need her running off to squeal. Besides, two for the price of one—Vittorio might like that." He raised his brows to his partner, who gave an unpleasant grin.

Bill tensed. "That's not Vittorio's way and you know it. She has nothing to do with any of this."

"What makes you think I care? She's just a dame. They're a dime a dozen as far as I'm concerned." The first man's dark eyes were cold. "Now. . ." He motioned with his gun for them to walk ahead of him. "It's time for you to take a little ride that's been long in coming. You, too, sister."

"You wanna find the real killer?" Bill stood his ground. "Tell Vittorio to take a good look at the Ferrelli family. I didn't kill Marco. I saved the man's life once; why would I kill him? I had no motive."

"Aw, go tell it to Sweeny."

"I'm not asking you to believe it, Alfonzo. I'm asking you to take me to Vittorio."

Sarah's heart froze. What was Bill doing? Vittorio would kill him before Bill ever opened his mouth; he'd told her so.

"He sent us to do the job." Alfonzo slightly waved his gun in a brisk movement. "You're trying my patience. Whether we do it here or somewhere outta the ways makes no difference to me. By the time those other picnickers get here, we'll be long gone."

Sasi's sudden barking startled them. Distracted, Alfonzo swung his head in that direction as the pup raced for him and grabbed a bite of his trousers hem. Sarah watched the other man aim at Bill and his finger move slowly on the trigger. She didn't stop to think, didn't stop to question. With all her strength, she pushed Bill out of the way.

In the next split second, the other man fired. Blinding pain tore through Sarah's side. A haze covered her eyes. The last thing she heard before sliding to the ground was Bill's panicked cry of her name.

Chapter 22

Before Vittorio's men could fire again, Bill rushed to his wife's side, grabbing her upper body close to him. Red soaked her yellow dress and spread onto his shirt.

"No, Sarah! No! Dear God, why?" His cries were tortured. *"Why?"*

A loud rustling stirred the bushes. Men's voices could be heard. "Bill?" Stewart called.

"Someone's coming," Lucio said. "More than one. Sounds like an army."

"Let's scram!"

The two mobsters ran off before a large group of men hurried into sight.

Bill heard exclamations of horror and surprise. Someone called out to go and get the doctor. Bill felt someone else take hold of his arm.

"Bill," Brent said urgently but quietly, "we need to get her back to the refuge."

He looked up, dazed.

"No, that's too far away," a woman said. "Bring her to my house. It's closer."

The need for immediate action pushed shock into a temporary corner of Bill's mind. One of the men moved forward to help pick Sarah up, but Bill shook his head to stop him. He scooped Sarah up into his arms and held her close. Her head lolled to the side like a broken doll's.

Throughout the next hour, Bill learned what unending torment felt like. While the doctor remained with Sarah beyond a closed door, Bill was made to wait in the parlor of the woman who'd offered her home. He dully noticed she was one of those who'd always snubbed Sarah. Bill didn't even know her name, didn't want to know. All the faces and voices formed a blur in this nightmare world into which he'd been thrust. All he wanted was Sarah, alive, well. . . .

He numbly heard Stewart's explanation of how Miranda had followed the two, seen the mobsters, and run to get help. If it hadn't been for her, they'd both be dead. At this point, Bill didn't want to live if it meant Sarah must die. That bullet should have been his.

What seemed like eternities passed as Bill waited. Darcy and Brent tried to encourage him, offering comfort. Charleigh and Stewart did the same, as did Pastor Wilkins. But Bill knew no comfort, didn't deserve it. His former criminal actions had done this. He alone was responsible.

Why did she push him out of the way? Why did she do that?

The question tormented his mind.

When the doctor finally entered the parlor, his face was grave. Bill's heart fell into a deep hole as he stood up to hear the words that he didn't want to hear but must.

"I successfully removed the bullet, but she shouldn't be moved." The elderly doctor patted his brow and beard with a handkerchief. "If she pulls through the night, there's a good chance she'll make it. I'm sorry, but that's all I can give you."

Bill curtly nodded, his throat so tight he couldn't speak.

"I wasn't able to save the baby. I'm very sorry."

Baby?

Bill stared, shock rooting him in place and fogging his mind. "Sarah was pregnant?" His words were hoarse.

"You didn't know?" The doctor seemed surprised, then averted his gaze as if uneasy.

Bill drew on every remnant of control he possessed. "May I see my wife?"

"Of course."

Bill entered the darkened room, closing the door behind him. Sarah lay upon the white sheets, her skin pale, her eyes closed as if she merely slept. A sheet covered her slight form to her bare shoulders. She looked like an angel. The thought terrified him.

He dropped down on one knee beside the bed. Gently, he laid his hand over her small one. "Oh, Sarah, forgive me. . . . Please forgive me." Hot tears clouded his eyes and rolled down his cheeks. He lowered his head to her arm, hoarsely repeating the words of contrition in a mindless chant. Minutes passed.

All that mattered now was that she live. . . . *Please, dear God, let her live.*

Bill straightened and looked at her as if to memorize her face. With his fingertips, he tenderly traced the graceful line of her cheek, her jaw. "Pretty Sarah, open your eyes; don't leave me. You can't leave me. I don't want to go on living without you." He pressed his lips gently to the corner of her still ones. A tear dripped onto her cheek. "You must live, sweetheart."

Seeing her beautiful hair imprisoned in the thick braid frustrated him. His hands trembling, he unwove the long silky strands, freeing them and spreading them to one side of her in a shimmering curtain. His gaze went to her flat stomach, and at the reminder, another stab of pain sliced through him. She must have known for months.

"Why didn't you tell me about the baby, Sarah? Did you think I wouldn't want it?" Gently he brushed tendrils of her hair from her temple. Memory of those occasions she'd asked if he liked children and seemed apprehensive about his offhand responses accused him. These past nights, when they'd discovered their love and she'd lain in his arms, he'd felt the slight swell of her stomach but thought it was weight gained due to her renewed appetite for food. What a fool he was!

He closed his eyes. "Oh, Sarah, Sarah. God willing, we'll create another baby. I do want children with you. Just please, don't die."

Time passed, but Bill remained. Brent came inside and laid a consoling hand to his shoulder, trying to urge him away from the bedside to eat something. Bill refused, and Brent finally left him alone to his tortured vigil. Night darkened the windowpane.

Throughout the bleak hours, Bill sat near her bed and replayed every sin, every crime he'd ever committed. That his Sarah should have been the one to suffer for all of them sliced through his conscience, tore through his heart. Why couldn't it be him lying there? He deserved it. Why couldn't it have been him?

He watched her face, took note of the shallow rise and fall of her chest, afraid to look away, as if by staring at her he could keep her alive. His prayers were without words but contained his entire soul. If she did come back to him, he would never again fail to tell her of his love for her, would tell it to her a hundred times a day.

Early into the morning, exhaustion overtook him, and he laid his head down beside her arm to rest. Her moan woke him what could have been minutes or hours later. Snatched from uneasy sleep, he raised his head in shock. Saw her lashes flicker. His heart skipped erratically as she slowly opened her eyes.

"Bill. . ." Her word was a mere breath.

"I'm here, baby." Tears threatened again, and he squeezed her hand tightly. "I'm here. Just hold on; don't leave me. You're going to get well, and we're going to have a great life together. I promise."

In the depths of her dark eyes shone a look of such intense love it took Bill's breath away. She nodded her head slightly against the pillow in confirmation and again closed her eyes.

How could he have ever doubted her love for him? Never again would he.

He waited until he was assured Sarah slept peacefully, then rose, his legs numb and shaky from sitting for so long. Brent met him when he came outside the door. A wave of gratitude that his brother had been with him throughout the whole night threatened Bill's dubious composure. Relief caused everything to converge upon him at once.

"Bill?"

"I feel she's going to make it."

"I'm relieved to know it." Brent looked uneasy. "Do you think we should ask for the police to post a guard on the event that those men will return?"

Averting his gaze from his brother to the gray light now coloring the window, Bill swallowed hard over the grief that clogged his throat and stared straight ahead.

"Bill?"

"There's no need for that. A life for a life." Bill gravely looked at his brother.

"Vittorio won't be bothering us again."

Without another word, Bill strode from the house. He kept walking until his legs burned, until his breath came fast and he could go no farther. Slumping down against a tree, he finally allowed the emotion to overtake him and wept for Sarah and the child he would never know.

Chapter 23

Bill sat and stared at the cracks in the porch. He heard someone come up beside him but didn't turn to look. For a long time, they remained silent.

"You need to stop taking all the blame," Charleigh said. "It wasn't your fault."

"How can you say that?" Head hung low, Bill threaded his fingers through his hair to the back of his scalp. "It was *only* my fault. If I hadn't joined up with those men years ago, none of this would have happened."

"Bill." She put a kind hand to his shoulder. "You simply can't go on like this. You haven't eaten, haven't slept. Forgive me for saying so, but you look terrible. You spend almost all your time sitting out here, staring at nothing. It's been almost three weeks. The doctor says Sarah's going to be fine. But she needs you to be strong right now; this has been very hard on her."

Bill swallowed hard. "How, Charleigh? How can I be strong for her when I feel as if my own soul and heart are crushed, when I know that all this happened because of me?" He looked at her, pleading. "Please. Tell me. How?"

She sank to the chair beside him, her manner one of gentle earnestness. "Only God can help you get through this, Bill. I know you're having a hard time trusting Him right now; I understand that. But you need to let go of the blame and stop looking at what you could have done differently in the past. We all make mistakes; we're human. Sometimes, unfortunately, we end up having to pay for those mistakes, as Stewart already told you. Even after we get right with God. But what's important is to continue the course, to put this all behind you, and go on."

"Put it all behind me?" Bill stared at her, incredulous. "We lost a child. My wife was shot and almost died."

"I know." Her eyes were full of sympathy. "And I know what I'm saying doesn't seem to make sense right now, but it really is the way not only to survive but to live a life of victory. The days will get better; I speak from experience. When you accept Jesus into your life, the storms do come, but so do the blessings. And they will come for both you and Sarah. Just don't give up on God."

She hesitated, as if unsure she should speak. "What Sarah did in pushing you out of the way and then taking that bullet reminds me of the love God showed for us, in that He took the punishment that should have been ours. I really think you've punished yourself long enough, Bill. God forgave you. He died on

237

the cross for you. Sarah forgave you, too."

Bill closed his eyes at that, emotion causing his throat to ache. Sarah had been nothing but gentle and loving, forgiving all his wrongs both past and present when he didn't deserve her forgiveness. In the cemetery now lay a small granite marker, an eternal testimony of his past sins, but she had never blamed him for the loss of their child or for any of his mistakes. And that sharpened his guilt almost to a point beyond what he could bear. He'd hardly been able to look at or be with her. Though it was all he wanted.

"Go to her. She needs you."

Bill nodded, resigned. He needed her, too, but still felt unworthy of her. He stood and went into the house, heaviness underlining his every step as he ascended the stairs.

When he opened their bedroom door, Sarah turned from the pillows to look at him. Such joy, such hope shone across her face and in her eyes, making Bill catch his breath. Gone were the days when she shielded her emotions; each nuance of expression told of her strong love for him.

"Sarah." Apprehension lifted from him as he quickly strode toward the bed and sat beside her, pulling her into his arms. Her head rested beneath his chin, and he fought the tears that now so often dwelled just beneath the surface. "I'm so sorry."

"Bill." Her hand reached up to press against his cheek, and she moved back as though to look at him. He stiffened his hold, not wanting her to see his tears. Regardless, they dripped onto her fingers.

"You have nothing to be sorry about," she said softly. "We have both suffered this loss. You aren't to blame."

He closed his eyes tightly. Would he ever believe that?

"I have felt so alone," she admitted. "Please don't go from me, too."

Her fearful tone sliced his heart, and he pulled away slightly, lifting his hands to cup her face. "Sarah, I will never leave you. Never. I've just been so confused, so upset. I didn't know how to sort out all that's happened to us. I still don't."

She nodded as though she understood. Tears ran from their eyes. They looked at one another seconds longer before he again drew her close. Weeping in each other's arms, they shared the pain of their loss.

While wrapped in one another's embrace, they experienced healing's first touch.

🙣🙢

"Sarah?"

At Bill's voice, she turned from entering the lake.

"I thought I'd find you here." He wrapped his arms around her waist in greeting and kissed her firmly. Pulling back, he gently slid a fragrant red blossom above her ear.

Sarah's heart leapt at his touch and his smile. Often he brought her roses in full bloom, since he'd told her about love's gentle fragrance. The continual bloom of their love filled her heart with song.

"Swim with me?" she asked.

He looked out at the lake. "Oh, well, why not?" He went to sit down and took off his shoes and socks. "The water shouldn't be too cold for early summer. At least I hope it isn't."

She giggled and pulled on his hand. "I have found that the cold can be invigorating."

The water was more than cold; it was frigid. Bill yelped and tried to shoot out of the lake, but Sarah tugged on his hand, pulling him in farther. "Do not cast a kitten or be such a high hat," she teased.

"Have a fit? Me? And pretty Sarah. . ." He changed his tactics, playing the predator to her prey. A flame kindled in his eyes, and his brows lifted with promise of sure retribution as he advanced a step toward her. "If you're going to call me a snob, then you'd better be willing to pay the consequences."

Squealing, she released his hand and splashed farther out until the water hit above her shoulders. He made a shallow dive after her. She didn't try very hard to escape, anticipating the moment of his sure victory.

He caught her and held her close. She melted against him. Soon neither of them felt the chill as he exacted his sweet revenge and she delighted in her defeat.

"I love you, Sarah," he whispered against her mouth long moments later. He pulled away to look into her eyes. "Every day that passes, I thank God that we're together. I hate what Vittorio did to us, but strange as it may sound, I think it bonded us even more. I never fully realized the extent of your love for me, or mine for you, until that day you took the bullet that should have been mine."

Sarah was surprised by his words. During her recovery all through the long fall and winter, and even into the spring, they hadn't spoken of that horrible day except briefly. Always, they tried to step around the subject that had brought them so much grief and loss.

She pressed her hand against his cheek. "I did not think; I only acted. I was afraid you would be killed."

"I almost did die when I heard that gun go off and saw you lying there."

Sarah remembered the pain, the heartache, the loss. Yet with Bill's love and encouragement, his tender care and touch, he had pulled her through that trying time, helping her to heal both in heart and in body. And she had helped him to heal as well. Together, they'd helped one another.

At first, fearful uncertainty that the men might return had tormented her, but Bill assured her that Vittorio had taken his vengeance. Bill knew these men, and he knew they would have observed from the shadows, learned of the private funeral, and would have looked to see the child's grave.

As though sensing her sudden melancholy, he tilted her chin so that she was looking into his turquoise-colored eyes. They gleamed with assurance, reminding her of inviting waters. "Don't be sad, pretty Sarah. We'll have a family some day. Whenever God thinks the time is right, we'll create another baby."

A slow smile tilted her lips. She took hold of his hand beneath the water and guided it to her flat stomach, pressing it there.

"The time is right."

Bill's eyes widened at her quiet words, and he stared for a few seconds before he spoke. "You don't mean..."

"Yes."

"Are you sure?"

She nodded. "I am."

Bill's boyish whoops and hollers made Sarah laugh in delight. Their joy rang out over all the lake. Scooping her up into his arms, he held her close, while she wrapped her arms about his neck.

"I love you, Bill."

"And I love you, my pretty Sarah, always and forever."

She met his kiss, revealing all the feelings she had for him, never again holding back. For in both God's love and Bill's, she had found her source of true strength.

Epilogue

Bill paced up and down the parlor. Outside, a wet snow fell. Each time he heard the creak of stairs, he halted his trek to dart a glance that way, but it was always only another of the children.

"Keep this up, guv, and we'll have to ship you off to Bedlam. I declare you must be wearing a hole in that rug." Darcy bounced her and Brent's newest baby, Madeline, over her shoulder. From the swell of her stomach, she would be expecting another child early in the summer. As would Charleigh, who walked in from the kitchen, bearing a huge pot of steaming water and towels over her arm.

"Let me get that for you, sweetheart." Stewart grabbed the pot and followed her upstairs. Bill noticed that since hearing news of the baby, Stewart had treated Charleigh like china, barely allowing her to lift anything at all. Much as Bill had treated Sarah.

"I don't recall ever seeing you this nervous about anything." Brent eyed Bill.

He threw his brother a disgusted look. "Don't you think the situation warrants it?"

Brent had the audacity to chuckle and settle back on the sofa, one of the twins sitting on each side of him. Clementine sat beside Beatrice, and both toddlers looked at the pictures in a book spread out on their legs. On the phonograph in the next room, Joel and Jimmy had put on a record that scratched out the tune "Ain't We Got Fun?"

Bill thought it highly inappropriate for the moment. Fun was the last thing he was having.

"Ah, but I've been through this event twice before, Bill. Truly, there's nothing to worry about."

"Aw now, guv'ner," Darcy teased as she came up behind him and laid a hand on his shoulder. "The way I heard tell it, you passed out cold when Robert Brent was born. Fainted dead away, he did." She winked at Bill in amusement.

"Yes, my dear. But Robert's presence was highly unexpected. I didn't know we were having twins."

Bill suddenly felt sick and dizzy at the same time. He'd heard twins ran in families. . .and Brent was his brother. The thought of having one was both terrifying and wonderful. The thought of two. . .

Suddenly from upstairs, the sound of a baby's lusty cry stopped everyone from what they were doing and had them glancing toward the ceiling.

241

Brent's smile widened as he looked at Bill. "Congratulations, big brother. It sounds as if you're a father."

The dizziness threatened to overtake Bill, and he grabbed the back of a chair.

"You all right, guv?" Darcy moved toward him.

"Just a little lightheaded."

She grinned. "Must run in the family."

Bill moved toward the staircase as if he were wading to it through deep water. He put his hand on the banister but just looked up the stairs. He heard a door open. Charleigh came out, and upon seeing him, her smile grew wide.

"I was just coming to get you. Come along." She motioned him upward, as if encouraging a nervous boy.

The weights that had grounded him released, and he charged up the staircase. She laughed and put a finger to her mouth. "Shhh."

"Oh, uh, sorry." Feeling suddenly awkward, he swallowed as he followed her into the bedroom he shared with his wife. The moment he saw Sarah, all hesitancy vanished.

Her face shimmered with perspiration; her hair was damp and clung to her, but the joy that glowed out of her dark eyes was unmistakable. "Bill." Smiling, she held out her hand to him, and he quickly moved to her side, sitting on the bed. He took her hand in both of his and brought it to his lips, closing his eyes.

"Sarah." He couldn't push anything out beyond that.

"Would you like to see your son?"

Son. Bill's heart went into double-time, and all he could do was nod.

She pulled down the thin sheet that had been protecting the wrapped bundle she held against her side in the crook of her arm. Bill stared in wonder at the tiny face, the closed eyes with their thick lashes. A thatch of dark hair covered his scalp. In awe, he brushed his finger along the baby's head, his soft cheek, to the little hand, which held tightly to a lock of Sarah's hair. How could a baby be so tiny?

Fierce love swamped Bill—for both the little fella who was flesh of their flesh and for his beautiful wife. "He's amazing. And I know the perfect name for him."

She looked at him, expectantly.

"Josiah."

Tears touched her eyes. "He would be honored."

"If it wasn't for your father, none of us would be here right now." His gaze was tender as he looked upon his wife, then down at his son. "Including this little guy."

"Josiah William." Sarah smiled. "It is a good name."

"God has been good to us, Sarah."

"Yes, Bill. He has."

Leaning forward, he touched his lips to hers, thankful for second chances and new beginnings.

A Bridge
Across the Sea

Dedication

Thank you to Jill Stengl, Therese Travis, and Adrie Ashford
for your invaluable help and constant support
as you cheered me along and critiqued chapters in record time.
Mom, that goes for you, too. You're incredible. . . .
Dedicated to my Lord and Savior, who guides me along unfamiliar paths
and makes a bridge across when there seems no other way.

Prologue

1928

eter, have you not heard a word I've spoken? Must I be harsh and reveal to you what we both already know? You ask for reasons why we cannot marry, yet those reasons should be obvious under the circumstances. Mummy would never abide my marriage to a man who is nameless.

Nameless. . .

Nameless. . .

"Excuse me, sir?"

Torn from the distressing memory of his last encounter with Claire, Peter Caldwell turned his head to look at the steward who had come up beside him.

"Yes?"

"Is everything all right?" The boy's eyes lowered to Peter's white knuckles clutching the ship's rail, then seemed to latch onto the cane hooked around his wrist, staring at the walking stick longer than necessary. "Are ye feeling well, sir?"

"Well?" Peter gave a dry chuckle.

He supposed he felt as well as a survivor of the *Titanic* disaster could feel when faced with the reality of sailing across the ocean again. Of course, he'd only been a small lad and remembered next to nothing of that time at sea. Once he'd feverishly worked to escape what little of the horror he did recall; now, ironically, the tragic sinking of sixteen years ago took him to America. He needed to discover what had happened that night so he could bury the vague memories that haunted his days.

Peter collected himself and eyed the lad, who looked only a few years younger than his own twenty-two. "Yes, thank you. I am well."

"It's only that you look a little green around the gills, sir. Travel on an ocean liner isn't for everyone, and anyone can be affected. Had a bit of the seasickness myself when I worked my first voyage, but it goes away after a spell. Would ye like me to direct you to the ship's physician?"

"No, thank you. Once I partake of some sustenance, I should feel better, I think. There's nothing quite like a good meal to soothe a man's stomach. Even at sea. Or so I've been told."

The steward laughed. "Aye, and this ship has the best gourmet food there is, though just between you and me, mate. . ." He leaned in closer as if to divulge a

245

secret. "My tastes run more toward the Italian variety."

"Italian? I can't say as I've tried that."

"You've never tried Italian food? Spaghetti? Or lasagna?"

Peter's mouth twitched. "To my knowledge, England doesn't contain a wealth of Old Italy. This is actually my first voyage. . .in a long time."

The boy's mouth dropped open. "Incredible. To be so well off a bloke as yourself and not to have indulged in the pleasures of pasta?" He shook his head as if Peter were missing out on something ideal. "Once we dock in Manhattan, you must try Marelli's. It has the best Italian food, I'll wager. Whenever we come to port, I eat there. And the blond waitress who works there? Cute as a button, she is." He winked and jabbed Peter in the ribs as if they were old shipmates.

Ignoring the steward's lack of protocol, Peter wondered how he'd gone from *sir* to *mate* in the span of seconds, but that was often the case. Strangers relaxed and let down their guards around him. He'd been told this was partly due to his dry wit. Not that humor in any form was a bad thing. His mother had said putting people at ease and making them laugh was a gift. . .his mother.

As he dwelt on the image, another woman's features came to mind. Peter sobered, averting his gaze to the waves rippling beneath him. The steward, obviously sensing the mood change, excused himself and left Peter to stare sightlessly out over the wide, unforgiving ocean.

He only prayed this voyage wasn't a mistake and that he would find the answers for which he'd been searching—both in his mind, since as a boy of seven he'd lost so much dear to him, and with his actions, since he'd purchased the ticket to New York and had given free rein to this burning desire to obtain truth. He had searched for the answers in England before this venture, but not with the present boldness that compelled him to dig deeper now.

It was too late to turn back the hands of time. His only recourse remained to press forward, and that was exactly what he intended to do. No matter the cost to his heart.

Chapter 1

Peter walked along the piers flanking the Hudson River, impressed by the massive ships docked there. As he shielded his eyes against the late-morning sun's glare and looked to the east, he noted the rigging of one ship in the process of being built. Beyond the docks, the Statue of Liberty emerged from the morning mist, her torch raised in silent hope. Seagulls cried out in mournful song as dockworkers toiled at their duties, and beyond that, the river glimmered as if it held its own secrets. The salty odor of fish permeated the foggy air.

Pulling his gaze away from the wharf, Peter focused on his destination. An old fisherman had given him directions to the simple building that housed a part of his past. The sign above the door read: WHITE STAR LINES LIMITED.

He hesitated before gripping the handle. One step farther through that door and he would forever terminate the possibility of letting go of the past. Buried secrets could cause pain once rocks were uncovered, as his father had warned before Peter left Liverpool. But they could also release him from the nightmare of ignorance that had held him bound for so many years.

A story from his childhood came to mind, and he wondered which would greet him when he opened the door: news of the lady for whom he had yearned, or the merciless tiger that would finish him off for embarking on this foolish quest. He thought of Claire and hardened his resolve to find the answers. Without further hesitation, he opened the door.

Inside, the room stood in disorder. No one occupied the desk piled awry with ledgers, papers, and packing crates.

"Hello?" Peter's greeting brought no answer. He looked around the room and toward a narrow corridor, also empty. "I say, is anyone about?"

The sound of shuffling shoes on the tiled floor preceded the appearance of an elderly bewhiskered gentleman. His clothes were worn, his shoulders bent, but the welcoming smile on his face seemed genuine. In his gnarled hands, he carried a mop and pail.

"Good morning. We don't get much business this early of a morning. I would think Mr. Fromby'll be here soon though." He set the pail down and went to work cleaning up a brown spill that Peter now saw beside the desk. "Please excuse the disorder. We're a lot more efficient than appearances show, I assure you. Since the White Star Lines Limited was included with the Royal Mail Steam

Packet Company last year—unofficially of course—things haven't settled down yet. Lots of shifting around, you understand."

Apparently the gentleman was a talker, something that could work in Peter's favor. "Perhaps you could help me? I'm seeking an old passenger list—sixteen years old, to be exact."

A gleam of interest shone in the old man's blue eyes. "That so? You a reporter?"

"A reporter?"

"Only ship that collected any interest from 1912 was the *Titanic*. I imagine that's the list you're wanting?"

"Yes, that's what I need. And this is for personal reasons. I'm not a reporter."

The man set the mop into the pail. "Well now, I would imagine that list would be in the archives room. I was here in the office that day." He shook his head. "A terrible day it was, too."

"Yes, I can well imagine. Is there any way I could see the list?"

"I'm not authorized to touch the records, or I'd help you, young fellow. You'll need to talk to Mr. Fromby. The White Star created a raw list for the hearings, both here and in Britain. That where you're from? You have the accent."

"Yes, near London, actually."

"Thought so. Don't get many Britishers in this office. I'm Roger, by the way. You writing a book?"

Peter was exhausted; leisurely chat held no appeal. The dream had revisited his mind last night, likely brought on by his quest, and he had slept little. "When do you expect Mr. Fromby?"

"Hard to tell with him. On Mondays, he usually doesn't show up 'til after lunchtime. Visits the piers and such in the morning. You won't get past his secretary though, and who knows where she is." He tapped his skull with a forefinger. "She's a bit touched in the head; don't trust nobody, which is wise in Manhattan, what with all the crime, I suppose. But she carries it to the extreme."

"Perhaps I'll check back later, regardless." Peter had braved his qualms and sailed across an entire ocean to reach his goal; a cagey secretary wouldn't prevent him from reaching it.

"You could always try, that's a fact. You find a place to stay?"

"Yes, actually. I have a room at the Waldorf-Astoria."

"A ritzy place, but then you look as if you can afford the extras." Roger's offhand comment didn't seem rude when matched with his wide grin; Peter had the feeling he was always one to speak his mind, no matter the occasion.

"Say. . ." His eyes lit up. "I might be able to help some at that. I know the names and locales of a few survivors who settled down in or around the city. People I've come to know over the years. I may be getting on in years, but my memory's still sharp as a tack." He grinned. "I could give the information to you, if you want to contact them for that book you're writing. Though I can't give you

Mr. Ismay's address; not long after he resigned as president of the White Star line, a year after the *Titanic* sank, he left the public eye. People didn't take too kindly to him surviving when the ship's own captain went down."

"I would appreciate any help you can give me." Uncomfortable about sharing his personal history with strangers and certain that if he did, the whole of New York City would know of it by nightfall, Peter didn't correct Roger's assumption that he was writing a book.

Hours later, armed with Roger's list, Peter hailed a cab that deposited him near Marelli's. The morning had been a disappointment. The one locale Peter had tried, when he finally found the place, yielded no results; the owners weren't home. Perhaps taking the ship steward's recommendation to sample an Italian meal might improve the afternoon's outlook.

As Peter approached the door, a man sped out of it.

"And you can take this back where it came from, too!" a woman yelled.

Startled, Peter swung his attention toward the restaurant door just as a square box came hurtling his way and struck him in the eye.

❧

Aghast, Melissa stood at the restaurant entrance and gaped at the tall stranger who stepped into the line of fire just as she threw Guido's gift back at his messenger. The go-between seized the opportunity to duck into his flashy black Lincoln and take off like a shot.

With his hand cupped over one eye, the stranger glanced at the retreating car, shifted his attention to the chocolate bonbons strewn over the ground, and then looked at Melissa. If she hadn't felt so awful for nailing him with the candy box, she might have giggled at the completely bamboozled expression on his face. A nice face, a part of her mind noted.

"I'm so sorry. Are you okay?"

His gaze dropped to the chocolates once more, then lifted to her. "Not your particular choice of flavor?"

Totally unexpected, the wry comment delivered in a crisp British accent made her eyes widen in incredulity. She gave a light laugh. In an instant, she felt at ease with this man, which then slowly put her on her guard. Melissa's trust had never been easily won by any man, and she suspected guilt prodded her to relax her defenses now. Despite this, she moved closer.

"Not my particular choice of suitor, either. Is it bad? Your eye, I mean?"

He pulled his hand away to let her see, and she winced. The corner of the box had caught him beneath his left eyebrow. On top of the bruised skin, a beaded line of red had appeared.

"Come inside and let me tend to that," she offered. "It's the least I can do after walloping you."

"I would appreciate it. I was intending to visit in any case. I was told I must sample the food here."

"Yes, it is good. But then, I'm biased in that regard."

She smiled and retraced her steps, then stopped when she noticed he wasn't following, and looked over her shoulder. He had stooped low, putting his weight on his cane, to scrape up the chocolates from the sidewalk and drop them back into the box.

"Oh, no. Please. You don't have to do that. Really, I feel bad enough as it is. I'll clean it up after we get you inside."

"Already finished," he said, collecting another handful and tossing them into the container. He rose with some difficulty and moved closer; it was then she noticed his slight limp and how he relied on the black cane to walk. He handed her the box. She took it, suddenly awash with shyness. Now that she wasn't focused on the incident or his wound, she couldn't help but notice how clear and bright his eyes were. And blue. As blue as the late-summer sky and lighter than her own. He appeared much younger than she'd first thought, too young to need a cane. She suspected he was no more than a couple of years older than she.

"Well. . ." Never at a loss for words, she suddenly couldn't find a one of them.

He stuck out his right hand. "Peter Caldwell, at your service."

"Melissa Reynolds," she said in a quick exhalation of air, still flustered. She gathered her wits and took his hand. . .strangely she found she didn't want to let go. Her heart stood still. His eyes flickered, and she broke contact, dropping her hand to her side.

What was she doing, acting all googly-eyed like some silly flapper—and to a complete stranger, yet? If her cousins saw, she would never hear the end of it.

"Your eye's getting worse every second we stand out here," she said to hide the rush of feeling that had surged through her at the strange connection she'd felt with him. "Come along, and I'll get you some ice. We don't have steaks here."

"Ice is preferable. I never was partial to raw meat."

At his careless quip, she again glanced at him, trying to figure him out, then gave a slight shake of her head and led the way inside. Relieved this was a slow time of the day—or she would never have gone off like a hothead and made a spectacle of herself earlier—she seated him at a table inside the empty restaurant.

"Just wait here, and I'll be right back." She handed him a menu from a nearby table. "And please, choose whatever you'd like. Your meal's on me."

"I could never dream of allowing such a thing."

"It would make me feel better, considering."

"It truly isn't necessary. I'm well aware that you didn't intend to wallop me—isn't that how you Americans say it?" His eyes teased, and she caught a breath.

"Well, yes, but you don't understand. My aunt Maria and uncle Tony own this restaurant, and I know they would also insist your meal be on the house. So no more arguments. *Capisci?*"

Before he could offer further objections, she headed to the kitchen to chip ice off one of the blocks in the walk-in freezer. Aunt Maria stood near the stove, stirring a huge vat of fragrant sauce. Spanish in heritage, she only grew more beautiful with each passing year. That she married an Italian and could cook better than any of Tony's sisters was the ongoing joke in the Marelli family.

Melissa felt her aunt watching her quick actions as she ducked into the freezer. Aunt Maria's eyebrows arched in curiosity when Melissa exited.

"For a customer," she explained, not yet willing to admit her embarrassing mistake. She felt a betraying flush swamp her face, which in retrospect was welcome after her mission in the freezer.

"*Mi niña*, I sense there is something you're not telling me."

Aunt Maria's use of her girlhood nickname made Melissa feel little more than a child, and as she did then, Melissa found herself defending her actions now.

"I didn't mean to hurt anyone."

"Oh, dear." Aunt Maria stopped stirring. "What have you done?"

"I, um, accidentally bashed a guy with the candy box I was throwing at one of Guido's henchmen."

The name of Vittorio's nephew made her aunt gasp. Alarm filled her dark eyes. "Oh, no. You must be careful. You do not want to get on that man's bad side. He is very dangerous."

"I know that." Melissa smiled to relieve her aunt's fears. "But I don't want to go out with him either, so how do you suggest I get the message across to him? A simple no didn't work—all ten times I tried it. Today was the third time he sent one of his thugs over with flowers or candy." She looked down at the melting ice in the cup. "I need to get back out there. Poor guy. He's going to have quite a shiner."

"Well, be sure and let him know whatever he wants is on the house."

"I already have," Melissa said with a smile and returned to the table.

Peter had removed his felt hat, which sat in the chair beside him, and Melissa could now see his hair was straight and dark blond. He read a piece of paper he held in both hands. When he lifted his gaze, stunned awareness filled his eyes, though he politely stood as she approached.

She waved him back down. "Is everything all right?"

"Your aunt Maria, she is Maria Marelli? A survivor of the *Titanic* disaster?"

A jolt of surprise shot through Melissa, transporting her back through time. She cleared her throat, glanced at the paper clutched in his hand, then looked back into his eyes. "Why do you wish to know?"

"Because she might be able to help me locate my family."

Chapter 2

Peter stared at the lovely woman before him. Shock clouded her cornflower blue eyes, and she shook her head of short blond curls, as though she struggled to follow his words. She gripped the back of a chair, as if she might pass out.

"Your family was on the *Titanic*?" she asked through stiff lips.

"Not those for whom I'm looking, no. But my mother and I were both passengers."

At this, she sat down with a swift thump. "You were on the *Titanic*?"

Peter wondered at her inability to fathom his words, when realization struck. "You were on the *Titanic* as well." It was a statement, not a question; her actions made it clear.

With a dull nod, she closed her eyes. "I celebrated my fifth birthday there." Her gaze grew unfocused as the seconds elapsed and she slipped into another time. "Such a party it was, too; I may have been very young, but I remember. My mother even secured a steward to play the part of a clown to entertain us, and the ship's musicians played nearby, in the adjoining room. A kind woman arrived late to the party, a passenger I wanted to be there, and she gave me a blanket for my new doll."

Her vague words opened a mist-shrouded memory inside Peter, and his eyes opened wider. "There was a waiter, a clumsy fellow. He knocked into the table and. . .something fell." He pulled his brows together in an effort to remember.

Her attention swung back to him. "The punch glasses," she said as if dazed. "He fell against a chair and grabbed the tablecloth. All the crystal went crashing to the floor. He was funnier than the clown." A quiet giggle escaped. "Mama was livid. She complained to the head steward that she suspected the man was inebriated."

"And the musicians began playing louder to cover her screeching—"

"Then the captain's mate came in to see what all the ruckus was about—"

"And she said if it were her ship, she'd make them all walk the plank."

Peter and Melissa stared at one another in wonder, each softly smiling as the tenuous bond drew them together.

"I liked stories of pirates, so perhaps that's why I remembered," Peter explained.

"Mama invited all the first- and second-class passengers' children to the Café

Parisian for my party. . .and you were there." She breathed the last words in awe, then blinked as if suddenly bashful, her gaze dropping to the cup she held. "Oh, dear. Your eye." Quickly, she poured ice into a napkin and bunched it up. She lifted the compress to his head but hesitated before contact could be made. Sensing her discomfiture, Peter held out his hand, and she gave the ice to him.

"Do you remember anything else about your time on the ship?" He pressed the cloth over his eye. The extreme cold burned his skin, but he kept the frozen napkin in place.

"Some things. Not a lot."

"What about that last night? Do you remember any of it?"

A haunted look swam through her eyes. "How could I forget?" she said simply.

He nodded and glanced at his cane propped against the table. "I bear a continual reminder; that night crippled me for life. Unfortunately, it crippled my memory, as well."

Her expression softened in sympathy. "I suffered no physical injuries, only emotional ones—as I'm sure every other survivor did. I still suffer from nightmares."

At the word *nightmare*, Peter tensed, thinking of his own. The one with his mother that always ended at the same spot. "I remember very little of that night, though some events, like your birthday party, are now clear to me. However, your party only became vivid after you spoke of it. Perhaps that's the key to unlocking the rest of what happened. Finding those who will speak of the events to spur the recollections."

"You *want* to remember?"

He nodded. "My mother died that night, and my family couldn't be found when we docked. It's one of the reasons I'm here."

Before she could respond, a dark-haired woman strode toward them, and Peter stood to his feet. Her hair was secured in a braid around her head reminiscent of an old-fashioned Mediterranean style. Peter guessed her to be in her midthirties, though her olive skin was still as fresh as dew and her cheeks bloomed with healthy pink.

"Missy, I wondered what was keeping you from giving me the new order." The words were delivered blithely in a melodic Spanish accent, and she then nodded to Peter with a smile. "You must forgive my niece; her aim has never been good. Please, sit down."

Peter looked back and forth between the women, amazed. While Melissa was as fair as a Scandinavian princess, her aunt was as dark as a Spanish *condesa*.

Peter focused his attention on the older woman and offered his hand in greeting. "Mrs. Marelli, allow me to introduce myself. I am Peter Caldwell, recently arrived from Great Britain. Your name was given to me from a worker at the White Star Lines Limited as one of those who survived the tragedy on the *Titanic.*"

Maria's eyes flashed wide in surprise, but she gave a short nod.

"I'm trying to locate anyone who was a passenger and might have known my mother or been acquainted with her on the ship." From his coat pocket, he withdrew a bound linen handkerchief and carefully unfolded it to show a gold oval locket resting within its snowy folds, one of two heirlooms he'd brought with him from England. He opened it to reveal a set of pictures, one on each side. Both were badly water damaged, but by some odd act of providence, the face of the woman wasn't harmed. Seawater had obliterated the other face.

"My mother put this around my neck that final night." Peter didn't know that speaking the words after so many years would produce within him such a sudden fount of emotion, and he cleared his throat before going on. "Shortly afterward, she left our cabin. I never saw her again."

Sympathy clouded Maria's brow. "I'm sorry for your loss." She took the locket and studied the picture for several seconds, then handed it back with an apologetic shake of her head. "She doesn't look familiar. But it has been so long, and I spent most of my time taking care of Missy, you understand. I was her *niñera*—her nanny."

His curiosity must have been evident.

"Aunt Maria and I aren't related by blood but through marriage," Melissa explained. "My mother married her brother when I was three, and Maria took care of me."

"Ah, I see." Still, he wondered that Maria should have taken on the role of servant to her brother's child. Perhaps in America, such protocol wasn't considered unusual.

Maria fondly smiled at the younger woman. "I think of Missy as a daughter; I always have." She looked at Peter. "Have you been in America long?"

"Only since yesterday when the ship docked."

"And you have found a good place to stay?"

Peter had a feeling that, like his adoptive mother, this woman would open her home to him and any other stranger in need. "Thank you, yes. I'm staying at the Waldorf-Astoria, though I've been out since early this morning on my quest. I was told on the ship I must try Italian food. Your restaurant was recommended to me."

Her brows sailed up at his mention of one of the most exclusive hotels in the city. "Since this morning, you have been searching? And here it is past noon. I assume from your words you have not eaten today?" She threw her hands up, and a stream of Spanish burst from her lips. Peter had the feeling he was being chided for not taking care of himself. "So, you never have had Italian food, Peter Caldwell? Then I must make you one of the best meals we have to offer."

"Please, don't go to any trouble on my account." He recalled what the steward on the boat had said. "A plate of spaghetti sounds like a splendid idea."

"*Sì, sì.* You shall have the spaghetti and more. Missy, keep our customer happy while I prepare his meal."

Both women grinned at Peter, and Maria hurried away.

"You might as well give up," Melissa said. "She is a force to be reckoned with when she's made up her mind."

"I don't want to put her out."

She gave a light laugh. "This is a restaurant, Peter! It's our job to serve you." She blushed. "I hope you don't mind if I call you Peter. I mean, since you were at my birthday party, I feel as if I know you."

"I would consider it an honor. And may I call you Missy? Or would you prefer Melissa?"

"Well, normally I only allow Maria to call me that since it sounds so babyish. But I guess I don't mind if you do, too."

"I rather like it." And he did. The nickname was as pert and delightful as the bearer; she was more than delightful actually. Missy had a fresh, delicate beauty about her china-doll-like features, and he felt as if he could stare into her pretty eyes all day. Realizing where his mind was taking him, he looked down at the paper in his hands, feeling a twinge of guilt. Claire had told him she couldn't marry him and why, but the only reason he'd journeyed to America on this search was to discover his heritage. He was already well on the road to finding answers and hoped soon the mystery of his past would no longer present a problem.

"The other names on the list," Missy said, breaking into his thoughts. "May I see them?"

"Of course." Peter handed the paper over and watched her expression, but no recognition lit her features.

"I was very young," she apologized, handing the list back. "Do you know your way around New York? Do you have a map of the area?"

"No, though I suppose I should purchase one. Especially to find this third place." He briefly looked at the paper to read the locale. "Coney Island. Do you know of it? Is this island far off the coast?"

She giggled, and he found he liked the sound. It didn't seem silly, flirtatious, or even childish; rather, her laugh was light and buoyant.

"It's a famous amusement park, a New Yorker's playground," she said. "You really don't know our city well if you've never heard of Coney Island, do you?"

"This is my first visit to America. I've lived my entire life in England, though I've traveled with my family to other parts of Great Britain."

Her brow wrinkled in puzzlement. "You said you couldn't find your family."

"My adoptive family. The truth is. . ." He hesitated, wondering why he found it easy to share matters with her that he'd guarded from others, even close friends, for years. Perhaps it had something to do with the fact that they'd both been passengers on the ill-fated ship.

"Yes, Peter?"

He saw only kindness in her eyes.

"The truth is, I don't know my given surname. That night wiped out a great deal of my memory, and the name which I'd associated with my mother the few times I heard her addressed by it wasn't on the ship's manifest, according to my adoptive father. I was too young to look at the time, of course."

She leaned forward, placing her fingertips against his sleeve in an unconscious gesture. "Oh, Peter. How awful for you!" She held his gaze a moment, then looked down at his sleeve as if just aware she'd touched him. Moving her hand away, she stared at the table, clearly embarrassed by her action.

Touched by her gesture, Peter wanted to relieve any qualms she might have concerning him and softened his voice a degree. "I'm not certain what I'm hoping to find or even if I'll find anything. So many years have elapsed. This entire venture might prove fruitless, but I won't know if I don't try."

She gave an encouraging smile and nod.

"Somehow, I know if I find any answers, they will be here, in America. In New York to be precise. I do remember. . ." He hesitated. "She told me I would meet my father in New York City."

"He didn't come to the dock to collect you when the *Carpathia* pulled in?"

"If he did, I wouldn't know it. I was in the infirmary, being treated for frostbite. But even if he had been in the same room with me, I wouldn't have recognized his face. He was never a part of my life. We were sailing to America to see him. And there's a good possibility. . ." Again he hesitated, uncertain why he was telling all this to a stranger. Yet speaking with Missy didn't feel like addressing a stranger. Due to the connection they shared, she seemed more than that. "There's a possibility that my mother never married. I need to know, to discover the truth. No matter what it leads to."

To Missy's credit, she didn't show one iota of shock, nor did she draw away in doubt the way Claire had when she'd learned of Peter's secret. Missy remained quiet a moment, her attention dropping to the list he held open in his hands. "And you feel that one of those six people might hold the key?"

"I can only hope so. Though what the key is, I don't know. Perhaps speaking with others will bring back the same clarity of memory you've given me and trigger a memory which will in turn, lead me to my family or at least the knowledge of one." He shrugged. "It's a bit far-fetched, I know. But I have nothing else to go by. I haven't any other method with which to start my search."

"I think if I were in your position, I'd do the same." Her expression became serious. . . ." This time she was the one to hesitate. "Peter, I'd like to help you, if you'll let me."

"Help me?" Stunned curiosity made him straighten in his chair.

"You don't know your way around the city. I know where most of the places are on that list—or at least how to get to them."

"I wouldn't wish to take advantage of your time."

"You wouldn't be. Besides, I offered." She gave a quirk of a smile. "This is a slow time of year for the restaurant. My uncle Tony's been suffering from arthritis in his elbow, and many of our patrons come only to hear him play the violin. He is quite the virtuoso. At this point, he's not playing, so that means business isn't as steady as usual; besides, our busiest hours are in the evenings, and as you can clearly see. . ." She waved a hand around the empty restaurant. "We aren't exactly at standing room only."

"But you know nothing about me except what I've told you." Were all American women so trusting of unknown foreign men?

"I know enough to sense you're not dangerous. Any man who offers a witty comeback after having been mistakenly knocked in the eye with a flying candy box from an irate blond can't be all that bad." She grinned. "And if you still think I'm a nut for offering to tag along with you, then let me reassure you here and now that I can take care of myself. Uncle Tony gave me a few boxing lessons when I was younger."

"You're joshing me."

"No, but then you don't know my uncle Tony." She giggled.

Her laughter was contagious, and he joined in then winced as a jolt of pain shot through his eye.

Her expression turned sympathetic. "Besides, you'll be doing me a favor. I have a personal reason I'd like to remain absent from the restaurant for a while."

"The man with the candy?" Peter asked.

"Almost." She grimaced. "He's just the associate. It's his boss I want to keep my distance from."

Peter wondered about the sudden hard glint in her eyes, but she then turned them on him and smiled again. "So what do you say, Peter, ole pal. Mind if I hook up with you on your hunt?"

"Ole pal?" He hitched up his eyebrows, and she chuckled.

"Well, we're *almost* kin, aren't we? The children of the *Titanic*? That has to count for something."

He studied her again, thinking what a pretty girl she was. As he dwelt on their conversation, his words grew curious. "On the voyage to America, a steward recommended this restaurant to me. At the White Star offices, a worker offered me the list of names, and your aunt's was one of six there."

"See? It must be fate that brought us together," Missy teased.

"Fate? Or a higher power?"

She ran her fingertip along the squares in the checked tablecloth before looking at him again. "Do you believe God ordains the paths of those here on earth? Or do you believe it's all left up to chance?"

He grew serious. "I was raised to believe and serve the Lord, but sometimes the answers to such questions are beyond my comprehension."

She gave a weak smile and nod. "That's about the size of it. We don't really know, do we, Peter? But for whatever purpose, destiny seems to have brought you here to us."

Her words alerted a hidden memory, but it faded into the mists of his mind before he could get a good grip on it.

"Peter? Are you okay?" She leaned forward.

He nodded, waving off her concern. "Just a thought. Nothing more."

"A thought?"

He looked into her curious eyes and smiled. "I suppose I cannot fight what is meant to be. If you'd like to come along on my hunt, I could certainly use a guide."

Her radiant smile made even the knock in the eye seem worthwhile.

Chapter 3

Melissa hurried through her toiletries at record speed the following morning. A tap sounded at her open door, and she turned to see.

Aunt Maria walked into her bedroom, her arms full of towels. "Are you sure about this, Missy?"

"You mean, will I be safe?" Melissa chuckled. "The man's a bona fide gentleman. Did you notice how he stood when each of us entered the restaurant? I've never seen a guy do that except in reel-to-reels at the picture show."

Her aunt gave a slight nod.

"And did you notice the tender way he spoke of his mother? He has a kind heart. Not something you find often in the men of New York City. At least not the men I know." Peter's mention of God had also surprised her, and that he would speak of his faith so freely. She, too, believed in God, but wasn't convinced of His guidance in people's lives, due in part to her own experiences.

"Exactly." Her aunt moved forward, breaking into Melissa's thoughts. "That is what I mean. Are you certain you're not using this only as an excuse to escape your problems regarding Guido?"

Melissa shrugged. "What if I am? Can you blame me?"

"No." Maria's expression softened. "But neither do I wish for you to mistake convenience for anything other than it is."

Melissa laughed in disbelief. "Aunt Maria, I'm going to be Peter's guide for a few days, probably no more than a week. The way you talk, you'd think I was planning my wedding list."

"Just be careful, mi niña. I have never known you to offer friendship to a man so quickly." Maria gave her a one-armed hug. "I trust you to listen to your head in this matter and not your heart."

"This, coming from you?" Melissa shook her head. "You're the one who's always prodded me to search for love."

"To be open to it, not to go running after it. It will come when it is time."

Melissa looked down at her dresser. "And I told you, Aunt Maria, you have nothing to fear. I just want to help him. Call it an act of charity, helping a fellow survivor. It feels right, somehow."

"Charity? Ah." Maria didn't sound convinced. "Just be careful, that is all I'm asking." She left the room and Melissa to her thoughts.

Melissa pondered the quiet warning. "Still, there is something about him," she said softly to herself.

Firming her lips into a tight line, she fluffed her curls with a brush. Perhaps the desire to aid Peter in his quest did stem from more than just the need to escape Guido's unwanted attentions, or her desire to assist a fellow survivor. But love? Impossible. She had only just met the man, after all. Helping Peter to discover the secrets that went down with the *Titanic* and could lead him to his unknown family might also help her to release her own phantoms of the past, especially those revolving around her mother.

Blissfully ignorant of the world's intrigues and cruelties, Melissa had drifted in her make-believe fantasy world with her niñera always by her side until that last night on *Titanic*. Melissa's innocent eyes had been forced open to harsh truths. Afterward, life swirled into a maelstrom of change, though the treatment she'd endured from one individual remained hopelessly the same.

An unbidden memory of her mother's tinkling laughter and a man's quiet voice outside Melissa's bedroom cabin door rushed to her, and she thumped the brush hard on the dresser. She winced, hoping the wooden handle hadn't scarred the fine oak.

"Missy." Her aunt's voice came from the corridor. "He is here."

Melissa positioned her matching blue hat atop her head at a jaunty angle, stuck the hatpin through the fabric, and grabbed her handbag. She hurried through the corridor leading to the spicy-aroma-filled kitchen, gave a quick nod to her cousin, Cecily, and hurried on into the restaurant, the rapid clicking of her pumps heralding her arrival.

Peter rose from his chair upon sight of her, and she noted the spark of appreciation in his eyes. Usually, she paid little interest to men's favorable attention to her appearance; this morning his notice felt welcomed.

"Hello. So, where should we start?" she cheerily greeted him. A thought struck. "Have you had anything to eat yet?"

"Your aunt's spaghetti and lasagna, while I enjoyed them, do not associate in my mind as breakfast food."

She giggled. "Silly. We do eat other foods here besides pasta. Well, not much, but some. If you're hungry, I noticed Cecily making eggs and bacon. I'm sure she wouldn't mind me begging off a platter."

"Cecily?"

"My uncle Tony's daughter. A cousin."

"If you're sure she won't mind, that would be splendid. I forewent the morning meal."

"I thought so," Melissa playfully chided. "While I understand your eagerness to start this day's activities, you really shouldn't skip eating to do so, Peter. I'll be right back." She hurried to the kitchen and soon returned, bearing a fragrant platter of food and a cup of coffee.

"Your eye looks somewhat better today." She set the plate on the table in front of him. At least the bruise wasn't as dark.

He smiled his thanks, and she noted how he closed his eyes and bowed his head before he took up his fork and began cutting into his egg. She slipped into the chair across from him and smiled as she watched him eat. He really was quite handsome, and he had such a penchant for manners.

He looked up at her. "Would you care for some?"

"Hm? No, I ate earlier."

"Ah." An uneasy smile lifted his lips as he gave a brief nod, then looked down at his food again. Once more he cut a piece of the fluffy egg and raised the fork to his mouth. His eyes lifted to hers and found her still watching.

"I'm sorry. I'm making you nervous, aren't I?" Melissa shifted position in her chair. "It's just that I find myself wondering what you looked like then. I'm trying to place your face at my birthday party."

"Well, I can satisfy your curiosity on that regard. I had very light hair—almost white if you can believe that—and I usually wore an old cap over it. I was skinny; often got myself into mischief."

"You know. . ." A sly smile spread across her face. "I was thinking about the party last night, and I remembered the waiter who knocked over the punch glasses argued that he tripped on something. Later, I found a marble by the wall. Only a few boys came to the party; the rest were girls."

Peter's face reddened as he took a sip of black coffee. "I did carry marbles in my pocket as a lad, but if the one you found was mine, I have no recollection of how it went missing."

Their gazes met, and slow smiles spread across their faces, turning to shared laughter.

"No recollection?" She lifted her brows.

"All right, perhaps there was a hole in my pocket. But no, I truly don't remember. And that's the problem in its entirety. I don't remember."

The words came lightly, his smile growing only a trifle melancholy, but they left an apparent change in the atmosphere. His plight touched Melissa's heart, and she no longer wished to tease him.

"We'll find your answers, Peter. Somehow, we will."

He gave a slight nod, gratitude filling his eyes. "Hearing you say it, I can almost believe it."

As she continued to stare at him, Melissa's heart twisted, and the impulse to take his hand in hers grew strong. Instead, she excused herself and rose from the table. While he finished his meal, she arranged for their cab.

❧

The first person on Peter's list, according to the address, worked at Macy's Department Store. Peter and Missy stood on the sidewalk and gazed up at the monstrous building that occupied the entire block of Seventh Avenue on the west, Broadway on the east, Thirty-fourth Street on the south, and Thirty-fifth Street on the north. One entire wall of plate glass, the width of a parlor, gave Peter a glimpse of mannequins on elaborate display, draped in the latest evening gowns.

"I love to window shop," Missy said to Peter as they walked under a canopy and toward the glass doors. "I've heard Macy's is the largest department store in the entire world."

Peter could believe it. "It's not Buckingham Palace, but it does come close."

Missy laughed. "There are dozens more like it throughout the city. Saks Fifth Avenue, which is in that direction. . ." Missy motioned across the street. "Altman's, and others."

A man in uniform held the door open and greeted them with a reserved smile. Peter blinked as he took in his first view of Macy's.

In one sweeping glance, he noticed scores of people who busied themselves in every corner of the store. Fashionable shopgirls waited on customers. Male clerks in dark, dignified suits walked the aisles. Everywhere Peter looked, items glittered and gleamed and filled racks and shelves. But the opulence of the store was what caused a moment's shock.

"My word," Peter said, shaking his head.

" 'Goods suitable for the millionaire, at prices in reach of the millions,'" a mustachioed man suddenly said, materializing at their elbows. "That was Rowland Macy's slogan, founder of Macy's. Now, sir, madam, how may I be of assistance to you this morning?"

"We would like to see ladies' shoes, please," Missy said before Peter could correct the man's assumption that they were married.

He gave them directions, and after a great deal of negotiating the crowded aisles, they approached a plush area lined with women's shoes in a range of colors and styles. A short, bespectacled man approached, his smile as polished as his surroundings. "Good morning. How may I be of service to you?"

"Good morning. We're looking for Mr. Frederick Delaney."

A glint of suspicion entered the clerk's eyes. "That's me."

"Splendid. Mr. Delaney, as a fellow survivor of the *Titanic,* I'm trying to find out any information you might have regarding this woman." Peter withdrew the locket from his coat, but the man darted a glance over his shoulder, as though afraid of discovery.

"Please. If Mr. Hobbs catches me not doing my job, I could get fired."

Missy picked up a navy pump. "I'd like to try this one on, if I may. Size 5."

"Of course, madam." He took the shoe and hurried beyond a drape covering the wall.

Peter curiously eyed Missy, and she shrugged. "If he's doing his work, he might be more inclined to listen."

He smiled in silent agreement. Mr. Delaney returned and took a place on the seat opposite the one Missy had taken. He slipped off her shoe, taking clinical hold of her ankle. His actions revealed a glimpse of her silk-stocking-clad leg. Peter looked at her shapely calf a moment before forcing his attention to a table of footwear, then to the locket in his hand. He opened it and held it suspended from the chain, lowering it in front of the clerk's face.

"Please, sir."

"There were more than two thousand passengers on that ship," the man argued. "I couldn't possibly remember. It's been sixteen years. And if she was in third class, I wouldn't have known her anyway."

"Please. I have reason to believe she was in first or second class." He looked at Missy, remembering his presence at her birthday party. "All I'm asking you to do is look. She. . .she was my mother. She went by the name of Franklin."

The man released a soft breath, then took the locket. "A lovely woman." He stared a moment more. "I don't recall her face. Sorry."

With a dejected nod, Peter closed the locket, slipping it back into his pocket.

"It's not that I don't care." Mr. Delaney's eyes grew sad. "Isidor Straus once owned this department store. After both he and his wife drowned that night, Isidor's brother and later his sons took over. I lost my business shortly after the sinking due to a bad investment, and I never could stop thinking about how it could have been me in Mr. Straus's place. Seeking a position here was my way of giving silent support to those men who lost their lives, to the families of those men. I could have been one of them, you see. But I jumped off before *Titanic* had taken on too much water, and I managed to swim to a boat. One of the very few who did." Tears rimmed his eyes, and Peter sensed the guilt that lay beneath the soft-spoken words. "I could have been one of them."

"Thank you, Mr. Delaney." Peter's own words came quietly. "I understand it's difficult for you to speak of this; I appreciate your time."

The man nodded, slipping the pump off of Missy's foot. "You didn't really want this, did you?"

A sheepish expression crossed her face.

"I didn't think so." Mr. Delaney smiled in a fatherly way, then grew alert, shifting his gaze to Peter. "You said 'fellow survivor' earlier. You were on the *Titanic*?"

Peter looked toward Missy. "Both of us were."

The man swung his surprised focus to Missy again, and she gravely nodded.

"My, my." Mr. Delaney sat back, eyeing them both. "It's a privilege to know two of the children who came through that horrible night, and to know you are alive and well. I helped to load the boats after the chaos began." He pulled out his handkerchief and blotted his eyes, his spectacles inching upward. "Have you visited the memorials?"

"Not as yet," Peter said. "But I plan to. I only arrived from England two days ago."

"You came all the way to America for this? My, my." Mr. Delaney shook his head in wonder. "Listen. I'll tell you what I *can* do. Leave a way that I can reach you, and if I remember anything, I'll be sure to contact you."

"I have a room at the Waldorf-Astoria." Peter reached for his fountain pen and pulled out a small tablet of paper he'd bought for his investigation. "You can reach me here." He scribbled off his name and room number, handing it to Mr. Delaney.

"Caldwell." The man's brows furrowed. "That name. It's very familiar."

"My adoptive mother and father were also on the Titanic." Peter watched the man carefully, not failing to notice Missy's sharp glance in his direction. "Lord Caldwell, he was a viscount at the time of the sinking."

"Oh, yes? I seem to remember the name, but beyond that. . ." He shrugged. "I *am* sorry."

"I appreciate your time." Peter took hold of Missy's elbow and guided her back to the aisle. She seemed pensive, and he wondered what was going through her mind now.

❧

Once back out on the sidewalk, Melissa studied the list.

"Where to next?" Peter asked.

"I recognize one other local address we could try. The others are going to take some time to reach. One is on Long Island; another at Coney Island. I suggest we tackle each of those on separate days. This street," she pointed to an address, "isn't far from here. We could try there next."

"That sounds like a good plan. May I ask a question?"

"Of course."

"How are you so knowledgeable when it comes to determining the locale of addresses on sight?"

She chuckled. "I had a horrible habit of getting lost when I was a child; my uncle Tony made me memorize street names, and some of the addresses are familiar to me because they're places I've been. Macy's for instance." She motioned to the building they'd just left. "Though I'll admit, anything not local will be harder to find; I'm not sure how good a guide I'll be then."

"That's all right. You're good company."

"Thanks. So are you." They shared a smile, then looked ahead again so as not to bump into other pedestrians. "Actually, Peter, you really should take a tour of the city while you're here. I know of some great spots that might interest you."

He nodded. "I could do that."

"Okay, my turn for asking a question."

He chuckled. "Turnabout seems only fair play."

"When you said you were adopted, I assumed you lived in an orphanage after the disaster. But what you told Mr. Delaney, about your adoptive parents being on the *Titanic*—that stunned me. Did you know them? Were they friends of your mother's?"

"No. If they had been, I'd have all the answers I need."

"Of course. I wasn't thinking." Melissa felt stupid for not realizing that.

"No, it's all right," he reassured. "My adoptive father, who was then no more than a stranger to me, buckled his life belt around me as well and jumped with me into the water that night. I don't remember any of it, only bits and pieces. I was told about it."

"Oh." She hesitated. "And his wife?"

"She made it to one of the lifeboats before the ship went down. They weren't married then—only childhood sweethearts who'd reunited on the *Titanic*. She lost her father that night, and Lawrence and Annabelle married days after the ship docked. Later they adopted me when no one came to claim me."

Melissa stopped walking suddenly.

"Missy?"

Alarm riddled his voice, but she could barely fathom it. "Annabelle?" She turned wide eyes to him. "Your mother's name is Annabelle?" Her gaze flicked to the side and widened further upon sight of a familiar black Lincoln slowly traveling along the street toward them. All thoughts of the past flew from her mind as she grabbed his free hand. "Come on! We've got to get out of here."

"What? Why?"

"I can't explain now. Just—come on!"

Although crippled, Peter did a remarkable job of keeping up with her. Still, with his limp and her high heels, they weren't fast enough, and dodging the crowds proved difficult. A number of pedestrians sharing the sidewalk aired angry retorts when the two jostled them as they ran past.

"So sorry." Melissa heard Peter call to those with whom they'd had a close skirmish. "Excuse us, please."

Rounding the corner, Melissa dove into the nearest shop, jerking Peter along with her. She halted abruptly and turned, but the force of her unexpected actions toppled Peter into her. To keep from falling, both grabbed each other at their waists in an instinctive gesture. They managed to find their balance, though Melissa's heart went off kilter. She forgot to breathe as, only inches away, Peter's startled blue eyes locked with hers.

Chapter 4

O h."

Missy's soft gasp broke Peter from the enticing harbor of her eyes, reeling him back to the present.

"Your idea of a tour through the city is more like a fifty-yard dash, isn't it?" he quipped.

"I. . .we had to get away."

Her words came breathlessly, and Peter realized his hands still framed her slim waist. But then, hers also still rested at his.

"Ahem."

The clearly disapproving sound startled them, and they turned their heads to see who shared the building. Peter saw they stood inside a haberdashery. Colorful ribbons filled the shelves, and bolts of material stood along the papered walls. The gray-haired woman behind the counter raised her eyebrows.

"Were you in need of sewing items?" she asked, a frost to her voice as she eyed them.

Peter released his hold on Missy, and she did likewise, both of them self-conscious as they put space between them.

"Thank you, no." Missy touched the back of her hat, straightening it. "We're just, um, taking a breath to rest."

"A breath to rest?" the woman repeated.

Peter raised his brows at Missy's choice of words, but her attention had gone to the shop's sole window. She peered beyond the white letters painted on the glass as if searching for something. Peter looked too, but nothing struck him as out of the ordinary. After a moment she exhaled a long, relieved sigh and turned to Peter. "It's safe now."

"Safe?"

"I'll tell you. Later." Her eyes flicked to the woman then back to him in a silent message. "Say, are you thirsty? How about an ice-cream soda? Do they have those in England?" With a smile, she walked outside, not waiting for his reply. Peter had no choice but to follow, though curiosity ate at him to understand her unusual behavior.

"There's a drugstore not far from here. I know the soda jerk who runs the fountain. We can walk." She headed in the direction from which they'd come.

"All right." Peter fell into step beside her, deciding to practice patience.

The next shop they entered sported a long counter with three high stools near one wall. A balding man in an apron stood in the narrow area of working space between the counter and an array of machinery, one with spigots. On either side, tall glasses stood in neat stacks.

"Hello, Melissa. The usual for you today?"

"Yes, thanks, Jim. For my friend here, too." She looked at Peter. "You don't mind if I order for you?"

"Not at all." Peter took a seat on one of the high stools, hoping he would like the "usual" as well as he liked spaghetti. He watched the man fill a cup from one of the spigots, add ice cream and syrup, put a lid on it, then shake it. He poured the mixture into one of the glasses and set it in front of Missy. She picked up a spoon and dipped into it. "Mmm. Perfect as always, Jim."

The man nodded with a smile and set about making another. Peter looked around the shop. Pharmaceutical items lined the shelves. Illustrated signs advertising cough elixirs and tonics plastered the walls.

He studied the brown liquid in the glass set in front of him, hoping "the usual" didn't contain any medicines.

"It's not some dark, foul-tasting potion," Missy teased. "Go on. Try it."

Peter took a bite. The zippy flavor blended with the ice cream to produce a pleasant taste. Well, if it was medicinal, at least it couldn't do him any harm.

"I take it you don't have soda fountains in England."

"I've never seen one. We live outside London, actually, and the surroundings are more rural." He thought of the verdant hills and dells, the slower pace of living, and the old-world flavor of the castles and manors. Quite unexpectedly, he found himself missing home.

"You have such a sad look on your face, all of a sudden."

"It's nothing, really." He smiled to reassure her. "Have you had your 'breath of rest'? Can you tell me what happened out there now?"

"Oh, yes. That." She fiddled with her glass, obviously flustered. Jim had moved to a back room, and they had the place to themselves. "Peter, I'm going to be completely honest with you, since you were so open with me when we met." She made a number of revolutions with her spoon through her soda then blew out a frustrated breath. Her blue eyes turned to his. "Where you come from, are there any gangsters?"

"Gangsters?" he asked, puzzled she should ask such a question.

"Men that are from the underworld, lawbreakers, mobsters, racketeers. . ."

"Yes, I know what they are. I imagine every society has men who choose a life of crime." He gave a slight shake of his head, not understanding where this was leading.

"I suppose. But Prohibition has only made things worse. The gangsters once committed their crimes behind the scenes; now they've come into the open, with drive-by shootings and such. They still try to hide a lot of it, like with the speak-easies, but very few of them are ever brought to justice."

Peter waited, hoping this would make sense soon.

"For years, a few members from one of those crime families have frequented my uncle Tony's restaurant. A man named Vittorio Piccoli is the mob boss, though as far as I know, he's never been to the restaurant. But his nephew Guido has, and he's taken an interest in me. He used to watch me when I was younger. I could always feel his eyes on me, and—" She pulled at her lower lip with her teeth. "Well, he's done watching. Let's just put it that way."

"Guido sent the candy," Peter inserted, beginning to understand.

She nodded. "I saw his car, and that's why I ran. I didn't want him to see me."

Something about her attitude gave him pause. "Do you have any ties to him, former or otherwise?"

"No. None at all. Only in his mind."

Her low, emphatic words erased the lingering doubt that she belonged to another, and he nodded.

"I thought you should know, since I'm palling around with you for a while. He, um, jealously guards whatever's his, and even though I'm not—his, I mean—things could get tricky."

"You're telling me I could be in danger."

"Yes." She gave a nervous shrug. "Not that I think you're the type to be intimidated, but I feel it's only fair to warn you. Vittorio's family isn't above murder to get what they want."

Though she'd acted with such independence, her eyes told all now. Fear touched the blue depths, making her vulnerable. A desire to protect her welled up inside him, and Peter covered her hand with his own. "Missy, I'm not without my own devices."

She looked doubtfully at his cane. "Wood wouldn't hold up well against bullets."

"Bullets?"

"Oh, yes. Tommy guns, revolvers—Vittorio and his bunch use them all."

He considered. "Perhaps it would be wise to invest in a handgun for protection." At her look of surprise, he explained, "I am well-versed in how to handle weaponry; from the time I was a boy, I was taught to shoot and hunt."

"My uncle Tony has a revolver; I could ask him."

He gave a nod of assent, then noticed her brow pucker with worry again.

"Don't be alarmed; when you're with me, I'll take care of you." He squeezed her hand in reassurance before letting go. "And I'm not frightened of Guido and his henchmen either."

"You really aren't, are you?" Puzzled wonder replaced the doubt in her eyes. "I'm not sure if that makes you the worst fool or the bravest man in New York

City. But somehow, I believe what you say."

They shared a quiet smile tinged with hope. Jim returned to the counter, and Missy straightened on her stool.

"So let's have a look at that list again." She unfolded the paper, studied it, then smiled. "Peter, have you ever been to the movies?"

☙❧

Their visit to the huge edifice that housed the motion-picture theater yielded no results. Hannah Metzler was absent that afternoon, but the woman at the ticket counter assured them she would be in to work the next day. When they couldn't locate the man who lived in Queens either, Peter decided to postpone the search. At Missy's invitation to stay and eat dinner at the restaurant, he politely declined. He didn't want to intrude on her generosity and time any more than he already had. Besides, he was exhausted. Lying down for an hour might help his mental acuity, which had begun to suffer.

Inside his luxurious hotel room, Peter removed his coat and shoes. He stared at his misshapen foot inside its wool sock and thought back to those grueling days after the disaster. Frostbite had destroyed part of his foot, and doctors had amputated two toes to save it. At the age of seven, he had learned to walk again, at first using a crutch, and later, as a young man, switching to a cane. Rather than grow embittered by his losses, he relied on humor to pull him through. His "angelic face," so called by his mother Annabelle, and his ready wit drew people to him even then. After mere minutes in his company, those who first pitied him forgot their sympathy and treated him as an equal. He'd been blessed with a great deal of love and support from his adoptive parents, which helped Peter not only to accept his situation, but also to deny self-pity and live each day to the fullest. Without Lawrence and Annabelle in his life, he might never have pulled through those trying days.

Peter stretched out upon the four-poster bed, his head cradled in the cloud of his feather pillow, and closed his eyes. Soon his thoughts faded away to nothing.

Inside corridor after empty corridor, Peter moved along the carpet as ice-cold water swirled around his bare ankles.

"Mummy?" Gaslights above flashed all around him, flickered, and went out. Incandescent fog metamorphosed into obscure shadows. "Mummy?"

Suddenly he was back in his stateroom, shivering in his nightshirt, awakened from sleep by his mother's insistent hand on his shoulder.

"Come, Peter. You must wake up."

"Why, Mummy?" He rubbed the sleep from his eyes and yawned. She stood before him, beautiful as ever in her brown and gold evening gown. Her dark hair was piled in ringlets atop her head but mussed. Her blue eyes were fearful and teary, though she remained calm.

"We must leave the ship. We're taking another boat."

"I'm tired."

"Not now, my pigeon. Stop your whining. You can go back to sleep soon." She hurried around the stateroom as she spoke, collecting his discarded knickers, shirt, and shoes. All of a sudden, she stopped, as if frozen, and dropped them all to the carpet. Her shoulders began to shake.

"Mummy?"

Outside the cabin, he heard shouting, crying. A heavy knock cracked the door, and she swung her gaze toward it in fear.

"Mummy?"

"You must always remember, Peter." She knelt in front of him as he stood with his back to a corridor wall. She slipped the locket over his head. Her eyes drilled into his. "It is important that you never forget. It is your destiny! Do you understand, Peter? It is what brought us here. . . ."

Destiny brought us. . . .

Do you understand Peter?

It is what brought us here. . . .

Destiny brought us. . . .

Abruptly caught up in a whirlpool of icy water, he was sucked down, alone, deep into a swirling mass of black ocean. He opened his mouth in a silent scream, shards of cold stinging his skin.

Mummy!

With a jerk, Peter awoke, sitting bolt upright on the hotel bed. His face had broken out in a sweat, and he struggled to regain even breaths. Eyes wide, he braced his hands on the mattress, trembling, remembering. The dream had always ended after the knock at the door, forcing him awake. This time, there had been more.

Missy's echo yesterday of his mother's words had jarred loose the memory of that night on the boat. He could still feel how his mother's eyes had bored into his as she placed the locket around his neck.

She had said it was his destiny. What was his destiny? What had Mother wanted him to remember?

His hand still shook as he checked his pocket watch. He had slept more than three hours. No outside glow muted his curtains; the sky had grown dark.

Food held no appeal; instead, he reflected on all Missy and Mr. Delaney had told him, the latter of which had been precious little. His gaze shifted to his valise, which held another item of worth. He turned on a light and retrieved the small box from where he'd secured it. He opened it, pouring a cascade of diamonds into his palm. The light stoked multi-sparkles in the facets. Only a fool would keep such a necklace in his room, and with all the talk of crime and gangsters, he didn't dare carry it on his person. Deciding to learn if the hotel had a safe, he replaced the jewelry in its simple cardboard box, dressed, and headed for the lobby.

Once he'd learned all he could in Manhattan, before he secured passage on a ship back to Liverpool, he would embark on the peculiar mission asked of him last week. Until that time, he planned to focus every waking moment on his own personal quest. Somehow, he must find the answers.

Chapter 5

Melissa was ready when Peter came to collect her the next day. He seemed quieter than usual, more intense, somehow, and eager to get started. Once they'd hailed a cab and climbed inside, she studied him.

"Is everything all right?"

"Hm?" He glanced at her as if wondering what she meant. "Oh, yes. Everything's chipper."

"Why don't I believe you?"

He chuckled. "All right, then. I had the dream last night. The one about the *Titanic*."

"Oh?" She hesitated to delve further, feeling like an interloper, though he'd offered the information.

"Yes. Strangely, your words from the first day in the restaurant mirrored the words in my dream. My mother told me destiny brought us here. I assume she meant to New York, that is, if the recollection of your words didn't spark an addition to my dream. I remembered her placing the locket around my neck, so I'm inclined to believe she did say those words."

Melissa furrowed her brow, sharing his frustration and pain. "As time progresses, you'll remember more, Peter. I'm sure of it. Just look at how much you've discovered in two days."

"I know. I must exercise patience. I've been ignorant of the truth for sixteen years. I can surely tolerate a few more days or weeks. Even months."

That he might extend his stay in Manhattan filled Melissa with pleasure. She remembered how he'd held her so close after their narrow escape the day before. She had thought Peter might even try to kiss her as they'd stood inside the entrance of the haberdashery, his large hands at her waist. She'd felt lost in his intense eyes and wasn't entirely sure she would have stopped him had he tried. Putting a rein on that memory, she then recalled the revelation that had stunned her before their mad dash down the sidewalk. Melissa opened her mouth to ask the question about Annabelle, but Peter spoke first.

"You never speak of your parents. Are they still living?"

"My mother is, but not my father." She worked to keep the chill out of her voice.

"Does your mother live in Manhattan?"

"No." The cab pulled up at the Roxy Theater and saved Melissa from having to explain. "Ah, here we are," she said brightly.

Distracted, Peter stared at the enormous edifice, of which they'd only viewed the lobby the day before.

"Wait 'til you see the inside," Melissa said.

She led him through the modest entrance and on into a cavernous lobby. An imitation galaxy of thousands of marquee lights glimmered from the foyer ceiling. Grecian statues lined the walls. In its gilt frame, an illustrated poster featured the Warner Brothers movie *Lights of New York*, and Melissa turned to him in excitement. "It's the first motion picture talkie all the way through."

"Talkie?"

"Not silent—it has sound and music."

"You've seen it?"

She shook her head. "It says so on the poster."

"Ah, yes." Peter noted the captions. "Well, once we've spoken to Mrs. Metzler, perhaps we should investigate as long as we're here. I've yet to see a motion picture."

Her heart jumped. This was beginning to seem much like a date, and she had mixed feelings about such a notion. But she gave a nod, and they headed into the theater. Upon querying a man in uniform, they learned Mrs. Metzler was cleaning in the auditorium. The movie wasn't set to show for another hour, but Peter secured tickets. After they gave their reasons for needing to enter the theater early, the manager gave them permission. Once they walked through the doors, their feet sank deeply into plush carpeting. Peter stopped and revolved in a slow circle to take in his surroundings.

"My word."

"I'm surprised you're impressed." Their voices echoed in the spacious arena, which housed thousands of seats on multitiered levels. "Surely the castles in England are much more awe inspiring."

"The castles in England are homes to the nobility. This public movie house is a *cathedral*. And your department store was also quite lavish."

She giggled. "New York City, for all her crime, certainly knows how to put on the Ritz with sparkle and glamour, I'll give her that. I've heard it said when they built the Roxy last year, they dubbed it the Cathedral of the Motion Picture."

"Not a difficult stretch of the imagination to reason why."

Mammoth curtains fronted the wide stage, and gilded stairways flanked either side. Urns bedecked numerous alcoves along the scrolled walls of the dual balconies, and costly drapery adorned the space behind each one. Opulent acres of lush carpeting spread out before them. An enormous crystal chandelier that must weigh tons gleamed high within the domed ceiling and cast twinkles of shimmering light over the huge rotunda—all of it similar to the opera house he'd visited in London.

Melissa noticed two women polishing seats nearby. "Peter."

He turned from studying the stage, and she motioned toward the women.

Set on his course again, he walked toward the workers, and Melissa followed. Upon inquiry, they located a small, buxom woman who proved to be Hannah Metzler, polishing near the stage with another woman. Unfortunately they also found Mrs. Metzler spoke little English. Regardless, Peter pulled his mother's locket from his coat, but when he mentioned the *Titanic,* she grew agitated and spoke in a foreign language Melissa didn't recognize. Tears swam to Mrs. Metzler's eyes. She rapidly patted her heart, shaking her head in denial, and hurried away from Peter and up the aisle.

"She lost all her family," the other woman explained with an accent not as pronounced. "She is one from third-class immigrants who survived, but her husband, her three sons. . ." The woman shook her head sadly.

Peter momentarily closed his eyes, his jaw working. "Please give her my most sincere apologies for troubling her."

"Yes, I do this. I hope you find what you seek," the woman said before turning back to her work.

He stared into space as if lost to his thoughts.

"Peter?" Melissa touched his sleeve. "Do you want to sit down?"

He nodded, giving her a shadow of a smile.

They chose a pair of seats midway to the stage. When he remained silent, Melissa laid her hand on his.

"Please, tell me what's troubling you."

❧

Peter took in a long breath and exhaled it softly. He propped his elbows on his legs. Steepling his fingers together, he lowered his forehead to them and rubbed his fingertips along his brow in a gesture of remorseful doubt.

"Peter?"

Missy's hand tentatively touched his back.

He straightened and looked at her. "I feel like the worst kind of heel for bringing to mind a tragedy that robbed so many of their lives. Yet conversely, I feel driven to pursue this. Am I wrong to do so?"

"It's only natural you'd want to find your family. Your reasons aren't selfish."

He shifted his gaze to the ornate wall of drapery hiding the stage. "At first, I'm ashamed to say, they were. I wanted to prove to a woman that I was worthy of her affections, though I myself wasn't certain if that were true. Being nameless in English society isn't a desirable attribute when one wishes to marry." He chuckled wryly. "Yet since last night, since the dream, I find it's no longer all about Claire. My purpose has altered; I need to find these answers for me. To find where it is—who it is—I come from. Does that sound selfish?" He turned his head to look at her again.

She lowered her hand from his back. "No, it sounds human." She hesitated. "This woman, Claire. . .do you love her?"

Taken aback by the question, Peter tried to frame his answer. "Our families are acquaintances; we grew up together, attended the same balls and parties. My past, before the *Titanic,* was something about which we never spoke. We British are actually quite reserved and shield our secrets well." Which made it that much more amazing he was sharing his problems with her now. Yet he'd carried them alone for so long; it eased his soul to speak of them.

She gave a slight understanding nod. He sensed she had put distance between them and regretted burdening her with his troubles. "Tell me of your family," he said suddenly, desiring to know.

Her eyes flickered with surprise. She averted her gaze to the seats in front of them, as if now wary. "What do you wish to know? You've already met my aunt Maria, and there's my uncle Tony. He was a widower when he met Aunt Maria. He's a kind man with an artist's soul. Both he and Maria have treated me like a daughter. My cousins—Tony's children from his first marriage—are younger than me. Lucio and Cecily. And Rosa is Maria and Tony's child. You'll meet them all soon, I'm sure."

"And your mother?" he asked softly.

"My mother?" she repeated bitterly, then gave a curt laugh. "I don't consider my mother part of my family."

His mouth opened in shock, and she looked down at her skirt.

"Maybe that sounds horrible, but she dumped me on Maria when I was eight and ran off with the man who became her fourth husband. The don—Don Ortega, Maria's brother—was her third. I suppose I should be grateful; at least she didn't divorce my father. He died and escaped any likelihood of that happening."

Peter heard the pain underlying her tone. "Missy. I'm sorry."

"Don't be. Mama loved money and whoever had the means to give it to her more than she loved me. I've come to accept it. And I'm thankful for Maria; she was more of a mother to me than the woman who gave me life."

Unsure what to do to quell the tide of bitter hurt he'd unleashed with his unknowing words, Peter took hold of her hand. Startled, she looked at him.

"Forgive me for opening an old wound and for speaking when I have no right, but your absence in her life is most certainly her loss."

Her expression softened in wonder. "Why, Peter. That's so sweet. I. . .thank you." Her lips softly parted, and Peter lowered his gaze to them.

He wanted to kiss her.

Astonished by the sudden thought, he did nothing but lift his eyes to hers. What might have happened, he never found out. Voices startled them both to the present as more people entered the theater. Peter withdrew his hand from

Missy's, then discovered he missed its warmth.

They talked of trivial matters until the curtain slid open and a hush filled the great rotunda. Silence fled as powerful notes of organ music resounded throughout the theater from a balcony high above. A film in black and white flickered across the screen. First, a cartoon entitled *Plane Crazy* featured an animated mouse named Mickey and was followed by a twenty-minute serial before the feature movie began. To Peter's consternation, he soon realized the talkie was a film about gangsters, and he looked over to Missy to see how she was taking it. Her expression was rigid, but when he whispered to her an offer to leave, she shook her head no.

The musical score included a blend of Tchaikovsky, Hebrew music, and popular ballads. Though the sound quality seemed unclear at times and tinny, he was nonetheless amazed to hear sound in a motion picture, to see a motion picture at all. Yet he couldn't enjoy it, not when Missy clearly was not. She jumped in her chair at the gunshots, and Peter could feel her tension crackling like electricity, which he suspected had nothing to do with the film. Finally, he took her hand and stood, leading her up the aisle and out of the theater.

"Peter?" she asked in bewilderment when they reached the lobby.

He stopped and turned toward her. "Tell me you wish to go back in there, and we will. But only if it's what you really want. And I suspect you don't."

She gave him a resigned half smile. "Am I that easy to read?"

Sensing her distress, he did his best to lighten the situation. "Not unless you make it a regular practice to embed nail prints into the chair cushions."

She chuckled. "Peter Caldwell, I like you."

"The feeling is mutual." He smiled. "Now would you like to go somewhere and get a bite to eat?"

"As long as it's not pasta." She laughed again, and he joined in. A doorman opened the door for them, and Peter waited for Missy to precede him onto the sidewalk.

"Well, well, if it isn't Melissa Reynolds."

At a woman's catty words, Peter turned to look behind them, as did Missy.

A brunette in a short, beaded, yellow dress that hung like a sack coolly returned Missy's gaze. Numerous strands of beads draped her neck. Along with the bright red lipstick she wore, the woman used paint on her face, a lot of it; unfortunately, it did nothing to smooth her features, made harsher by her cropped hair.

Chapter 6

"Florence." Melissa managed a civil greeting, though her lips thinned when the flapper gave Peter a slow appraisal.

"Tall, not so dark, but oh-so-definitely handsome." Florence arched her brow. "Aren't you going to introduce me to your friend, Melissa?" Her attention never left his face.

Melissa would rather take him by the arm and haul him away, but courtesy demanded she honor the request. "Peter, this is Florence. Florence, Peter."

"Well, hel-looo, Peter." She took his hand to shake and, in Melissa's opinion, held it longer than necessary. "So, you new in town?"

"Just arrived from London, actually."

Florence squealed. "And just listen to that accent! A classy British gent, unless I miss my guess. But even gentlemen have their vices, eh?" She sidled closer. "If you're interested in the goods, I can score you some hooch."

"Hooch?"

"You know, booze. Liquor," she explained when he only shook his head in ignorance.

Melissa clenched her teeth at the bold flirtation Florence forced her to witness. "You're barking up the wrong tree, Florence. I suggest you go find a different one to yap at." She glanced at Peter. "We really should be leaving."

"Guido's not going to like it that you're out two-timing him," Florence sneered.

"I'm not two-timing anyone."

"No? He seems to think you two are an item, though why, I couldn't even begin to imagine." The sweep of Florence's cold gaze left no doubt in Melissa's mind that the flapper thought Melissa not worth the trouble. If Melissa could convince Guido of that, she would gladly do so.

Instead of shooting off with another retort, Melissa took Peter by the arm as she'd wanted to do in the first place, turned her back on Florence, and resumed walking toward the streetcar stop.

"Did you just call me a tree?" Peter asked.

Despite her annoyance, Melissa smiled. "An American expression. I told her to leave you alone, more or less." Suddenly she realized how that could be taken. "Believe me. You don't want to get involved with bootleggers."

"I have no intention of doing so."

"I'm glad to hear it." She hadn't thought him the type to be interested in obtaining illegal liquor. "About what happened back there—I'm sorry about Florence." The woman was no friend, but Melissa felt an apology was in order regarding Florence's brazen behavior.

"Don't be concerned. It's nothing new to me, though her particular mode of fashion isn't something I'm accustomed to seeing in England."

An odd prick of resentment toward those unknown women needled Melissa. Nothing new? She gave him a sidelong glance. Well, why should she be surprised others found him attractive? And didn't he tell her he was almost engaged? Her mind wandered further. That woman rejected him, but he must feel strongly about her, must care deeply to have asked her to marry him. The idea discouraged her, and Melissa put a swift check on such thoughts. Maria had been right to warn her yesterday. To curb this nonsense, she pointedly chose to introduce the subject of his girlfriend.

"Tell me about Claire."

He looked at her in some surprise. "Claire?" he asked as if he'd forgotten her name. "What do you wish to know?"

That seemed an odd response. Didn't people in love look for each and every opportunity to praise the attributes of the one to whom their heart was linked? Her cousins did; as for Melissa, she'd never been in love so didn't know.

"Is she pretty?"

"Yes, quite so. Beautiful actually."

"Mm. That's nice." His answer didn't improve Melissa's frame of mind. "I assume her family is also titled?"

"Her father holds a seat in the House of Lords, as does my own."

"Ah." She didn't know much about British aristocracy, except that the king ruled England, but Peter's reference to the House of Lords sounded very regal.

She tried to think up another question to ask about Claire, then realized she didn't really want to know.

"So, if your father is in the House of Lords now, that means you'll be taking his place one day. Right?"

"No, that honor will go to my younger brother."

"Your younger brother?" She may not understand much about the peerage, but she did know the eldest was supposed to inherit. At least that's how it happened in most societies she'd read about. She assumed Peter was the eldest since his parents had both adopted him and married after the *Titanic* disaster.

They came to a stop where the streetcar would collect them. He looked at her then. "I'm not a blood heir, so I cannot inherit the title or any of the privileges that come with it." Not an ounce of regret filled his words. "Edward will make a fine earl when that day arrives; he's viscount now."

"And what about you, Peter? What will you do?"

"Do?"

"Once your mission is done here? Once you leave New York."

"Why, I'll go back to England, of course."

"Of course."

Thankfully the streetcar rattled up to them on its tracks, and Melissa turned her face away to hide the flames she knew burned her cheeks. But she couldn't put a brake on the sudden hope that hurtled through her mind of wishing that day would never come.

❧

Not desiring to be rude and reject a second dinner invitation, Peter acquiesced to Missy's request that he dine at the restaurant. Once he escorted her home, he returned to his hotel room to change into evening wear and afterward took time to jot a message to send home, assuring everyone he'd arrived safely and all was progressing well under the circumstances.

His mother had worried when she learned he would embark on a voyage to America. If the memory of the *Titanic* disaster had been as vivid to him as it was to her, he might have felt the same and avoided ocean travel. Even without the full memory of that night, it had taken a good deal of fortitude to board a vessel that traveled the same route as the *Titanic*.

As the first ribbons of sunset unfurled over the bustling city, Peter entered Marelli's. Amazed to see the restaurant teeming with life, he stood in the entrance to absorb the difference.

Patrons filled almost every table, and poignant music rippled from the strings of the violin played by a dark, mustachioed man with superlative talent. A single globed candle glowed on each table of the darkened room. Delicious spicy aromas brought the air to life, reminding Peter he'd not eaten since lunch.

A young girl, possibly fourteen, with long curly dark hair and wearing a frilly white blouse and long black skirt came up to him.

"Allo, you must be Melissa's Peter." She giggled. "I am Rosa, Maria and Tony's daughter. Come, we have a special table reserved for you."

A special table? Peter followed the girl to a booth near the back of the restaurant where the musician played. Fronds of plants atop the ledges brought a feeling of the outdoors to the surrounding booths. Each private cubicle gave the mood of a clandestine meeting.

Once seated, he glanced around the restaurant, failing to see a familiar face. "Is Missy in the vicinity?"

Rosa handed him a menu with a shy smile. "She asked that I take care of you. She will be out soon."

"Thank you."

"My pleasure." She giggled again, moving away.

Peter smiled and opened the menu to peruse the Italian cuisine. He debated trying something different this time. Perhaps the fettuccine Alfredo or the *caponata,* described as a spicy eggplant dish, or even the *baccalà* dish of salted cod. As he weighed the choices, Rosa returned bearing a platter with huge hunks of what Peter had learned was mozzarella cheese. In her other hand, she carried a plate with a crusty loaf of fresh-baked bread and set both before him.

He ordered the fettuccine Alfredo, deciding to live adventurously and sample a new entrée each time he came. He hadn't intended to make a habit of dining here since the Waldorf-Astoria also boasted fine culinary establishments, but here the food rated superb, the atmosphere was always pleasant, and the Marellis were a friendly lot. Not to mention that Missy was a person he would like to know better.

The violinist ended his performance, taking a seat at a nearby table. A boy appeared with a guitar and perched on the edge of a stool. Then Peter saw Missy and forgot all about food.

Looking as if she'd been immersed in a moonbeam, Missy moved to stand beside the guitar player, who settled the instrument across his knee. Her white lace blouse shimmered, matching the string of pearls at her throat and in her ears. A dark skirt flowed over her slim waist and hips, offsetting her fair beauty. Her face glowed like dew under the moonlight; her hair glimmered like radiant stars. Peter reasoned the white spotlight added to the ethereal effect, but he was nevertheless amazed.

The guitar player strummed the strings softly, producing the most beautiful, haunting music that heated Peter's blood and brought chills to his skin. Missy began to sing, and the chills increased. Peter stared, totally bedazzled, his mouth falling open.

A hint of sultriness laced the sweetness of her voice, the drawn-out notes clear and strong, at the same time muted and soft. Peter didn't understand the foreign words, Italian or Spanish, but he judged from the wistful expression on her face that this must be a song about love. She put all of herself into her aria, which seemed to nestle into his heart and make its home there.

Once the last soft note wavered into oblivion, Peter could only continue to stare. Enthusiastic applause burst forth all around him, and he realized it wasn't her uncle Tony's prowess with the violin that brought patrons to this restaurant as Missy had said, or even the guitar player, as skillful as he'd been; Missy was the sparkling lure that captured their clientele.

She smiled her thanks to the audience, then noticed Peter and moved his way, but he couldn't seem to wrap his mind around the present. Couldn't remember when he'd heard such an exquisite voice. The greeting that fell off his tongue seemed lackluster in comparison to the uplifting experience that still buoyed his heart.

"That was lovely."

"Thank you." She inclined her head shyly. "May I sit down?"

Her words reminded Peter of his uncommon bad manners. "Of course, please do." He stood as he spoke, jarring the table and causing the flame in the candle to shiver.

She gave a delicate laugh. "Please, Peter. Sit down and enjoy your meal."

"Will you join me? For dinner, I mean."

She hesitated the barest moment. "I'd love to."

"I've already ordered, so once you decide, you'll have to tell Rosa." He almost groaned at his ineptitude; she did after all know the workings of their family restaurant far better than he did.

"Rosa knows what to bring me." Her words were gracious; her manner kind. "Before I forget, I want to ask if you'd like to attend services with us tomorrow."

"Services?"

"Church. Tomorrow *is* Sunday."

"Of course. And yes, thank you. I would." He was beginning to resemble a callow youth out for his first night in high society. Deciding it would be in his best interest to put the bread and cheese to good use and engage his mouth, Peter took a portion of both.

"The song, it was beautiful," he said when he'd gathered his wits about him enough to speak again.

"It's a Latin song of love; the boy who played guitar is Lucio, my uncle Tony's son. He's very skilled."

"Yes, he is. Have you had training? You sound as if you have."

The violin player strode to the table, preempting her answer. A stocky man of medium height, he bore the dark coloring and lively dark eyes of all the Italians Peter had met. "You must be Peter," he said, his accent strong. He thrust out his hand in greeting. "Welcome to our humble restaurant," he said as he shook Peter's hand.

"You have a wonderful place."

"*Grazi, grazi.* Please, sit down. My Maria has told me some of your story. I hope all turns out well for you."

He spoke with them a few minutes more before his attention shifted to another table, and he moved that way to speak with the two men there.

"Your family is quite grand."

"Thank you. They've made me feel wanted."

Her wistful eyes twisted his heart, and he felt he should change the subject. "Regarding my previous question—have you had vocal training?"

"No." Her eyes grew shuttered, and she tore away a hunk of bread. "Mother sang in the Metropolitan Opera; I suppose that's the one trait she gave me, the ability to sing. . . . So tell me, does a visit to Coney Island sound good for Monday?" She bit into the bread.

"Yes, that sounds lovely." Her quick change of subject and forced smile told him the subject of her mother wasn't open to discussion. He couldn't help but see the irony: He endeavored to do all within his power to gather information about his mother, while Missy worked with equal fervor to dispense with the memory of hers. Perhaps this quest would help them both lay their ghosts to rest.

Chapter 7

On Monday, Peter and Melissa paid a nickel apiece to take the subway to the famed New Yorkers' playground of Coney Island. After services the day before, she had suggested they make a day of it at Coney Island once they located Horace Miller, the man who could hold a key to Peter's locked past.

Peter enthusiastically agreed, yet when Melissa mentioned that many also found pleasure at the beach there and suggested they take advantage of the bathhouses to change clothes and indulge in a swim, he adamantly refused. After a gap of tense silence, he shared with her the cause of his crippled state, stumbling over his sentences and avoiding her eyes as if sure she would be disgusted. But Melissa's feelings had been far from disgust, and when Peter looked up, his eyes opened wider to see the tears that trickled down her cheeks.

"Missy?"

"You went through so much," she had explained, "for one so young. More than many of us had to bear."

To her shock, he had lifted his hand and wiped away her tear with the pad of his thumb. "Don't cry for me." His smile had been encouraging. "Long ago I accepted the things I couldn't change. I'm all right. Really."

She had nodded, his touch and tender expression doing strange things to her heart and robbing her of her voice.

Now, she watched him as they exited the subway and he studied their surroundings with curious interest. Her sundry difficulties couldn't begin to compare with the great travail he'd suffered, yet he so often seemed without a care, as he did now. She wished she could exhibit optimism despite all odds. Even as they approached the Bowery, the four-block alley running from Steeplechase to Feltman's Arcade, delight animated Peter's face at the overabundance of glitzy penny arcades and open game booths that challenged a man's skill while encouraging him to empty his pockets of nickels. Bordering this were terrifying rides that brought shivers of fear and screams of delight from their passengers.

Mechanical pianos played swinging jazz numbers and vied with the shouts of barkers calling over each other to attract prospective customers. Concession stands offered an assortment of tempting foods, and the mouthwatering aroma of fire-roasted hot dogs and warm bread wafted through the air.

"First, we should find Mr. Miller," Peter said.

He spoke as if he would say more. When he didn't continue, Melissa prodded, "And then?"

"And then. . ." He gave her a sidelong glance, his boyish smile in place. "We play."

Melissa giggled, not surprised that she'd been correct in her assessment of his character and that he was still a boy at heart.

After asking directions from a hot-dog vendor, they found the shooting gallery where Horace Miller spun his spiel, encouraging passersby to engage in hitting his targets. Painted metal ducks ran past on a mechanical track at the far end of the booth. Mr. Miller, a brown derby rakishly angled over his high brow, eyed Peter and Melissa like a snake would field mice.

"Well, sir," he said, appraising Peter, "you look like a gent who can handle a rifle well. Step right up and try your luck. Only ten cents for ten shots; hit half the targets, and you can win your lady a gen-u-ine Kewpie doll."

"Actually, I was hoping you could help me in another area. I'm here to seek out information. Am I correct in presuming that you're Mr. Miller?"

The man's gregarious attitude hardened to coldness. "You're not here to take a shot?"

"No."

"Then beat it." He swung his thumb to the side for them to go.

"I just want to ask a couple of questions; I won't take much of your time, only a few minutes."

"What are you, some kind of cop? I ain't got the time to say nothin' to no copper."

"I'm not a cop. I understand you sailed on the *Titanic*, and I seek information, to discover anything you can tell me about this woman." Peter withdrew the locket.

At Peter's mention of the ship, the man's eyes livened with a flash of shock, then narrowed. "Look, bub, you want me to look at that there picture, then you lay out a dime."

Peter nodded and extracted the coin, setting it on the waist-high wooden planking between them.

The man pocketed the coin and held out his hand for the locket. Peter hesitated before handing it to him. Mr. Miller took a long look at it. "Can't say as I recall anyone like her in third class, but then it's been awhile."

"You were in third class?" Peter asked.

"Yeah." The man grew embittered as he returned the locket. "I was one of them gutter rats who made it. They wouldn't let us immigrants up 'til all the swells had been taken care of. Even our women and children were left below, locked in like animals. By the time they allowed us up, most of the lifeboats were gone. More of our women and children were lost than saved."

Melissa sensed by the man's attitude that his words were personal. "Did you lose someone close, Mr. Miller?"

Her quiet words, the first words she'd spoken, made him swing his attention her way. He stared a moment, and his face slackened. "My grandmother. She was so sure that coming to America would be the start of a great new life. It's all she talked about for years."

"I'm so sorry for your loss."

Her sincere words produced a faint nod, the hint of a smile, before he turned to Peter and handed him a rifle. "You gonna take that shot or not?"

"It's not necessary. Thank you for your time." As Peter turned away, Melissa caught his eye and gave a slight tilt of her head toward the booth, sensing that his cooperation might give the barker a boost. Peter looked at her a moment, then turned back. "On second thought, I will take a shot."

Melissa watched as he leaned his cane against the booth, lifted the rifle, and took careful aim. Five rapid explosions knocked five ducks down with loud metal pings. A few passersby stopped to stare in amazement.

Both the barker and Melissa turned to Peter, their mouths agape.

He handed back the rifle and shrugged, his expression self-conscious as he faced Melissa. "I did mention that I learned to hunt."

❧

While others vied for a place in line to try their chance at shooting the metal ducks, Peter took Missy's arm and steered her through the crowd. They walked close, but Peter sensed her distance and wondered what was running through her mind. The shooting gallery had required a simple aim really, nowhere near as difficult as the clay pigeons catapulted into the air which he'd mastered as a lad. Yet Peter now felt perhaps he should have purposely missed a couple of the targets, though Missy had accepted the Kewpie doll with a grateful smile.

He worked to cover his own disappointment. He'd known all along that on a ship of more than two thousand souls, bearing three different classes, the likelihood of finding even one of six people on the list who might have known his mother was slim to nothing. Still, he had hoped for some information by this time.

From her excited words of the previous day, Peter knew Missy wanted to partake in the fun of Coney Island. Peter could also use the relaxation. He made a choice to take pleasure in this day spread out before them and in this fantasy land thickly riddled with roller coasters, Ferris wheels, carousels, and other alluring rides that promised to make one's heart soar one instant, then drop the next.

He smiled at Missy. "What do you wish to do first?"

"First?" The gaiety of their surroundings began to take hold, and her eyes sparkled. "I noticed a house of mirrors earlier; I'd like to go there."

"Then go there, we shall." He formally crooked out his arm toward her, and smiling, she wrapped hers through it.

As lighthearted as children, they wended their way through aisles of warped mirrors that stood taller than they did and laughed at their crazy reflections. Afterward, they lived dangerously and rode the Cyclone, a roller coaster whose tracks spiraled into a figure eight with plummets at terrific speed. Once they exited the train of linked cars, it took them both awhile to find their balance again, then they decided to eat lunch.

For a penny a piece, they feasted on clams drenched in butter at one of the many restaurants. They spoke of nothing and everything and, as if in silent accord, made no mention of the *Titanic* or of their quest or of gangsters. This remained a day to be enjoyed, and they both shed their troubles and took in all they could of the innumerable amusements.

If Peter had secured a room in one of the plush hotels nearby and stayed a week, he still wouldn't have covered all that Coney Island had to offer. They visited a house of wax and braved various rides, staying away from the seedier establishments, the havens to gamblers and those of low morals.

The setting sun highlighted the clouds with bright pink as they, along with hundreds of others, promenaded along the wide boardwalk that stretched over half the length of the area. To the right, a strip of brown beach ran alongside, and a number of bathers took advantage of the Atlantic Ocean.

When they grew weary of walking, they stopped at Feltman's Pavilion for Mr. Feltman's famed invention of pork sausages encased in rolls. The hot dogs took the edge off their hunger, and afterward, they rode a carousel of painted horses. By the time they left the pavilion, the sky had darkened to faded ink, but Coney Island was lit up as if it were Christmas. Hundreds of thousands of bright electrical lights rimmed the massive rides and fanciful towers, spires, and minarets on the Oriental-style buildings.

They walked along with the crowds, carried away by the magic of Coney Island as they observed the blur of activity around them.

"Are you willing to try one more ride before we take the subway home?" Missy asked, a twinkle in her eye.

"Of course."

Eagerly, she took Peter's hand and led him through the crowd to the towering Wonder Wheel. It stood like a revolving beacon beside the ocean, the ride brightly lit up with hundreds of incandescent lights. Deciding against one of the inside cars that slid on curved tracks toward the center and then back with each revolution of the wheel, they opted instead for one of eight stationary cars that rimmed the outside of the monstrous Ferris wheel. Evidently, their choice of seating wasn't popular, for when the attendant couldn't find two more takers to the stationary car, he closed their door.

The wheel hoisted them higher into the air, then stopped as people boarded the lower cars. Finally, they reached the top, the wheel coming to a swift halt again.

Missy exhaled a breath. "Oh, Peter, look."

All of Coney Island lay spread out before them, a glittering panorama of festive white lights against a backdrop of dark ocean and sky. "It's like a fairy tale," she exulted softly.

They sat close on one side of the car. She turned to look at him at the same moment he looked at her, their faces only inches apart.

Wrapped inside the magic of their surroundings, they stared at one another. His gaze flicked down to her lips, then slowly returned to the oasis of her blue eyes. Her lips softly parted, and he lifted his fingertips to skim her silken jaw. "A fairy tale," he repeated on a whisper, lowering his head toward hers as he moved his hand away.

Before their lips could touch, the wheel gave a sudden lurch and went into motion. Peter drew back, stunned by both actions. Uneasy and a trifle embarrassed, he shifted position, averting his attention to the nighttime playground. A span of electric silence charged the air between them, while outside their car, people shrieked from the inside cars zipping along their tracks. Organ music played somewhere far below, but up so near the stars, all seemed muted.

Missy cleared her throat. "I . . ." Her words trailed off, as if she'd lost them.

Uncomfortable to discuss what had almost happened between them, Peter took the advantage. "After this ride has ended, we should return to Manhattan. It's late, and I want to get an early start in the morning."

"About that . . ." She looked down at her skirt and cupped one knee, digging her fingers into it nervously. "I can't go with you tomorrow."

"I see."

"It's not that I don't want to." Swiftly she met his gaze. "I promised my aunt I would help her with some things around the restaurant."

"I understand. You don't have to explain, Missy."

Peter changed the subject and soon had her laughing again, though he sensed her mood was forced. When he dropped her off at the restaurant, he knew something had altered between them but didn't dwell on the situation until he reached the solitude of his hotel room.

He regretted both his spontaneous attempt to kiss her and his lack of success in that attempt. But this time, any pang of guilt that prodded his conscience, whispering that he'd betrayed Claire, seemed far more subdued than before. As Peter lay stretched out on the bed, studying the carved ceiling, he began to question his situation. For weeks he'd dwelt on the past and what resolution it might unleash, but now he pondered his future and what mysteries it might contain. And to his shock, Claire was no longer a part of his personal aspirations.

Chapter 8

"Missy, if you scrub that spot any harder, you will dig through the floor and into the earth."

Melissa straightened from her crouched position on hands and knees and glanced at her aunt, who had just walked into the kitchen where Melissa scrubbed the floor. She dipped the scrub brush into the sudsy water again and continued scrubbing.

"Mi niña." Maria squatted beside her. "What is the matter?"

"Matter? Nothing's the matter. I thought you wanted the restaurant to have a thorough cleaning."

"Sí. But why today? You said you wanted to help Peter."

"I did." Melissa hesitated. "I do. I just felt it was time to get this done now. That's all."

Aunt Maria didn't force the issue but gave Melissa a concerned glance before she left the room. Melissa crawled to the next dry spot of flooring to give it a scrupulous cleaning with the bristles.

She didn't know what bothered her. Well, yes she did. When Peter had almost kissed her on the Ferris wheel, the desire for his kiss astonished her, confused her, even alarmed her. She needed this time away from him to sort through her feelings. Things between them were going too fast for strangers who'd known each other only a matter of days, yet she felt as if she'd known him a lifetime. She had always shied away from the prospect of falling in love. Not that Melissa thought herself unlovable; through tender care over all these years, Maria had proven that Melissa was, indeed, worthy of love. Nor did Melissa worry she would fail at marriage, because she would never treat a man the selfish way her mother had treated her husbands.

No. Most of her unease stemmed from Guido and his unwanted notice of her; he had singled her out to wait on him since she'd turned fourteen. As the years progressed, so had his attention toward her, and she feared what he might do to her and those she loved. But Peter was nothing like Guido. He was a gentleman—kind, funny, attractive. Yet didn't his heart belong to Claire? Wasn't his love for her what had brought him to America? Despite the fact that Claire had refused him, wasn't his main initiative for his quest to win her back?

Her heart conflicted, Melissa tried to link answers to questions that weren't hers to ask. She clenched her teeth and scrubbed the floor harder. If all that mattered to the woman was his name, Claire didn't deserve a man like Peter. But that didn't change the fact that soon, very soon, Peter would return to England, to his home and family, and to Claire, while Melissa would remain in New York, and life would resume its usual course.

The thought was not at all satisfying.

Melissa threw herself into her work all day. When evening came, she fell into bed exhausted, but morning brought no relief from her discontent. Noon came and went, and she looked up often, expecting Peter to enter the restaurant. He usually came well before noon, but it had rained earlier, and that had slowed traffic. As the day stretched on, Melissa realized he wasn't coming. Now instead of the distance she'd sought between them, she desired his presence.

She waited on tables that night, her attention going to the door every time it opened. Her work suffered, reflecting her turmoil. When she mistook an order and brought the wrong entrée to a table, the customer grew belligerent. Lucio signaled the time had come for her to sing, but her voice carried little of the life it normally possessed.

Alone in her bed, she brought the covers up to her chin and closed her eyes. "I've hurt him. I know I have. My stupid insecurities pushed him away. Please. . .let him come back." She wasn't aware she'd phrased her longing into a prayer until after she'd uttered it, and that made her think. She would like to believe what Maria taught, that God was a guiding force in people's lives, but too many disappointments clouded such hopes. A whisper from the past she wished to forget taunted the fringes of her mind.

"I haven't the time to be saddled down with a daughter; besides, Clark doesn't like children. You take her, Maria. She likes you."

Melissa closed her eyes, and a tear escaped.

The next day seemed endless. More rain fell, and again, Peter didn't come.

On the fourth day, Melissa attacked her duties with dogged resignation. He wasn't coming; she might as well accept it and resume her life. She readied tables with stark efficiency, took orders from the few customers who visited, and taste-tested sauces. She made no more mistakes, but neither did she smile, and Maria softly scolded her, reminding her that no customer liked a grouchy waitress. Her warning seemed odd, since the restaurant had served only two tables of guests, both parties now gone.

That afternoon, Melissa spread a clean cloth over a table, fixing it so it hung evenly. She bent at the waist to smooth out the wrinkles.

"Hello, Missy."

At the sound of Peter's voice, she jumped up and whirled around so fast she was surprised she didn't injure herself. The joyful relief upon seeing him almost had her rushing forward to hug him.

"Peter." She blinked. "I wasn't expecting you." Of all the things she wanted to say, that wasn't one of them.

"I'm sorry I haven't been around lately."

His voice sounded hoarse. She studied him further and noticed the dull haze in his eyes. "Are you all right?"

"I was ill, but I'm doing better now, thank you. The morning after we visited Coney Island, I caught a nasty bug. Today I didn't feel as if the entire world was in constant upheaval, so I felt it safe to leave my room."

He'd been ill! She hadn't chased him away.

Relief gave way to concern as she moved forward. Without thinking twice, she pressed her fingers to his brow and frowned. "You still feel a bit feverish. You shouldn't have left your bed so soon."

As she retreated a step, he gave a slight lurch forward and grabbed the back of a chair. She grasped his arm to help support him.

"You can barely stand!"

"No, I'm all right, really." His actions jerky, he moved to sit down.

"No, you're not, Peter." Determined, she set her jaw. "You don't eat right, you barely sleep, and now you come out of your sickbed and into this damp cold." She softened her demeanor. "Peter, these people aren't going anywhere. I sincerely doubt they'll be moving away within the next week. Please, go back to your hotel room and get some rest. Ask them to bring you a bowl of chicken soup; it's a good remedy. If we had some here, I'd make it for you, but we don't have any chicken, only veal. We can resume the hunt when you're feeling better."

He opened his mouth to argue, but something in her expression must have stopped him for he gave a resigned nod. "All right. You win, Missy. I do feel better than I did, but I certainly could use more rest."

Glad that she'd persuaded him to see reason, she was nevertheless concerned that he'd given in so quickly. "Are you certain you can make it back to your hotel on your own?"

"I got here, didn't I?"

She breathed out a worried laugh. "Barely, from the looks of you." A sudden thought hit. "Lucio has to run some errands for my uncle. I'll ask him to accompany you to the hotel."

"I wouldn't wish to impose. I'll be all right."

"I insist. I wouldn't get a wink of sleep tonight otherwise."

She turned away to mask the sudden torrent of emotion at the thought of him lying helpless in the street with the rain pounding down on him. "I'll go ask Lucio now. Stay put." She gave him a warning glance. "I mean it. I don't want to come back here and find you gone. Capisci?"

He nodded as if dazed, and Melissa wondered if her gentle order sounded as fraught with hidden meaning to him as it did to her. She didn't want him to go, not now or in the future. How long he remained in her life depended on the success of his quest, and Melissa felt a harsh twinge of guilt for her sudden wish that his search would never end.

※

Peter recovered after two more days of bed rest. When he lay awake, he relived the memory of Missy's resolute plea that he take care of himself. In her eyes, he had seen reflected the same desire that brought him to the restaurant that afternoon. Perhaps he'd been foolish to attempt such an undertaking before he'd made a full recovery, and in retrospect, he hoped his thoughtless action hadn't contaminated anyone else.

But the quest that urged him on had equaled his longing to see her again, and his muddled mind hadn't been able to reason out the consequences. He had missed her company and had gone to her. What astounded him more was that she had missed him. He'd seen that truth written in her jubilant expression during those first few seconds when she'd swung around to face him. Heard its revelation in her quiet, emphatic words that he mustn't go.

He couldn't remember ever having missed Claire and, in fact, hadn't thought about her in days. A modicum of remorse gave way to a magnitude of doubt as he dwelt on the matter now.

A glance at his pocket watch showed him the day was fast getting away from him. Eager to embark on his quest and to see Missy again, he hailed a taxicab to take him to the restaurant.

Again, Missy's eyes sparkled upon seeing him. "You look wonderful," she breathed. "I mean, you seem so much more rested. Your color is good, too."

Her own color had heightened, and he smiled. "Are you agreeable to traveling to Long Island today to find Patience Arbunckle?"

"Oh, yes. You've already eaten?"

He nodded, and her grin grew wide. "Good. Let me get my coat."

They took a cab to Pennsylvania Station and from there boarded a train into Long Island. Looking out the window, Peter eyed the vista of beaches and box-like suburban homes. A quiet haven nestled away, Long Island appeared nothing like Manhattan. No skyscrapers towered in almost every available space of sky as they did in the city. Mile after mile of uninterrupted countryside and beaches flew past the train window.

"You might already know this," Missy said from beside him, "but last year, Charles Lindbergh flew his *Spirit of St. Louis* nonstop from this island to Paris in the first transatlantic flight. All of Manhattan gave him a ticker-tape parade upon his return. My cousins and I went to see; it was quite something."

"I read about that and found it quite extraordinary. Perhaps one day passengers will fly across the ocean in airplanes instead of taking voyages on ships."

"Now that would be interesting," Missy agreed. "But I find it unlikely that such an idea would catch on with the masses."

"Oh, I don't know." He grinned. "I would try it."

She regarded him with an assessing smile. "I believe you would."

They found directions to the small lakeside hotel where Patience Arbunckle resided, as easily as they found the woman who ran the place. Bearing a gregarious charm yet stately elegance, Patience and her friend, Beth Ryan, led them to a table overlooking Lake Ronkonkoma, and they sat down to take tea.

"Legend has it that the lake contains special healing powers," Patience stated as they looked out over its blue waters. "It was formed by a retreating glacier. Whether the claims are true or not, it brings tourists in by the droves, and naturally, I'm pleased with that. My grandfather built this hotel and once told me the lake is bottomless, but I confess, I've never tested the waters so wouldn't know. I'm not much of a swimmer." Her eyes twinkled. "Now, how can I help you, Mr. Caldwell? You mentioned on the telephone that your visit here today concerns the RMS *Titanic*."

"The *Titanic*?" Patience's friend Beth uttered in shock.

"Yes, I understand you were a passenger, Mrs. Arbunckle."

"A very young one," she explained. "I was fourteen then and traveling with my family. We had gone to Europe on vacation and were returning home."

Peter hesitated to ask the question uppermost in his mind. She must have sensed it, for she nodded sadly. "My mother, my sisters, and I, all of us were rescued. My father was one of the brave men who stayed behind. He had no choice; they wouldn't allow men inside the lifeboats. Not on our side of the ship; perhaps if we had been on the other side. . ." Her smile grew melancholy. "But then, there's no use speaking of the past and what can't be changed, is there?"

"Actually, I've come to ask you to remember, if it isn't too painful for you."

"Oh?" She regarded him with surprise. "Are you a writer?"

"No." He handed her the locket and motioned for her to open it. "That was my mother. I was hoping you might remember her face or having had any acquaintance with her."

"Oh, my. It's been so many years. I can barely remember what I ate for dinner last night." She gave a light laugh but studied the picture. She shook her head. "I'm sorry. Her face isn't familiar to me."

"I understand." Peter took the locket, no longer disappointed by the outcome, having half expected it. Sixteen years was too great a time for a person to remember a casual acquaintance aboard a ship of thousands.

"May I see it?" Miss Ryan held out her hand. Peter detected the lilt of an Irish accent in her words, but it was her tense manner that caught his attention.

Curious, he opened the locket and handed it to her across the table. She looked down and inhaled a startled gasp.

Alert to her obvious recognition, he asked, "Were you on the *Titanic*? Did you know her?"

"No. I'm sorry." Her sympathetic brown eyes grew troubled. "But a year ago, I worked for a family on the island, not far from this hotel. I'd run on hard times, and I took a job as one of their maids. Such a sad home it was. One of the most lavish on the island, but not a moment's peace or happiness could be found there. The poor woman drifted in her husband's shadow. He was quite the tyrant, you see, a steel magnate, and he could scare a person clear into next week."

Peter remained patient, though he wanted to hurry the woman along in her memory.

"My job was to clean the upstairs rooms, and one room was always kept locked, though I was given a skeleton key and required to clean it every day. I even had to change the bedding to keep it fresh! Well, I did what was expected of me, though I don't mind tellin' you every ghost story I'd ever heard went flyin' through my head when I was in that room. Some of the other maids said they'd heard quiet sobbing from behind the locked door, though I never did. But in that house, who can tell what goes on?"

She shivered. "Later I learned the room belonged to their only son. He was involved in an automobile accident the night before the *Carpathia* pulled into the harbor. The roads were slick with rain, and he lost control. He died two days later."

A sense of startled unreality grabbed hold of Peter as her gaze locked with his. "Naturally, since the locked room was never occupied, the whole situation piqued my curiosity. I can still vividly recall the items I dusted every day. You might say I committed them to memory. There was a photograph on the dresser that I remember in detail. This woman was in it, and she wore this very locket."

Chapter 9

Peter, are you all right?"

Melissa hesitated, uncertain what to do to help him. Five minutes after leaving Mrs. Arbunckle's hotel, Peter still stood silent beside the lake, studying its waters as if trying to see far beneath them.

"Peter?" She moved his way, when he suddenly turned, startling her into stopping.

"All right? No, I'm not all right."

His feelings didn't surprise her, but that he aired them did. All former reserve disappeared as he bared his heart and soul to her. A haze of pain clouded his eyes.

"I put all my misgivings behind me and sailed across an entire ocean, only to discover that my father is dead."

"Were you hoping to find him alive?"

"Yes. Yes, I was. That might sound absurd under the circumstances; after all, he refused to have anything to do with my mother and myself. Otherwise, he wouldn't have been absent for all those years and would have had some place in our lives. Yet a part of me hoped that we might lay all misconceptions and hard feelings to rest. . .that we could surmount the difficulties."

Melissa's heart ached at the raw pain in his voice. "Peter, you don't know for sure that the family Miss Ryan worked for is your own."

Her attempt at encouragement fell flat as he sadly shook his head. "She recognized my mother from that picture."

"But it's been over a year since she worked at the Underhills. Perhaps the woman in the photograph only looked like your mother."

"She recognized the locket, too."

Melissa drew her brows together, thinking. "All right, then what about what she said—that their son was in an accident the night before the *Carpathia* pulled into port?"

"What about it?"

"Maybe he was going to meet the ship. To meet you."

"We don't know that for certain." Wary hope filled his voice.

"No, but the very fact Miss Ryan brought it up seems important. She'd obviously heard it mentioned when she worked there. The date coinciding with the *Carpathia*'s arrival must have significance for it even to be mentioned and linked to his accident."

He looked at her a long moment, then dipped his head and nodded in weary resignation. "It's possible. I'll give you that."

"You'll never know unless you ask them."

He gave a wry laugh. "Truer words were never spoken, yet what if my father was right and a scorpion lies beneath the rock I uncover? Perhaps the tiger will have its way after all, and the lady behind the door was only a boy's dream."

Melissa didn't understand his odd words and assumed he spoke of his adoptive father. How she wished these lake waters could heal the heart as well as the body! Both she and Peter could use a plunge. She moved toward him, putting her hand to his arm in silent support, and he turned to look at her.

"Whatever happens, you're not alone, Peter. Remember that."

His gaze took in every inch of her face, and she held her breath.

"I will."

Twenty minutes later, as they stood at the front door of the sprawling mansion that belonged to the Underhills, Peter replayed Missy's encouraging words. A housekeeper answered the bell and at first refused to admit them, but Peter pleaded for an audience. His manner and clothes must have convinced her he was no peddler, for she told them to wait a moment and closed the door. Soon it opened again, wider this time, and she motioned for them to enter.

Peter worked to control his breathing, though his pulse rate threatened to skyrocket through the carved ceiling. This might all be merely happenstance; Miss Ryan might have mistaken his mother for an old memory of a similar-looking woman in a faded photograph.

The housekeeper led them to a paneled study. Though it bore the comforts of a fire, the austere brown furnishings seemed as cold and harsh as the bearded gentleman who appraised them from a mahogany chair. He closed his book but didn't rise. Strong in build despite his advanced years, he reminded Peter of a polar bear, with his snow-white hair and pale skin.

"You wished to see me?" Mr. Underhill's greeting lacked any welcome.

"I was told you might be able to help me," Peter rasped, and he cleared his throat. "Sixteen years ago I lost my mother when the *Titanic* foundered; I think you might know her."

"Indeed?" Mr. Underhill's tone left no doubt that he thought such a possibility utter nonsense.

Peter had come too far to back down now. He opened the locket and held it out to the man. Mr. Underhill didn't accept it, giving only the barest and most indifferent of glances to the treasured oval.

"I've never seen this woman."

"Perhaps you're mistaken; please look again." Peter worked to hide his annoyance.

"I told you I don't know her. Now if you would be so good as to leave my home, my housekeeper will show you the door."

Peter sensed something amiss, judging by the man's uncooperative attitude alone; Missy also looked at the man askance, confusion on her face. Other than demand Mr. Underhill take a long look at the photo, which Peter had no intention of doing, he had no recourse but to do as the man wished and leave.

"Please, sir," Missy said, surprising Peter. "We're not asking for a lot. Just for you to take a good look at the photograph."

"What is it you hope to gain?" Mr. Underhill changed his tactic, first looking at Missy, then at Peter. "You have come, perhaps, with the claim of being a long-lost relation? Don't bother. We had one son, and he's dead. He had no child, and we have no grandson."

"I don't recall making mention of any such possibility. I thank you for your time." Peter's words came clipped, and he signaled to Missy that they should go.

Once out of the oppressive room, Peter didn't draw a breath of relief until they were outside. Too many uncertainties clamored inside his mind for him to make normal conversation, though he sensed Missy's frequent glances his way.

They'd gone about fifty feet down the sidewalk when a slight, feminine voice called for them to stop. Peter turned to see a petite woman dressed in a fine, black lace dress, her silver hair upswept. She pressed a hand to her heart and walked closer, eyeing Peter.

"May I see that locket?"

Her words came out in mere breaths, as if she'd rushed to catch up with them. She continued staring at Peter as he handed her the locket, then looked down at it. She stared at the oval a long time, and Peter observed her carefully. A number of emotions flitted across her face, but he had difficulty classifying any of them.

"Did you know her?" he asked quietly.

She didn't answer right away, but after a moment, she looked up. "No, I never knew her." What looked like regret filled her green eyes as she placed the locket into his palm. "I'm so sorry." Her words seemed more than a courtesy. She clasped his hand with her other one in sympathy, her strong grip surprising Peter.

"Millicent?"

She glanced over her shoulder toward the house. "I must go. I hope you find what you're looking for. You seem like such a nice young man. Perhaps—"

"Millicent!"

All of them looked toward the porch. Mr. Underhill moved through the door, his stance forbidding.

"I must go." She gave Peter one last glance. "Good-bye."

Peter stared after her. Once she reached the steps, Mr. Underhill took hold of her arm, glared at Peter one final time, then turned with the woman into the house.

"What do you make of that?" Missy echoed Peter's thoughts.

"Peculiar, to say the least." Peter forced the words through a tight throat. "Her actions seemed almost guilt ridden."

"You think you're related, don't you? That they're your grandparents."

He blew out a weary breath steeped in frustration. "I don't know what to think. Sometimes, I'm almost sorry I started this venture."

"Well, at least you can put this part of your quest behind you." Missy's words did little to comfort, though he smiled in gratitude for her attempt.

"Perhaps it's time to abandon the entire hunt."

She didn't respond immediately. "Whatever you decide, you can be grateful for one thing, Peter."

"Oh, what's that?"

"You might be a different man today had you been raised by the Underhills. A man not in possession of so many admirable qualities."

Her words struck a chord of truth within him, but he centered on her last words. "You think I have admirable qualities?"

A flush of pink tinted her face. "Yes. Of course." She averted her gaze to the mansion. "And my praise doesn't come easily; I can't say the same about many men."

"Let's walk." Wanting to learn more about her, he broached a new subject as they retraced their steps. "Did you know your father?"

She shook her head. "He died when I was two. I only have his name to remember him by; I don't even possess a picture like you have of your mother." Sadness tinged her voice, but she threw him a tepid smile. "The men of my mother's acquaintance could hardly be described as admirable. Even Maria's brother—the don—wasn't without his vices. He had a hot temper, though I suppose one couldn't really blame him since he had to deal with my mother every day. I later learned we were sailing on the *Titanic* because he had sent her home to New York and away from Spain. He never came to the States any time after that." Her voice grew vague; then she suddenly turned to him.

"Oh—something I've wanted to ask, but I kept forgetting. The woman who raised you, you said her name was Annabelle. Is that right?" At his nod, wonder filled her eyes. "Remember when I said that I invited a woman to my birthday party on the *Titanic*? Her name was Annabelle; I remember because I named my doll after her. She was different than the other adults on the ship; she talked to me like I was important. Do you think my Annabelle could be the same person as your mother?"

"From your description, there's a very good chance they could be the same. Annabelle treats everyone with the same measure of kindness, whether they are a servant or a lady. When I was in the infirmary on the *Carpathia*, she came to see me though we were strangers, and she held me while I cried. Since that night, she's helped to fill in the gap left in my life, she and Lawrence both."

"Peter, if those people *are* your grandparents, I doubt they would have given you half the love and support your adoptive parents gave you and that you needed so badly, considering all the losses you suffered." Her tone grew tentative. "It's almost as though God had a hand in placing you with the right people."

"Thank you, Missy. That helps to take away some of the sting of my father's rejection. And the Underhills'."

She gave a brief nod. "So, where do we go from here? Since you believe you found them, do you still want to visit the others on the list?"

"Yes, I suppose so. I still have too many unanswered questions, and if I don't seek out those people, I'll never know if one of them might have held a key to any of them. Queens adjoins Long Island, correct?" At her nod, he continued, "Then I imagine we should try there next."

Chapter 10

Queens proved to be a disappointment. Mr. Jack Frohmann had moved to New Jersey the previous month, and his neighbor had no forwarding address. Melissa noticed Peter worked hard to bury his disappointment and keep the positive outlook that she'd helped him rediscover at the lake.

That had been the first time she'd ever seen him so discouraged and prepared to give up. Under the circumstances she couldn't blame him, and if Mr. Underhill hadn't unnerved her so badly, she might have worked up enough courage to tell him exactly what she thought of his belittling attitude toward Peter. She'd wanted to shake Mrs. Underhill, to make her admit to Peter what he so needed to hear to help him fit that absent link onto the chain of his life. Like Peter, Melissa felt almost certain the Underhills were his grandparents, judging by their peculiar behavior alone.

"Rather than visit Mr. Harper, the last person on the list, I think I'd prefer to spend the rest of the day visiting memorials. Would you care to come along?"

"Of course."

Melissa didn't understand why he should suddenly feel the need to ask, nor did she question why she agreed so readily. Any time spent with Peter she considered a gift, and she realized she was fast coming to care for him. She wanted so badly for him to succeed in his quest, and when he ran up against a brick wall, she felt his discouragement and pain as if they were her own.

They returned to Manhattan to visit the memorials erected to those outstanding passengers of the *Titanic*. First they shared a late lunch at a small café; then they viewed the *Titanic* Memorial Lighthouse, which sat perched atop the roof of the Seaman's Institute, where the crew's survivors had stayed during their recovery. A man passing by them on the street stopped to watch and told them that at the stroke of noon every day, a ball at the top of the imitation lighthouse dropped down to signal the hour to boats in the harbor.

The Wireless Operators Memorial in Battery Park faced the inner harbor and the Statue of Liberty. Inscribed with the names of men, the granite stone had been erected as a commemoration to their heroism and their futile but courageous efforts to make contact with a ship closer than the *Carpathia*. Next, Melissa and Peter traveled to a V-shaped park at Broadway and 106th Street, where the statue of a graceful lady reclined near a reflecting pool, her head propped on one hand, her other hand framing her cheek in a winsome manner. The memorial plaque paid homage to Isidor and Ida Straus. Melissa stroked the folds of the statue's gown, thinking about the former owners of Macy's and the words of the shoe clerk, Mr. Delaney. Ida Straus had given up her seat in a lifeboat, claiming she'd lived fifty years with her husband and would not leave him.

Awed by such devotion, Melissa felt a tear slip from her eye. It would take a very special man to make a woman want to sacrifice her life just to remain by his side for what could only amount to minutes for both of them. Without conscious thought, Melissa's glance lifted to Peter.

He looked at her at the same time, and she felt her face warm.

"These people had a trait you don't often see," he said.

"What's that?"

"The courage to die, to face death with equanimity."

She nodded. "They had more than that, I think. They had each others' love to support them in their crisis; without that love, I wonder if they could have been so strong."

His admiring gaze only added to the fire in her cheeks.

Taking a taxicab to Central Park, they found upon one wall another memorial in honor of William T. Stead, a British journalist.

"The original is on the Thames in London," Peter said. "I've seen it as well. See there at the bottom—" He pointed to a figurine of a medieval knight on the left corner and one in long robes in the opposite corner. "Those two statuettes symbolize courage and charity, two attributes that were demonstrated by many that night."

Melissa studied the small statues.

"Mr. Stead wrote of passenger-liner accidents in the years before the *Titanic*; how ironic that he experienced all of what he wrote but didn't live to tell about it."

Melissa shuddered; so many ironies and coincidences seemed connected with that night and with Peter's life now. On Long Island, she hadn't really thought about it, but now she found it amazing that Miss Ryan had happened to be at the hotel just when Peter showed Mrs. Arbunckle the locket, and that she'd been a maid at the Underhills, though the venture to their mansion hadn't brought about much success.

Melissa saw a pattern, and the consistencies gave her pause. Maybe Maria was right and God in His heaven did care enough to direct the everyday course of His children on earth. Perhaps He stood at the helm of Peter's quest even now, without either of them realizing it.

"Missy?"

The concern in Peter's tone made her lift her head.

"Are you still with me?" When she only stared, he explained, "You seem so far away."

She preferred not to speak of what had been on her heart. Not yet. Not until she had time to dwell on it further. "Tell me about London, Peter. About England. I was too young to remember much of the short time we were there."

"What do you wish to know?"

"Everything. Does the king always wear his crown?"

He laughed as though delighted, and Melissa smiled, realizing how silly that sounded. "I meant when he travels in public, of course."

"On the occasions I have seen him, he did wear it, yes. I cannot account for any other times." He moved closer and took gentle hold of her arm. "Let's find a place to sit down, shall we? Then I'll satisfy your curiosities about England to your heart's content."

"You want to sit here?" Melissa looked at the trees around them.

"Why not? It is a park. And surely where there is a park, there's also a bench."

She refrained from telling him that Central Park was also a hangout for thieves and bums. After witnessing him fire the rifle, she had the feeling he could take care of them both. At first, it had made her uneasy to witness his prowess with the weapon; the man was a sharpshooter, no mistake about it. Guns made her nervous, but perhaps it was really Guido and his mob that unsettled her.

They found a bench on which to rest, and Peter filled her mind and heart with tales of the beauty of his homeland. She could almost experience the relics of castles and view the morning mist breaking up along the glens and moors, could almost feel the ancient mystery of the land where kings and queens resided. And she envisioned knights of old who fought in tournaments and rescued their ladies fair.

She decided that, one day, she would visit Great Britain. She didn't know how she could accomplish such a feat, but she wanted to know more about the land from which this amazing man came, wanted to know more about him.

After her frightening experience on that April Sunday of 1912, when the *Titanic* had sunk below the depths of the icy sea, New York City had become the cradle which had nurtured the child Melissa had been. The city had taught her, opening her eyes to some harsh realities, and it also had helped her to mature. But she'd had enough of the gangsters and crime that had increased since Prohibition started, and she wanted an end to that life. She wanted to experience peace.

As though Peter read her mind, he broke off from his tale concerning his visit to Windsor Castle, his expression sincere. "You should come to visit England; I think you would love it there. And of course, you would be our guest."

She smiled. "I can think of nothing I'd like better."

❧

Peter felt certain he had read more into Missy's words than what she'd meant. Since that afternoon when she spoke of her desire to visit England, Peter had replayed the entire conversation in his mind. Dreams of Missy filled his sleep, and when he awoke, she was his first thought. A glance at his pocket watch showed him he must hurry, and he dressed quickly and ate breakfast in a hotel restaurant.

His list had narrowed down to one last passenger he wanted to question. First, however, he planned to visit the White Star offices the moment they opened and attempt once again to get a look at the passenger list. In Liverpool, the secretary had been uncooperative in locating the copy used in the British hearings, and when pressed, the man had claimed he was unable to locate it; Peter hoped his efforts to obtain the list from the American hearings would be rewarded.

Mr. Fromby's secretary, Mrs. Little, was as intimidating as Roger had painted her to be. She looked up at Peter suspiciously over the edges of her half-moon glasses. "May I help you?"

Her tone seemed contrary to the greeting, as if she'd rather kick him back out the door he'd just entered. Peter tipped his hat and gave her his most charming smile. The frost in her eyes melted a fraction.

"I was here last week. Your janitor, Roger, told me that you might be of some assistance to me. I seek the passenger list belonging to the *Titanic*, especially those passengers in first and second class." Quickly he produced the locket and opened it, forestalling a negative response. "This was my mother. She died that night and left me with a mystery to solve. I wish only to look at the names to see if I'm able to locate a familiar one."

As the woman surveyed the locket and Peter for what seemed an eternity, Peter's disappointment rose. At last she spoke.

"Roger told me about your visit. He also spoke with Mr. Fromby, who's away on business at the moment. Mr. Fromby consulted with his associates, and they've agreed to grant your request. If you'll wait right here, I'll return presently."

Peter could only stare in surprise that she'd given him the permission he'd sought. He'd been ready to engage in polite warfare and could barely grasp that the surrender had come without any need to parley.

She soon returned and handed him a sheaf of papers. Peter took the thin stack and stared at it, disbelief mingling with an odd sense of profound sentiment. In his hands were the names of many; names once linked to the faces of people young and old, wealthy and poor, all who shared two common traits: Each of these passengers once possessed individual hopes and dreams. And each one of them as a group had shared the fear and loss that tragic night.

"You can sit over there in that chair." As if she understood his hesitation, Mrs. Little's words came tentatively, breaking into Peter's thoughts.

Peter nodded his thanks. Once seated, he turned to the surnames beginning with the letter F. Just as his father had said, he found no woman by the name of

Franklin listed among the passengers, though a man's name was there. Had Peter's memory been faulty? He'd forgotten so much; what if he'd misunderstood the name the few times he'd heard it, as well? Not many children at the age of seven possessed knowledge of their mother's first name or even their surname. He'd never been addressed by his surname at that age—not that he could remember.

His hand began to shake as he ran his index finger down the columns. Fillbrook. . .Flegenheim. . .Flynn. . .Fortune. . .Fox. . Franklin, Mr. . .Funk. . . Fynney. Nothing. He closed his eyes and drew a deep breath, thinking. As if some unknown force directed him, he felt compelled to flip back a page to the beginning of the list of surnames beginning with F and search there. Duran. . .Eitmeiler. . . Enanader. . .Fahlstrom. . .

His focus halted on the next name, and a sense of unreality pervaded his soul, even while truth whispered to his heart:

Farlan, Miss Lily
Farlan, Master Peter W.

Tears clouded his eyes, and the words swam before him. Gently, he brushed his fingertip over the fine black print.

His mother's name was Lily.

Despite what this proved—that she'd never married, and he was indeed nameless—the little boy who'd never had the chance to say good-bye reached out now to cling to this snippet of his mother's existence. In so doing, the memory of being held in her arms comforted him, and he knew if he possessed nothing else, he once had had his mother's love.

Chapter 11

The moment Melissa saw Peter enter the restaurant, she knew something of great magnitude had occurred. Bittersweet knowledge filled his blue eyes, and his smile seemed to falter.

"Peter, what's wrong?"

"My last name was *Farlan,* not *Franklin.*"

She let out a soft sigh in understanding. "You saw the list? You went to the White Star offices this morning?"

He nodded. "My mother never married; it was as I thought all along. I have no legitimate father."

Melissa held a stunned breath—stunned because of the revelation that catapulted through her head with his admission. With this new turn of events, Claire would never accept him as a prospective husband. Now that he knew the truth, Peter could be free, if he so chose. But what of his heart? Would it forever be bound to the woman who'd denied it?

"Such things don't matter," she said to cover the strength of her emotions at the worry that all his searching would come to nothing if he didn't learn to let go of Claire. "It doesn't make you any more or less the man you are, the remarkable man you've become."

His smile was tinged with both gratitude and regret. "With you as my champion, things don't seem quite so bleak."

"Good." She moved to collect her coat from the chair. "Do you still intend to visit Mr. Harper?"

"I see no reason to do so. I know the truth of who I am now."

She didn't like the defeated tone that underscored his words; this attitude was so unlike him. "Since he's the last one on the list, I say we should go. His home is closer than the others were; we can at least go there and see what he has to add, if anything."

"The day I first met you, I went to see him but received no answer to my knock. I tried again on my way from the hotel a few days ago."

"That doesn't mean he's not home now."

"All right, Missy." His words were resigned. "We'll try."

"Don't give up yet, Peter. God didn't bring you across an entire ocean to abandon you when you need Him most."

He regarded her with surprise. "I thought you didn't believe in guidance from a higher source."

"I said I wasn't sure what to believe. But the more I think on this, the more inclined I am to think a divine hand must have arranged the times and places: first your meeting on the ship with that steward who suggested our restaurant, then your meeting with Roger who just happened to remember all those people and gave you a list of where to find them. True, not every tip paid off, but then again, we don't know what all might have been set in motion. Maybe God intended that we be there for them. Like that woman at the movie theater, maybe she needed the reminder of the tragedy so she could finally release any unhealthy grief she still suffered. Who knows?" She shrugged.

Peter stared at her as if he'd never seen her before.

"I know this all sounds a bit far-fetched, but I just can't let go of the idea. Too much has happened to chalk it up to mere coincidence. Remember the message at the service last Sunday? About how God desires to give His children every good thing, but sometimes He waits to act so that more people can receive the blessing?" At Peter's nod, she went on. "Maybe that's what's happening now, Peter. God waited to act, to inspire you to go on this quest so He could bring this all together in His way and His time, so that many could benefit and not just one."

Her words tumbled out in her excitement, but she hadn't been able to get the idea out of her mind since the revelation first hit her. "And what's more, I don't think you're supposed to quit your search until you fit the last piece in place. Does that make any sense, or do I sound completely batty?"

At this, he laughed, the delight in his voice genuine. Melissa could have cheered to hear him sound at ease again.

"Actually, Missy, I believe it makes a great deal of sense. My mother Annabelle raised me to believe in God's guidance, though as I've mentioned before, I've questioned its existence. During some of those times, she gave as an example the story of how she believed He had helped her to locate a little girl who went missing that night. The girl had run back to her cabin to hide beneath her bed, and Mother found her."

Missy smiled through the tears that sprang to her eyes. "Peter, *I* was that girl."

"You, Missy?"

She nodded, remembering. "I was so scared. Maria dragged me out of the cabin, and before we reached the top deck, I realized I didn't have one of my dolls. I pulled away from her and ran back. Everything was falling apart everywhere. Water had risen to the lower levels, lights exploded all around me, and sparks flew, things crashed and broke apart—people were screaming, some were hurt and bleeding. It was horrible; I was so frightened. I found our cabin—Maria had left the door open—and I crawled underneath the bed to hide. Annabelle found me there. When I was old enough to understand, I realized she saved my life. I never forgot that—or her."

"And Lawrence saved mine." Peter looked at her in wonder and slowly shook his head. "It would seem God has woven our lives together almost from the start, in more ways than one and without either of us knowing about it. If I had any doubts regarding the possibility of God's guidance before this, the truth of His intervention is becoming more difficult to counter with cold logic."

Melissa had thought nothing more could stun her; she was wrong. "It's almost as if He made a bridge across the sea to bring you here." *And to bring us together,* she finished silently. For now she admitted what she'd been afraid to face before: She had come to love Peter.

As they continued to gaze at one another, she sensed the fragile bond that linked them strengthen. And though he made no move toward her, in Melissa's heart, she felt as if they'd connected.

❧

At Jacob Harper's residence, a woman in her thirties answered the door. Her face looked haggard; her eyes kind. Peter introduced himself and explained his mission.

"I'm so sorry," she said. "I'm Maude Harper; Jacob Harper was my father. He died a few weeks ago."

"May I offer my condolences? And please, forgive me for troubling you." Discomfited, Peter took Missy by the arm and moved to go.

"No. Wait." Maude motioned they should step inside. "It's all right. Really. And please excuse the disorder. I've been boxing up his possessions; the lease is up, you see, and I have to move everything out of here or risk losing it. He was such a packrat." Her laugh was shallow and choked, a failed attempt at lightness.

Peter nodded, yet couldn't help but notice Miss Harper's red-rimmed eyes. He felt uneasy bothering the woman at such a difficult time, even though she'd invited them inside.

"I can return another time," he said.

"I'm afraid there won't be another time. I'll be moving to Connecticut to stay with my aunt. Please, it's all right. I want to show you something."

Curious despite himself, he acquiesced, and the woman excused herself.

Peter shared a look with Missy and saw reflected in her eyes the same sympathetic disquiet. The woman soon returned, turning a slim book over in her hands and peering at its black and gold binding.

"Father always wanted to be a novelist; he was constantly gathering tidbits of useless information to create characters he planned to use someday. He did the same on the *Titanic.*" She handed Peter the book. Opening it, he noted that a man's strong handwriting filled the pages. "He carried this in his coat pocket all the time, and that night was no different. He was one of the lucky few who found a lifeboat. The officers who loaded those earlier boats didn't know better, I suppose. They allowed men on too, but only on that side of the ship.

"Later, Father said he felt guilty for taking what could have been a woman's seat—very few knew there weren't enough lifeboats at the time—and though this may sound selfish, I'm glad he did get off the ship. I don't think I could have survived losing him, too. I had just lost my mother the previous year," she explained.

"All that aside. . ." She looked down at the book Peter held. "He kept that, always saying he planned to write a story of what those days were like. He never did; I just don't think he had the heart to do so."

Peter nodded, thinking about all the sacrifices of that night. He closed the book and held it out to her, but she made no move to take it.

"I want you to have it. It won't do me any good. There's already so much I have to remember him by, and I probably won't be able to keep half of his possessions. Please," she stressed when Peter hesitated. "I think he would've wanted you to have it; if you knew my father, you'd know it would have cheered him to think his scribblings could bring about some good. That's what he wanted to do, you see. Inspire people and make them think. He wanted to be a writer, to reach the people." She gave a rueful laugh. "Though I'm afraid he was somewhat scatter-brained with the way he recorded the information. Still, if you can make sense of his meanderings, they might help you find the answers you lack."

Moved, Peter pocketed the journal and clasped her hand with both of his. "Thank you. Your gift is most appreciated."

Once they were on the sidewalk, Missy turned to him. "May I see it?"

"Of course. Let's sit down first." They entered nearby Central Park, and he handed her the book. She flipped through the first few pages. "He's dated everything, showing the place and time of meeting and a physical and character description of the passengers. Amazing. Listen to this: 'Although many on board desire little to do with the magnanimous Mrs. J. J. Brown, whose mouth one finds can be considered almost as wide as her heart, I would warrant that a more noble woman could not be found on the ship.' It goes on to give a physical description of her—hair brassy red, eyes blue. . . ." Missy looked up and froze, then glanced away.

"Perhaps we should return to the restaurant. I find that I'm suddenly hungry." She stood.

Confused, Peter also stood while casting a glance in the direction Missy had looked. Two men stood conversing with one another. Upon closer appraisal, Peter recognized them as restaurant patrons to whom Tony had spoken on the first night Peter heard Missy sing. Tony had left Peter's table quite abruptly to speak with the men.

"Who are they?" Peter noticed one of the men glance their way.

"Don't look at them," she whispered, staring in another direction. "Just walk with me and pretend you didn't see them. They're Guido's men."

"Will they cause trouble?"

"From past experience, they'll report to Guido that they saw me here. You have nothing to worry about."

"I'm not worried for myself, Missy. I'm concerned for you."

"Other than grab me and run, they wouldn't do anything, and I'm sure they wouldn't even do that. They only follow their boss's orders. I'm not sure they were even following me; it might just be dumb bad luck we ended up where they are, but I know they've seen me now."

Clenching his jaw, Peter put his hand to the small of Missy's back and guided her out of the park and away from their view.

He wanted answers to the mystery of Guido, and he felt that her uncle Tony was the place to start.

Chapter 12

Once Missy left to prepare for the restaurant's evening customers, Peter sought out Tony. Maria sent Peter to a back office, where he found the man sitting at a desk, his head clutched in his hands.

"Mr. Marelli?"

The man straightened, eyeing Peter with surprise. He smiled nervously to cover his earlier agitation. "Please, call me Tony."

"Very well. Tony." Peter motioned to the other chair. "May I?"

"Of course." If Tony was curious as to the reason for Peter's visit, he didn't show it.

Peter took a seat. "I wish to know more about this man, Guido Piccoli."

Wariness glinted in Tony's eyes, and he gave an indifferent shrug. "He is one of my customers."

"A dangerous customer who's formed an attachment to Missy, one she clearly doesn't return. What I wish to know—is Missy in any real danger?"

Tony's act of ignorance slipped. He shut his eyes and hung his head. "The Piccolis get what they want. Who's to say what will happen with them always calling the shots?"

Peter felt alarmed at the man's obvious dismissal of the situation. "Can't you do something to stop his harassment? Alert the authorities?"

Tony let out a humorless laugh. "Vittorio's family is untouchable. They have connections with those who run most of New York, and they have informers—spies—everywhere."

Recalling Tony's actions that first night and how he rushed to the table to speak with the two men, Peter asked quietly, "How did you get involved with them, Tony?"

Tony looked up, surprised. A second look of resignation crossed his dark features. "Do not tell Maria. My father was indebted to them, and when I first started this restaurant, Guido helped, though I did not ask for his help. Now he feels I am indebted to him for life. It is the way with these people. They give small favors, then expect much in return."

"And now Vittorio's nephew wants Missy for his bride."

"The family does not marry outside of their own kind." Pained disgust clipped Tony's words.

"Then why. . ." Understanding rang clear in his mind, and Peter's jaw hardened.

"We cannot let that man get hold of her, Tony. I don't want her to travel anywhere in the city alone; you or I or Lucio must be with her at all times. Guido's men were at Central Park today. Missy claimed it was all coincidence, but I'm not certain it was."

Tony dropped his head into his hands. "Maria would never forgive me if something happened to Melissa."

Peter hesitated. "She told me you own a handgun. I'd like to carry it for her protection."

"Of course. It was my father's, so it is somewhat old."

"Anything is better than nothing."

Tony regarded him steadily. "You love her."

Said aloud, the words didn't shock Peter as much as he thought they would. He'd played them over and over in his mind while in his hotel room. "Yes, I love her."

Tony nodded. "This is good. You are a strong man and will be good for Melissa. She's been hurt—in her feelings—by men all her life. You are not one of them. She loves you, too." Tony gave a quick nod of emphasis.

"She told you that?" Peter could barely frame the words.

"No, I see it. In her eyes." Tony's smile was sad. "She will be missed, but it is good for her to go from this place. You will take her back with you? To England?" He raised his thick brows.

Peter wasn't exactly sure what he'd planned, but this conversation had gotten entirely out of hand. Yes, he'd pondered a future with Missy, but he didn't want to share those thoughts with her uncle. Not yet. "Missy might not want to leave New York," he said in a weak attempt to satisfy the man's curiosity when Tony continued to stare as if awaiting an answer.

"She will want to go."

Later at his hotel, Peter couldn't rest. Tony's words played continuously in his mind. He read a few pages from Mr. Harper's notebook, but his thoughts wandered. The bold, sloppy handwriting became harder to decipher, and Peter felt a headache coming on. Deciding he needed air, he took a walk along the wharf and stared out to sea.

"Are you planning to throw yourself in, or wondering how to bail yourself out?"

At the smooth words delivered with a trace of French accent, Peter swivelled to stare at the man who'd come up behind him. Gray streaked his fair hair, and lines crisscrossed his sharp features, but his eyes seemed kind.

"Pardon?"

The man nodded toward the ocean. "You look as if you carry a millstone around your neck."

"I have a lot on my mind."

"Tell me to mind my own business if you'd prefer, but I've found it sometimes helps to talk with a stranger. You never need see the person again so don't have to fear what they think of you. I run a soup kitchen not far from the wharf. Why not come with me and enjoy a bowl?"

"I wouldn't wish to take away food from those in true need of it."

The Frenchman laughed. "Believe me, we cook up plenty. And it's good, too; my wife knows her spices well."

Peter nodded, uncertain if it was the stranger's friendly attitude or his own need to confide in another individual that led him to accept the invitation.

The soup kitchen appeared little more than a hovel, but the air simmered with the spicy aroma of soup. The handful of dockworkers in the place seemed happy.

While he ate the clam chowder, which was every bit as good as the man claimed, Peter told his story from the beginning, without naming any names but Guido's. His host listened intently, his blue eyes sparking with surprise when Peter spoke of sailing on the *Titanic* and of running away from gangsters.

"That is quite a story," his host said after a long moment. "May I share a piece of advice?"

"Of course."

"Do not second-guess Guido and his bunch. I've had many dealings with men such as these. For all their foolishness, they are smart and will act when you least expect them to. I know this from experience. Before accepting Christ, I was one of them. A dangerous criminal, a lowlife of the worst sort. I worked for Vittorio at one point in my life."

Peter found such a thing hard to believe, but his host nodded, his eyes solemn.

"*Oui.* It is true. Ironically, the woman I hurt the most was also the one who helped me the most. She taught me about absolute forgiveness, and her friend showed me an act of undeserved kindness. It was in jail that I grew to understand both, and later I found true freedom."

A towheaded boy ran up to their table and spoke quickly in French; the man answered him, then turned to Peter.

"I apologize. I must leave you. My wife needs me." He shrugged in a blithe manner, his eyes twinkling in amusement. "Probably to open a jar. I will pray that God gives you all the guidance you need in this matter."

As the child led the man away by the hand, Peter realized he'd never even thought to ask his host's name.

When Peter returned to his hotel, the clerk at the front desk stopped him.

"Mr. Caldwell, while you were out, a woman rang for you. She left a message." From a slot he withdrew a note and handed it to Peter.

Certain it must be from Missy, he tried to hide his alarm. She'd never contacted him at his hotel before tonight, and he worried that the threat of Guido might have been what prompted the call.

In the elevator, he unfolded the note and read:

Please meet me at the Japanese Teahouse in Manhattan tomorrow at noon. I have something I would like to share with you.

Respectfully yours,
Mrs. Lorne Underhill

Chapter 13

Melissa noticed Peter bounce the crown of his hat against his leg as they stood outside the painted screen enclosing the room and waited for the oriental woman in the red kimono to slide the door along its track. Smiling, she motioned they were to take off their shoes first.

Melissa felt Peter's shock and saw him jerk back when the woman knelt as if she would do it for him. "It's all right," Melissa said to the waitress. "I'll take care of it."

The woman bowed, as she'd done often since they'd met at the front of the Japanese restaurant. She gave Peter an uncertain look before gracefully scurrying away.

Missy knelt before Peter.

"Missy, no. Don't."

Anxious dread laced his voice, but she sensed he wouldn't be able to do this task and keep his balance, since no chairs were in the vicinity on which to sit. "She won't be looking at your feet," she whispered. Before he could argue further, she untied and slipped off his shoe, then did the same with the other one. Her heart clenched at the sight of his misshapen sock, but she guarded her pity well as she stood and slipped out of her own black pumps, depositing them next to his shoes. "What is it you British like to say? Pip pip, keep a stiff upper lip, and all that?"

He rewarded her with a low laugh. The tenderness softening his eyes made her wish for a moment that Mrs. Underhill wasn't on the other side of the screen. He slid the door open for Melissa to precede him.

Within the screened area, a circular table sat low to the floor, pillows of all colors piled around it. Mrs. Underhill sat on one of them, looking decidedly uncomfortable with her legs tucked up close to her body and the hem of her black skirt pulled tight to cover every inch of her stockings. Melissa had the feeling her choice of a meeting place stemmed from the need for discretion rather than the desire for cuisine.

After stiff greetings all around, Peter relied on his cane to lower himself to a sitting position and laid his hat on another pillow. Melissa sank to the pillow beside him, and both stared at Mrs. Underhill across the table.

Such wistfulness touched her expression as she stared at Peter that it took Melissa's breath away.

"You have your father's eyes," she said at last. "I can see him inside you."

The Japanese woman returned at that moment, bearing a platter with a variety of small dishes and postponing any reply as she gracefully laid each one in its spot on the table. An electric tension shivered in the air, and Melissa noted the stunned look on Peter's face. They had guessed his lineage, but hearing they'd been correct still brought surprise.

Once the waitress left with more bows and smiles and closed the door behind her, Peter leaned forward.

"Why?"

The pained fury encased in that one soft syllable left no doubt as to his meaning. Mrs. Underhill bowed her head a moment before looking at Peter again.

"My husband is a very harsh man. Clayton—your father—loved Lily, but my husband wouldn't budge in his decision. He had his own plans for our son, and they didn't include marriage to a foreigner. But Clayton opposed him and married your mother, bringing her with him to America."

Peter inhaled a swift lungful of air. "They were married?"

"For a time." Mrs. Underhill studied her blue-veined hands clasped on the table. "My husband deceived Lily, even staging a scene that made Clayton appear unfaithful, and she left your father, returning to England. Clayton never got over her and despised his father more with each passing year. But one thing frightened him more than losing your mother; he feared poverty, and he knew my husband would cut him out of the will should he flee to England."

She released a sigh of sad resignation. "Later, I learned Lily had been pregnant when she left, and they had been communicating for years; a friend of Clayton's acted as a go-between, and the letters were mailed to his bungalow. On the night before the *Carpathia* pulled in to port, Clayton admitted the truth and told me Lily was coming to him with their child. He was so fearful that you both might not have survived the sinking of the *Titanic* and that he was too late. I never was so proud of him as when he vowed that he would do all he must to make a living for the two of you, and that he would have his family with him again. That was the night my son grew up.

"Unfortunately, my husband overheard his declaration, and they had a horrible row. Clayton stormed out of the house, and that was the last I ever saw him."

She fumbled for a handkerchief from her purse and pressed the bunched cloth against her eyes. Melissa felt her own eyes water. The food sat forgotten as they each became lost in their thoughts.

Mrs. Underhill cleared her throat and pulled a wrapped bundle from her handbag, handing it across the table to Peter. "These are all the letters your mother wrote to your father." She reached into her bag again. "And this is their picture. He kept it on his bureau. They're yours now."

Peter took the framed oval, the size of his hand, and stared at it without comment. Melissa leaned in to look, struck by the resemblance Peter bore to the man in the photograph. The woman most definitely was his mother; she even wore the same dress she had for the picture contained in the locket, and Melissa wondered if the daguerreotypes had been taken the same day.

"Peter. . ."

The yearning in the woman's voice had him lift his gaze.

"I wanted you, wanted to find you. But my husband. . ." Tears filled her eyes again, and she cut off her words, shaking her head in despair.

"I understand." He gave her a slight smile of assurance, but Melissa knew him well enough to sense its stiffness.

"Do you? I hope you really do and you're not just saying that to make me feel better. I don't deserve it, but I knew I wouldn't be able to sleep tonight if I didn't meet with you. I had to see you once more. Clayton would have wanted you to know the truth." She stood suddenly. "I must get back before I'm missed. And please, don't think too harshly of us. Your grandfather's had a hard life; he wasn't always a steel tycoon, and I. . .well, I've never had enough courage to stand up to him and tell him he was wrong, to insist we search for you. Clayton's death devastated me, and I barely spoke to anyone for weeks. But I did want you, so very much." Her words thickened, and she pressed the handkerchief to her mouth, hurrying from the screened room without another word.

Peter stared at the plate in front of him.

"Peter?" Concerned, Melissa laid a hand on his sleeve.

"I'm all right. Actually, I feel sorrier for her than I do for myself."

"I know what you mean. And I find myself more grateful than ever that you weren't raised in that household." Melissa did sympathize with the woman and her plight yet couldn't help but feel a twinge of righteous indignation on Peter's behalf. "Well. . ." She looked toward the untouched food. "Should we eat as long as we're here?"

"You can eat if you'd like. I'm not all that hungry."

"Neither am I."

His eyes met hers. "Thank you for coming with me today, for supporting me. I didn't want to do this alone."

"Hey, we're a team, remember? I'm with you every step of the way." Her light response belied the rapid beating of her heart. They sat close, and almost without her realizing it, the atmosphere changed. She looked deeply into his eyes, feeling she could drown there, then down to his lips, hoping he would try to kiss her again.

Instead he looked away and cleared his throat, breaking the moment. "We should go." He struggled to use his cane to help himself up.

"Here, let me. Sitting on the floor doesn't make it easy to rise gracefully." She laughed as her own scramble to her feet grew awkward.

She grasped his hand with both of hers and pulled hard, while he relied on her support to get a decent footing. But her silk stockings slid on the floor, and she couldn't maintain a good foothold. Suddenly, she found herself pulled down and sprawled on top of him.

Startled, they stared into each other's eyes.

"I'm sorry," she breathed. "Did I hurt you?"

"Missy, you couldn't hurt me if you tried." Peter's gaze grew serious. "Unless, of course, you told me to go away and never come back. Now that. . .that would hurt me."

She inhaled softly at his candid words. "Put your mind at rest then, because that's never going to happen. Haven't you figured out yet that I've completely fallen for you?"

They moved toward one another at the same time. Their lips met, and Missy's heart sang with its first note of love.

The sound of the door sliding on its track, followed by a nervous titter of laughter, broke them apart. They both turned their heads toward the door, where the Japanese woman laughed delicately behind her fingertips.

"So sorry," she said. "I come back soon." She left, sliding the door closed again.

Peter groaned. "Before whatever reputation you have left is hopelessly tarnished by the gossipmongers, I think it wise for us to get up off this floor. I have a feeling we've just become the new topic of conversation."

She laughed and crawled off him. When she held out her hand again, he shook his head, instead using both his cane and the table to stand.

"Chicken," she teased.

"No." He struggled to his feet. When he almost lost his balance, she put out her arm to aid him, and he turned to her, his eyes steady. "I simply know my limits."

His words teased, but his eyes didn't, and she felt a shiver of pleasurable warmth rush through her.

"Peter, what just happened between us?"

He studied her as if now cautious. "What do you think happened?"

"I think. . . ." She bit her lower lip. "I think I just told you how I feel about you, but I'm still uncertain where you stand."

"Where I stand?"

"How you feel about me." Embarrassment warmed her face. "I'm new at this sort of thing, so if I sound naive, it's because I am."

At her second outburst of nervous laughter, his expression grew serious. "How I feel about you. . ."

She swallowed hard as he drew closer.

"I cannot sleep for thinking of you. Though I spend all my days with you, I find it's not enough. I take every opportunity to travel to your restaurant, foregoing a marvelous eatery within my own hotel, just to see your face and hear your voice each night." With each sentence he spoke, her eyes widened farther, but he didn't stop there. "The thought of returning to England without you is unbearable, and I've found myself trying to think up excuses to stay in New York a little while longer now that my quest is over and I've found my answers. But I found more than that, Missy. I found you."

"I. . ." She was speechless.

"And I don't ever want to let you go." His final words were a breath upon her mouth as he lowered his head and kissed her, making her heart drop then soar with stunned delight. The gentle brush of his warm lips against hers grew stronger, and she lifted her arms to wrap them around his neck. She pressed in closer, but he edged away.

"We should go. This would be a splendid time to take a walk in the fresh air."

Giddy from the warmth of his kisses, she giggled and nodded, hardly daring to believe her dreams were really coming true.

Always before, something had come along to pop her fantasy balloon of the life she yearned for; always she'd lost her idyllic dream before it even began. First, with her mother's stinging rejection of her as the child she'd been. Later, with a gangster's unwelcome desire for her as the woman she'd become. Her life had never been happy or normal, even though that had been her dream and all she'd ever wanted.

She would not lose her dream with Peter.

Chapter 14

As the days slipped into weeks, Peter and Missy's love for each other flourished, while his concern for her sharpened. Neither Guido nor his associates had made an appearance at the restaurant for some time, and while that should produce relief and alleviate his worries, it did the opposite. He couldn't help but recall the words of his mystery host at the soup kitchen: *Don't second-guess Guido and his bunch. For all their foolishness, they are smart and will act when you least expect them to.*

"Peter?"

Missy's voice broke into his thoughts, and he looked up from Mr. Harper's journal he'd opened, though he hadn't been able to concentrate on it. With a mischievous smile, she moved toward him in the empty restaurant and sank to his lap, her mood playful as she plucked off his hat and tossed it to the table.

"Why are you being such a Gloomy Gus today, hm?" She kissed him lightly on the lips. "Ever since you arrived, you've been brooding. It's so unlike you, Peter."

He looked into her beautiful blue eyes, shining with the same love he felt for her. "Missy, will you be my wife?"

"Of course."

"And you will come back with me to England?"

"Tu casa es mi casa." She cradled his jaw with her hands and kissed him again.

He pulled back. "I'm serious, Missy. I wish to marry you. Today."

Her eyes widened. "Peter, I. . .don't know what to say."

These past weeks, they'd spoken of the future when they might one day marry, but their light talk had been in fun, sharing in the fantasy. He'd never formally proposed to her. These strong feelings for Missy he'd experienced since coming to America were a first for him, too, and now he followed the urgings of his heart. Placing his hands at either side of her waist, he lifted her to stand, then dropped to one knee before her. He took her hand in both of his and looked up at her.

Shocked wonderment crossed her features, but the anticipation in her eyes encouraged him to continue.

"Melissa Reynolds, without you I am half a man, and I want to be whole again. You've taken my heart; it is yours. Now I ask you to take all of me. Say we can we be together for a lifetime, whole in each other, our hearts beating as one." He pressed his lips against her hand, closing his eyes, the depth of his emotion threatening to overwhelm him. "With you by my side, I will have found my greatest treasure."

She dropped to her knees before him. "Oh, Peter—yes!" Her hands went to either side of his face, and she drew his head down to kiss him. "Yes, I'll marry you, yes, yes. . ." She kissed him twice more then drew away. "Only. . ."

"Only?" His elation at her response began to fade.

"I can't marry you today. The state has laws. We'll have to wait—I've heard it takes days to get a license." Her eyes sparkled. "Next week is Thanksgiving. The day after Thanksgiving, I'll marry you."

He leaned in close to kiss her again, this sharing of their hearts slow and tender. A smattering of giggles broke them apart, and they looked up to see Rosa enter the room, followed by a clearly agitated Maria. Her dark brows arched high. Both Missy and Peter hurried awkwardly to their feet.

"There is an explanation for this, sí?" Maria waved her arm toward the front of the restaurant. "Perhaps you wish to give our customer a sideshow?"

Missy inhaled a sharp breath, her face going pink, and Peter felt just as awkward to realize that an elderly man had slipped into the restaurant, his smile wide as he looked their way.

"I'm not one bit offended, Maria," the man said. "I rather enjoy watching a good proposal."

"Proposal?" Maria swung her gaze to Missy.

"Yes, Maria." Missy's smile brightened her entire face, though her manner seemed nervous. "Peter and I are getting married!"

"Ah, mi niña!" Maria strongly embraced Missy, then did the same to Peter. She surveyed them both, an arm around each of their waists. "You do not know how happy this makes me. I have waited long for this day."

"Really, Maria?" Missy's expression seemed doubtful.

"Sí. Really, Missy."

Relief flitted across Missy's features. Maria smiled, then clapped her hands together. "I will make a special meal! Daniel, today your dinner will be on the house."

"Well, now," the newcomer said. "It seems as if my timing was perfect after all."

They all laughed, and Peter watched Missy, admiring her beauty and spirit. Still, his niggling worry persisted.

Next week, she would be safe, and he comforted himself with that thought. After their wedding, he would take her with him to Ithaca, New York, where he would embark on his final undertaking. They would remain until late spring or early summer, once any threats of ice on the ocean melted. Then they would sail home to England.

Only a week longer, and she would be safe.

❧

Thanksgiving Day on Thirty-fourth Street was a sight to behold. Crowds of thousands lined the streets in anticipation of the big parade. Children squealed and squirmed, eager for their first view of the floats. Parents hushed and held on to the smallest of their youngsters, while the older ones banded together in groups, pushing toward the front, hoping to get a good place in line.

From 145th Street and Convent Avenue, to 110th Street and Eighth Avenue, on to Thirty-fourth Street and Broadway, the promised three-hour parade brought New Yorkers out by the masses. Exhilaration zipped through the icy air, and though snow lightly frosted the heads of the waiting crowd, it couldn't dampen their excitement.

Melissa stood with Peter, her gloved hand encased in his as they waited with the rest of the crowd and craned their heads at the first faint strains of band music—trumpets, horns, and drums.

"It's coming," a young boy cried out. "The parade is coming!"

The people cheered and waved pennants, their arms, and their hands. Caught up in the excitement, Melissa and Peter did the same. Her smile was bright for another reason; beneath her glove, a diamond engagement ring circled her finger. Peter had told her four days ago when they went to pick it out that even though their engagement would be short, he wanted her to have it all. She had stared at him in some amazement.

"But if you're not an heir to the title, can we afford such an extravagance?"

He had laughed and kissed her cheek, mentioning that his father, Lawrence, had put aside a yearly allowance for him. "But I love to paint, and my dabblings have fetched a good price among those lords and ladies interested."

"You paint? What do you paint?"

"Landscapes, though I've done a few portraits; I'm told I'm quite good, actually."

"I believe it. You would succeed in anything you put your mind to, Peter."

"You think so? I'd like to paint you one day. You inspire me. In fact, I wish I had a canvas with me this very moment."

She had giggled. "Yes, I can just see you setting up camp on the sidewalk right here in front of Macy's, with your easel and your paints."

Now as she stood beside him, viewing the parade, her dreams sailed through her heart on ribbons of promise, much like the massive helium balloons that billowed and floated past the skyscrapers. She looked to the sky to see the first one approach.

Marchers carried ropes that secured the balloons and kept them from flying away before it was time. This was the second year Macy's had used them. Last year, the balloons burst once they were released, and she hoped the man in charge had fixed the problem and it wouldn't happen again. It had been rather disconcerting to see Felix the Cat blown to smithereens.

Melissa pointed out to Peter the mammoth colorful toy-soldier balloon floating above a few live camels and elephants guided by their trainers. She thought she heard her name and looked over her shoulder. To her surprise, she glimpsed Rosa's face and red hood about twenty feet away. The young girl looked around, as though searching for someone, and Melissa tugged Peter's sleeve, motioning to her cousin. "We should go to her," she yelled above the cheering crowd and blaring music. Still he couldn't hear and shook his head, leaning in closer. She cupped her hand around his ear. "Rosa is over there. We should go to her. She looks lost."

He straightened and nodded, his gaze going to where she pointed. Hand in hand, they slowly made their way through the press of bodies. Many parade-goers acted disgruntled or mouthed irate comments that Melissa was glad she couldn't hear. She tried to keep a good grip on Peter's hand, but people pushed between them. She felt the pull of her arm as she attempted to hold on and then the sudden loss of his touch.

"Peter?" She tried to turn around, but a heavyset man terminated her efforts as he shoved into her. People moved closer to see the next float. "Peter!"

Abandoning her efforts and hoping he hadn't lost sight of her and could catch up, she focused ahead.

"Rosa!" she called, the name a bare scrape of sound amid the sudden clamor of numerous cymbals crashing. Her cousin showed no sign of having heard her.

Someone grabbed Melissa's arm. "Hey!"

Another strong hand grabbed her other arm. "Don't make a sound, and we'll let your boyfriend live. Understand?" a male voice rasped in her ear.

Fear knotted her throat, but she gave an abrupt nod.

"Good girl. Now, walk with us real nicelike and no funny business. You try anything, and my friend Bernardo here will introduce your British boyfriend to the darker side of Manhattan. Got it?"

She swallowed hard. In the close press of bodies, she felt the outline of a revolver in the man's shoulder holster. Again she nodded.

"You're one real smart doll. Come on. The boss wants to see you." Gruffly, he and his friend forced Melissa to walk with them toward the back of the crowd.

Through the fear swirling round her mind, one thought broke through and soared upward in a silent plea. *Please, God, don't let anything happen to Peter.*

❧

The moment Missy's hand slipped from his, a thread of worry wound around Peter's mind. He struggled through the crowd. Because of his limp, his endeavors proved difficult, especially with those who made no move to let him pass and grew belligerent when he shoved through anyway, as if by moving aside and allowing him to obstruct their view for mere seconds they would miss the entire parade.

Worry thickened into dread when Peter could find no sign of Missy. In desperation, he scanned the faces of those around him but spotted no green velvet hat or brown coat. He managed to quicken his pace and came up beside Rosa.

"Where's Missy?" he asked in greeting.

Her expression of pleasure to see him faded into anxiety. "Melissa? I thought she was with you."

"We became separated." Again, he searched the area, scanning faces and forms. The tail end of one of the marching bands passed, and hearing became easier. "Where are your parents?"

"Papa wasn't feeling well, and Mama wanted to stay and work on preparations for the wedding."

The wedding. Peter swallowed down the metallic taste of fear and fought to keep it from spiraling out of control. He took hold of her upper arm in a tight grip so as not to lose her. "Come, you must help me find her. We'll stay together, but you look in that direction, I'll look in this one."

She nodded and walked with him as Peter retraced his steps. He stumbled, almost tripping over something. Rosa bent to pick up the object. As she straightened, alarm threatened to consume him when he saw what she held.

"Melissa's purse." Her brown eyes were very wide and scared.

Any hope that foul play wasn't involved quickly dissolved into despair. "Rosa, can you find your way back home on your own?"

"Sí. I came alone."

"I want you to go home. Now."

"But the parade, it is not over. And Melissa, she is lost."

"Just do as I say." He softened his brusque words with a faded smile of encouragement. "Please. You must tell your parents what happened. They need to notify the police."

Her eyes widened even more. "I will go now."

Peter watched her thread her way to the buildings at the back; then he turned to ask several people if they'd seen Missy, giving a brief description of her. The few who cooperated in giving him an answer said they hadn't been paying any attention to those around them, only to the parade.

Dear God, how will I find her?

He worked his way to the back where another street intersected. Glad to see it reasonably empty, he hurried as fast as he was able, hoping to find a taxicab. Frantic, he had no idea how to begin his search—or where. He sucked in a deep breath, forcing himself to think.

First he would return to the restaurant, speak with Tony, and find out where Guido lived. Wherever that man hid, Peter felt certain he would find Missy there.

The thugs on either side of Melissa forced her to walk between the buildings and down an empty street, then bundled her into the back of a waiting Lincoln. She quickly slid over the seat, but before she could get a grip on the opposite door handle, one of Guido's men jumped in beside her and grabbed her arm.

"Any more of that and we'll have to tie you up. Behave!"

She detested being spoken to like a child, especially from this ruffian who could hardly be described as acting mature. "Where are you taking me?"

He leered. "The boss wants to see you, and I aim to follow orders. And lady, if that means I have to knock you out cold to get you there, then that's what I'll do."

Melissa sank back, crossing her arms over her chest out of cold, fear, and anger.

"That's better." He nodded to the man in front, who turned to the steering wheel. The car took off like a shot, throwing Melissa's head back against the seat. Her guard, a husky Italian with a wide forehead and eyes that were dark both in color and intent, pulled a silver flask from his pocket and unscrewed it, taking a large swig. He pulled it away from his mouth, offering the bootleg liquor to Melissa, but she wrinkled her nose in disgust and turned her head away.

He laughed and made a snide comment. Melissa chose not to rise to the bait. At some point, she might be able to escape from these men. Until then, she dared not annoy them at the risk of having her hands and feet tied.

The thought that her wedding day was tomorrow struck her, and she squeezed her eyes shut, refusing to let these bullies see her reduced to tears.

Dear God, please open a way of escape.

Chapter 15

I told you, I don't know." His hands cupping his head, Peter threaded his fingers through his hair in frustration. "She was directly in front of me."

The police inspector asking questions chewed on the end of his cigar and pinpointed Peter with shrewd eyes. "So you're saying you didn't see anyone nab her?"

"No, I didn't."

"Well, now, in a crowd of thousands, it doesn't seem so unusual that you two got separated. Happens all the time. She's probably out there right now, walking around Macy's and trying to find you."

Grabbing Missy's purse, Peter rose from his chair and approached the man, who seemed intent on finding excuses for why he shouldn't start a search. He held it up. "I found this on the ground. It's her handbag. Now I don't know if you understand anything about women, Inspector, but a woman would not simply drop her handbag and leave it lying on the ground for it to be trodden upon."

"In the press of the crowd, she might not have realized she dropped it until it was too late."

"That is highly unlikely."

The man took a puff from his cigar.

"Why aren't you out there looking for her?" Peter tried to cage his frustration, but with every minute that passed with Missy unaccounted for, irritation was fast breaking through the iron bars of his reserve. "Instead of asking me these ridiculous questions, you should be out trying to catch the criminal who abducted her. I'll even give you a name—Guido Piccoli. Once you find him, I'm certain you'll find Missy."

Peter sensed Tony stiffen beside him. A cold look crusted the inspector's eyes. "You have proof he took her, evidence of some kind?"

"No." Peter felt any credence his words might have received dissipate like smoke. "Just a hunch."

"A hunch, he says." He glanced at the uniformed officer beside him, and both men had the audacity to smile. "Mr. Caldwell, we can't just go around arresting people without grounds to do so. It's like I said, she probably got lost and will be walking through that door any minute."

"I can't believe this." Peter began to pace, then faced them. "So you're not going to do anything?"

"We can't very well act unless we establish that a crime has been committed. If she hasn't returned by morning, give us a call." He tipped his hat to Maria, who stood pale and trembling in the circle of Tony's arms. Rosa sat in a chair by Maria, her downcast gaze focused on the floor.

All manner of words soared to Peter's lips as the policemen made their exits, but he dared not utter a one of them.

"You should not have mentioned Guido," Tony said. "I have no proof, but I think for many months some on the police force are owned by Vittorio. His family rules many in New York. If this is so, and these policemen take orders from him, they will not work hard to find her."

Then whom could a person trust? Peter wanted to ask but didn't when he observed the pained horror in Maria's eyes.

"Tomorrow was your wedding day," she said sadly, taking his hand in both of hers.

"I'll find her." Peter tried to reach through her fear and make her believe. "I promise."

"How?" Tony asked. "Where will you go?"

"Do you know where Guido lives?"

"No, I don't. I'm sorry."

Peter nodded and picked up his hat, setting it on his head. "Then I must go see someone who does." His gaze again went to Maria. "I *will* find her."

❧

The Packard stopped in front of a ritzy establishment that Melissa assumed lay on the outskirts of Manhattan. The glow of incandescent light flooded the windows of both stories beyond the closed draperies. They'd taken back streets, often rough with ruts, and Melissa had lost track of their course. She wondered if the roundabout route was intentional, if Guido had warned his men about her excellent sense of direction and aptitude for finding locales. He would know anything about her that Uncle Tony might have chosen to share over the years.

Pity for her uncle seeped into her heart. She didn't blame Tony for his respectful fear of the nephew of the infamous Vittorio; every man who knew the family or knew of them dreaded what they could do. All except Peter. If he feared them, he hadn't shown it. Still, her aunt had taught her that even the bravest of men possessed a measure of fear but had learned the secret of how to conquer it by not allowing it to inhabit them.

Melissa prayed for that same courage.

One of her two abductors knocked on the door in a signal. Almost immediately, a flapper opened it, the shoulders of her red-fringed dress askew, her eyes half closed and bleary from too much whiskey, if her breath was anything to go by. She gave Melissa a cursory glance, then let out a laughing snort.

"You know where to take her, boys."

They walked farther into the mansion, and Melissa caught sight of a parlor before they went through a door and into an empty room, a man's study, by the look of the brown and gold furnishings and the massive desk off in a corner. One of the men moved to the paneled wall, reaching behind the fireplace mantel.

The entire wall moved outward as if on a hinge, and Melissa gaped. Both men forced her into a dark corridor beyond; the wall closed behind them. A cord was pulled, and a light bulb flickered on, weakly shining down on them. On both sides of the corridor, tall racks held wine bottles. They continued along the hidden passageway to a crude wooden door. From beyond it, Melissa heard loud jazz music, laughing, and talking.

One of the men knocked, again using a signal. A wooden slat in the door shot to the side, revealing a square opening and a pair of eyes. Melissa took an involuntary step back. The ogre who held her left arm tightened his grip as if afraid she might run. *Run?* she thought wryly. *Where?* Even if she could get back to the mock-fireplace door, she had no idea how to open it.

The wooden slat shot back into place, the sound of a heavy bolt scraped across the door, and it opened wide.

Melissa coughed, and her eyes watered at the rank smell of cigarette smoke. The entire room, lavish with its red and gold furnishings, lay smothered in a cloud of smoke that made it seem cheap. Women, most of them flappers judging by their brash clothes and attitudes, sat with men, danced with them, drank with them. Uniformed waiters glided past several small tables and chairs, carrying trays of drinks. Couples in embrace occupied two sofas, and a group of men gambled with a roulette wheel in a far corner. The place lay smothered in a pit of darkness; the lamps and the lights of the chandelier turned down low.

Spared from having to associate with the speakeasy's inhabitants, Melissa was hurried along as her jailers escorted her to the back of the huge room and to another door. She ignored the curious glances many flappers turned toward her, as well as the interested stares their male companions gave.

One of her abductors used the same knock. The door swung open, and a tall man, at least two heads taller than Melissa, glared at them. His gaze dropped to Melissa, and he motioned them inside with a quick jerk of his head.

She walked into another plush room and abruptly halted.

In a chair in front of the fireplace, Guido sat with lazy elegance. His gaze slowly swept over her, and then he smiled, like a sleek panther that had triumphed over its prey.

꧁꧂

Peter found the soup kitchen with little trouble. His former host proved more difficult to locate. Men and women crowded the area, but Peter soon spotted the man's familiar tall form and hurried his way.

"Hello," the Frenchman said with a smile. "I did not expect to see you here again."

"I need your help," Peter greeted. "Guido and his men have taken my fiancée, and I need you to help me locate them."

A grave look swept into his host's eyes, and he cast a glance around as if afraid of being overheard. "We can't talk here. Come outside."

Peter walked with him to the door. The moment the salty tang of ocean air hit his face, Peter turned to him. "I need you to tell me where Guido's home is located."

"Why do you think I would know?" Wariness touched the words.

"You told me you were one of them once; did you know Guido, too?"

"It was a long time ago, and I worked for Vittorio, not Guido. But if you think you can just march into their home and take your fiancée back, you are sadly mistaken, *mon ami*."

Peter pulled his coat to the side to reveal Tony's concealed gun. The Frenchman only raised his brows and laughed. "You seriously think you can do damage with that relic? These men have machine guns and all the latest in handguns—many of them."

"I have to find her and bring her back. I won't rest until I do."

He surveyed Peter a long moment. "There is a speakeasy ten miles from here. A wealthy widow's home. If Guido wanted to hide someone, I think he would choose that place. He spends much time there, I am told." He went on to give detailed directions, and Peter felt thankful he'd spent so much time searching through Manhattan and recognized many of the street names. Yet one matter disturbed him.

"I thought you didn't know Guido."

"*Non.* I never said that. He was only a young man when I quit working for the family, still much of a boy."

For the first time, Peter wondered if he could really trust this man; Tony had told him that the underworld had spies everywhere.

As if reading his mind, the Frenchman straightened. "I am not giving you false information, nor would I become the informer and rat on you. As God is my witness, I have no evil intent. You already know what danger you face."

"Why did you quit working for the family?"

"I had become the next name on the list."

"The list?"

"They intended to kill me; an associate warned me, and I escaped."

Peter's eyes narrowed. "And you're not afraid they'll find you now?"

He chuckled dryly. "They would never think to look for me in this place." He waved his hand toward the mission. "Years have passed; they have forgotten one insignificant Frenchman."

From what Tony had told him, Peter doubted Guido or his family would forget anything. He stared at the man before him a moment longer before nodding, satisfied. "Thank you for your help." He turned to go.

"You are really going to do this alone?"

"I have no choice."

His host gave a swift nod and stuck out his hand. Peter took it, and both men clasped forearms.

"Then I will pray for you, mon ami. For in order to succeed, you will surely need guidance as you have never needed it before."

Chapter 16

Melissa remained quiet, though every nerve ending stood on alert. Guido sat in casual elegance, his Italian good looks belying the hard glint in his eyes that spoke of his ruthlessness. With unhurried grace, he poured amber liquid into a crystal glass. He rose and approached, holding the glass out to her.

"You look parched, my dear Melissa. Have a drink to quench your thirst."

Giving no thought to her actions, she knocked the glass from his hand with one sweep. It went crashing to the floor, and liquid splashed up onto the wall.

"No, thank you," she said with ultra politeness, though her tone oozed a chill that frosted the room. "I'm not interested in anything you have to offer."

His eyes narrowed; his jaw hardened. After tense seconds, he gave the slightest nod as if he'd figured her out and smiled, though there was no warmth to his expression. He looked past Melissa. With an abrupt jerk of his head, he motioned for his lackeys to leave the room. Melissa swallowed, made uneasier now that the two of them were alone.

"That's one quality I've always admired about you, Melissa. You have such fire and spirit encased in that cool, blond veneer."

To escape his close proximity, she sought the warmth of the fire. Pulling off a glove so as to warm her hands, she tried to appear unruffled, but her pulse beat rapidly in her throat, giving her fear away. One thing stood in her favor; Guido seemed to admire women of courage, and she had no intention of falling to her knees and begging for him to release her like some melodramatic heroine from a silent movie. If she kept her wits about her, by some miracle she might persuade him to see reason and return her to her family.

"Maybe you'd care to tell me why your thugs spirited me away from an absolutely delightful parade, only to bring me to this dark, dreary place." Careful to keep her tone civil, she arched her eyebrows in question and pulled off the other glove. As she did, she realized her mistake. Guido's eyes clouded as dark as a thunderstorm at the flash of her ring. He rushed her way and grabbed her by the shoulders.

"He'll never have you, Melissa—you're mine! I've waited for you to grow up for a long time."

Disconcerted, fear clotted her throat, and she held the flaps of her coat together. "I never belonged to you; I don't want to belong to you. My pastor teaches that light can't live with darkness. Neither will survive that kind of union. We serve two different masters, Guido. I serve the Almighty God; you serve the god of mammon."

His chuckle was dark. "What? So pious all of a sudden?"

"Which proves you know nothing about me. I respect God, even if I don't always understand His methods. I could never live this kind of life."

His hands dropped from her shoulders. "Ah, but Melissa, I would give you everything you could ever want. Fur coats, a house of your own, a car with your own chauffeur. . ." He sauntered behind her, reaching around to trace her jaw with his knuckle. Her mouth dry with alarm, she jerked her head away from his touch. He moved his finger lower to glide across her neck. "Diamonds, pearls, rubies. . .whatever your heart desires to decorate that white throat—it's yours."

"I'm not interested in the accumulation of such goods if I have to sell my soul to gain them."

He came around to face her again, his expression amused. "So you think I am the devil?"

"I think you act like the devil. You could do so much good with all your money and power, but instead you choose to cause others only pain and harm."

He lost his seductive quality and straightened, almost defensive. His black eyes glittered. "I give the people what they want."

"That's just a poor excuse to feed their bad habits and to supply yourself with even more money in the process. And you know it."

He laughed. "You really are such a child. It is time you grew up and opened your eyes to the reality of the world. It's not some fairytale land of your daydreams. It's harsh, it's cruel, and if people choose to indulge in a few harmless pleasures to lighten their loads, then what harm is there in that?"

His words brought to mind her own cherished dream, and she furrowed her brow as once again she realized her fantasy balloon had been blown to smithereens. There would be no wedding for her tomorrow.

"You will change your mind," he said with confidence. "Spend a night or two locked inside this room without food or water, and you may find the prospect of my company isn't so disagreeable."

"Never."

Her emphatic declaration only made him laugh. "We shall see, Melissa. We shall see."

She was fast growing to despise that name.

❧

Peter sat in the back of the taxicab, wishing to increase the vehicle's speed, though the cabbie drove as fast as the car could manage down several dark, rutted streets and past buildings of questionable repute.

Looking out the side window, Peter grew alert. "Stop!"

The driver hit the brakes with a screech, then looked back at Peter with a doubtful expression on his craggy face. "You want to get out here?"

"I see someone I need to talk with."

"Okay, fellah. That'll be a buck-eighty."

"I'll be coming back directly."

The cabbie shook his head. "I ain't stickin' around these parts; you want me to drop you somewhere else, I will. You want out now, the fare's up. I've been robbed in this area before, and I ain't temptin' fate again."

"Very well." Peter firmed his jaw and paid the man, then approached the woman who'd just exited one of the ramshackle buildings that looked as if it should be condemned.

"Well, well. If it isn't the English prince come to visit us common peasants," Florence said in greeting. "Did ya lose your proper lady, or are you out looking for some real fun?"

Peter ignored her snide words. "I need you to help me get into the speakeasy that Guido runs."

Her eyes widened. "Oh, no. Nothin' doin'." She gave an incredulous laugh. "You realize his men know what you look like? You wouldn't be able to get within a hundred yards of that place and not be spotted. And I've got a newsflash for you, Mr. Royal Bucks—Guido doesn't like you."

"I mean to do my best to find a way inside. He's abducted Missy."

"Is that a fact? Well, I'm sorry, but I'm not getting involved."

"If you'll help me," he said before she took more than three steps away from him, "we'll both get what we want."

She turned, her eyes sparking with curious interest. "Oh, how's that?"

"You'll have Guido, and I'll have Missy."

Taken aback, she reeled before making a quick recovery, but she didn't deny that she cared for the mobster, though Peter couldn't begin to fathom why.

"If you're caught, it's curtains for you. And you know what that means?" she asked.

Peter nodded. "No matter; I have to do this."

In disbelief, she stared at him, as if just coming to a realization. "You really love her."

"She's my life," he said simply.

A wistful flicker touched her eyes but quickly vanished. Clearly agitated, she looked at him, looked away, and shook her head. "I can't believe I'm doing this," she muttered under her breath, then said to him, "I can get you through the door, but after that, you're on your own. If you're caught, I had nothing to do with any of it."

"Agreed."

"Oh, all right then." She shook her head, giving him a weak smile. "So tell me, are all British gentlemen knights in armor in disguise?"

She found them another cab. Fifteen minutes later, the driver pulled up to the drive of a two-story mansion.

After Peter paid the man and the cab took off, Florence eyed Peter in appraisal, as if she found him wanting. "First thing we need to do is make you look like you've had a night out on the town." She studied his clothes, frowning, and popped off his hat. With one hand she mussed his hair so that it hung over his forehead, then slapped his hat back on his head. Her brow wrinkled in displeasure. "Button up your coat. . .no, mismatch the buttons to the holes. Make it hang crooked. Hmm. . ."

Peter stood silent, allowing her to continue her ministrations. She tugged his collar high up around his neck, then lowered her assessing gaze to his cane. "Can you lose that? It's a dead giveaway."

"I'll need the support. I may stumble otherwise."

"That's the whole idea, Romeo, just until we get through the door and mix with the crowd. You can lean on me—that'll give your disguise even more of a convincing effect. Gretta expects that of the men I bring to her establishment."

"*Her* establishment?"

"Guido uses Gretta's home for a cover. Look, do you wanna do this or not?"

"Most definitely." All Peter could think about was the danger Missy was in.

They walked to the door, keeping to the shadows. At Florence's order, Peter hooked his cane in his waistband and again buttoned his coat. Florence anchored her arm around Peter's waist, supporting him. "Lean on my neck," she whispered. "And lower that hat. If she sees those clear blue eyes of yours, she'll know right off the bat she's being hoodwinked. Your face is too angelic looking as it is, but your eyes give away the fact you haven't been drinking."

A dark-haired woman dressed in flapper style, much like Florence, opened the door to a signal knock.

"He looks like he's had too much already," Gretta said after the two women exchanged greetings.

Peter hoped he wasn't overacting the part required of him. He sensed the woman's mistrust and lowered his head.

"Now, Gretta," Florence said with a carefree laugh. "When is it *ever* too much?"

That got the woman laughing, and she opened the door wider to let them inside. Soon Peter found himself in a large den, and Florence quickly shut the door behind them. "One more hurdle, and you're through," she said in an undertone as she tripped a hidden lever and the fireplace wall opened.

"My word." Stunned, he stared at the dark corridor beyond and shook his head.

"Come on, Sir Knight," Florence urged, putting her arm around him and supporting him as he walked beside her.

Another bolted door barred their entrance at the end of the long corridor. A secret knock and a brief appraisal by the hulking man inside the door, and Peter entered what appeared to be a den of iniquity. Jazz music zinged through the crimson and gold room from a player piano. Women in skimpy fringed dresses showed the tops of their stockings as they kicked their heels high to do the Charleston. For a moment, Peter hesitated; he'd never been inside such a place and felt ill that Guido had brought Missy here. What manner of evil had he subjected her to? Peter clenched his teeth, fighting down a surge of anger.

"I'll just leave you over there by the wall—there's a door at the back that leads to a private parlor. I have a feeling if she's anywhere, he would've put her in there. I don't see her out here."

They staggered through the room, and Peter leaned heavily against Florence until they reached the wall. No one paid them any attention, since several others stumbled about the room in the same condition. "This is where I leave you off, Romeo. From this point on, I'm out of the picture."

"Thank you." He hoped his eyes conveyed the depth of his gratitude. "You're a very kind woman, Florence."

"Yeah, sure." She gave a wry snort, but her expression lost a bit of its hard edge. "Just don't let the word get around, or it'll ruin my reputation. Good luck."

It would take much more than luck. Only God's intervention could help him in this situation, and Peter knew it. He hadn't planned beyond this moment and had no idea how he would get Missy out of this place. He certainly couldn't bring her through this room full of people or past the gun-toting guards posted near the doors. With relief, he saw the door at the back was unguarded.

At the fringes of the dim room, Peter unbuttoned his coat and carefully removed his cane. One thing stood in his favor: with all the revelry and loud music, he would be surprised if anyone noticed him.

He moved to the door and tried the handle. It wouldn't budge.

Chapter 17

Missy stood by the fireplace where Guido had left her and surveyed the furnishings of her gilded prison. A small chandelier glittered from the ceiling. Decorated in red and gold like the room next door, this parlor reminded her of a room a Greek palace might contain. A massive gold-framed painting of women in Grecian dress hung on one rose-papered wall, and a plush matching sofa stood angled in the center. Little else filled the room. No windows lined the walls for her to slip out of; no other doors lay in wait for her exit.

She shivered, drawing her coat tighter around her, and rubbed her arms. The fire in the grate couldn't dispel the chill closing in around her heart. He would be back, whether tonight or tomorrow, and she sensed the next time he wouldn't be so tolerant of her refusal. Guido always took what he wanted, but when he returned, she would be ready for him.

She scanned the room for a weapon and noticed a heavy brass candlestick on one of the side tables that flanked the sofa. If Guido came back tonight to carry out his intent, she would show him she wasn't some docile lamb to be naively led to the slaughter. Now that she stood alone in the locked room and the shock of her abduction had faded, fear also had lost its razor edge.

The candlestick base was slim enough to slip the article inside her deep coat pocket and heavy enough to knock anyone out. She pulled the tapered candle from its holder and slid the candlestick inside her coat. Confident that she at least had that to use in defense, she wandered to the sofa and sank onto it.

No magazines or books sat on either of the two tables, and Missy sought about for something to pass the time. Thoughts of Peter and her terminated wedding day weakened her and brought tears, so she forced her mind to other things. She had to stay emotionally alert and strong; she couldn't afford to break down now, not until this was over. And it *would* be over.

She recalled other memories, ones that helped firm her resolve and kept a sharp point on her indignation. Her mind touched upon the memory of her mother abandoning her to run off with her fourth husband, and for the briefest moment, Missy wondered where her mother was, if she was well, and if a number five had been added to her list of conquests. Her mother's desire for men's attention almost made Missy pity her. She recalled that last night on the *Titanic,* and how, when she had left her bed to ask for a drink, she had caught the cabin steward in her mother's arms. Painful as was the memory of her mother's stinging slap delivered after taking Missy back to bed, it did not hurt like the words hissed in her face, claiming Missy was always in the way.

As the minutes passed, though Missy had no clock to show her just how many, apathy once more gave way to apprehension, and she turned to prayer again.

"Father, I am so frightened, but I know somehow You will protect me from Guido. Keep my family and Peter safe, and please help me find a way out of this place." She gave a cursory glance to the four rose-colored walls surrounding her. "There must be a way. . . ."

Thinking of the false fireplace, she moved toward the mantel. If the other room hid a passage, this room might, too. She ran her hands over the carved marble, but her fingers didn't make contact with a hidden lever or knob. Not ready to admit defeat, she tried again, more slowly this time, sliding her fingertips over every inch of the smooth surface, pressing any recesses she found. Biting her lower lip in contemplation, she turned to look at the rest of the room. Her attention went to the door. To her alarm, she noticed the knob turning.

She dipped her hand into her pocket and withdrew the candlestick. Hiding it behind her back, she watched as the door swung slowly open.

❧

Peter used the key Florence had given him. Earlier, he'd spotted her across the room and made eye contact, signaling the door was locked. In tense amazement, he'd watched as she nodded and moved toward a tall man in a black, pinstriped suit and fedora, who looked like one of the mobsters. She flirted with him while pulling his coat lapels together and drew him out to dance with her. A few minutes later, she walked past Peter, slipping the key into his pocket. Peter assumed she must have used sleight of hand to retrieve it, because he'd watched the entire time and the man never handed the key to Florence.

A commotion at the front brought Peter's head around in worry that he'd been caught. A strange pair walked into the speakeasy—an ugly woman in a knee-length, brown fur coat and a man with a black beard down to his chest. Something about them and their loud demand for two gin and tonics seemed unusual, but he didn't stop to consider. Quickly, he slipped into the room, praying Missy would be there, and closed the door behind him. Even over the jazz music, he heard the sound of metal striking stone and swung his gaze to the right.

Missy stared at him, her eyes wide, a candlestick rolling near her feet.

She rushed toward him at the same time he went to her. Her hands grabbed either side of his head, and he reached for her as she peppered fervent kisses across his mouth and jaw. His relief at finding her safe made his own response just as intense, and he kissed her over and over again, wondering if the tears he felt against his cheek were hers or his own.

"Are you both completely loco?" Florence asked, having followed him in and closed the door. "Someone could walk into this room any second, so if you two lovebirds can stop your pecking now, we really should get you out of here."

Missy turned in shock, moving her hands to circle Peter's arm. "Florence? What are you doing here?"

"Believe me, I've asked myself that question for the past half hour, ever since your lover boy roped me into doing this." She looked at the closed door as if afraid it would suddenly swing open. "We don't have a lot of time. I think someone spotted me slipping the key out of Bernardo's pocket. I don't know if they'd rat on me or not, but I don't want to take any chances."

Peter slipped his arm protectively around Missy. "Can you get her a disguise, a scarf or something of that nature? Her blond hair is sure to draw attention, as light as it is."

"Oh, you can't go back out there. That would be suicide."

"Then how?" Missy sounded confused. "There's no other way out."

"Honey," Florence said with a dry chuckle, "there's always a way out if you look hard enough."

Florence walked toward the fireplace just as the door banged open. One of Guido's men burst inside. Peter pushed Missy down to safety behind the sofa and pulled out Tony's gun before the guard could reach for his. He'd never shot a man and didn't think he could now. Instead, he aimed for the chandelier chain and fired. The crystal light crashed down on the hoodlum's head, and he sank, unconscious, to the floor.

Florence raced to shut the door and wedged the sole chair in the room beneath the knob. "You've both got to get out of here, now!" Even as she spoke, the door shook on its hinges with the force of the blows aimed against it. "This chair won't keep them out long."

"But how do we get out?" Missy looked at the walls as though she expected a door to materialize before them.

"The left andiron—twist it to the right. And hurry!" Florence added when the wooden door almost shattered.

Missy sped to the fireplace and twisted the gold andiron. A click sounded, barely discernable over the banging against the door. She looked around the room to locate the source, then toward Florence, her face a mask of confusion.

"The painting—push on it. The passage'll take you to a room on the other side of the house that leads to a door outside. But you have to hurry. They know about the passage—it was created in case of a raid."

Peter pushed on the painting, and it swung inward. He stepped over a two-foot high ledge that was part of the wall and turned to help Missy, just as the door crashed inward, the chair flew aside, and Florence screamed.

Chapter 18

Shocked, Missy looked back. Bernardo caught her eye and raced for the opening, grabbing her arm before she could escape.

"Oh, no you don't!" He yanked on her arm so hard he almost pulled her off her feet. Missy acted before she thought. Wrenching back her other arm, she swung with all she had in her, and her fist connected with his eye. He let go and staggered backward, cupping his hand over it. Before he could lurch at Missy again, Florence hit him over the head with the crystal decanter, and he sank to the floor.

Peter stared at Missy, his mouth agape.

She shrugged self-consciously and shook her stinging hand. "I did mention my uncle once gave me boxing lessons."

Despite the gravity of the situation, Peter grinned, then turned his attention to Florence. "Come on!" he urged, holding out his hand.

"Oh, no." She shook her head. "But you two had better skedaddle before Guido and his big ape get back. These two bozos were easy enough to tangle with, but the others are much more dangerous."

High-pitched whistles suddenly pierced the air, and ladies screeched from the next room. Florence's jaw dropped.

"What is it?" Missy asked.

"A raid! The feds have found the place."

"Then you haven't got a choice now!" Peter grabbed Florence's arm and hauled her inside the passageway. He closed the door hidden behind the painting, leaving them in the dark and muting the sounds of pandemonium from the other side.

"Can you lock it?" Peter asked.

"No." Florence's voice shook.

"How will we see?" Missy whispered. "Is there a light somewhere?"

"It's too risky to pull the switch. If someone else comes inside, they'd see us right away. We're just going to have to walk blind and use the wall to feel our way. This passage leads straight to the room with the outside door."

"How do we know the feds haven't surrounded the place?" Missy asked the woman behind her.

"We don't."

Missy didn't like the sound of that. She and Peter were innocent of any nefarious activities associated with the speakeasy, but their presence here argued otherwise. And she didn't want to spend the night in jail on the eve of her wedding.

She closed her eyes, continuing to follow Peter, one hand on his shoulder, the other using the rough rock wall to guide her. In this pitch black, whether she left her eyes opened or closed didn't matter. The popping of gunfire sounded far beyond the painting, and she swallowed hard, praying they wouldn't be found, hoping the federal agents would be successful in their raid.

She forced her spirits to rally; five minutes ago, her prospects had been glum, and she'd entertained the possibility of having to protect her virtue. She hadn't been sure when, if ever, she'd see Peter again, and now she had him with her. Whatever further trial challenged them, at least they were together again.

An eternity seemed to pass before Peter came to an abrupt stop. "We've reached a dead end; I can't go any farther, and I can't find a handle."

"That's the door," Florence said. "Just push hard on it; there is no handle."

Peter did so, and the pitch black lightened to gray as a moonlit room opened before them. They left the passage and closed what looked like part of the paneled wall. When Peter shut it, Missy couldn't see any sign of a door.

"Hurry!" Florence ordered. "But try to be quiet."

They sped across the room to an opposite door, the rapid taps of Peter's cane the only sound on the tiles.

"Can't you keep that thing quieter?" Florence asked in fearful exasperation.

"Sorry." Peter's tone was apologetic.

"Never mind. We'll be outside soon enough, and it won't matter."

Cautiously, she cracked open the last door and peered out. After several seconds she relaxed and pulled it wider. "It's safe."

They moved across the grounds, cutting a path toward some trees at the back of the mansion. From the front, they could hear men and women screaming irate words, and Missy assumed the police were busy hauling the flappers and other drinkers outside to the paddy wagon.

They left the open area and moved toward the shadows of the trees. Suddenly a pair of headlights switched on, spotlighting them. As one, they swung around in shock. An automobile sat concealed within the shadows of trees opposite the road, no more than ten feet away.

❧❧

Peter blinked hard against the glare, drawing Missy close to his side. Florence clutched his other sleeve. The headlights switched off, and the door swung open. A shadowy figure emerged. Peter tensed and reached for Tony's gun, prepared to do battle.

"I figured you could use a getaway car," a man said, his smooth voice breaking the electric silence.

Peter almost laughed in relief. "It's all right," he said to the women as he hurried them toward the car. "He's a friend."

The Frenchman opened the door for them to pile in the back and hurried to resume his place behind the wheel. The car took off at a crawl in the opposite direction from the mansion. Once they were blocks away, he switched on the headlights again and picked up speed. "Where do you wish me to take you?"

"Marelli's Restaurant," Missy said.

"No." Peter looked at her. "It will be the first place Guido looks."

"Your hotel?"

He shook his head. "They know who I am; they could find us there, too."

"Then where?"

"They would never find you at the soup kitchen," their driver said.

"Brilliant!" Peter smiled. "I'll leave the women there and return to the hotel for my things. I'll make a call to your aunt while I'm there, Missy, assuring her you're safe, and then I'll take you to Ithaca."

"Ithaca?" The Frenchman grew alert.

"An acquaintance of my mother's lives near there, someone she met on the *Titanic*. They manage a children's reform school, so I believe Missy will be safe in such a secure environment."

Their driver gave no reply, and Peter continued to discuss the details of their plans. Once they arrived at the soup kitchen, their host excused himself to find his wife.

"Well, toodle-oo! I wish you the best." Florence walked away from the car in the opposite direction.

"Wait, don't go," Peter said. She turned to him, her eyes wary, and he continued. "You don't have to go back to Guido and the rest of them."

"I don't, huh? And where else would I go?" She swung her hand to take in the nearby wharf. "Should I take a dive in the ocean?"

Peter's eyes were steady as he walked up to her. "You said something earlier that had great merit. 'There's always a way out if you look hard enough.' It's as I said, Florence, you don't have to go back."

She chuckled wryly at her own words used against her. "You know nothing about me or where I come from, oh privileged prince. I'm not like you; I never had a decent bone in my body. I fought tooth and nail for everything I got, but now it's mine, and I'm happy just as I am." The waver to her biting words proved she wasn't as callous as she tried to make it appear. "Besides, there's no way out for the likes of me. There just isn't."

"There is," Missy said, her expression gentle as she came to stand beside Peter. "The only way out is up."

Before Florence could follow with another retort, a lovely brunette, big with child, approached them. "Hello. You must be Peter. I'm Janine. My husband's told me so much about you." She smiled at Missy and Florence, including them in her greeting. Peter made introductions, and Janine waved her hand toward the soup kitchen door.

"Please, come inside and rest," she said, directing her words to Florence, and Peter wondered how much of their conversation Janine had overheard. "You've all been through so much tonight. My husband will speak soon; you should stay and listen. His words are very powerful."

"Speak?" Peter asked.

"He ministers to those who come here to eat. He tells his story and gives them hope. When we first met, he had just been released from prison and was a hard nut to crack. Believe me!" She laughed. "My father and I helped him find his direction. When Father died, my husband took over the soup kitchen and married me." Her eyes sparkled. "That was seven years ago, and every year just gets better."

Peter exchanged a tender look with Missy, anticipating the start of their future together. By the expression in her eyes, she shared the same thought.

Between the three of them, they managed to convince Florence to stay for one bowl of soup. The room had grown more crowded, but Janine led them to a table at the front. Three small children with curly blond hair sat at the edge of one of the plank seats. Peter recognized the oldest boy as the one who'd interrupted their conversation the first time he'd been to the soup kitchen. The smallest of the children, a girl, slid off the bench and ran to Janine, who lifted her up, and Peter realized these must be her children.

Halfway into their meal, Janine's husband moved to the front of the room to speak. Peter was moved, awed, and shocked upon hearing his new friend's history, though he knew the Frenchman had been a gangster. But he found it difficult to believe this calm man standing before him had conned, deceived, assaulted, and even murdered—and had done it all not to just one but many. His forthright, quiet words held no restraint and touched hearts. Peter noticed Florence reach for her handkerchief to blot her eyes. When their host spoke of his long, difficult journey to find God, she let the tears stream down her face, no longer bothering to stanch their flow. Peter lifted a silent prayer that she would find the peace their host had.

The Frenchman concluded his testimony with an invitation for salvation, and several rough-looking men went toward him and asked for prayer. With head bowed, Florence shook with suppressed sobs but didn't move from the table. Janine sank beside her, wrapping her arm around the flapper's shoulders, saying nothing, only holding her.

Peter swallowed over the emotion of the moment and squeezed Missy's hand. She turned to him, her eyes brimming with tears.

"I need to return to the hotel and check out. Will you be all right here?"

She nodded. "You'll find a telephone and call Aunt Maria? She must be so worried."

"Of course. I'll return shortly." He kissed her cheek.

At the hotel, Peter made quick work of packing his valise and checking out of his room, also collecting his box from the hotel safe. At the front desk, a quick call to Maria reassured the woman, and she agreed that Peter must get Missy out of town with all haste and not bring her home. To his relief, he didn't spot any of Guido's men and wondered if the feared gangster remained unaware of Missy's escape because of the raid. Once he returned to the soup kitchen, he noticed Missy in conversation with Janine and stepped back outside to give the women some time to talk. He strode a short distance away, looking out over the dark ocean.

With no one about, he leaned against one of the wharf's pilings, withdrew the box from his pocket, and stared at it, thinking of his next mission.

"Mon ami, something troubles you?"

Startled, Peter swung around, losing his hold on the box. It fell to the ground, the lid popped off, and the string of diamonds spilled at his feet. His host moved swiftly, before Peter could use his cane to bend over and collect the necklace.

Holding the gems up to his eyes, his host studied the sparkling facets a long moment, then turned to Peter, his expression flabbergasted. "Where did you get this?"

Confused by his demanding tone, Peter held out his hand for the jewels. "I assure you; no foul play was involved. It belongs to my mother. In England."

"Your mother?" He stared at Peter as if he'd struck him. "What is her name?"

"Lady Annabelle Caldwell. Why do you ask?"

It took him a moment to respond, and when he did, his voice was hoarse. "Merely curious." He handed the diamonds back to Peter, searching his face a moment, then picked up the box and offered that, too. "I apologize for startling you. My wife often tells me I am too silent. A word of caution: this area is filled with destitute men. If you do not wish to invite trouble, I advise you to keep that well hidden."

Peter placed the necklace inside the box, pocketing it. His friend was right; he had been foolish to unearth it from his coat. Several feet farther, and it could have ended up in the ocean.

"I came to tell you that you're welcome to stay overnight, though it might be crowded and not as comfortable as you're accustomed to."

"Thank you for your hospitality, but I've already made arrangements for two rooms at a hotel near Penn Station. Our train leaves in the morning. If you could drive us there, I would be most obliged."

"Of course."

341

Inside, Peter and Missy said their good-byes.

Florence took Peter aside. "Thank you," she said, her eyes steadier and more sincere than Peter had ever seen them. Her earlier tears had done damage to her powdered face, but he'd never seen it look softer. "No one ever cared enough to grab me like you did and make me come with you. You're quite a guy, a real prince." She grinned. "I hope you and Melissa have a happy life together."

"And you? What of your life?" Since he'd forced Florence to escape with them, he felt somehow responsible for her welfare.

"Janine has offered to shelter me here for a while. You were right; I can't go back. Guido's men know I was the one who helped you spring Melissa."

"And for that you have my undying gratitude." He took her hand and on impulse kissed the back of it, as he would for any lady of noble bearing. "I wish you the very best, Florence."

Flustered, she remained speechless a moment, then shook her head and smiled. "You really *are* a prince."

"And I want to add my thanks for helping Peter find me," Missy said coming up beside him.

Disconcerted, Florence found it hard to look Missy in the eye. "No hard feelings about. . .you know?"

"No hard feelings." Her expression sincere, Missy hugged Florence good-bye.

The drive to the hotel started silently, each of them immersed in their own thoughts.

"Do you think she'll be all right?" Missy finally asked.

"We'll make sure she is," their host assured. "Don't worry. We'll take care of your friend."

Soon they pulled up to the front of the hotel. Once they climbed out of the vehicle, their host looked at Peter from his rolled-down window.

"You have found much in your quest, mon ami, and have learned many things that have given you both joy and pain. Before we part, I want to share with you a piece of advice Janine's father once told me: 'It is not where you come from that's important; rather it is who you are and what you make of yourself.'"

Moved, Peter shook his friend's hand, then realized something extraordinary. "With all that we've been through together, I don't even know your name."

He chuckled. "It's Eric."

"Eric. . .?"

"Just Eric." He smiled at both of them, tipped his hat to Missy in farewell, and drove away.

Chapter 19

When Peter first told Missy they would be staying at a children's reformatory, she'd been anxious about what to expect, but Lyons' Refuge was nothing like she'd imagined.

Once they'd taken the train to Ithaca, Stewart and Charleigh Lyons met them at the station. Missy's first thought was that the striking couple—she with her red hair and he with his gray at the temples—were much too kind to be jail wardens, not that she'd ever met any.

Children overran the farm, which seemed more of a country haven than a disciplinary institution. As Missy and Peter exited the car, the smaller ones came running up to see, followed by older boys and girls who approached more slowly, their expressions every bit as curious. Most of the children were darlings—though Missy doubted she would ever remember all their names—and she dreamed of the day she and Peter would have little ones of their own.

Missy soon met the other guiding forces who ran the reformatory: Brent and Darcy Thomas and Bill and Sarah Thomas, each of them remarkable in their own way. As the afternoon wore on, her qualms evaporated and a measure of much-needed peace stole into her heart.

That evening, Charleigh and Darcy, both of them originally from London, dominated Peter, obviously thrilled to have a fellow countryman with whom to discuss the latest news from home. Missy watched a moment, admiring how Peter patiently fielded the women's excited questions. Then, without bringing attention to herself, she slipped outside to the porch.

Though the crisp air chilled her face, the muted softness of the snow on the acres of ground brought with it a calm she hadn't felt in a long time. Above, the moon shone full and bright, bringing with it a tranquility all its own. The door opened, and Missy turned to see who'd joined her.

"It's awfully cold out here," one of the older girls of the refuge noted, a brunette with a vivacious personality. The smattering of light freckles across her nose only added to her appeal.

"Yes, but right now, I like the cold if it means I can look at a view like this. . . . Miranda, right?"

The girl nodded. Missy placed her at sixteen or seventeen.

"Are you one of Darcy's, Charleigh's, or Sarah's?"

Miranda laughed. "None of the above, though I think of all three of them as my mothers. But let me help you. The twins, Robert Brent and Beatrice, belong to Darcy and Brent, as do Madeline, Lizzy, Roger, and Matthew. Clemmie, Stewart Jr., and Scottie are Charleigh and Stewart's, and Sarah and Bill are the parents of Josiah, David, Hannah, and Esther. All the rest of the children are reformers like me."

"Reformers?"

"We took a vote a few years ago and decided to call ourselves that. Not only are we being reformed, but also we are the next generation who plan to initiate reforms for the betterment of society. Soon, thanks to Mrs. Lyon's father and his scholarship program, I'll go to college. Once I earn my teaching degree, I'll return to the refuge and give back some of what these wonderful people have given to me."

"And believe you me, that day won't come soon enough!"

Both women jumped as a robust, good-looking young man came around the side of the porch, his arms full of firewood.

"Clint, you shouldn't sneak up on a person like that!" Miranda scolded, though Missy noted the light in her eyes as she watched him take the stairs.

"Who's sneaking?" His smile was wide. "I made about as much noise as humanly possible without calling out to announce myself."

"Where's Joel? I thought he was with you."

"He's packing." Clint looked at Missy. "Joel's one of the oldest boys at the refuge; we're all pretty proud of him. He's enlisted in the army, and we're giving him a sendoff tonight. You guys got here just in time to join the fun."

"That's wonderful." Missy continued to be amazed by those whose lives had been improved by this place. From the little she'd seen, a few of the newer residents experienced difficulties, but most of the older ones seemed mature and emotionally stable.

"Did I hear Darcy mention that you're planning to have your wedding here soon?" Miranda asked.

"Yes, once my aunt arrives. We decided to wait until she can come."

Clint moved in close to the girl. "One day, maybe we'll have our own wedding here, eh, Miranda?"

Pink flames leapt to the girl's cheeks. "Clint, hush! You're incorrigible." She pushed him away, but Missy noticed the slight smile that tilted her lips. "I really need to get back inside and help Clemmie make that sweet bread. She's taking Joel's leaving really hard; she has such a crush on him for being almost ten," she explained to Missy. "I just wanted to make sure you're okay."

"I'm fine." Missy gave a reassuring smile. As the two youngsters retreated inside the house, Missy's mind approached the memory of last night.

Today she *was* fine, but once they'd arrived at the hotel the previous evening and Peter had escorted her to her room, she'd fallen apart.

The aftermath of all she'd experienced hit her hard once they were alone, and she'd been unable to prevent the release from coming. Mortified, she'd buried her face in her hands so Peter wouldn't see her tears.

He had drawn her close and held her long, kissing her hair, whispering warm reassurances of her safety, telling her he would only be in the next room and would keep watch over her. She hadn't wanted him to release her, but when he bid her good night, she had regained a semblance of control.

"Hullo, what are you doing out here?"

At the sudden sound of his voice, her heart jumped, and she turned.

Peter closed the door behind him. "Just taking a breath to rest?"

She grinned at his teasing words. "Did you talk things over with Charleigh?"

"I'm waiting until tomorrow for that; the house is abuzz with this farewell party they've planned." He moved to stand beside her, and for an undisturbed moment, they stared at the scenery together. He pulled Mr. Harper's book from his pocket. "There's something in here I think might interest you. I read the remainder of this on the train; you were sleeping, and I didn't want to wake you."

Missy almost felt afraid to take the book, as if by doing so, the past might unfurl and entangle her in its folds. Joining with Peter on his quest to uncover his answers hadn't involved her history; she feared that whatever he wanted her to discover in this book did.

"It's all right. I think you'll find it well worth the effort."

His eyes shone with tenderness, and she took the journal, slipping it into her coat pocket. Then she slipped her arms around his neck and kissed him hard, burying her misgivings in the warmth of his arms.

"Whatever would I do without you, Peter?"

"It's a good thing you'll never have to find out, because like it or not, you're stuck with me."

She grinned. "Oh, I definitely like it," she whispered and kissed him again.

An hour later, everything remained in an uproar. Missy offered her help, and when the women discovered she'd worked in a restaurant for more than half her life, they gratefully put her to work. She helped set the three tables in the big dining room, observing the refuge's inhabitants as she did.

Joel, the guest of honor, was a handsome young man, and from his rakish smile and the comic mischief in his blue eyes, Missy assumed he knew the ladies found him attractive. He reminded Missy of Peter, with the same blue eyes and almost angelic quality to his features, but Joel seemed a little too wild. And from what Missy could tell, Clemmie wasn't the only girl at the refuge infatuated with the fair-haired man and his charismatic charm.

Two girls, reformers both younger than Miranda, helped Missy set the tables. She was surprised the items even made their way to the tablecloth and didn't go crashing to the floor, since the girls couldn't seem to take their eyes off Joel for a moment. He stood by the window, oblivious to their infatuated stares, and spoke with a short, redheaded young man.

Missy giggled, realizing the girls' smitten behavior reflected how she had conducted herself around Peter. No wonder Maria thought she'd lost all sense!

Joel turned to look at her and approached the table. Missy sensed the girl standing nearest her almost drop the plate. Instead, Fran drew it to her chest and held it there.

"Miss Reynolds," Joel addressed her, "since you lived in the Big Apple, perhaps you can settle an argument. Was Arnold Rothstein shot at the Park Central Hotel or at the Waldorf-Astoria? My friend Herbert here insists it was the Waldorf, but I remember reading about it being the Park Central Hotel."

She sensed no spitefulness in his clear eyes, but she tensed at the question. Only those in charge at the refuge knew of her abduction and close escape from gangsters, and she wondered why so many men enjoyed discussing crime and the mobs that terrorized New York. She had overheard many a conversation as she'd waited on tables in her uncle's restaurant.

"It was the Park Central."

"See there!" Joel turned a triumphant smile on his friend. "I knew it."

Herbert grumbled, and Missy's mind revisited past days. Her hand shook, almost knocking a glass over onto the plate. If it had been the Waldorf-Astoria where the mobster Mr. Rothstein had met his demise three weeks earlier, Peter might have been caught as an innocent bystander in the crossfire. She couldn't wait to get out of New York State and put all this behind them.

For a moment, Missy wondered how she would handle ocean travel. The memories of that last night on the *Titanic* had never departed, but to stay in New York? That wasn't an option since Guido had become a real threat, and no longer a distant admirer.

Delectable food soon covered the tables, and good company filled the room. Joel, Herbert, Tommy, Lance, and Clint, the oldest boys at the refuge, linked arms and sang along with the phonograph. They mangled popular tunes such as "S'Wonderful" and "I Wanna Be Loved by You" in an absurd manner, giving everyone a good laugh. Missy thought the five young men should be on vaudeville. Caught up in the merriment of the evening, she recognized other show tunes played, and when Peter asked if she would sing for them, Missy readily agreed.

She looked through the stack of records, finally deciding on a selection to which she knew the words by heart. She handed the record to Clemmie, a pert redhead with intelligent green eyes, who'd taken on the task of changing records.

Missy opened her mouth and sang the first lines of the love song. She couldn't help but notice everyone's frank amazement. At the audience reaction, a twinge of embarrassment tugged at her as it always did, and she turned her attention to Peter, focusing only on him.

The song mirrored Missy's heart, and she sang it from the depths of her soul. She made the words her own as she explained how she'd always scoffed at love before, but the first time she'd glimpsed his blue eyes, the moment his hand clasped hers, her heart had stood still. And from then on, she'd belonged to no other.

After she let the last clear note fade into the air, wild applause burst throughout the room, and a few boys whistled through their fingers. Joel's voice rose above the commotion.

"That was some of the best singing I've ever heard," he enthused, then turned to Herbert. "Was it just me, or did you get the feeling they were the only two people in the room?"

Missy felt a blush color her face at his mischievous teasing but didn't look away from Peter. "We were," she mouthed to him, and he smiled.

Chapter 20

M r. Lyons, Mrs. Lyons, are you sure it wouldn't be too great an imposition? Missy and I can easily find a chapel, since we have a license."

"Nonsense, Peter. We've never had a wedding at the refuge; I should love preparing for such an event, and I know Darcy will, too." She leaned forward. "And you really must call us Charleigh and Stewart."

He gave a slight nod to the lovely redhead, though he felt odd addressing the older couple in such a manner. Still, they had a way of making him feel comfortable, as if their home were his, and since Charleigh, as well as Darcy, was British, Peter felt a connection to them.

"Tell me, how's your mother?" Charleigh smiled. "I haven't heard from her in years. We only exchanged letters twice, and that was shortly after I married Stewart and we started the refuge. Have you other siblings? She had Gwen and Edward at the time."

"Yes. There are now seven children, actually." Reminded of the real reason he'd sought out Charleigh, he withdrew the box from his pocket. "She sends her best wishes. . . ." He removed the lid and laid the box on the kitchen table in front of her. "And this."

Months ago, when his mother had asked him to deliver the necklace, Peter's curiosity had been piqued. He'd expected a surprised or confused reaction, certainly, but now felt alarmed when every ounce of color drained from Charleigh's face.

"Darling, are you all right?" Stewart left his chair and dropped to his knee beside her, putting his hand to her back.

She picked up the string of diamonds, peering at them more closely, then dropped the glittering necklace on the table as if it were a snake and might bite her.

"Why would she do this? Why?"

Pain filled her voice, confusing Peter. "It belonged to her mother." He related all he knew. "She put aside other jewelry for the girls to inherit, but she said this particular necklace gave her heartache because it reminded her of the *Titanic* and of losing her father. I never saw her wear it and believe she kept it hidden away all these years. She did say one other thing." He hesitated, hoping his mother's confusing message wouldn't cause further upset. "She mentioned you once sought this for all the wrong reasons, and now she wants to give it to you for the reasons that are good and right."

"Good and right?" Charleigh shook her head, tears brimming in her green eyes. "Whatever does she mean?"

"I cannot say for certain, since she didn't share anything further, but perhaps. . . perhaps she meant for you to sell it and use the money to help you here with your school." Though if that were true, Peter wondered why she hadn't asked Lawrence to invest financially instead.

A dawning look filled Charleigh's eyes. "And perhaps this is Annabelle's way of showing she's completely forgiven me."

"Forgiven you?"

Charleigh nodded. "On the *Titanic*, my associate and I stole this very necklace. The night of the disaster, I took it from his cabin, and weeks later, after I was presumed dead, I returned it to your mother."

Stunned, Peter couldn't respond.

"Peter," Stewart spoke into the silence. "You mentioned you came here early because of your escape from gangsters. For reasons not mine to disclose, I need to ask—did you tell anyone of your destination? Anyone at all?"

With a look of alarm, Charleigh turned to her husband. "Several crime families inhabit Manhattan, Stewart. You don't actually believe it could be Vittorio?. . .Is it?" She addressed her question to Peter.

Recognizing the name of the mobster, Peter felt uneasy. "Not Vittorio, no. But his nephew Guido and his men abducted Missy."

"Oh, my."

Peter didn't understand their reactions, but the news clearly upset them. He rose from his chair. "We don't wish to impose, and evidently we've unknowingly brought trouble to your household. If you can recommend a hotel, I should appreciate it."

"Sit down, Peter." Stewart's voice was grave. "We don't want you to go anywhere. Under the circumstances, perhaps you should know the truth. Excuse me a moment."

Confused, Peter watched him leave the room.

"Don't look so distressed." Charleigh's voice trembled, but kindness filled her eyes. "You and Missy are both welcome here. We wouldn't dream of having you stay anywhere else."

Mildly reassured, Peter nodded.

Soon Stewart returned with both Bill and Brent. In features, the brothers could be twins, but similarities stopped there. Bill's face and arms were bronzed though it was late November, and his hair grew long. Brent reminded Peter of one of his professors, with the precise clothing and manner to match, and it came as no surprise that he taught at the refuge. Where Brent was slender and refined, Bill seemed more a man ready to tackle the outdoors. Peter found it odd how Bill's Polynesian wife, Sarah, was so quiet and elegant, while Brent's fun-loving wife, Darcy, was gregarious to the point of being brash.

Charleigh rose from the table to start a pot of tea. Bill took a seat across from Peter and came straight to the point. "Stewart mentioned you had dealings with someone we're both acquainted with, and he asked me to share some of my history." His expression grim, he clasped his hands on the table in front of him. "Before I met my wife, I used to work for a crime ring run by Vittorio. I was framed for his son's murder and had to flee for my life, but they found me and almost killed my wife. They did kill our unborn child."

Peter stared, bewildered. "You're the second man I've met who once worked for Vittorio—he's the only one I told of our destination," he added to Stewart. "No one else knows except Missy's aunt, and she only knows I took her to an acquaintance of my mother's in Ithaca. If I hadn't felt he was trustworthy, I wouldn't have spoken so freely to him, I assure you."

Stewart drew his brows together. "Who is this man?"

"He runs a soup kitchen, a mission. He's married with children, and his sole purpose in life is helping people and spreading the gospel."

Stewart nodded, seeming relieved.

"You say he worked for Vittorio," Bill said, his manner still just as tense. "How do you know you can trust him?"

After all Bill and his wife had been through, Peter understood the man's caution, and he shared all he knew. "He had a most amazing testimony. He was once a con artist, a mobster, and a murderer, but his prison guard had a habit of speaking the Word along with a desire to save souls. He also told me the woman he'd wronged the most was the one who taught him forgiveness, and if she'd not done that, he might not have listened to the guard. But he did, and it changed his life. While visiting his establishment, I observed a number of people seeking salvation upon hearing his witness and going to him for prayer. I truly don't think you need worry about his motives."

Stewart nodded. "I'm convinced."

"Well, I'm not," Bill insisted. "Didn't he give you his name? Since he worked for Vittorio, I might know him."

"Yes, of course. His name is Eric."

The teakettle crashed to the floor, and the men swung around to look at Charleigh. "Eric?" Her face had gone almost white.

"What was his last name?" Stewart demanded, his manner now as intent as Bill's.

"He didn't give it."

"Eric," Charleigh whispered, grabbing the counter for support and covering her mouth with her other hand.

Stewart hurried to her side to wrap his arm around her. "Charleigh, we don't know for sure it's him."

"Tell me." Charleigh spoke as if she'd not heard him. "Did he speak with a French accent? Is he blond and tall? Dark blue eyes?"

A sense of unreality swept through Peter's confusion. "Yes."

Her eyelids fluttered closed, while Stewart's jaw hardened, and suddenly Peter understood.

"You were the woman he wronged, the one who forgave him."

Charleigh gave a stiff nod.

"And your friend who showed him an act of kindness?"

"What?"

Peter explained, and she moved to sit down. "Darcy gave him money to buy a coat. He was sick and didn't have one. It was snowing." She spoke in a monotone.

Dumbfounded, Peter stared at the table, and his mind clicked the scattered pieces together. "Now it makes sense. Both of you reacted with the same shock upon seeing the necklace. He was your accomplice, the one on the *Titanic*." Peter wondered why Eric hadn't shared with him that he, too, was on the ship.

"Eric saw the necklace?" Horrified confusion filled her voice. "And he knew you were bringing it here?"

"Yes." Their anxiety caused him doubt. "He told me if I didn't want to invite danger from destitute men, I should keep it well hidden."

Charleigh gave a humorless laugh. "He should know."

"We've only one way to learn the truth," Stewart said with grim determination. "Can you find this soup kitchen? Will you take us to him?"

"What of Missy?" Peter stalled. "I can't leave her here alone, and I certainly can't take her back to Manhattan."

"She'll be fine. Brent and Bill will be here, as well as the older boys. Besides, if the man we know as Eric is the one whom you told of your destination, he would tell no one else, especially if his desire is to get the necklace. . .or to gain revenge."

Peter desperately tried to follow the conversation. "Revenge? For what?"

Charleigh had recovered, but her smile was grim. "For losing what he had— me and the necklace. And for us putting him in prison."

❧

Missy frowned, shaking her head. "I don't want you to go back there without me. I could wear a wig; no one would recognize me."

"No, Missy." Frustrated, Peter pushed a hand through his hair, stepping away from her.

She followed. "You promised you would never leave me, that we would stick together. We're a team, remember?" She knew she was being unreasonable but couldn't help herself. She didn't want to be separated from Peter again and couldn't quell the fear that it might be permanent this time.

351

"We are a team, yes." He dropped his cane and placed his hands on either side of her head, tilting her face up, his eyes intense as he looked into hers. "But I would never forgive myself if something happened to you, if one of Guido's informers should somehow see you and report to him. I love you, Missy. I'd give my life for you, and I refuse to put you in a potentially dangerous situation."

She felt her heart melt. "I love you too, Peter. It's only because I love you so much that I want to go with you." She sensed him begin to tense again and added, "But I'll stay. I need to do a few things before the wedding, so I suppose it is best." She searched for something positive to say. "I can't believe Aunt Maria is finally coming, though five days seems like forever. I know she's had to be careful not to give our location away on the chance she's followed, but this waiting's been hard."

"For me, too." He touched his lips to hers in a light kiss. "I'll be back tonight, I promise."

"I'll hold you to that. But I *am* going along with Brent and Darcy to drive you to the station."

"About that. . ."

She gathered her brows, sensing she wouldn't like what was coming.

"Charleigh's decided she's going too, though Stewart is none too happy about it. I'm afraid there won't be room in the car now since Bill is also going. He and Eric were friends, only he knew him as Philip, and oddly enough, they both saved each other's lives," Peter explained.

Sidetracked for a moment within this odd triangle in which they'd found themselves, Missy shook her head. "It's all so strange, isn't it? I, for one, don't believe there's a cruel bone in Eric's body; he was so kind to us and so sincere with those who prayed with him."

"I agree. But after all the Lyons have been through regarding him, I suppose they feel they must do this to put their minds at rest."

Missy smiled, and Peter's expression grew curious.

"What?"

"I was just thinking: it all goes back to that message—how sometimes God waits for His perfect timing to bring things to pass so that many can be blessed and not just a few. Perhaps in your quest, He used you as the catalyst to bring about something more important than you ever dreamed."

He looked at her in awe. "Missy, you're an amazing woman. I never thought of that, but I think you're right."

An hour later, once Peter left with the others for the station, Missy grew discouraged. Later when Darcy and her husband returned, Darcy noticed Missy standing at the window in the parlor and slipped her arm around her.

"Aw, cheer up, luv. He'll be back tonight. Won't he, Brent?"

"I've been given instructions as to the precise time of their return."

Missy smiled, trying to appear brave. "It's just hard to be apart, even for a day."

"Ah, young love," Darcy said on a sigh. "How well I remember."

Brent smiled at his wife. "And it only improves with age."

"It does at that, guv'ner. It does at that!"

Darcy laughed, and Missy looked on with a smile. They were still so much in love, and watching them gave her hope. Marriage wasn't easy; she'd learned that by witnessing her mother's failures. But Missy *would* succeed because she fervently wanted a life with Peter. She would work hard to be the wife he needed.

Missy excused herself and went upstairs to the room she'd been given. Closing her eyes, she sank to her bed and drew the comforter around herself, trying to crowd out the chills of fear.

As a child, whenever someone had left her for a time, she had grown anxious they might not return. She recalled those few days Peter had been absent from her life because he'd been ill. At the time, her insecurities had caused her to doubt that he would return. And though she felt confident in his love now, niggling questions persisted, despite her best efforts to quell them.

From the moment they'd met, she had brought Peter physical pain, and later she'd only added to his emotional anguish. Guido's men almost killed him because of her! She wouldn't blame Peter if he changed his mind and never came back, but her heart entreated his return.

"Dear Lord, I need to learn to trust. Help me. I don't know how, and I desperately want to. You gave Peter guidance; help me to trust."

A calm drifted into her spirit as she focused on His strength, which seemed to enfold and comfort her. She grew so relaxed that she stretched out on the bed and fell asleep.

When she awoke, Mr. Harper's journal was the first thing she saw. A current of guilt jetted through her.

She had promised to read the journal but had put the book aside and concentrated on other matters concerning Peter and their upcoming wedding. Now with him gone, she had no more excuses.

Missy picked up the book from the bedside table, stared at it a long moment, then opened the frayed cover. As she struggled through the first pages, she noticed little order to the entries. They meandered here and there and would often leave off, commence with the introduction of a new person, then reintroduce an older subject pages later.

Her earlier trepidation led to amusement as she tried to follow the ambiguous scribblings of a writer. Far into the book, she found what she'd nervously anticipated:

Doña Ortega—Scandinavian blond, blue eyes, full-figured, mid-20s; traveling alone with small daughter and maid. Reserved to the extreme of being snobbish, therefore fitting in quite well with all other matrons of whom

I've made acquaintance; I sense pain in her eyes—involving her ill-behaved daughter? Her missing husband? Seating arrangements have placed us at same table throughout voyage; perhaps I will learn answers then.

Ill-behaved? Missy frowned. The following paragraph introduced yet another passenger. Intrigued despite her desire to resist, Missy flipped a few pages until she found more:

Doña Ortega—has habit of pressing three fingers to her temple when upset. Is upset often. Daughter—Missy—spitting image of mother. I sense tension between them but cannot place cause for it. Perhaps my earlier assessment of child was unfair; if I had belonged to such a mother, I might also have made myself scarce by habitually running away. Child carries doll everywhere, went so far as to ask steward for chair to place doll in. Her comment brought laughter from all those at our table, all except her mother. The manner in which the doña narrows eyes at doll—perhaps not a gift from her?

Missy's eyes widened as she relived her childhood through an adult passenger's eyes. She flipped through several pages until she found more:

I was put in a most awkward position today after having fallen asleep in chair against alcove wall in reading room. I awoke to hear voices. On other side of wall in adjoining alcove, the doña spoke with Mrs. J. J. Brown (who could mistake that strong voice?). Am amazed Mrs. Brown able to crack through the doña's icy exterior but have found her to be an amazing woman. Felt some shame for not making my presence known by clearing my throat. Instead, I remained quiet and eavesdropped. Soon, I determined the conversation was brought on by the disastrous outcome of a birthday party the doña had planned for her daughter, after which Missy made herself scarce by running away to hide. She is quite adept at this.

Doña Ortega—a very insecure woman (*note: would make good character type for planned novel, perhaps one of the sisters?). She's certain husband will take daughter away; claims he seeks Missy's love with his gifts, including doll. The peculiar thing is child and the don are not blood-related, so why such fears? The doña admitted she's a poor excuse for a mother (few could disagree) and Missy would do better with anyone else, and I quote, "I'm afraid to keep her, and I'm afraid to lose her. In my own way, I love her, but I don't think that love will ever equal what she needs." One can only pity a creature like that.

In shock, Missy stared at the page until it blurred. Mother had told a passing stranger that she loved Missy but, for whatever reason, had neglected to tell Missy the same. Faced with the truth of her mother's insecurities, Missy could only wonder. She'd never thought of the statuesque Doña Ortega as being anything other than a strong, cold woman, a former prima donna who asserted complete control of every situation. To find out otherwise brought a trickle of compassion, a feeling she'd never felt toward her mother. Like Missy, the doña had struggled with personal doubts and fears, and that made Missy not only begin to understand her mother a little better but also feel connected to her in a way she never had been before.

Chapter 21

Eric exited the soup kitchen door, his expression calm and not the least bit surprised. His next words proved it.

"I thought you might come. You're looking well, Charleigh."

Charleigh gave a barely discernable nod. She searched his face, as if trying to associate it with the memory from her past, then turned her shocked gaze to his four-year-old daughter clasped at his side. From big blue eyes, Lynette observed the newcomers with shy interest while keeping her arms firmly fastened around her father's neck.

"Bill, it's good to see you again." Eric stuck out his hand, and Bill shook it.

"You, too, Phil, er. . .Eric. I want to thank you for the warning you sent years ago. About Vittorio."

Eric nodded. "Of course."

Peter had a difficult time trying to determine Charleigh's feelings, but Stewart's blazing eyes and clenched mouth told all.

"If this is what you're after," Stewart said, pulling the diamond necklace from his pocket and shoving it in Eric's face, "take it! It will save you coming to the refuge to torment our women and children again." The little girl's eyes widened as she stared at the jewels sparking glimmers of colored fire in the morning sunlight.

Eric sighed. "I don't want your necklace."

"Then what *do* you want?"

Eric didn't answer right away. He kissed Lynette's temple, set her down on the ground, and told her in French to go to her mother. Once she'd scampered off, he regarded them gravely.

"I want peace among us, and since you ask, Stewart, I want your forgiveness."

"Forgiveness?" Stewart's contained rage altered into open disbelief. "After all that's happened—after you broke into our home and held a gun on my wife— you expect me to *forgive* you?"

"Non, I do not expect it. I humbly ask for it. Whether you choose to give forgiveness or not is your decision alone." When Stewart gave no answer and all four of them continued to stare, Eric motioned to the building behind him. "Please, let us leave the street and continue this discussion inside."

Peter hesitated. "I'll have to decline. We're here for only a few hours, and I must attend to other matters. How is Florence?"

Eric smiled. "She is doing much better, mon ami. She helps Janine with the children while Janine serves our guests."

Peter nodded, satisfied.

Bill turned Peter's way. "Would you like some company?"

Although surprised, Peter sensed Bill felt what he did, that Eric and the Lyons needed time alone to talk. "That would be splendid. I want to visit the restaurant and collect Missy's things." He also wanted to find out what had occurred since their escape and if Missy remained in danger from Guido or if the man had been thrown into jail after the raid.

An hour later, his worst fear was realized.

"Guido wasn't at the speakeasy when the raid took place," Tony said while Maria went to Missy's room to gather her things into a trunk. "Two of his men came to question me about Missy; they watched the restaurant for three days but caused no trouble and have not been here since." He looked around the almost empty restaurant and leaned in closer. "I hear my customers talk. One of them is a fed, Moe Smith, who brought with him his partner, Izzy." He shook his head. "They wear bizarre disguises to sneak into suspected speakeasies, and that night from what I hear, Moe wore a dress."

"Really?" Peter raised his brows in incredulous amusement. He remembered the strange couple who'd entered the speakeasy before he'd found Missy. The ugly woman in the fur coat had looked more like a man with dark bushy brows and a strong jaw, and the companion had also seemed out of place with his long beard. He wondered if they had been the two agents.

"An anonymous call led them to a speakeasy; I heard him say the tipster revealed that Guido had kidnapped a woman, and I know this must be our Missy."

Peter straightened in his chair, alert. He had told only one man about his plan to go there and rescue Missy. "Eric," he mouthed to Bill across the table. Eric's ex-associate smiled and nodded.

Once Maria returned to the table, Peter regarded her warmly. "I'm relieved to know your family is well. Now, I have a favor to ask, something to which I hope you'll both be agreeable."

❧

Missy could barely sit still as she glanced at the mantel clock for what must be the fifth time in as many minutes. The train should have arrived thirty-five minutes ago; what was taking so long?

At last, the whir of a car's engine sounded, and she raced for the door, ready to throw herself into Peter's embrace. She stopped short when the door opened and a familiar, dark-haired woman exited the vehicle.

"Aunt Maria!" She ran to Maria's open arms and hugged her. "Everyone's all right?" Missy pulled away. "Tony? The children?" At Maria's nod, Missy exhaled in relief. "But how—you said you were coming on Saturday."

"Peter thought you might not wish to delay the wedding any longer than you have already." Maria's eyes sparkled with joy. "I have brought your trunk with all your things."

"Herbert, you and Clint take the trunk to Missy's room, please," Missy heard Brent instruct behind her.

Missy turned her attention toward the car as Peter exited. His gaze seemed both affectionate and uncertain. "I hope you don't mind."

"Mind?" She laughed and rushed forward to hug him, not caring what anyone thought. "You mad, impulsive Englishman! Why should I mind? It's what I've wanted all along."

"Actually," he whispered, for her ears alone, "I didn't just do it for you; it's what I wanted as well."

"Oh, this is smashing!" Charleigh trilled. Missy noted that her face seemed to glow with a peace she'd not seen before and assumed all had gone well with Eric. Before she could ask about their trip, Charleigh moved toward the stairs. "I'll ring the minister and see if he's free tomorrow."

"I can't wait to see Darcy's face when we ask her to bake a wedding cake tonight," Stewart said, and he, too, seemed more relaxed than Missy had ever seen him. Peace replaced the former lines of stress on his face, and his eyes sparkled with exuberance.

"Oh, please, no," Missy said, keeping one arm around Peter. "Under the circumstances, I don't need a cake."

"Are you kidding?" Bill smiled at her. "My sister-in-law looks for every excuse invented to bake. She won't mind a bit, I'm sure." Sarah came out onto the porch, and Bill hurried toward her, and she to him. The two embraced as if they'd been apart for weeks and not one day. Oblivious to everyone but each other, they tenderly kissed.

Missy smiled. "It will be like that for us, too, I know it."

"I have no doubt in my mind," Peter said with a grin. Two of Bill and Sarah's children came running out the door, squealing as they ran to embrace their father. With the focus on the Thomas family, Missy moved closer to Peter and kissed him, hardly daring to believe that tomorrow this wonderful man would be her husband.

Chapter 22

Peter donned his best clothes, knowing that in less than an hour, his sweet Missy would become his wife. Taking this moment of solitude to collect his thoughts, he moved to the bedroom window and stared out over the distant treetops.

He felt no compunction whatsoever at the idea of taking Missy as his bride and sharing a life with her. But Guido still lurked out there, and though Stewart had reassured him they remained safe at the refuge, Peter wouldn't breathe easy until they were well away from New York. Still, God had guided him this far; that much was apparent. And Peter knew He wouldn't abandon them now. Peter thought back to the previous day.

When he'd returned with Bill to the soup kitchen, they'd both been amazed to see Eric and Janine sitting at a table with the Lyons and having a friendly chat. Peter had pulled Eric aside. "You were the tipster who called the feds about the raid, weren't you?"

Eric released a short breath of amusement, then gave a magnanimous shrug. "I figured you could use a little help. Was I wrong?"

"No." Peter chuckled in disbelief, shaking his head. "Why didn't you tell me you were on the *Titanic*?"

"Ah, mon ami. That is a time in my life I wish to forget. When I realized you were Annabelle's son..." He shook his head in remembered bewilderment. "I felt doubly gratified to know I had given you my assistance."

"And I thank you for all your help."

Eric gave a short nod. "You, too, have helped me. Through your quest to find your family, God has brought reconciliation to all of us." He looked toward Charleigh and Stewart, who were in deep discussion with Janine.

"And I *have* found a family here." Peter thought of all those who'd offered him support these past weeks. "More of a family than I ever dreamed possible."

Still amazed at how God had used his quest to help his new friends breach a wall that spanned almost two decades of pain, remorse, and fear, Peter recalled how Stewart had shaken Eric's hand in good-bye. Charleigh had hugged Janine and then tentatively did the same with Eric, wishing them both well. From that moment on, Peter had sensed a difference in the Lyons, as if they'd found a long-sought peace and had finally embraced freedom.

A knock at the door broke him from his thoughts.

Peter opened it to one of the reformers, a young man named Tommy. They shared one similarity, drawing Peter to the boy who was only a few years younger than he. Tommy had a clubfoot and often seemed unsure of his place in the world.

"Mr. Thomas sent me up to ask if you needed anything," he explained.

Peter regarded him. "Now that I think about it, I do need something. How would you like to be my best man, Tommy?"

The boy's eyes widened. "You mean it?"

"Of course. Missy has asked Stewart to walk her down the aisle, and I could use someone to stand beside me."

"Sure, I'll do it." Tommy's eyes lit up. "That would be swell. So you guys are traveling south along the coast?"

"Yes. To Florida, actually. I decided it would be best to leave New York for the months we must wait before we sail for England."

"I envy you. Any week now, the blizzards should start, and you don't want to be in upstate New York in the dead of winter."

He gave a mock shiver, and Peter laughed, clapping him on the shoulder. "Are you ready to go downstairs?"

"I'm the one who should be asking you that. You're really not a bit nervous, are you? I knew one other guy who married—Samuel, one of the original reformers—and he was as nervous as a barnyard cat perched on a fence and staring down a pack of hungry dogs."

"Really?" Peter chuckled. "I suppose when a man finds treasure, as I have, he's eager to claim it."

"Yeah, I guess. I wish I'd find a treasure of my own some day."

"You will." Peter gave an encouraging smile.

"Aren't you even the slightest bit uneasy about married life?"

Peter turned the question over in his mind, then smiled. "I learned something these past months, Tommy. With God's guidance in our lives, we're destined to succeed."

❧

"Aunt Maria, it's so beautiful." Awed, Missy smoothed her hand over the creamy white lace of the Spanish-styled wedding gown she wore.

"I took the dress in quite a bit, but I think it fits well."

"It's perfect." Missy turned to hug her aunt. "Thank you for allowing me the honor of wearing your wedding gown."

"Missy, it pleases me so much to do this. You have always been like a daughter to me."

Her words brought with them the memory of her mother, and Missy sobered.

"Mi niña, she does love you." Maria correctly guessed Missy's thoughts. The previous evening, unable to sleep from excitement, Missy had spent hours talking with Maria about what she'd found in the journal and about the past. "She just does not know how to express that love."

Missy pondered her aunt's words, coming to a decision. "Do you know where she is now?"

"Up until three years ago, I did. I read in the newspaper that she joined an opera company and was touring with them."

Missy turned to examine her dress in the mirror and fluffed the flounces of the skirt. "If she contacts you, will you let me know? I—I think I would like to write her."

The admission made Maria gasp; for years, Missy had refused even to speak of her mother. But now. . .now it was time to let go. She didn't want to enter her new life with Peter burdened by bitterness from her past.

Maria's eyes filled with tears. "Sí, I will write you."

"And you must come visit us, too." Missy grinned. "I can't wait to see my first castle!"

In three days, she and Peter would take the train to Florida, and later, they would set sail for England. But first. . .Missy took a deep breath, focusing on the present, and nodded to Maria. "I'm ready now."

Ten minutes later, she glided into the white and pink beribboned parlor on Stewart's arm in rhythm with a melodious tune playing on the phonograph. Missy's gaze locked with Peter's dazed one the entire time she moved to take her place beside him before the minister.

Gazing into Peter's blue eyes, she found herself. Taking his hand, she came to life, and in anticipating their future together. . .her heart stood still.

Epilogue

One year later

Who would've ever believed that the baby blanket you gave me as a birthday present for my doll seventeen years ago would one day swaddle your first grandchild?" Missy spoke softly, gazing upon the sleeping infant in her arms with all the love a mother could possibly bear. She looked up at her mother-in-law and noted the tears filming her green eyes.

The years had been kind to the Countess, Lady Annabelle Caldwell, bringing with them a distinct softness to her features and a slight silvering to her dark hair. During the past year in which Missy had lived in England with Peter in one wing of the Caldwells' sprawling manor, Missy had resumed her acquaintance with the woman who'd once been so kind to her on a ship full of strangers. She felt blessed to regard Annabelle not only as her mother-in-law but also as a dear friend.

"I cannot believe the blanket is still in such good condition," Annabelle murmured, fingering its snow-white folds.

"Once I quit playing with dolls, I put it away to keep it safe." Missy laughed softly so as not to wake her sleeping son. "Aunt Maria put into that trunk every item I possessed, and I'm glad now she did." She thought about her aunt's most recent letter and was thankful Guido hadn't terrorized the family upon his failure to locate Missy, apparently accepting Tony's explanation that she'd run away.

"Including the dolls I've seen on the bureau in your bedroom?" Annabelle teased, breaking into her thoughts.

Warmth flushed Missy's cheeks, and she grinned. "One day I'll give them to my daughters, especially the doll called Annabelle. She was my most treasured possession at that time because she reminded me of you."

The countess laid her hand on Missy's shoulder. "I know I've told you this often, but I thank God every day for bringing you into Peter's life, and I pray you both will be as happy as Lawrence and I have been. To think that the small sassy girl I knew on the *Titanic* is now a member of my family." She shook her head. "I am continually amazed by the way God works things out and brings people together."

"Sassy?" Missy's brows sailed upward.

Annabelle laughed. "Yes, sassy. But loveable and sweet, too."

"Missy?" Gwen stood in the nursery door. Of all her sisters- and brothers-in-law, Missy felt closest to the sixteen-year-old girl. The eldest of the children born after Annabelle and Lawrence had adopted Peter, Gwen possessed striking looks and a quiet manner. "Peter asked me to tell you he's ready for you."

"Thank you." Missy placed a kiss on her son's forehead, then carefully transferred him to his grandmother's waiting arms. Still, she hesitated, wondering if he might soon wake up hungry.

"Go on. Clayton will be fine. And be certain not to overtire yourself, dear."

"I won't." Missy looked back one last time to see the charming picture of Annabelle smiling tenderly at her grandson.

On the way downstairs, she met her father-in-law coming up. The earl's thick hair was heavily sprinkled with silver, but despite his years, he retained his trim, strong build. Nor had age diminished his height. He towered almost a foot above Missy. His ice-blue eyes were striking in his distinguished face, and from the day she'd met him, Missy had found Lord Caldwell to be as wonderful as Peter had claimed. Both he and Annabelle had welcomed her into their family as if she'd always belonged there.

"Are you feeling well?" he asked.

"Perfectly."

"Don't let that son of mine tire you out." He glanced up toward the top landing, and Missy smiled.

"She's in the nursery with Clayton."

"Ah, thank you, my dear." The earl took the stairs quickly, eager to find his wife, and Missy was just as eager to locate her husband.

She exited the front door and inhaled a swift breath at the sight before her. She'd been in England almost a year, but the scenery never ceased to amaze her.

Beyond the sprawling green lawn, far in the distance, a stone castle stood on a hill. Everywhere on the Caldwell estate, trees grew in abundance, and the fragrance of sweet summer roses perfumed the air. But the sight of her husband sitting beneath the elm tree was what brought a smile to Missy's face.

When she came within a few feet of his easel, Peter saw her and rose from his stool. He pulled her close, and she wrapped her arms around his waist, pressing her cheek against his shirtfront to feel his steady heartbeat and breathe in the clean scent of him.

"Are you sure you're up to this?" he asked, his voice laced with tender concern.

"Peter!" She laughed and drew slightly away. "I had the baby two weeks ago; I'm fine."

"You'll tell me if you get tired?"

"Yes."

"Then come." With a smile, he took her hand and escorted her to the stool he'd set up in front of the easel. She sat down and looked at the castle over her shoulder.

"Will you paint the castle into the background?"

"Yes, of course. My princess must have her castle." He arranged her upper body, positioning her hands in her lap, then tilting her head until her pose satisfied him. "I have always wanted to paint your portrait, Missy."

"I know. But just remember, I warned you, Peter. I'm not sure I'll be a very good subject."

"On the contrary, my dear. I'm afraid I won't be able to do justice to your beauty."

Reveling in his compliment, she shook her head. "I might move."

"Then I'll merely have to arrange your pose again."

He trailed his fingertips along her jaw to her chin, tilting it just so, and bent to touch his lips to hers. Pleasurable tingles of warmth spread through Missy as their kiss blossomed into an expression of mutual love. Her heart soared to the heavens, as light as a cloud.

With Peter, she had at last found the fulfillment of all her dreams.

A Letter to Our Readers

Dear Readers:

In order that we might better contribute to your reading enjoyment, we would appreciate your taking a few minutes to respond to the following questions. When completed, please return to the following: Fiction Editor, Barbour Publishing, Inc., P.O. Box 719, Uhrichsville, OH 44683.

1. Did you enjoy reading *New York Brides* by Pamela Griffin?
   ❑ Very much—I would like to see more books like this.
   ❑ Moderately—I would have enjoyed it more if _____
   _____
   _____

2. What influenced your decision to purchase this book?
   (Check those that apply.)
   ❑ Cover   ❑ Back cover copy   ❑ Title   ❑ Price
   ❑ Friends   ❑ Publicity   ❑ Other

3. Which story was your favorite?
   ❑ *Heart Appearances*   ❑ *A Bridge Across the Sea*
   ❑ *A Gentle Fragrance*

4. Please check your age range:
   ❑ Under 18   ❑ 18–24   ❑ 25–34
   ❑ 35–45   ❑ 46–55   ❑ Over 55

5. How many hours per week do you read? _____

Name _____

Occupation _____

Address _____

City_____ State _____ Zip _____

E-mail_____

If you enjoyed

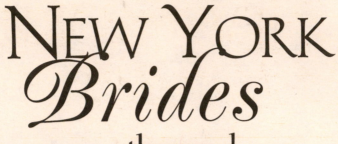

NEW YORK
Brides

then read

KENTUCKY
Brides

**Three Romances Complicate
a Simple Way of Historic Life**

Into the Deep by Lauralee Bliss
Where the River Flows by Irene B. Brand
Moving the Mountain by Yvonne Lehman

If you enjoyed

NEW YORK *Brides*

then read

OKLAHOMA *Weddings*

**HARDWORKING MEN AND SOFTHEARTED WOMEN
MEET IN THREE NOVELS**

In His Will by Cathy Marie Hake
Through His Grace by Kelly Eileen Hake
By His Hand by Jennifer Johnson